WE FEW

DAVID WEBER
JOHN RINGO

We Few

Copyright © 2005 by David Weber & John Ringo

A Baen Books Original

Baen Publishing Enterprises
P.O. Box 1403
Riverdale, NY 10471
www.baen.com

ISBN: 0-7434-9881-X

Cover art by Kurt Miller

First printing, April 2005

Library of Congress Cataloging-in-Publication Data

Weber, David, 1952-
  We few / by David Weber & John Ringo.
      p. cm.
  "A Baen Books original."
  ISBN 0-7434-9881-X
    1. Princes--Fiction. 2. Life on other planets--Fiction. 3. Kings and rulers--
  Succession--Fiction. I. Ringo, John, 1963- II. Title.

  PS3573.E217W4 2005
  813'.54--dc22

                                                            2004029931

Distributed by Simon & Schuster
1230 Avenue of the Americas
New York, NY 10020

Production by Windhaven Press, Auburn, NH
Printed in the United States of America

10 9 8 7 6 5 4 3 2 1

This one's for Gena and Lindsey,
without whom I would never have
survived to get it written.

========

Of Alexandra VII's three children, the youngest, Roger Ramius Sergei Alexander Chiang MacClintock—known variously to political writers of his own time as "Roger the Terrible," "Roger the Mad," "the Tyrant," "the Restorer," and even "the Kin-Slayer"—did not begin his career as the most promising material the famed MacClintock Dynasty had ever produced. Alexandra's child by Lazar Fillipo, the sixth Earl of New Madrid, whom she never married, the then-Prince Roger was widely regarded prior to the Adoula Coup as an overly handsome, self-centered, clothes-conscious fop. It was widely known within court circles that his mother nursed serious reservations about his reliability and was actively disappointed by his indolent, self-centered neglect of those duties and responsibilities which attached to his position as Heir Tertiary to the Throne of Man. Less widely known, although scarcely a secret, was her lingering distrust of his loyalty.

As such, it was perhaps not unreasonable, when the "Playboy Prince" and his bodyguard (Bravo Company, Bronze Battalion, of the Empress' Own Regiment) disappeared *en route* to a routine flag-showing ceremony only months before an attack upon the Imperial Palace, that suspicion should turn to him. The assassination of his older brother, Crown Prince John, and of his sister, Princess Alexandra, and of all of John's children, combined with the apparent attempt to assassinate his Empress Mother, would have left Roger the only surviving heir to the throne.

What was unknown at the time was that those truly behind

1

the coup were, in fact, convinced that Roger and his Marine bodyguard were all dead, as his assassination had been the first step in their plans to overthrow Empress Alexandra. By hacking into the personal computer implant of a junior officer aboard the Prince's transport vessel, they were able, through their unwilling, programmed agent, to plant demolition charges at critical points within the vessel's engineering sections. Unfortunately for their plans, the saboteur was discovered before she could quite complete her mission, and the ship, although badly crippled, was not destroyed outright.

Instead of dying almost instantly in space, the "Playboy Prince" found himself marooned on the planet of Marduk . . . a fate some might not have considered preferable. Although legally claimed by the Empire and the site of an Imperial starport, it was obvious to the commander of his bodyguard, Captain Armand Pahner, that the system was actually under the *de facto* control of the Caravazan Empire, the ruthless rivals of the Empire of Man. The "Saints'" fanatical attachment to the principle that humanity's polluting, ecology-destroying presence should be excised from as many planets as physically possible was matched only by their burning desire to replace the Empire of Man as the dominant political and military power of the explored galaxy. Their interest in Marduk was easily explainable by the star system's strategic location on the somewhat amorphous boundary between the two rival star nations, although precisely what at least two of their sublight cruisers were doing there was rather more problematical. But whatever the exact details of their presence in the Marduk System might be, it was imperative that the Heir Tertiary not fall into their hands.

To prevent that from happening, the entire crew of Roger's transport vessel, HMS *Charles DeGlopper*, sacrificed their lives in a desperate, close-range action which destroyed both Saint cruisers in the system without ever revealing *DeGlopper*'s identity or the fact that Roger had been aboard. Just before the transport's final battle, the Prince and his Marine bodyguards, along with his valet and his chief of staff and one-time tutor, escaped undetected aboard *DeGlopper*'s assault shuttles to the planet. There, they faced the formidable task of marching halfway around one of the most hostile, technically habitable planets ever claimed by the Empire so that they might assault the spaceport and seize control of it.

It was, in fact, as virtually all of them realized, an impossible mission, but the "Bronze Barbarians" were not simply Imperial Marines. They were the Empress' Own, and impossible or not, they did it.

For eight endless months, they fought their way across half a world of vicious carnivores, sweltering jungle, swamp, mountains, seas, and murderous barbarian armies. When their advanced weapons failed in the face of Marduk's voracious climate and ecology, they improvised new ones—swords, javelins, black powder rifles, and muzzle-loading artillery. They learned to build ships. They destroyed the most terrible nomadic army Marduk had ever seen, and then did the same thing to the cannibalistic empire of the Krath. At first, the horned, four-armed, cold-blooded, mucus-covered, three-meter-tall natives of Marduk seriously underestimated the small, bipedal visitors to their planet. Physically, humans closely resembled oversized *basiks*, small, stupid, rabbitlike creatures routinely hunted by small children armed only with sticks. Those Mardukans unfortunate enough to get in the Empress' Own's way, however, soon discovered that *these basiks* were far more deadly than any predator their own world had ever produced.

And along the way, the "Playboy Prince" discovered that he was, indeed, the heir of Miranda MacClintock, the first Empress of Man. At the beginning of that epic march across the face of Marduk, the one hundred and ninety Marines of Bravo Company felt nothing but contempt for the worthless princeling whose protection was their responsibility; by its end, Bravo Company's twelve survivors would have fixed bayonets to charge Hell itself at his back. And the same was true of the Mardukans recruited into his service as The *Basik's* Own.

But having, against all odds, captured the spaceport and a Saint special operations ship which called upon it, the surviving Bronze Barbarians and The *Basik's* Own faced a more daunting challenge still, for they discovered that the coup launched by Jackson Adoula, Prince of Kellerman, had obviously succeeded. Unfortunately, no one else seemed to realize Empress Alexandra was being controlled by the same people who had murdered her children and her grandchildren. And, still worse, was the discovery that the notorious traitor Prince Roger Ramius Sergei Alexander Chiang MacClintock was being hunted by every member of the Imperial military and police establishments as the perpetrator of the attack on his own family.

Despite that . . .

—Arnold Liu-Hamner, PhD,
from "Chapter 27: The Chaos Years Begin,"
The MacClintock Legacy, Volume 17, 7th edition, © 3517,
Souchon, Fitzhugh, & Porter Publishing,
Old Earth

I*mprimis*, they nuked the spaceport.

The one-kiloton kinetic energy weapon was a chunk of iron the size of a small aircar. He watched it burn on the viewscreens of the captured Saint special operations ship as it entered the upper atmosphere of the planet Marduk and tracked in perfectly. It exploded in a flash of light and plasma, and the mushroom cloud reached up into the atmosphere, spreading a cloud of dust over the nearer Krath villages.

The spaceport was deserted at the moment it turned into plasma. Everything movable, which had turned out to be everything but the buildings and fixed installations, had been stripped from it. The Class One manufacturing facility, capable of making clothes and tools and small weapons, had been secreted at Voitan, along with most of the untrustworthy humans, including all of the surviving Saint Greenpeace commandos who had been captured with the ship. They could work in the Voitan mines, help rebuild the city, or, if they liked nature so much, they could feel free to escape into the jungles of Marduk, teeming with carnivores who would be more than happy to ingest them.

Prince Roger Ramius Sergei Alexander Chiang MacClintock watched the explosion with a stony face, then turned to the small group gathered in the ship's control room, and nodded.

"Okay, let's go."

The prince was a shade under two meters tall, slim but muscular, with some of the compact strength usually associated with professional zero-G ball players. His long blond hair, pulled back in a ponytail, was almost white from sun bleaching, and his handsome, almost beautiful, classic European face was heavily tanned. It was also lined and hard, seeming far older than his twenty-two standard years. He had neither laughed nor smiled in two weeks, and as his long, mobile hand scratched at the neck of the two-meter black and red lizard standing pony-high by his side, Prince Roger's jade-green eyes were harder than his face.

There were many reasons for the lines, for the early aging, for the hardness about his eyes and shoulders. Roger MacClintock—Master Roger, behind his back, or simply The Prince—had not been so lined and hard nine months before. When he, his chief of staff and valet, and a company of Marine bodyguards had been hustled out of Imperial City, thrust into a battered old assault ship, and sent packing on a totally nonessential political mission, he had taken it as just another sign of his mother's disapproval of her youngest son. He'd shown none of the diplomatic and bureaucratic expertise of his older brother, Prince John, the Heir Primus, nor of the military ability of his older sister the admiral, Princess Alexandra, Heir Secondary. Unlike them, Roger spent his time playing zero-G ball, hunting big game, and generally being the playboy, and he'd assumed that Mother had simply decided it was time for him to steady down and begin doing the Heir Tertiary's job.

What he hadn't known at the time, hadn't known until months later, was that he was being hustled out of town in advance of a firestorm. The Empress had gotten wind, somehow, that the internal enemies of House MacClintock were preparing to move. He knew that now. What he still didn't know was whether she'd wanted him out of the way to protect him ... or to keep the child whose loyalty she distrusted out of both the battle and temptation's way.

What he did know was that the cabal behind the crisis his mother had foreseen had planned long and carefully for it. The sabotage of *Charles DeGlopper*, his transport, had been but the first step, although neither he nor any of the people responsible for keeping him alive had realized it at the time.

What Roger *had* realized was that the entire crew of the *DeGlopper* had sacrificed their lives in hopeless battle against the Saint sublight cruisers they had discovered in the Marduk System when the crippled ship finally managed to limp into it. They'd taken those ships on, rather than even considering surrender, solely to cover Roger's own escape in *DeGlopper's* assault shuttles, and they'd succeeded.

Roger had always known the Marines assigned to protect him regarded him with the same contempt as everyone else at Court, nor had *DeGlopper's* crew had any reason to regard him differently. Yet they'd died to protect him. They'd given up their lives in exchange for his, and they would not be the last to do it. As the men and women of Bravo Company, Bronze Battalion, The Empress' Own, had marched and fought their way across the planet they'd reached against such overwhelming odds, the young prince had seen far too many of them die. And as they died, the young fop learned, in the hardest possible school, to defend not simply himself, but the soldiers around him. Soldiers who had become more than guards, more than family, more than brothers and sisters.

In the eight brutal months it had taken to cross the planet, making alliances, fighting battles, and at last, capturing the spaceport and the ship aboard which he stood at this very moment, that young fop had become a man. More than a man—a hardened killer. A diplomat trained in a school where diplomacy and a bead pistol worked hand-in-hand. A leader who could command from the rear, or fight in the line, and keep his head when all about him was chaos.

But that transformation had not come cheaply. It had cost the lives of over ninety percent of Bravo Company. It had cost the life of Kostas Matsugae, his valet and the only person who had ever seemed to give a single good goddamn for Roger MacClintock. Not Prince Roger. Not the Heir Tertiary to the Throne of Man. Just Roger MacClintock.

And it had cost the life of Bravo Company's commanding officer, Captain Armand Pahner.

Pahner had treated his nominal commander first as a useless appendage to be protected, then as a decent junior officer, and, finally, as a warrior scion of House MacClintock. As a young man worthy to be Emperor, and to command Bronze Battalion. Pahner had become more than a friend. He'd become the father Roger had never had, a mentor, almost a god. And in the end, Pahner had saved the mission and Roger's life by giving his own.

Roger MacClintock couldn't remember the names of all his dead. At first, they'd been faceless nonentities. Too many had been killed taking and holding Voitan, dying under the spears of the Kranolta, before he even learned their names. Too many had been killed by the *atul*, the low-slung hunting lizards of Marduk. Too many had been killed by the *flar-ke*, the wild dinosauroids related to the elephant-like *flar-ta* packbeasts. By vampire moths and their poisonous larva, the killerpillars. By the nomadic Boman, by sea monsters out of darkest nightmares, and by the swords and spears of the cannibalistic "civilized" Krath.

But if he couldn't remember all of them, he remembered many. The young plasma gunner, Nassina Bosum, killed by her own malfunctioning rifle in one of the first attacks. Corporal Ima Hooker and Dokkum, the happy mountaineer from Sherpa, killed by *flar-ke* almost within sight of Ran Tai. Kostas, the single human being who'd ever cared for him in those cold, old days before this nightmare, killed by an accursed damncroc while fetching water for his prince. Gronningen, the massive cannoneer, killed taking the bridge of this very ship.

So many dead, and so far yet to go.

The Saint ship for which they'd fought so hard showed how brutal the struggle to capture it had been. No one had suspected that the innocent tramp freighter was a covert, special operations ship, crewed by elite Saint commandos. The risk in capturing it had seemed minor, but since losing Roger would have made their entire epic march and all of their sacrifices in vain, he'd been left behind with their half-trained Mardukan allies when the surviving members of Bravo Company went up to take possession of the "freighter."

The three-meter-tall, horned, four-armed, mucus-skinned natives of The *Basik*'s Own had come from every conceivable preindustrial level of technology. D'Nal Cord, his *asi*—technically, his "slave," since Roger had saved his life without any obligation to do so, though anyone who made the mistake of treating the old shaman as a menial would never live long enough to recognize the enormity of his mistake—and Cord's nephew Denat had come from the

X'Intai, the first, literally Stone Age tribe they had encountered. The Vasin, riders of the fierce, carnivorous *civan*, were former feudal lords whose city-state had been utterly destroyed by the rampaging Boman barbarians and who had provided The *Basik*'s Own's cavalry. The core of its infantry had come from the city of Diaspra—worshipers of the God of Waters, builders and laborers who had been trained into a disciplined force first of pikemen, and then of riflemen.

The *Basik*'s Own had followed Roger through the battles that destroyed the "invincible" Boman, then across demon-haunted waters to totally unknown lands. Under the banner of a *basik*, rampant, long teeth bared in a vicious grin, they'd battled the Krath cannibals and taken the spaceport. And in the end, when the Marines were unable to overcome the unexpected presence of Saint commandos on the ship, they'd been hurled into the fray again.

Rearmed with modern weaponry—hypervelocity bead and plasma cannon normally used as crew-served weapons or as weapons for powered armor—the big Mardukans had been thrown into the ship in a second wave and immediately charged into the battle. The Vasin cavalry had rushed from position to position, ambushing the bewildered commandos, who could not believe that "scummies" using cannon as personal weapons were really roaming all over their ship, opening shuttle bay doors to vacuum and generally causing as much havoc as they could. And while the . . . individualistic Vasin had been doing that, the Diaspran infantry had taken one hard point after another, all of them heavily defended positions, by laying down plasma fire as if it were the rank-upon-rank musketry which was their specialty.

And they'd paid a heavy price for their victory. In the end, the ship had been taken, but only at the cost of far too many more dead and horribly injured. And the ship itself had been largely gutted by the savage firefights. Modern tunnel ships were remarkably robust, but they weren't designed to survive the effect of five Mardukans abreast, packed bulkhead-to-bulkhead in a passage and volley-firing blast after blast of plasma.

What was left of the ship was a job for a professional space dock, but that was out of question. Jackson Adoula, Prince of Kellerman, and Roger's despised father, the Earl of New Madrid, had made that impossible when they murdered his brother and sister and all of his brother's children, massacred the Empress' Own, and somehow gained total control of the Empress herself. Never in her wildest dreams would Alexandra MacClintock have closely associated herself with Jackson Adoula, whom she despised and distrusted. And far less would she ever have married New Madrid, whose treasonous tendencies she'd proven to her own satisfaction before Roger was ever born. Indeed, New Madrid's treason was the reason she'd never married him ... and a large part of the explanation for her distrust of Roger himself. Yet according to the official news services, Adoula had become her trusted Navy Minister and closest Cabinet confidant, and this time she had announced she *did* intend to wed New Madrid. Which seemed only reasonable, the newsies pointed out, since they were the men responsible for somehow thwarting the coup attempt which had so nearly succeeded.

The coup which, according to those same official news services, had been instigated by none other than Prince Roger ... at the very instant that he'd been fighting for his life against ax-wielding Boman barbarians on sunny Marduk.

Something, to say the least, was rotten in Imperial City. And whatever it was, it meant that instead of simply taking the space-port and sending home a message "Mommy, come pick me up," the battered warriors at Roger's back now had the unenviable task of retaking the entire Empire from the traitors who were somehow controlling the Empress. The survivors of Bravo Company—all twelve of them—and the remaining two hundred and ninety members of The *Basik*'s Own, pitted against one hundred and twenty star systems, with a population right at three-quarters of a trillion humans, and uncountable soldiers and ships. And just to make their task a bit more daunting, they had a time problem. Alexandra was "pregnant"—a new scion had been popped into the uterine replicator, a full brother of Roger's, from his mother's and father's genetic material—and under Imperial law, now that Roger had been officially attainted for treason, that fetus became the new Heir Primus as soon as he was born.

Roger's advisers concurred that his mother's life would last about as long as spit on a hot griddle when that uterine replica-tor was opened.

Which explained the still dwindling mushroom cloud. When the Saints came looking for their missing ship, or an Imperial carrier finally showed up to wonder why Old Earth hadn't heard from Marduk in so long, it would appear a pirate vessel had pillaged the facility and then vanished into the depths of space. What it would *not* look like was the first step in a counter coup intended to regain the Throne for House MacClintock.

He took one last look at the viewscreens, then turned and led his staff off the bridge towards the ship's wardroom. Although the wardroom itself had escaped damage during the fighting, the route there was somewhat hazardous. The approaches to the bridge had taken tremendous punishment—indeed, the decks and bulkheads of the short security corridor outside the command deck had been sublimed into gas by plasma fire from both sides. A narrow, flexing, carbon-fiber catwalk had been built as a temporary walkway, and they crossed it carefully, one at a time. The passageway beyond wasn't much better. Many of the holes in the deck had been repaired, but others were simply outlined in bright yellow paint, and in many places, the bulkheads reminded Roger forcibly of Old Earth Swiss cheese.

He and his staffers picked their way around the unrepaired holes in the deck and finally reached the wardroom's dilating hatch, and Roger seated himself at the head of the table. He leaned back, apparently entirely at ease, as the lizard curled into a ball by his side. His calm demeanor fooled no one. He'd worked very hard on creating an image of complete *sang-froid* in any encounter. It was copied from the late Captain Pahner, but Roger lacked that soldier's years of experience. The tension, the energy, the anger, radiated off him in waves.

He watched the others assume their places.

D'Nal Cord squatted to the side of the lizard, behind Roger, silent as the shadow which in many ways he was, holding himself up with the long spear that doubled as a walking stick. Theirs was an interesting bonding. Although the laws of his people made him Roger's slave, the old shaman had quickly come to understand that Roger was a young nobleman, and a bratty one at that. Despite his official "slave" status, he'd taken it as his duty to chivvy the young brat into manhood, not to mention teaching him a bit more of the sword, a weapon

Cord had studied as a young man in more civilized areas of Marduk.

Cord's only clothing was a long skirt of locally made *dianda*. His people, the X'Intai, like most Mardukans the humans had met, had little use for clothing. But he'd donned the simple garment in Krath, where it was customary to be clothed, and continued to wear it, despite the barbarism of the custom, because humans set such store by it.

Pedi Karuse, the young female Mardukan to his left (since there was no room for her behind him), was short by Mardukan standards, even for a woman. Her horns were polished and colored a light honey-gold, she wore a light robe of blue *dianda*, and two swords were crossed behind her back. The daughter of a Shin chieftain, *her* relationship with Cord was, if anything, even more "interesting" than Roger's.

Her people shared many common societal customs with the X'Intai, and when Cord saved her from Krath slavers, those customs had made her the shaman's *asi*, just as he was Roger's. And since Roger had been squared away by that time, Cord had taken up the training of his new "slave," only to discover an entirely new set of headaches.

Pedi was at least as headstrong as the prince, and a bit wilder, if that were possible. Worse, the very old shaman, whose wife and children were long dead, had found himself far more attracted to his "*asi*" than was proper in a society where relations between *asi* and master were absolutely forbidden. Unfortunately for Cord's honorable intentions, he'd taken a near-mortal wound battling the Krath at about the same time he entered his annual "heat," and Pedi had been in charge of nursing him. She'd recognized the signs and decided, on her own, that it was vital he be relieved of at least that pressure on his abused body.

Cord, semiconscious and delirious at the time, had remembered nothing about it. It had taken him some time to recognize what was changing about his *asi*, and he'd only been aware that he was going to be a father again for a handful of weeks.

He was still adjusting to the knowledge, but in the meantime, Pedi's father had become one of Roger's strongest allies on the planet. After a futile protest on the shaman's part that he was far too old to be a suitable husband for Pedi, the two had been married in a Shin ceremony. If the other Shin had noticed that Pedi was showing signs of pregnancy—developing "blisters" on her back to hold the growing fetuses—they had politely ignored it.

Despite the marriage, however, Pedi's honor as Cord's *asi* still required her to guard the shaman's back (pregnant or no), just as he was required to guard Roger. So Roger found the two almost constantly following him around in a trail. He shook them off whenever he could, these days, but it wasn't easy.

Eleanora O'Casey, Roger's chief of staff and the only surviving "civilian" from *DeGlopper*'s passengers, settled into the seat to his right. Eleanora was a slight woman, with brown hair and a pleasant face, who'd had no staff to chief when they landed on Marduk. She'd been given the job by the Empress in hopes that some of her noted academic skills—she was a multidegree historian and specialist in political theory—would rub off on the wastrel son. She was a city girl, with the flat, nasal accent of Imperial City, and at the beginning of the march across the planet, Roger and everyone else had wondered how long she would last. As it had turned out, there was a good bit of steel under that mousy cover, and her knowledge of good old-fashioned city-state politics had proven absolutely vital on more than one occasion.

Eva Kosutic, Bravo Company's Sergeant Major and High Priestess of the Satanist Church of Armagh, took the chair across from Eleanora. She had a flat, chiseled face and dark brown, almost black hair. A deadly close-in warrior and a fine sergeant major, she now commanded Bravo Company's remnants—about a squad in size—and functioned as Roger's military aide.

Sergeant Adib Julian, her lover and friend, sat next to her. The onetime armorer had always been the definitive "happy warrior," a humorist and practical joker who got funnier and funnier as things looked worse and worse. But his laughing black eyes had been shadowed since the loss of his best friend and constant straight man, Gronningen.

Across from Julian sat Sergeant Nimashet Despreaux. Taller than Kosutic or Julian, she had long brown hair and a face beautiful enough for a high-class fashion model. But where most models had submitted to extensive body-sculpting, Despreaux was all natural, from her high forehead to her long legs. She was as good a warrior as anyone at the table, but she never laughed these days. Every death, friend or enemy, weighed upon her soul, and the thousands of corpses they'd left behind showed in her shadowed eyes. So did her relationship with Roger. Despite her own stalwart resistance and more than a few "stumbles," she and Roger could no longer pretend—even to themselves—that they hadn't fallen hard for each other. But Despreaux was a country girl, as lower-class as it was possible to be in the generally egalitarian Empire, and she'd flatly refused to marry an emperor. Which was what Roger was inevitably going to be one day, if they won.

She glanced at him once, then crossed her arms and leaned back, her eyes narrowed and wary.

Next to her, in one of the oversized station chairs manufactured to fit the Mardukans, sat Captain Krindi Fain. Despreaux was tall for human, but the Mardukan dwarfed her. The former quarryman wore a Diaspran infantryman's blue leather harness and the kilt the infantry had adopted in Krath. He, too, crossed his arms, all four of them, and leaned back at ease.

Behind Fain, looming so high he had to squat so his horns didn't brush the overhead, was Erkum Pol, Krindi's bodyguard, senior NCO, batman, and constant shadow. Not particularly overburdened intellectually, Erkum was huge, even by Mardukan standards, and "a good man with his hands" as long as the target was in reach of a hand weapon. Give him a gun, and the safest place to be was between him and the enemy.

Rastar Komas Ta'Norton, once Prince of Therdan, sat across from Krindi, wearing the leathers of the Vasin cavalry. His horns were elaborately carved and bejeweled, as befitted a Prince of Therdan, and his harness bore four Mardukan-scaled bead pistols, as also befitted a Prince of Therdan who happened to be an ally of the Empire. He'd fought Roger once, and lost, then joined him and fought at his side any number of other times. He'd won all of those battles, and the bead pistols he wore were for more than show. He was probably the only person in the ship who was faster than Roger, despite the prince's cobralike reflexes.

The outsized chair next to Rastar was occupied by his cousin, Honal, who'd escaped with him, cutting a path to safety for the only women and children to have survived when Therdan and the rest of the border states fell to the Boman. It was Honal who had christened their patched-together mixed force of humans and Mardukans "The *Basik*'s Own." He'd chosen the name as a joke, a play on "The Empress' Own" to which the Bronze Battalion belonged. But Roger's troopers had made the name far more than a joke on a dozen battlefields and in innumerable small skirmishes. Short for a Mardukan, Honal was a fine rider, a deadly shot, and even better with a sword. He was also insane enough to win one of the battles for the ship by simply turning off the local gravity plates and venting the compartment—and its defenders—to vacuum. He was particularly fond of human aphorisms and proverbs, especially the ancient military maxim that "If it's stupid and it works, it ain't stupid." Honal was crazy, not stupid.

At the foot of the table, completing Roger's staff and command group, sat Special Agent Temu Jin of the Imperial Bureau of Investigation. One of the countless agents sent out to keep an eye on the far-flung bureaucracy of the Empire, he had been cut off from contact by the coup. His last message from his "control" in the IBI had warned that all was not as it appeared on Old Earth and that he was to consider himself "in the cold." He'd been the one who'd had to tell Roger what had happened to his family. After that, he'd been of enormous assistance to the prince when it came time to take the spaceport and the ship, and now he might well prove equally vital to regaining the Throne.

Which was what this meeting was all about.

"All right, Eleanora. Go," Roger said, and sat back to listen. He'd been so busy for the last month handling post-battle cleanup chores and the *maskirova* at the spaceport that he'd been unable to devote any time to planning what came next. That had been the job of his staff, and it was time to see what they'd come up with.

"Okay, we're dealing with a number of problems here," Eleanora said, keying her pad and preparing to tick off points on it.

"The first one is intelligence, or lack thereof. All we have in the way of information from Imperial City is the news bulletins and directives that came in on the last Imperial resupply ship. Those are nearly two months old, so we're dealing with an information vacuum on anything that's happened in the interim. We also have no data on conditions in the Navy, except for the announced command changes in Home Fleet and the fact that Sixth Fleet, which is normally pretty efficient, was last seen apparently unable to get itself organized for a simple change of station move and hanging out in deep space. We have no hard reads on who we might be able to trust. Effectively, we're unable to trust anyone in the Navy, especially the various commanders who've been put in place post-coup.

"The second problem is the security situation. We're all wanted in the Empire for helping you with this supposed coup. If any *one* of the *DeGlopper's* survivors goes through Imperial customs, or even a casual scan at a spaceport, alarm bells are going to ring from there to Imperial City. Adoula's faction has to believe you're long dead, which makes you the perfect bogeyman. Who better to be wanted for something he didn't do, covering up the fact that they were the real perps, than someone who's dead? But the point remains that without *significant* disguise mod, none of us can step foot on any Imperial planet, and we're going to have real problems going anywhere *else* that's friendly with the Empire. Which means everywhere. Even the Saints would grab us, for any number of reasons we wouldn't like.

"The third problem is, of course, the actual mission. We're going to have to overthrow the current sitting government and capture your mother *and* the uterine replicator, without the bad guys making off with either. We're also going to have to prevent the Navy from interfering."

"'Who holds the orbitals, holds the planet,'" Roger said.

"Chiang O'Brien." Eleanora nodded. "You remembered that one."

"Great Gran's former Dagger Lord daddy had a way with words," Roger said, then frowned. "He also said 'One death is a tragedy; a million is a statistic.'"

"He cribbed that one from a much older source," Eleanora said. "But the point is valid. If Home Fleet comes in on Adoula's side—and with its current commander, that's a given—we're not going to win, no matter who or what we hold. And that completely ignores the insane difficulty of actually *capturing* the Empress. The Palace isn't just a collection of buildings; it's the most heavily fortified collection of buildings outside Moonbase or Terran Defense Headquarters itself. It might *look* easy to penetrate, but it's not. And you can be sure Adoula's beefed up the Empress' Own with his own bully boys."

"They won't be as good," Julian said.

"Don't bet on it," Eleanora replied grimly. "The Empress may hate and detest Adoula, but her father didn't, and this isn't the first time Adoula's been Navy Minister. He knows good soldiers from bad—or damned well ought to—and either he or someone else on his team managed to take out the rest of the Empress' Own when they seized the Palace in the first place. He'll rely on that same expertise when he brings in his replacements, and just because they work for a bad man, doesn't mean they'll be bad soldiers."

"Cross that bridge when we come to it," Roger said. "I take it you're not just going to give me a litany of bad news I already know?"

"No. But I want the bad to be absolutely clear. This isn't going to be easy, and it's not going to be guaranteed. But we do have some assets. And, more than that, our enemies do have problems. Nearly as many problems as we have, in fact, and nearly as large.

"The news we have here is that there are already questions in Parliament about the Empress' continuing seclusion. The Prime Minister is still David Yang, and while Prince Jackson's Conservatives are part of his coalition, he and Adoula are anything but friends. I'd guess that a lot of the reason they seem to be hunting so frantically for you, Roger, is that Adoula is using the 'military threat' you represent as the leverage he needs as Navy Minister to balance Yang's power as Prime Minister within the Cabinet."

"Maybe so," Roger said, with more than a trace of anger in his voice, "but Yang's also a lot closer to the Palace than we are, and *we* can tell what's going on. Yang may actually believe I'm dead, but he knows *damned* well who actually pulled off the coup. And who's controlling my mother. And he hasn't done one pocking thing about it."

"Not that we know of, at any rate," Eleanora observed in a neutral tone. Roger's eyes flashed at her, but he grimaced and made a little gesture. It was clear his anger hadn't abated—Prince Roger was angry a lot, these days—but it was equally clear he was willing to accept his chief of staff's qualification.

For the moment, at least.

"On the purely military side," O'Casey continued after a moment, "it seems clear Adoula, despite his current position at the head of the Empire's military establishment, hasn't been able to replace all of the Navy's officers with safe cronies, either. Captain Kjerulf, for example, is in a very interesting position as Chief of Staff for Home Fleet. I'd bet he's not exactly a yes-man for what's going on, but he's still there. And then there's Sixth Fleet, Admiral Helmut."

"He's not going to take what's happening lying down," Julian predicted confidently. "We used to joke that Helmut got up every morning and prayed to the picture of the Empress over his bed. And he's, like, prescient or something. If there's any smell of a fish, he'll be digging his nose in; you can be sure of that. Sixth Fleet's going to be behind *him*, too. He's headed it for years. Way longer than he should have. It's like his personal fiefdom. Even if they send someone out to replace him, five gets you ten that the replacement has an 'accident' somewhere along the line."

"Admiral Helmut was noted for some of those tendencies in reports I've seen," Temu Jin interjected. "Negatively, I might add. Also for, shall we say, zealous actions in ensuring that only officers who met his personal standards—and not just in terms of military capability—were appointed to his staff, the command of his carrier and cruiser squadrons, and even to senior ship commands. Personal fiefdoms are a constant concern for the IBI and the Inspectorate. It was only his clear loyalty to the Empress, and the Empire, that prevented his removal. But I concur in Sergeant Julian's estimate of him, based on IBI investigations."

"And there's one last possibility," Eleanora continued. Her voice was thoughtful, and her eyes were half-slitted in a calculating expression. "It's the most . . . interesting of all, in a lot of ways. But it also depends on things we know the least about at this point."

She paused, and Roger snorted.

"You don't need the 'cryptic seer' look to impress me with your competence, Eleanora," he said dryly. "So suppose you go ahead and spill this possibility for us?"

"Um?" Eleanora blinked, then flashed him a grin. "Sorry. It's just that a fair percentage of the Empress' Own tends to retire to Old Earth. Of course, a lot take colonization credits to distant systems, but a large core of them stays on-planet. After tours in the Empress' Own, I suppose backwaters look a bit less thrilling than they might to a regular Marine retiree. And the Empress' Own, active-duty or retired, are loyal beyond reason to the Empress. And they're also, well . . ." She gestured at Julian and Despreaux. "They're smart, and they have a worm's eye view of the politics in Imperial City. They're going to be making their own estimations. Even absent what we know, that Roger was on Marduk when he was supposedly carrying out this attempted coup, they're going to be suspicious."

"Prove I was out here, not anywhere near Sol . . ." Roger said.

"And they're going to be livid," Eleanora said, nodding her head.

"How many?" Roger asked.

"The Empress' Own Association lists thirty-five hundred former members living on Old Earth," Julian replied. "The Association's directory lists them by age, rank on retirement or termination of service, and specialty. It also gives their mailing addresses and electronic contact information. Some are active members, some inactive, but they're all listed. And a lot of them are . . . pretty old for wet-work. But, then again, a lot ain't."

"Anybody that anyone knows?" Roger asked.

"A couple of former commanders and sergeants," Despreaux answered. "The Association's Regimental Sergeant Major is Thomas Catrone. No one in the company really knew him when he was in. Some of us crossed paths, but that doesn't begin to count for something like this. But . . . Captain Pahner did. Tomcat was one of the Captain's basic training instructors."

"Catrone's going to remember Pahner as some snot-nosed basic training enlistee, if he remembers him at all." Roger thought about that for a moment, then shrugged. "Okay, I doubt he was a snot-nose even then. It's hard to imagine, anyway. Any other assets?"

"This," Eleanora said, gesturing at the overhead and, by extension, the entire ship. "It's a Saint insertion ship, and it's got some facilities that are, frankly, a bit unreal. Including some for bod-mods for spy missions. We can do the extensive bod-mods we're going to require for cover with those facilities."

"I'm going to have to cut my hair, aren't I?" Roger's mouth

made a brief one-sided twitch that might have been construed as a grin.

"There were some suggestions that went a bit beyond that." Eleanora made a moue and glanced at Julian. "It was suggested that to ensure nobody began to suspect it was you, and so you could keep your hair, you could change sex."

"*What?*" Roger said in chorus with Despreaux.

"Hey, I also suggested Nimashet change at the same time," Julian protested. "That way—*oomph!*"

He stopped as Kosutic elbowed him in the gut. Roger coughed and avoided Despreaux's eye, while she simply rolled a tongue in her cheek and glared at Julian.

"We've come to an agreement, however," the chief of staff continued, also looking pointedly at Julian, "that that extreme level of change won't be necessary. The facilities are extensive, however, and we'll *all* be retroed with a nearly complete DNA mod. Skin, lungs, digestive tract, salivaries—anything that can shed DNA or be tested in a casual scan. We can't do anything about height, but everything else will change. So there's no reason you can't keep the hair. Different coloration, but just as long."

"The hair's not important," Roger said frowningly. "I'd considered cutting it, anyway. As a ... gift. But the time was never right."

Armand Pahner had cordially detested Roger's hair from first meeting. But the funeral had been a hurried affair in the midst of the chaos of trying to keep the ship spaceworthy and simultaneously clear the planet of any sign the Bronze Barbarians had ever been there.

"But this way you can keep it." Eleanora kept her own tone light. "And if you didn't, how would we know it was you? At any rate, the body-mod problem is solved. And the ship has other assets. It's too bad we can't take it deep into Imperial space."

"No way," Kosutic said, shaking her head sharply. "One good look at it by any reasonably competent customs officer, even if we could get it patched up, and he's going to know it's not just some tramp freighter."

"So we'll have to dump it—trade it, rather—with someone we can be sure won't be telling the Empire what they traded for."

"Pirates?" Roger grimaced and glanced quickly at Despreaux.

"I'd hate to support those scum in any way. And I wouldn't trust them a centimeter."

"Again, considered and rejected," Eleanora replied. "For both of those reasons. And also because we're going to need a considerable amount of help pirates simply aren't going to be able to provide."

"So who?"

"Special Agent Jin now has the floor," the chief of staff said, rather than responding directly herself.

"I've completed an analysis of the information that wasn't wiped from the ship's computers," Jin said, tapping his own pad. "We're not the only group the Saints have been messing with."

"I'd think not," Roger snorted. "They're a pest."

"This ship, in particular," Jin continued, "has been inserting agents, and some covert action teams, into Alphane territory."

"Aha." Roger's eyes narrowed.

"Into whose territory?" Krindi asked in Mardukan. Because the humans' personal computer implants could automatically translate, the meeting had been speaking the Diaspran dialect of Mardukan with which all the locals were familiar. "Sorry," the infantryman continued, "but I've been getting up to speed on most of your human terms, and this is a new one."

"The Alphanes are the only nonhuman interstellar polity with which we have contact," Eleanora said, descending into lecture mode. "Or, rather, the only one which isn't *predominately* human. The Alphane Alliance consists of twelve planets, with the population about evenly split between humans, Altharis, and Phaenurs.

"The Phaenurs are lizardlike creatures—they look something like *atul*, but with only four legs and two arms, and they're scaly, like the *flar-ta*. They're also empaths—which means they can read emotions—and, among themselves, they're functional telepaths. Very shrewd bargainers, since it's virtually impossible to lie to them.

"The Altharis are a warrior race that looks somewhat like large . . . Well, you don't have the referent, but they look like big koala bears. Very stoic and honorable. Females make up the bulk of their warriors, while males tend to be their engineers and workers. I've dealt with the Alphanes before, and the combination is . . . difficult. You have to lay all your cards on the table, because the Phaenurs can tell if you're lying, and the Altharis lose all respect for you if you do."

"But the critical point, for our purposes, is that we have information the Alphanes need," Jin continued, picking up the thread once more. "They need to know both the extent of Saint penetration—which they're going to be somewhat surprised about, I suspect—and the true nature of what's going on in the Empire."

"Even if they do need to know that, and even if we tell them, that doesn't necessarily mean they're going to help us," Roger pointed out.

"No," Eleanora agreed with a frown. "But they can, and there are reasons they may. I won't say they *will*, but it's our best hope."

"And do you have any suggestions about how we're going to penetrate the Empire?" Roger asked. "Assuming we can convince the Alphanes to help us, that is?"

"Yes," Eleanora said, then shrugged. "It's not my idea, but I think it's a good one. I didn't at first, but it makes more sense than anything else we've come up with. Julian?"

Roger looked at the noncom, and Julian grinned.

"Restaurants," he said.

"What?" Roger frowned blankly.

"Kostas, may he rest in peace, gave me the idea."

"What does Kostas have to do with it?" Roger demanded, almost angrily. The bitter wound of the valet's death had yet to fully heal.

"It was those incredible meals he'd summon up out of nothing but swamp water and day-old *atul*," Julian replied with another smile, this one of sad fondness and memory. "Man, I still can't *believe* some of those recipes he came up with! I was thinking about them, and it suddenly occurred to me that Old Earth is always looking for the 'new' thing. Restaurants spring up with some new, out-of-this-world—literally!—food all the time. It's going to require one helluva lot of funding, but that's going to be a problem for anything we do. So, what we do, is we come to Imperial City with a chain of the newest, most you've-got-to-try-this-new-place, most brassy possible restaurants serving 'authentic Mardukan food.'"

"You've wanted to do this your whole life," Roger said, wonderingly. "Haven't you?"

"No, listen," Julian said earnestly. "We don't just bring Mardukans and Mardukan food. We bring the whole schmeer. *Atul* in cages. *Flar-ta. Basik.* Tanks of *coll* fish. Hell, bring Patty! We throw a grand opening for the new restaurant in Imperial City that's the talk of the whole planet. A parade of *civan* riders and the Diasprans bearing platters of *atul* and *basik* on beds of barleyrice. Rastar chopping the meat off the bone right there in the restaurant for everyone to watch. Impossible to miss."

"The purloined letter approach," Kosutic said. "Don't hide it, flaunt it. They're looking for Prince Roger to come sneaking in? Heaven with that! We'll come in blowing trumpets."

"And do you know how good a restaurant is for having meetings?" Julian asked. "Who thinks about a group of former Empress' Own having one of their get-togethers in the newest, hottest restaurant on the face of the planet?"

"And we've got the whole *Basik*'s Own right there in the heart of the capital," Roger said, almost wonderingly.

"Bingo," Julian agreed with a chuckle.

"Just one problem," Roger noted, with another of those quick, one-side-of-the-face smiles. "They're all lousy cooks."

"It's *haute cuisine*," Julian said. "Who can tell the difference? Besides, we can scrounge up cooks on the planet. Ones that are either loyal to us, or don't know what's going on. Just that they were hired to go to another planet and cook. That place in K'Vaern's Cove, the one down by the water—you know, the one Tor Flain's parents own. That's a whole *family* of expert cooks. Ones we can trust, come to think of it. And how many humans *speak* Mardukan? It was only your toot and Eleanora's that let us get by at first. Then there's Harvard."

"Harvard?" Roger asked.

"Yeah, Harvard. If you trust him," Julian said seriously.

Roger thought about that for a long time. They'd discovered Harvard Mansul, a reporter for the Imperial Astrographic Society in a cell in a Krath fortress the Marines had captured. He'd been almost pathetically grateful to be rescued, and to have his prized Zuiko tri-cam returned more or less unharmed. Since then, he'd been attached to Roger like a limpet. Not for safety, but because, as he'd frankly admitted, it was the story of all time. Marooned prince battles neobarbarians and saves the Empire . . . assuming, of course, that any of them survived.

But Mansul wasn't in it solely for the story. Roger felt confident about that. He was not, by any means, scatterbrained, and he was loyal to the Empire. And furious at what was happening at home.

"I think I trust him," the prince said finally. "Why?"

"Because if we send Harvard back early, he thinks he can get a pretty good piece—maybe a lead piece—into the *IAS Monthly*. He's got good video, and Marduk is one of those 'I can't believe worlds like that still exist' places the IAS loves. If we hit right after the IAS piece, it'd make for that much better publicity, and he's willing, more than willing, to help. Obviously, he'll hold off on the *big* scoop. And he can do some other groundwork for us in advance. We're going to need that."

"Why do I have the feeling Captain Pahner is watching us," Roger said with a crooked smile, "and clasping his head and shaking it. 'You're all insane. This isn't a plan; this is a catastrophe,'" he added in a slightly deeper voice.

"Because it isn't a plan," Kosutic replied simply. "It's the germ of a plan, and it *is* insane, because the whole idea is insane. Twelve Marines, a couple of hundred Mardukans, and one scion of House MacClintock taking on the Empire? No plan that *isn't* insane will save your mother and the Empire."

"Not quite," Eleanora said, carefully. "Well, there's one other approach that *might* do either of those. Government-in-exile."

"Eleanora, we talked about this." Julian shook his head stubbornly. "It won't work."

"Maybe not, but it still needs to be laid on the table," Roger said. "A staff's job is to give its boss options. So let me hear this option."

"We go to the Alphanes and lay out everything we know," Eleanora said, licking her lips. "Then we make a full spectacle of it. Tell the whole story to anyone who'll listen, especially the representatives of other polities. On the side, we dump them the data we got from the ship, by the way. There are already questions in Parliament about your mother's condition—we all know that. This would make it *much* harder for her to conveniently die of 'remnant trauma from her ordeal.' We've got Harvard, who's a known member of the Imperial press, to start the ball rolling, and others. will come to us to follow it up. That much I can absolutely guarantee; the story's a natural."

"And what we'll have is a civil war," Julian said. "Adoula's faction's in too deep to back out, and they're not going to go down smiling. They also control a substantial fraction of the Navy and the Corps, and they *own* the current Empress' Own. We do this, and Adoula either sits tight on Imperial City, declaring a state of martial law in the Sol System while the various fleets have internal squabbles and duke it out in space. Or, maybe even worse, he runs back to his sector with the baby, your mother being dead, and we end up in a civil war between two pretenders to the Throne."

"He's going to get some portion of the Navy, no matter *what* we do," Eleanora argued.

"Not if we capture the king," Julian countered.

"This isn't a chess game," Eleanora said mulishly.

"Wait." Roger held up his hand. "Jin?"

The agent raised an eyebrow and then shrugged.

"I agree with both," he said simply. "All of it. Civil war and all the rest. Which will mean, of course, the Saints will be busy snapping up as many planetary systems as they can manage. The flip side, which, curiously, neither of them mentioned, is that it means all of us will be relatively safe. Adoula wouldn't be able to touch us if we were under the Alphanes' protection. And if they offer it, it will be full force. They're very serious about such things. You can live a full life, whether Adoula is pushed out or not."

"They didn't mention it because it's not part of the equation," Roger said, his face hard. "Sure, it's tempting. But there are too many lives on the trail for any of us to ever think about turning aside because it's 'safer.' The only question that matters here is where our duty lies? So how do you evaluate *that* question?"

"As one with too many imponderables for a definite answer," Jin replied. "We don't have enough information to know if the insertion and countercoup plan is even remotely feasible." He paused and shrugged. "If we find that it's impossible to checkmate Adoula, and we're still undetected, we can back out. Go back to the Alphanes—this all assumes their support—and go for Plan B. And if we're caught, which is highly likely given that the IBI is *not* stupid, the Alphanes will be authorized to release the entire story. It won't help us, or your mother, most likely, but it will severely damage Adoula."

No," Roger said. "One condition we'll have to have on their help will be that if we fail, we *fail*."

"Why?" Julian asked.

"Getting Adoula out of power, rescuing Mother—those are both important things," Roger said. "I'll even admit I'd like to live through accomplishing them. But what's the most important part of this mission?"

He looked around at them, and shook his head as all of them looked back in greater or lesser degrees of confusion.

"I'm surprised at you," he said. "Captain Pahner would have been able to answer that in a second."

"The safety of the Empire," Julian said then, nodding his head. "Sorry."

"I've contemplated not trying to retake the Throne *at all*," Roger said, looking at all of them intently. "The *only* reason I intend to try is because I agree with Mother that Adoula's long-term policies will be more detrimental to the Empire than another coup or even a minor civil war. Give Adoula enough time, and he'll break the Constitution for personal power. *That's* what we're fighting to prevent. But the long-term good of the Empire is the *preeminent* mission. Much, *much* more important than just making sure there's a MacClintock on the Throne. If we fail, there will be no one except Adoula who can possibly safeguard the Empire. He won't do a good job, but that's better than the Empire breaking up into small pieces, ripe for plucking by the Saints or Raiden-Winterhowe, or whoever else moves into the power vacuum. We're talking about the good of three-quarters of a *trillion* lives. A major civil war, with the half-dozen factions that will fall out, would make the Dagger Years look like a pocking *picnic*. No. If we fail, then we fail, and our deaths will be as unremarked as any in history. It's not heroic, it's not pretty, but it *is* the best thing for the Empire . . . and it *will* be done. Clear?"

"Clear," Julian said, swallowing.

Roger leaned his elbow on the station chair's arm and rubbed his forehead furiously, his eyes closed.

"So we go to the Alphanes, get them to switch out the ship for one that's less conspicuous—"

"And a bunch of money," Julian interjected. "There's some technology on here I don't think they have yet."

"And a bunch of money," Roger agreed, still rubbing. "Then we take the *Basik*'s Own, and Patty, and a bunch of *atul* and *basiks* and what have you—"

"And several tons of barleyrice," Julian said.

"And we go start a chain of restaurants, or at least a couple," Roger said.

"A chain would be better," Julian pointed out. "But at least one in Imperial City. Maybe near the old river; they were gentrifying that area when we left."

"And then we *somehow* parlay that into taking the Palace, checkmating Home Fleet, and preventing Adoula from killing my mother," Roger finished, looking up and gesturing with an open palm. "Is *that* what we have as a plan?"

"Yes," Eleanora said in an uncharacteristically small voice, looking down at the tabletop.

Roger gazed up at the overhead, as if seeking guidance. Then he shrugged, reached back to straighten his ponytail, pulled each hair carefully into place, and looked around the compartment.

"Okay," he said. "Let's go."

"Hello, Beach," Roger said.

"I cannot *believe* what your guys did to my ship!" the former Saint officer said angrily. She had soot all over her hands and face and was just withdrawing her head and shoulders from a hole in a portside bulkhead.

Amanda Beach had never been a Saint true-believer. Far too much of the Saint philosophy, especially as practiced by the current leadership, was, in her opinion, so much bullshit.

The Caravazan Empire had been a vigorous, growing political unit, shortly after the Dagger Years, when Pierpaelo Cavaza succeeded to its throne. And Pierpaelo, unfortunately, had been a devotee of the Church of Ryback, an organization dedicated to removing "humanocentric" damage from the universe. Its creed called for the return of all humans to the Sol System, and the rebuilding—in original form—of all "damaged" worlds.

Pierpaelo had recognized this to be an impossibility, but he believed it was possible to reduce the damage humans did, and to prevent them from continuing to seek new frontiers and damaging still more "unspoiled" worlds. He had, therefore, started his "New Program" soon after ascending to the throne. The New Program had called for a sharp curtailment of "unnecessary" resource use via ruthless rationing and restrictions, and a simultaneous aggressively expansionist foreign policy to prevent the "unholy" from further damaging the worlds they held by taking those worlds away from them and transferring them to the hands of more responsible stewards.

For some peculiar reason, a substantial number of his subjects had felt this was a less than ideal policy initiative. Their disagreement with his platform had led to a short, but unpleasant, civil war. Which Pierpaelo won, proving along the way that his particular form of lunacy didn't keep him from being just as ruthless as any of his ancestors.

From that time on, the Saints, as they were called by everyone else in the galaxy, had been a scourge, constantly preaching "universal harmony" and "ecological enlightenment" while attacking any and all of their neighbors at the slightest opportunity.

Beach, in her rise through the ranks of the Saint Navy, had had more than enough opportunities to see the other side of the Saint philosophy. What it amounted to was: "The little people deserve nothing, but the leaders can live as kings." The higher-ups in the Saint military and government lived in virtual palaces, while their subjects were regulated in every mundane need or pleasure of life. While extravagant parties went on in the "holy centers," the people outside those centers had their power turned off promptly at 9 P.M., or whatever local equivalent. While the people subsisted on "minimum necessity" rationing, the powers-that-were had feasts. The people lived in uniform blocks of concrete and steel towers, living their lives day in and day out at the very edge of survival; the leaders lived in mansions and had pleasant little houses for "study and observation" in the wilderness. Always in the most charming possible locations in the wilderness.

For that matter, she'd long ago decided, the whole philosophy was cockeyed. "Minimum resource use." All well and good, but who belled the cat? Who decided that this man, who needed a new heart, deserved one or did not? That this child—one too many—had to die? Who decided that this person could or could not have a house?

The answer was the bureaucracy of the Caravazan Empire. The bureaucracy which insured that *its* leadership had heart transplants. That *its* leadership had as many children as they liked, and houses on pristine streams, while everyone else could go suck eggs.

And she'd poked around the peripheries of enough other societies to see the real black side of Rybak. The Saints had the highest population growth of any human society of the Six Polities, despite a supposedly strictly enforced "one child only" program. Another of what she thought of as the "real" reasons they were so expansionist. They also had the lowest standard of living and—not too surprisingly; it usually went hand-in-hand—the lowest individual productivity. If there was nothing to work towards, there was no reason to put out more work than the bare minimum. If all you saw at the end of a long life was a couple of children who were doomed to slave away their lives, as well, what was the point? For that matter, Caravazan cities were notorious for their pollution problems. Most of them were running at the bare minimum for survival, mainly due to their shitty productivity, and at that level, no one who could do anything about it cared about pollution or the inherent inefficiency of pollution controls.

She'd visited Old Earth during an assignment in the naval service, and been amazed at the planet. Everyone seemed so *rosy*. So well fed, so happy—so smugly complacent, really. The streets were remarkably clean, and there were hardly any bums on them. *No* bums who'd lost hands or arms because of industrial accidents and been left out to die. A chemical spill was *major* news, and nobody seemed to be working very hard. They just *did*, beavering away and getting tons of work done in practically no time.

And Imperial *ships*! Efficiently designed to the point of insanity. When she'd asked one of their shipbuilders why, he'd simply explained—slowly, in small words, as if to a child or a halfwit—that if they were less efficient than their competitors, if their ships didn't get the maximum cargo moved for the minimum cost, both in power usage and in on/off loading speeds, then their customers would go to those competitors.

Lovely rounded bulkheads and control panels, for safety reasons . . . which were considered part of overhead. Control runs that took the shortest possible route with the maximum possible functionality. Engines that were at least ten percent more efficient in energy use than any Saint design. Much less likely to simply blow up when you engaged the tunnel drive or got to max charge on the capacitors, for that matter. And *cheap*. Comparatively speaking, of course; no tunnel drive ship was anything but expensive.

Saint ships, on the other hand, were built in government yards by workers who were half drunk, most of the time, on rotgut bootleg, that being the only liquor available. Or stoned on any number of drugs. The ships took three times as long to build, with horrible quality control and lousy efficiency.

The *Emerald Dawn* was, in fact, a converted Imperial freighter. And it had been converted by a quiet little *Imperial* yard that was happy for the work and more than willing to avoid unnecessary questions, given the money it was being paid. If the work had been done in one of the ham-handed Saint yards, the quality loss would have been noticeable.

In fact, if the *Dawn* had been a Saint ship, those idiot Mardukans would probably have blown it all the way to kingdom come, instead of only halfway.

Amanda sometimes wondered how much of it was intentional. The official purpose of the Church of Ryback was to ensure the best possible environmental conditions. But if they actually *succeeded* in being as "clean" as the Imperials against whom they inveighed so savagely, would people see that level of "contamination" as that great a threat? Would the workers even care about the environment? Could the Church of Ryback sustain itself in conditions where the environment was clean *and* people went to bed hungry every night?

Her commander in the *Dawn*, Fiorello Giovannuci, on the other hand, had been a real, honest, true-believer. Giovannuci wasn't stupid; he'd seen the hypocrisy of the system, but he ignored it. Humans weren't perfect, and the "hypocritical" conditions didn't shake his belief in the core fundamentals of the Church. He'd been in command specifically because he was a true-believer despite his lack of stupidity; no one *but* a true-believer ever got to be in command of a ship. Certainly not of one that spent as much time poking around doing odd missions as the *Dawn*. And when the *Basik's* Own's assault was clearly going to succeed, he'd engaged the auto-destruct sequence.

Unfortunately for his readiness to embrace martyrdom, there'd been a slight flaw in the system. Only true-believers became ship commanders, true, but the CO wasn't the only person who could *shut off* the auto-destruct. So when Giovannuci had been . . . removed by the ever-helpful Imperials, Beach had been in nowise unwilling to turn it off.

Giovannuci himself was no longer a factor in anyone's equations, except perhaps God's. He and his senior noncommissioned officer had tried to murder Roger with "one-shots"—specialized, contact-range anti-armor weapons—after surrendering. The sergeant had died then, but only Armand Pahner's sacrifice of his own life had saved Roger from Giovannuci's one-shot. Unfortunately for Fiorello Giovannuci, the *Dawn's* entire cruise had been an illegal act—piracy, actually, since the Saints and the Empire were officially at peace—and that was a capital offense. Then, too, the accepted rules of war made his attempt to assassinate Roger after surrendering a capital offense, as well. So after a scrupulously honest summary court-martial, Giovannuci had attained the martyrdom he'd sought after all.

As for Amanda Beach, she had no family in the Caravazan Empire. She'd been raised in a state creche and didn't even know who her *mother* was, much less her father. So when the only real choice became dying or burning her bridges with a vengeance, she'd burned them with a certain degree of glee.

Only to discover what a hash the damned Empies and their scummy allies had made of her ship.

"Six more centimeters," she said angrily, rounding on the prince and holding up her thumb and forefinger in emphasis of the distance. "Six. And one of your idiot Mardukans would have blown open a tunnel radius. As it is, the magnets are fried."

"But he didn't blow it open," Roger noted. "So when are we going to have power?"

"You want *power*!? This is a job for a major dockyard, damn it! All I've got is the few spaceport techs who were willing to sign on to this venture, some of your ham-handed soldiers, and *me*! And I'm an *astrogator*, not an engineer!"

"So when are we going to have power?" Roger repeated calmly.

"A week." She shrugged. "Maybe ten days. Maybe sooner, but I doubt it. We'll have to reinstall about eighty percent of the control runs, and we're replacing all the damaged magnets. Well, the worst damaged ones. We're way too short on spares to replace all of them, so we're having to repair some of the ones that only got scorched, and I'm not happy about that, to say the least. You understand that if this had been a *real* freighter that wouldn't even be possible? Their control run molycircs are installed right into the ship's basic structure. We're at least modded to be able to rip 'em out to repair combat damage, but even in our wildest dreams, we never anticipated *this* much of it."

"If it had been a real freighter," Roger said, somewhat less calmly, "we wouldn't have *done* this much damage. Or had our butcher's bill. So, a week. Is there anything we can do to speed that up?"

"Not unless you can whistle up a team from the New Rotterdam shipyards," she said tiredly. "We've got every trained person working on it, and as many untrained as we can handle. We've nearly had some bad accidents as it is. Working with these power levels is no joke. You can't smell, hear, or see electricity, and every time we activate a run to check integrity, I'm certain we're going to fry some unthinking schlub, human or Mardukan, who doesn't know what 'going hot' means."

"Okay, a week or ten days," Roger said. "Are you getting any rest?"

"*Rest?*" she said, cranking up for a fresh tirade.

"I'll take it that that means 'no.'" Roger quirked one side of his mouth again. "Rest. It's a simple concept. I want you to work no more than twelve hours per day. Figure out a way to do that, and the same for everyone else involved in the repairs. Over twelve hours a day, continuous, and people start making bad mistakes. Figure it out."

"That's going to push it to the high end on time," she pointed out.

"Fine," Roger replied. "We've got a new project we need to work out, anyway, and it's going to mean loading a lot of . . . specialized stores. Ten days is about right. And if you blow up the ship, we're going to have to start all over again. As you just noted, you're an astrogator, not an engineer. I don't want you making those sorts of mistakes just because you're too pocking tired to avoid them."

"I've worked engineering," she said with a shrug. "I can hum the tune, even if I can't sing it. And Vincenzo is probably a better engineer than the late chief. At least partly because he's more than willing to do something that's not by the Book but works. Since the Book was written by the idiots back on Rybak's World, it's generally wrong anyway. We'll get it done."

"Fine. But get it done *after* you get some rest. Figure out the schedule for the next day or so, and then tuck it in. Clear?"

"Clear," she said, then grinned. "I'll follow anybody that tells me to knock off work."

"I told you to cut back to twelve hours per day," Roger said with another cheek twitch, "not to knock off. But now, tonight, I want you to get some rest. Maybe even a beer. Don't make me send one of the guards."

"Okay, okay. I get the point," the former Saint said, then shook her head. "Six more damned centimeters."

"A miss is as good as a mile."

"And just what," Beach asked, "is a 'mile'?"

"No idea," Roger answered. "But whatever it is, it's as good as a miss."

Roger continued down the passageway, just generally looking around, talking to the occasional repair tech, until he noticed a cursing monotone which had become more of a continuous, blasphemous mutter.

"Pock. Modderpocking Saint modderpocking equipment . . ."

Two short legs extended into the passage, waving back and forth as a hand scrabbled after the toolbox floating just out of reach.

" . . . get my pocking wrench, and *t'en* you gonna pocking work . . ."

Sergeant Julio Poertena, Bravo Company's unit armorer when the company dropped on Marduk, was from Pinopa, a semitropical planet of archipelagoes, with one small continent, that had been settled primarily from Southeast Asia, and he represented something of an anomaly. Or perhaps a necessary evil; Roger was never quite certain how the Regiment had actually seen Portena.

While the Empress' Own took only the best possible soldiers, in terms of both fighting ability and decorum, the Regiment did allow some room in its mental framework for slightly less decorum among its support staff, who could be kept more or less out of sight on public occasions. Staff such as the unit armorer. Which had been fortunate for Portena's pre-Marduk career, since a man who couldn't get three words out without one of them being the curse word "pock" would never have been allowed, otherwise.

Since their arrival on Marduk, however, Poertena had marched all the way across the world with the rest of them, conjuring miracles from his famed "big pocking pack" times beyond number. And, when miracles hadn't been in the offing, he'd produced serious changes of attitude with his equally infamous "big pocking wrench." More recently, as one of the Marines' few trained techs, he'd been assisting with the ship repairs...in, of course, his own, inimitable fashion.

Roger leaned over and tapped the toolbox, gently, so that it drifted under the scrabbling hand on its counter-grav cushion, apparently all on its own. The hand darted into it and emerged dragging a wrench that was as long as an arm. Then, the hand—with some difficulty, and accompanied by more monotone cursing—hauled the giant wrench into the hole, and there was a series of clangs.

"Get in *t'ere*, modderpocker! Gonna get you to pocking—"

There was a loud zapping sound, and a yowl, followed by more cursing.

"So, *t'at's* t'e way you gonna ...!"

Roger shook his head and moved on.

"Get *up* there, you silly thing!" Roger shouted, and landed a solid kick behind the armored shield on the broad head.

Patty was a *flar-ta*, an elephant-sized, six-legged Mardukan packbeast, that looked something like a triceratops. *Flar-ta* had broad, armored shields on their heads and short horns, much shorter than those of the wild *flar-ke* from which they were clearly descended. Patty's horns, however, were just about twice normal *flar-ta* length, and she obviously had more than her share of "wild" genes. She was a handful for most mahouts, and the Bronze Barbarians had long ago decided that the only reason Roger could ride her was that he was just as bloody-minded as the big omnivore. Her sides were covered in scars, some of which she'd earned becoming "boss mare" of the herd of *flar-ta* the Marines had used for pack animals. But she'd attained most of those scars with Roger on her back, killing the things, Mardukan and animal, that put them there.

Now she gave a low, hoarse bellow and backed away from the heavy cargo shuttle's ramp. She'd had one ride in a shuttle already, and that was all she was willing to go for. The long, sturdy rope attached to the harness on her head prevented her from drawing too far away from the hatch, but the massive shuttle shuddered and scraped on its landing skids as she threw all six-legs into stubborn reverse.

"Look, Roger, try to keep her from dragging the shuttle back to Diaspra, okay?" Julian's request was just a little hard to understand, thanks to how hard he was laughing.

"Okay, beast! If that's how you're gonna be about it," Roger said, ignoring the NCO's unbecoming enjoyment.

The prince slid down the side of the creature, jumped nimbly to the ground via a bound on a foreleg, and walked around her, ignoring the fact that she could squash him like a bug at any moment. He hiked up the ramp until he was near the front of the cargo compartment, then turned and faced her, hands on hips.

"*I'm* going up to the ship in this thing," he told her. "*You* can either come along or not."

The *flar-ta* gave a low, high-pitched sound, like a giant cat in distress, and shook her head.

"Suit yourself."

Roger turned his back and crossed his arms.

Patty gazed at his back for a moment. Then she gave another squeal and set one massive forepaw on the shuttle ramp. She pressed down a couple of times, testing her footing, then slowly eased her way up.

Roger gathered in the slack in the head rope, pulling it steadily through the ring on the compartment's forward bulkhead. When she was fully in the shuttle, he secured the rope, anchoring her (hopefully) as close to the centerline as possible. Then he came over to give her a good scratching.

"I know I've got a kate fruit around here somewhere," he muttered, searching in a pocket until he came up with the astringent fruit. He held it up to her beak—carefully, she could take his hand off in one nip—and had it licked from his palm.

"We're just going to take a little ride," he told her. "No problem. Just a short voyage." You could tell a *flar-ta* anything; they only knew the tone.

While he was soothing her, Mardukan mahouts had gathered around, attaching chains to her legs and harness. She shifted a few times in irritation as the chains clicked tight against additional anchoring rings, but submitted to the indignity.

"I know I haven't been spending much time with you, lately," Roger crooned, still scratching. "But we'll have lots of time on the way to Althar Four."

"What the hell are you going to do with her aboard ship?" Julian asked as he entered the compartment through the forward personnel hatch and picked up a big wicker basketful of barley-rice. He set it under Patty's nose, and she dipped in, scooping up a mouthful of the grain and then spraying half of it on the cargo deck.

"Put her in hold two with Winston," Roger answered, using a stick to reach high enough to scratch the beast's neck behind the armored shield. The big, gelded *flar-ta* was even larger than Patty, but much more docile.

"Let's hope she doesn't kick open the pressure door," Julian grumbled, but that, at least, was a false issue. The cargo bay pressure doors were made out of ChromSten, the densest, strongest, *heaviest* alloy known to man . . . or any other sentient species. Even the latches and seals were shielded by too much metal for Patty to demolish.

"I don't think that will be a problem," Roger said. "*Feeding* her now. *That* might be."

"Not as much as feeding the *civans*," Julian muttered.

"Quit that!" Honal slapped the *civan* on its muzzle as it tried to take a chunk out of his shoulder. It was never wise to allow one of the ill-tempered, aggressive riding beasts to forget who was in charge, but he understood why it was uneasy. The entire ship was vibrating.

Cargo was being loaded—*lots* of cargo. There were flash-frozen *coll* fish from K'Vaern's Cove, kate fruit and *dianda* from Marshad, barleyrice from Diaspra and Q'Nkok, and *flar-ta, atul* and *basik*—both live examples and meat—from Ran Tai, Diaspra, and Voitan. There were artifacts, for decoration and trade, from Krath, along with gems and worked metals from the Shin. All of it had been traded for, except the material from the Krath. In the Krath's case, Roger had made an exception to his belief that it was generally not a good idea to exact tribute and simply landed with a shuttle and ordered them to fill it to the deckhead. He was still bitterly angry over their attempt to use Despreaux as one of their "Servants of the God"—sentient sacrifices to be butchered living and then eaten—and it showed. As far as he was concerned, if *all* of their blood-splattered temple/slaughterhouses were stripped of statuary and gilding, so much the better.

Honal couldn't have agreed more with his human prince, except, perhaps, for that bit about "not a good idea" where tribute was concerned. But he understood perfectly how the continuous rumble of the loading, not to mention the strange smells of the damaged ship and the odd light from the overheads, combined to make the *civan,* never the most docile of beasts at any time, nervous. And when *civan* got nervous, they tended to want to spread it around. Generally by making anyone around them afraid for their lives.

Civan were four-meter tall, bipedal riding beasts that looked something like small tyranosaurs. Despite their appearance, they were omnivorous, but they did best with a diet that included some meat. And they were often more than willing to add a rider's leg or arm to that diet. On the other hand, they were *always* willing to add an *enemy's* face or arm to the menu, which made them preeminent cavalry mounts. If you could get them to distinguish friend from foe, that was.

The Vasin were experts at creating that distinction, which had made them the most feared cavalry on the Diaspran side of the main continent of Marduk. Up to the coming of the Boman, that was.

The Boman had been a problem for generations, but it was only in the last few years that they'd organized and increased in numbers to the point of becoming a real threat. The Vasin lords, descendents of barbarians who had themselves swept down from the north only a few generations ahead of the Boman, had been established as a check on the fresh barbarian invasion from the northern Plains. They'd been paid in tribute from the more civilized areas—city-states like Sindi, Diaspra, and K'Vaern's Cove—to prevent people like the Boman from causing mischief to the south.

But when the Boman had combined under their great chief, Kny Camsan, they'd swept the severely outnumbered Vasin cavalry from the field in waves of infantry attacks. The fact that the Vasin cities' food supplies had been systematically sabotaged (for reasons which had, presumably, made sense to his own warped thinking) by the particularly megalomaniacal ruler of Sindi, one of the cities they were supposed to be defending, had effectively neutralized the Vasin's traditional strategy for dealing with that sort of situation. With their starving garrisons unable to stand the sieges which usually outlasted the Boman's ability to maintain their cohesion, the Vasin castles and fortified cities had been overwhelmed, their garrisons and citizens slaughtered to the last babe in arms. And after that, the Boman had continued on to conquer Sindi and put its miscalculating ruler and his various cronies to death in the approved, lingering Boman style.

They undoubtedly would have destroyed K'Vaern's Cove and the ancient city of Diaspra, as well, but for the arrival of Roger's forces. The Marines' core of surviving high-tech gear and their thousands of years of military experience and "imported" technology—pike formations, at first, and then rifles, muskets, artillery, and even black powder bombardment rockets—had managed to hold together an alliance against the Boman and break them in the heart of their newly conquered citadel of Sindi.

The entire occupied area had been recovered, with the Boman forces scattered after hideous casualties and either forced to resettle under local leadership or driven back across the northern borders. Even the Vasin castles, what was left of them, had been retaken. The last Boman remnants had been driven out as soon as the humans took the spaceport and, reassured that there were no

Saints around, could use their combat shuttles and heavy weapons against the barbarians.

Honal and Rastar could have returned to their homes. But one look at the ruined fortifications, the homes they'd grown up in and in which their parents, families, and friends had died, was enough. They'd returned to the spaceport with Roger and turned their backs upon the past. The Vasin—not only the force Honal and Rastar had led out of the ruins of Therdan to cover the evacuation of the only women and children to survive the city's fall, but all that had been gathered from all of their scattered people's cities—were now surrogates of Prince Roger MacClintock, heir apparent to the Throne of Man. Most of the survivors remained on Marduk, relocated to new homes near Voitan and provided with locally produced Imperial technology to ensure their survival and well being. But Rastar's personal troops were committed to the personal service of the human who had made their survival as a people possible. Where Roger went, they went. Which currently meant to another planet.

Honal had to admit that if it weren't for the circumstances which made leaving possible—his entire family was dead, as well as Rastar's—he would have felt only pleased anticipation at the prospect of following Roger. He'd always had a bit of the wanderlust, probably inherited from his nomadic forefathers, not to mention his Boman tribute-bride mother. And the chance to see another planet was one very few Mardukans had been given.

On the other hand, it meant getting the *civan* settled aboard a starship. It had been bad enough on those cockleshell boats they'd used to cross the Western Ocean, but starships were even worse, in a way.

For one thing, there was that constant background *thrum*. He was told it was from the fusion plants—whatever they were—that fed power to the ship, and that they'd been charging the "capacitors" for the "tunnel drive" (more odd words) for the last two days. And the gravity was different from Marduk's. It was lighter, if anything, which allowed for some interesting new variations on combat training. And, like most of the Mardukans, Honal had developed a positive passion for the game of "basketball." The humans, on the other hand, had insisted that the Mardukans had to use baskets which were mounted at two and a half times regulation height the instant they saw the Mardukan players soaring effortlessly through two-meter jump shots in the reduced gravity. But if the Mardukans enjoyed the lighter gravity, the *civan* didn't like it—not at all, at all. And they were taking out their dislike on their grooms and riders.

Honal looked around the big hold at the other riders settling the *civan* in their stalls. Those stalls had been custom-made by the "Class One Manufacturing Plant" which had been shipped from the spaceport to Voitan. They were large enough for the *civan* to pace around in, or lie down to sleep, and strongly made from something called "composite fibers." And there were attachment points on the floor—the *deck*—of the hold, to which the structures had been carefully secured.

The stalls were also roofed, and much of the material the *civan* were going to be eating on the voyage was stuffed into the vast area above them. Huge containers of barleyrice and beans had been hoisted into the area and stacked in tiers. There was water on tap in several spots, and arrangements had been made to dispose of the *civan's* waste. He'd been told that human ships occasionally had to move live cargo, and from the looks of things, they'd figured out how to do it with the normal infernal human ingenuity.

An open area on the inner side of the hold had been fenced off to provide space in which they could work the *civan*. It was big enough for only a few of the beasts to be exercised or trained at once, but it was better than they'd managed on the ships of the Crossing, where the only exercise choice had been to let them swim alongside the ships for short periods. Still, with only one working area available, the grooms and riders were going to be working around the clock to keep them in decent shape.

The clock. That was another thing that took getting used to. The Terran day, which the ship maintained, was only two-thirds as long as Marduk's day. So just about the time it felt like early afternoon, the ship lights dimmed to "nighttime" mode. He'd already noticed the way it affected his own sleep, and he was worried about how the *civan* would react.

Well, they'd make it, or they wouldn't. He loved *civan*, but he'd come to the conclusion that there were even more marvelous transportation options waiting beyond Marduk's eternal overcast.

He'd lusted after the humans' shuttles from the instant he'd seen them in flight, and he'd been told about, and seen pictures of, the "light-flyers" and the "stingships" available on Old Earth. He wondered just how much they cost . . . and what he was going to be earning as a senior aide to the Prince. A lot, he hoped, because assuming they survived for him to collect his pay, he was bound and determined to get himself a light-flyer.

"How's it going?" a voice asked, and he looked up as Rastar appeared at his shoulder.

"Not bad," Honal replied, raising a warning hand to the *civan* as he sensed the lips drawing back from its fangs and its crest folding down. "About as well as can be expected, in fact."

"Good." Rastar nodded, a human gesture he'd picked up. "Good. They think they'll finish loading in a few hours. Then we'll find out if the engines really work."

"Won't that be fun?" Honal said dryly.

"Engaging phase drive—" Amanda Beach drew a deep breath and pressed a button "—now."

At first, the image of the planet below seemed unchanged on the bridge viewscreens. It was just the same slowly circling, blue-and-white ball it had always been. But then the ship began to accelerate, and the ball began to dwindle.

"All systems nominal," one of her few surviving engineering techs said. "Acel is about twenty percent below max, but that's right on the numbers, given our counter-grav field status. Runs one, four, and nine are still out. And charge rate on the tunnel capacitors is still nominal. Nine hours to full tunnel drive power."

"And eleven hours to the Tsukayama Limit," Beach said, with a sigh. "Looks like it's holding. We'll find out when we try to form a singularity."

"Eleven hours?" Roger asked. He'd been standing by in the control room. Not because he felt he could do anything, but because he thought his place was here, at this time.

"Yeah," Beach said. "If everything holds together."

"It will," Roger replied. "I'll be back then."

"Okay." Beach waved a hand almost absently as she concentrated on her control board. "See ya."

✧   ✧   ✧

"I've just had a suspicion I don't much care for," Roger said to Julian. He'd called the sergeant into his office, the former captain's office, once the phase drive had turned out to work after all.

"What kind of suspicion?" Julian crinkled his brow.

"How in the hell do we *know* Beach is headed for Alphane space instead of Saint space? Yes, she seems to have burned her bridges. But if she pops out in a Saint system with the ship—and me—they're going to be somewhat forgiving of any minor lapses on her part. Especially given conditions on Old Earth."

"Ack." Julian shook his head. "You've picked a fine time to think about that, O My Lord and Master!"

"I'm serious, Ju," Roger said. "Do we have anyone left who knows *anything* about astrogation?"

"Maybe Doc Dobrescu," Julian suggested. "But if we put somebody on the bridge to watch Beach, she's going to know damn well what we suspect. And I submit that pissing her off would be the worst possible thing we could do right now. Without her, we're *really* up the creek and the damncrocs are closing in."

"Agreed, and it's something I've already considered. But beyond that, my mind is a blank. Suggestions?"

Julian thought about it for a moment, then shrugged.

"Jin," he said. "Temu Jin," he clarified. Gunnery Sergeant Jin, who'd made the entire crossing of the planet with them, had died in the assault on the ship.

"Why Jin?" Roger asked, then he nodded. "Oh. He's got the whole ship wired, doesn't he?"

"He's in the computers," Julian said, nodding in turn in agreement. "You don't have to be on the bridge to tell what the commands are, where the ship is pointed. If Dobrescu can figure out the stellar positions, and where we're supposed to be, then we'll know. And none the wiser."

"So now you want me to be a star-pilot?"

Chief Warrant Officer Mike Dobrescu glowered at the prince in exasperation. Dobrescu liked being a shuttle pilot. It was a damned sight better job than being a Raider medic, which was what he'd been before applying for flight school. And he'd also been damned good at the job. As a chief warrant with thousands of hours of no-accident time, despite surviving several occasions where accidents really had been called for, he'd been accepted as a shuttle pilot for the small fleet that served the Imperial Palace.

Not too shortly afterwards, he'd been loaded aboard the assault ship *Charles DeGlopper* and sent off to support one ne'er-do-well prince. Okay, he could adjust to being back on an assault ship. At least this time he was in officers' country, instead of four to a closet, like the rest of the Marines. And when they got to the planet they were headed to, he'd be flying shuttles again, which he loved.

Lo and behold, though, he'd flown exactly *once* more. One hairy damned ride, with internal hydrogen tanks and a long damned ballistic course, and then landed—damned nearly out of fuel—in a *deadstick* landing on that incomparable pleasure planet, Marduk.

But wait, things got worse! There being no functional shuttles left, and him being the only trained medic, he was stuck back in the Raider medic business, making bricks out of straw. Over the next eight months, he'd been called upon to be doctor, vet, science officer, xenobiologist, herbalist, pharmacologist, and anything *else* that smacked of having two brain cells to rub together. And after all *that*, he'd found out he was a wanted man back home.

It really sucked. But at least he was back to having shuttles under his fingertips, and he was damned if he was going to get shoved into another pigeonhole for which he had no training and less aptitude.

"I cannot astrogate a starship," he said, quietly but very, very definitely. "You don't have to do the equations for it—that's what the damned computers are for—but you do have to *understand* them. And I don't. We're talking high-level calculus, here. Do it wrong, and you end up in the middle of a star."

"I don't want you to *pilot* the ship," Roger said carefully. "I want you to figure out if *Beach* is piloting it to Alphane space. Just that."

"The ship determines its position in reference to a series of known stars every time it reenters normal-space between tunnel jumps," Jin said. "I can find the readouts, but it's a distance estimate to the stars based on something called magnitude—I'm not familiar with most of the terms—and it gives their angles and distance. From that, the astogrator determines where to go next. They tune the tunnel drive for a direction, charge it up, and they go. But without any better understanding of how they establish their starting position in the first place, I can't begin to figure out where we are, or which direction we're going. For that matter, I only vaguely know which direction Old Earth and the Alphane Alliance—or Saint space—*are* from here."

"Turn right at the first star, and straight on till morning," Dobrescu muttered, then shook his head. "I had a course in it—one one-hour course—in flight school, lo these many eons ago. I forgot it as fast as it was thrown at me. You just don't need it for shuttle piloting. We did a little of it on that ballistic to Marduk, but I was given the figures by *DeGlopper*'s astrogator before we punched the shuttles. I don't think I can figure it out. I'm sorry."

"You look sorry," Roger said, shaking his head, and gave another of those one-cheek grins. "Okay, go ask around. I know Julian and Kosutic don't know any of it. Ask the rest of the Marines if any of them even have a clue. Check with *all* of them, because we really, really need a crosscheck on her navigation. I want to trust her, but *how far* is the question."

"Well, until we get to the Alphanes, at least," Julian said.

"Oh?" Roger lifted one eyebrow at the sergeant. "And who, pray tell, is going to pilot the ship from Althar Four to Old Earth?"

"Come!" Roger called, looking up from a hologram of ship's stores with a pronounced sense of relief.

He hated paperwork, although he realized he had to get used to it. His "command" was now the size of a small regiment—or, at least, an outsized battalion—including shipboard personnel and noncombatants, and the administrative workload was one of some magnitude. Some of that, thankfully, could be handled by the computers. It was much easier now that they had all the automated systems up and running. But he still had to keep his finger on the pulse and make sure his subordinates were doing what *he* wanted them to do, not just what *they* wanted to do.

He hadn't realized how much of that Captain Pahner had handled before his death, and eventually, he knew, he'd shuffle much of it off onto someone else. But before he could deputize and delegate any of it, he had to figure out what was important

right now, in addition to wracking his brain for every detail of
the Imperial Palace he could recall. He knew exactly how essential all of that was, but that didn't make him enjoy it one bit
more, and he tipped back his chair with alacrity as the cabin
hatch opened.

Julian and Jin stepped through it, followed by Mark St. John,
the surviving member of the St. John twins. Mark still shaved
the left side of his head, Roger noted with a pang. By now, it
was long-ingrained habit, but it had grown out of an early order
from a first sergeant who'd been unable to tell the two of them
apart.

The twins had been two of the more notable characters of the
trek across the planet. They'd maintained a permanent, low-level
sibling argument every step of the way—whether it was who Mom
liked more, or who'd done what to whom in some bygone day,
they'd always found something to argue about. They'd also covered
each other's backs, and made sure they got through each encounter
alive. Right up until the assault on the ship, that was.

The two of them had had more experience with zero-G combat
than anyone else in the company, and they'd found themselves
detailed to take out the ship's gun emplacements.

Mark St. John had come back, injured but alive. His brother
John, had not.

John had been a sergeant, a hard-working, smart, capable, NCO.
Mark had always been more than willing to let his brother do
the thinking and mental heavy-lifting. He was a good fighter, and
that, as far as he was concerned, was enough. Roger would take
any of the surviving Marines at his back in any sort of firefight,
or with swords or assegais, come to that. But he wasn't sure he'd
trust Mark's brains on a bet. Which was why he was surprised
to see him with the other two.

"Should I take it you found an astrogator?" Roger raised one
eyebrow and waved at chairs.

"Sir, I'm not an astrogator, but I know stars," St. John said,
remaining at a position of parade rest as Jin and Julian sat
down.

"Tell me," Roger said, leaning further back.

"Me and John," St. John said, with a swallow. "We was raised
on a mining platform. We were shuttling around near the time

we started walking. Stars're all you got to go by when you're out in the beyond. And later, we had astrogation in school. Miners don't always have beacon references to go by. I can pilot and steer by stellar location. Give me the basic astro files, and I can figure out where we are, at least. And which way we went to get there. I know the basics of tunnel navigation, and I can read angles."

"We're entering the first jump in—" Roger consulted his computer implant "toot" and frowned. "About thirty minutes. Did Jin show you what he has?"

"Yes, Your Highness. But I only had time to glance at it. I'm not saying I can tell you off the top of my head. But by the time we're ready for the *next* jump, I'll know if we're headed in the right direction."

"And if we're not?" Roger asked.

"Well, I think then some of us should have a talk with Lieutenant Beach, Sir," Julian said. "Hopefully, that talk will be unnecessary."

"Preparing to engage tunnel drive," Beach said. Normally, that announcement would have come from the Astrogator. Since she didn't have one, she was conning the ship from the astrogation station so she could handle it herself.

"Engaging—now," she said, and pressed a button.

The background thrum of the engines rose in key, climbing higher and higher as a rumble sounded through the ship. Roger knew it had to be his imagination, given the meters upon meters of bulkheads and hatches between him and the cargo hold, but he was almost certain he could hear a distant trumpeting.

"Somehow, I'm willing to bet Patty doesn't much care for this bit," he said softly, and Beach gave him a smile that looked slightly strained.

The engine sound rose and entered a period of prolonged high-pitched vibration. Then it passed.

"We're in tunnel-space," Beach said. The external viewscreens had gone blank.

"That didn't sound right, though," Roger observed.

"No, it didn't," Beach sighed. "We'll just have to find out if we come out in the wrong spot. If we do, and if no major damage's been done, we'll be able to compensate on the next jump."

"How many jumps?" Roger asked lightly.

"Eight to the edge of Alphane space," Beach replied. "Two of them right on the edge of Saint territory."

She didn't look particularly happy about that, which didn't surprise Roger a bit. Each of the jumps, which lasted six hours and took the ship eighteen light-years along its projected course, required a standard day and a half of charting and calibration—not to mention charging the superconductor capacitors. In *Emerald Dawn*'s case, just charging the capacitors took a full forty-eight hours, although ships with better power generation, like the huge carriers of the Imperial Navy, could recharge in as little as thirty-six hours. But they all had to recalibrate and chart between jumps, and Beach was the only qualified bridge officer they had to see to it that it was all done properly.

"Fourteen?" Roger repeated with a sour chuckle. "Well, let's hope the drive holds together—especially through the ones close to the Saints. And that we're in *deep* space."

Ships, especially merchant ships on their lonely sojourns, tended to move directly from system to system, as much as possible. They couldn't hyper into any star system inside its Tsukayama Limit, but as long as they popped back into normal-space no more than a few light-days out from their destination, someone would come out and tow them home in no more than a week or so if their TD failed.

Warships, which more often than not traveled in squadrons and fleets, tended to move from deep space point to deep space point. In the *Dawn*'s case, deciding exactly how to plan their course was an unpleasant balancing act. Too far out, and the failure of the tunnel drive—a real possibility, given the cobbled-together nature of their repairs—would maroon them, probably for all time, in the deeps of space. But too close in to a Saint star system, and there was the chance of a Saint cruiser's wandering out to look over the unexpected, unscheduled, and—above all—*unauthorized* tunnel drive footprint which had suddenly appeared on its stellar doorstep.

"I'm in favor of deep space," Beach said with a grimace. "And, yes, let's hope it holds together."

Despreaux stepped onto the bridge and made a crooking gesture at Roger with one finger. Her smile, he noticed, had a definitely malicious edge.

"My advisers tell me it's time to get my game face on," he said to Beach. "So you won't have the pleasure of my company for a while."

"We'll try to manage," Beach said, with a grin of her own.

Roger worked his jaw muscles and stared into the mirror. The face that stared back at him was utterly unfamiliar.

The Saint mod-pods were liquid-filled capsules into which a patient was loaded for body sculpting. They doubled as autodocs, and two of the four *Dawn* carried were still filled with Marine casualties from the assault. Roger had slipped into one of the other two and been hooked to a breathing apparatus. Then, as far as he was concerned, he'd simply gone to sleep ... until he'd been reawakened in recovery by an unhappy-looking Despreaux.

Her expression hadn't been because of anything wrong with the ship—they'd made the first two tunnel transfers while he was out, and everything was still functioning. It was because of his looks.

The face looking back at him was wider than his "real" face, with high, broad cheekbones and far more pronounced epicanthic folds around eyes which had been transformed into a dark brown. He also had long, black hair, and his hands seemed shorter. They weren't, but they'd become broader in proportion, and he was markedly heavier in the body than he ought to have been. It felt wrong, like in ill-fitting suit.

"Hello, Mr. Chung," he said in someone else's voice. "I see we're going to need a new tailor, as well."

Augustus Chung was a citizen of the United Outer Worlds. The UOW was even older than the Empire of Man, having been a brief competitor for stellar dominance against the old Solarian Union. It still maintained "ownership" of Mars, some of the more habitable of the Sol System's moons, and several outworlds in Sol's vicinity—enough to retain its independence from the Empire and be officially considered the sixth inter-stellar polity. Its territory, however, was entirely surrounded by Imperial star systems.

The UOW survived mainly because of its value as an area where deals which weren't strictly legal among Imperial worlds could be transacted. And citizens of the UOW did not fall under normal

Imperial law. Furthermore, it would be difficult for the Imperials to look up much data on Augustus Chung, because UOW personal data was not readily available to Imperial investigators. In fact, it would take a formal finding of guilt in an Imperial court to pry any information about him out of the UOW. And if things got that far, it wouldn't matter.

Augustus Chung was a businessman. That was what his documents said, anyway—founder, president, and CEO of "Chung Interstellar Exotic Imports Brokerage, LLC." He'd been a purser on various small merchant vessels before going into the "import/export brokerage" business. His sole fixed business address was a post office box on Mars, and Roger wondered what was in it. Probably stuffed with ads for herbal remedies.

Chung was, in other words, a covert agent identity which had been "stockpiled" by the Saints. In fact, over a hundred such identities were available on the ship, which must've taken considerable work to set up. Given the logistics involved, Chung probably had just enough "reality" to survive a light scrutiny. It was a very nice cover . . . and one the Imperial Bureau of Investigation would recognize as such the instant anything attracted its attention and it ran a real check.

"A *tailor*? Is that all you can say?" Despreaux demanded, looking into the mirror beside him.

"Well, that . . . and that I'm looking forward to seeing what Doc comes up with for *you*," he said. He smiled at her in the mirror, and, after a moment, she smiled back and shrugged.

"All he told me is that I'm going to be a blonde."

"Well, we'll make a pretty pair," Roger replied, turning and feeling his footing, carefully. Chung's body was just as muscular as his normal one and, if anything, a tad more powerful. Higher weight, mostly muscle. Broad chest, heavy pectorals, massive shoulders, flat abdominals. He looked like an underweight sumo wrestler. "Assuming I can find a good tent-maker," he added.

"It looks . . . good." Despreaux shrugged again. "Not you, but . . . good. I can get used to it. He's not as pretty as you are, but he's not exactly ugly."

"Darling, with all due respect, *you're* not the girl I'm worried about."

Roger smiled broadly. It felt strange these days, but Chung was a smiler.

"What?" Despreaux sounded confused.

"Patty is *not* going to like this."

Neither did Dogzard.

The Mardukan dog-lizard was defending the middle of Roger's stateroom, hissing and spitting at the intruder into her master's territory.

"Dogzard, it's me," Roger said, pitching his voice as close to normal as he could.

"Not to her, you're not," Julian said, watching carefully. He'd seen Dogzard rip a full-grown Mardukan to shreds in battle, and he was not at all happy about seeing Roger down on one knee with the dog-lizard in its present state. "You don't even *smell* the same, Boss; entirely different genetic basis on your skin."

"It's me," Roger said again, holding out his hand. "Shoo, *doma fleel,*" he added in the language of the X'Intai. It meant something like "little dog," or "puppy." When Roger had picked up the stray in Cord's village, it had been less than a quarter of its current six hundred-kilo size, and the runt of the village.

He continued talking to the dog-lizard in low tones, half in Mardukan, half in Imperial, until he had a hand on her head and was scratching her behind the ears. Dogzard gave a low, hissing whine, then lapped at his arm.

"She is having a moment of existential uncertainty," Cord said, leaning on his spear. "You are acting as if you were her God, but you neither sound nor smell like her God."

"Well, she's going to have to get used to it," Roger replied. Patty had been, if anything, worse. But when he'd climbed onto her back, despite her hissing and spitting, and slapped her on the neck with his sword, she'd gotten the message.

"Okay, Dogzard. That's enough," he added sternly, standing up and waving at the door. "Come on. There's work to do."

The beast looked at him uncertainly, but followed him out of the room. She'd gotten used to life being strange. She didn't always like it, but the good news was that, sooner or later, whenever she followed her God, she eventually got to kill something.

✧   ✧   ✧

"Despreaux?" Pedi Karuse said.

"Yes?" The tall, blonde sergeant walking down the passage stopped, her expression surprised. "How could you tell?"

"The way you walk," the Shin warrior-maid said, falling in beside her. "It's changed a little, but not much."

"Great," Despreaux said. "I thought all us humans looked alike to you?"

"Not friends," Pedi answered, working her back in discomfort, and eyed the sergeant thoughtfully. "You look as if you were four months pregnant, but on the wrong side. And you lost two of your litter. I'm sorry."

"They're not pregnancy blisters," Despreaux said tightly. "They're tits."

"You had them before, but they were . . . smaller."

"I know."

"And your hair's changed color. It's even lighter than my horns."

"I know."

"And it's longer."

"I *know*!"

"This is bad?" Pedi asked. "Is this ugly to humans?"

"No," Despreaux said, just a tad absently. She was busy staring hard at one of the passing civilian volunteers . . . who didn't notice for quite some time because he was *not* looking at her eyes. When he did notice, he had the decency to look either ashamed or worried.

"So what's the problem?" Pedi asked as the civilian scurried off a bit more rapidly than he'd appeared.

"Oh . . . damn." Despreaux's nostrils flared, and then she gave her head a brisk shake.

"Okay," she said then, pointing at her chest, "these are like baby *basik* to an *atul*. Men can *not* seem to get enough of them. I was . . . medium to small before. Probably a little too pretty, too, honestly, but I could *work* with that. These, however," her finger jabbed at her chest again, "are *not* medium to small, and the problems I've got now go way beyond 'a little too pretty.' Just getting a guy to look me in the eye is damned hard. And the hair color—! There are *jokes* about girls with this kind of hair.

About how stupid they are. I've made them myself, God help me. I had a *fit* when Dobrescu showed me the body profile, but he swore this was the best personality available. The bastard. I look like.... God, it's too hard to explain."

Pedi considered this as they walked down the passage, then shrugged.

"Well, there's really only one thing that matters," she finally said.

"What?"

"What Roger thinks of it."

"Oh, good God."

Roger's eyes looked downwards—once—and then fixed resolutely on her face.

"What do you think?" Despreaux asked angrily.

She looked like she could have posed as a centerfold. Long legs were a given, too hard to change. Small hips and waist rising to ... a really *broad* rib cage and shoulders. Slim neck, *gorgeous* face—if anything, even more beautiful than she had been. Bright, nearly purple eyes. Hair that was probably better than his had been. Nice ears. And—

"Christ, those are *huge*," was what he blurted out.

"They're already killing my back," Despreaux told him.

"It's ... as good as you were before, just entirely different ..." Roger said, then paused. "Christ, those are *huge*."

"And all this time I thought you were a leg man," Despreaux said bitingly.

"I'm sorry. I'm *trying* not to look." He shook his head. "They've *gotta* hurt. The whole package is fantastic, though."

"You don't want me to *stay* this way, do you?" Despreaux said desperately.

"Errrr ..." Roger had grown up with an almost passionate inability to communicate with women, which more than once had landed him in very hot water. And whatever he felt at the moment, he realized this was one of those times when he should be very careful about what he said.

"No," he said finally and firmly. "No, definitely not. For one thing, the package doesn't matter. I fell in love with you for who you are, not what you look like."

"Right." Despreaux chuckled sarcastically. "But the package wasn't bad."

"Not bad," Roger admitted. "Not bad at all. I don't think I would have been nearly as attracted if you'd been severely overweight and out of shape. But I love you for *you*. Whatever package you come in."

"So, you're saying I *should* keep this package?"

Roger started to say no, wondered if he should say yes, and then stopped, shaking his head.

"Is this a 'does this dress make me look fat' thing?"

"No," Despreaux said. "It's an honest question."

"In that case, I like them both," he confessed. "They're totally different, and I like them both. I've always been partial to brunettes, especially leggy ones, so the hair is a wash. But I like a decent-sized chest as much as any straight guy. Those are, honestly, a bit too large." Okay, so it was a little white lie. "On the other hand, whether you marry me or not, your body is *your* body, and I'm not going to tell you—or ask you—to do anything with it. Which do you prefer?"

"Which do you think?" she asked sarcastically.

"It was an honest question," Roger replied calmly.

"My *real* body. Of course. The thing is . . . I guess the question I'd ask if I were trying to trap you is: Does this body make me look fat?"

"No," Roger said, and it was his turn to chuckle. "But you know the old joke, right?"

"No," Despreaux said dangerously. "I *don't* know the old joke."

"How do you get guys to find a kilo of fat attractive?" he said, risking her wrath. She glared at him, and he grinned. "Put a nipple on it. Trust me, you don't look fat. You do look damned good. I suppose I do, too, but I'll be glad to get my old body back. This one feels like I'm maneuvering a grav-tank."

"This one feels like I'm maneuvering two blimps in front of me," she said, and smiled at last. "Okay, when this is over, we go back to our own bodies."

"Agreed. And you marry me."

"No," she said. But she smiled when she said it.

✦   ✦   ✦

"Mr. Chung," Beach said, nodding as Roger came onto the bridge.

"Captain Beach."

Roger looked at the repeater plot. They were in normal-space, building charge and recalibrating for the next jump. That one would be into the edge of Saint territory.

"So, have you found someone to crosscheck me?" Beach asked an offhand manner.

"Yes," Roger replied, just as offhandedly.

"Good." Beach laughed. "If you hadn't, I would've turned this damned ship around and dropped you back on your miserable mudball planet."

"I'm glad we see eye to eye," Roger said, smiling thinly.

"I don't know if we do or not." Beach gazed at him for a moment, then tossed her head at the hatch. "Let's go to my office."

Roger followed her to her office, which was down the passage from the bridge. It had taken some damage in the assault, but most of that had been repaired. He grabbed a station chair and sat, wondering why it had taken this long for the "conversation" to occur.

"We're fourteen light-years from the edge of what the Saints consider their space," Beach said, sitting down and propping her feet in an open drawer. "We're in deep space. There's exactly one astrogator on this ship: me. So let's be clear that I'm holding all the cards."

"You're holding *many* cards," Roger responded calmly. "But let me be clear, as well. In the last nine months, I've become somewhat less civilized than your standard Imperial nobleman. And I have a very great interest in this mission's success. Becoming totally intransigent at this time would be, at the very least, extraordinarily painful for you. I'd taken you for an ally, not a competitor, although I'm even willing to have a competitor, as long as we can negotiate in good faith. But failure of negotiations will leave you in a position you *really* don't want to occupy."

Beach had raised an eyebrow. Now she lowered it.

"You're serious," she said.

"As a heart attack." Roger's newly brown eyes gave a remarkable

imitation of a basilisk's. "But as I said," he continued after a
moment, "we can negotiate in good faith. I hope you're an ally, but
that remains to be seen. What do you *want*, Captain Beach?"

"Most of what I want, you can't give me. And I was raised
in a hard school. If it comes down to force, you're not going to
like the results, either."

"Agreed. So what do you want that I *can* give you?"

"What are you going to get from the Alphanes?" Beach countered.

"We don't know," Roger admitted. "It's possible that we'll get
a jail cell and a quick trip to Imperial custody. I don't think so,
but it's possible. We'll be negotiating, otherwise. Do you want
money? We can negotiate you a more than fair fee for your services, assuming all goes well. If we fully succeed, and I believe
we will, we'll be freeing my mother, and I'll be Heir Primus to
the Throne. The next Emperor of Man. In that case, Captain,
the sky is the limit. We *owe* you—*I* owe you. Do you want your
own planet?" he finished with a smile.

"You do know how to negotiate, don't you?" Beach smiled in
turn.

"Well, I really should be letting Poertena handle it, but you
wouldn't like that," Roger told her. "But, seriously, Captain, I do
owe you. I fully intend to pay that debt, and since it's an open
one, you can draw on it enormously. Right now, I have virtually
nothing you could want. Even this ship is going to have to go
away—you know that?"

"Oh, yeah. You can't get this thing anywhere *near* Sol. We
could only hang around the fringes, where it was easy to bribe
the customs officials."

"So we can't give you the ship; we're going to need it to trade
to the Alphanes."

"But you're going on to Old Earth?"

"Yes."

"Well . . ." Beach pursed her lips, then shrugged. "What I want,
as I said, you can't give me. Now. Maybe ever." She paused and
made a wince. "How . . . Who are you going to use as a captain
on the Old Earth trip?"

"I don't know. The Alphanes will undoubtedly have at least
one . . . discreet captain we can use. But he or she will be one

of *their* people. Are you volunteering to captain the ship to Sol? And if so, why?"

"I will want money," Beach said, temporizing. "If you fully succeed, a *lot* of money."

"Done." Roger shrugged. "A billion here, a billion there, and sooner or later, you're talking real money."

"Not *that* much." Beach blanched. "But ... say ... five million credits."

"Agreed."

"In a UOW numbered account."

"Agreed."

"And ..." She made a face and shook her head. "If— What are you going to do about the Caravazans?"

"The Saints?" Roger leaned back in his chair with a tight smile. "Captain, right now we're wondering if we can make it to Alphane territory in one piece! After that, we have the little problem of springing someone from a fortified palace and somehow keeping the Navy from killing us. I'm in no position to discuss *anything* about the Saints, except how we're going to sneak by them."

"But in the long run," Beach said, half-desperately. "If you become Emperor."

"I'm not going to start a unilateral war against the Caravazan Empire, if that's what you mean," Roger replied after a moment. "I have ... many reasons I don't care for them, but they pale beside the damage such a war would cause." Roger frowned. "What do you have against the Saints? You *were* one."

"*That's* what I have against them," Beach said bitterly. "And so, I will ask this of you. If you see the opportunity, the one thing that I'll ask—screw the money!—the *one* thing that I ask is for you to take them down. All the way. Conquer the whole damned thing and kill the leaders."

"Not all of them," Roger said. "That's not how it's done." He gazed at her for several seconds, his expression almost wondering, and she half-glared unwaveringly back at him.

"So that's the deal, is it?" he asked finally. "For captaining the ship, for turning off the self-destruct, you want me to invade the Caravazan Empire?"

"If the time comes," Beach said. "If the time is right. Please.

Don't hesitate. Don't ... do it by half measures. Take the whole thing. It's the *right* thing to do. That place is a cesspool, a pit. Nobody should have to live under the Saints. Please."

Roger leaned back and steepled his fingers for a moment, then nodded.

"If we succeed, if I become Emperor, *if* war comes with the Saints—and I won't go looking for it, mind you—then I will do everything in my power to ensure that it's a war to the knife. That not one member of the Saint leadership is left in power over so much as a single planet. That their entire empire is either transferred to a more rational form of government, or else absorbed by the Empire of Man or other less irrational polities. Something close to that anyway. As close as I can get it. Does that satisfy you, Captain?"

"Entirely." Beach's voice was hoarse, and her eyes glittered with unshed tears. "And I'll do whatever you need done to ensure that day comes. I swear."

"Good," Roger said, and smiled. "I'm glad I didn't have to break out the thumbscrews."

"Hey, 'Shara,'" Sergeant Major Kosutic said, sticking her head into Despreaux's stateroom. "Come on. We need to talk."

Kosutic was a blonde now, too, if not nearly as spectacularly so as Despreaux. She was also her regular height, with equally short hair, and a more modest bosom. She was stockier than she had been—she looked like a female weightlifter, which was more or less how she'd looked before, actually—but her stride was a little more ... feminine, now. Something about the wider hips, Despreaux suspected. The transformation hadn't changed her pelvic bones, but it had added muscle to either side.

"What does Julian think of the new look?" Despreaux asked.

"You mean 'Tom?'" the sergeant major said in tones of minor disapproval. "Probably about what Roger thinks of yours. But 'Tom' didn't get the big bazoombas. I've detected just a hint of jealousy about that."

"What is it with men and blonde hair and boobs?" Despreaux demanded angrily.

"Satan, girl, you really want to know?" Kosutic laughed.

"Seriously, the theories are divergent and bizarre enough to keep conspiracy theorists babbling happily away to themselves for decades. 'Mommy' fixation was an early one—that men want to go back to breast-feeding. It didn't last long, but it was popular in its time. My personal favorite has to do with the difference between chimps and humans."

"What do *chimps* have to do with anything?"

"Well, the DNA of chimps and humans is really close. Effectively, humans are just an offshoot of chimpanzee. Even after all the minor mutations that have crept in since going off-planet, humans still have less variability than chimps, and on a DNA chart we just fall in as a rather minor modification."

"I didn't know that," Despreaux said. "Why do you?"

"Face it, the Church of Armagh has to make it up as we go along." Kosutic shrugged. "Understanding the real *why* of people makes it much easier. Take boobs."

"Please!" Despreaux said.

"Agreed." Kosutic smiled. "Chimps don't have them. Humans are, in fact, the only terrestrial animal with truly pronounced mammary glands. Look at a cow—those impressive udders are almost all functional, milk producing plumbing. Tits? Ha! Their . . . visual cue aspect, shall we say, has nothing to do with milk production per se. That means there's some other reason for them in our evolutionary history, and one theory is that they developed purely to keep the male around. Human females don't show signs of their fertility, and human children take a long time, relatively speaking, to reach maturity. Having a male around all the time helped early human and prehuman females with raising the children. The males probably brought in some food, but their primary purpose was defending territory so that there was food to be brought in. In addition, human females are also one of the few species to orgasm—"

"If we're lucky," Despreaux observed.

"You want to hear this, or not?"

"Sorry. Go ahead."

"So, that was a reason for the female to not be too upset when the male was always having a good time with her. And it was another reason for men to stick around. Tits were a visual sign that said: 'Screw me and stick around and defend this territory.'

Can't be proven, of course, but it fits with all the reactions males have to them."

"Yeah," Despreaux said sourly. "*All* the reactions. They're still a pain in the . . . back."

"Sure, and they're effectively as useful as a veriform appendix these days," the sergeant major said. "On the other hand, they're still great for making guys stupid. And *that* is what we're going to talk about."

"Oh?" Despreaux's tone became decidedly wary. They'd reached the sergeant major's stateroom, and she was surprised to see Eleanora waiting for them. The chief of staff had been modded as well and was now a rather skinny redhead.

"Oh," Kosutic confirmed. She closed the hatch and waved Despreaux onto the folded-down bed next to Eleanora, who looked at her with an expression which mingled thoughtfulness and determination with something Despreaux wasn't at all sure she wanted to see.

"Nimashet, I'm going to be blunt," the chief of staff said after a moment. "You have to marry Roger."

"No." The sergeant stood back up quickly, eyes flashing. "If this is what you wanted to talk about, you can—"

"Sit down, Sergeant," Kosutic said sharply.

"You'd *better* not use my *rank* when talking about something like this, *Sergeant Major!*" Despreaux snapped back angrily.

"I will when it affects the security of the Empire," Kosutic replied icily. "Sit. Down. Now."

Despreaux sat, glaring at the senior NCO.

"I'm going to lay this out very carefully," Eleanora told her. "And you're going to listen. Then we'll discuss it. But hear me out, first."

Despreaux shifted her glower to the chief of staff. But she also crossed her arms—carefully, given certain recent changes—and sat back stiffly on the bed.

"Some of this only holds—or matters—if we succeed," Eleanora said. "And some of it is immediately pertinent to our hope of possibly pulling off the mission in the first place. The first point is for everything—current mission and long-term consideration, alike. And that point is that Roger literally has the weight of the Empire on his shoulders right now. And he loves you. And I think you love him. And he's eaten up by the thought of losing you, which raises all sorts of scary possibilities."

Desperaux's surprise must have shown, because the chief of staff grimaced and waved one hand in the air.

"If he *fails*," she said, "if we go with the government-in-exile program and he becomes just some guy who was *almost* Emperor, you'd marry him, wouldn't you?"

Despreaux looked at her stony-eyed for two or three heartbeats, then sighed.

"Yes," she admitted. "Shit. I'd do it in a second if he was 'just some guy.' And I'm setting him up *to* fail so I can do just that, aren't I?"

"You're setting him up to fail," Eleanora agreed with a nod. "Not to mention contributing to the mental anguish he's in right now. Not that I think for a moment that you've been doing either of those things intentionally, of course. You're not manipulative enough for your own good, sometimes, and you certainly don't think *that* way. But the effect is the same, whether it's intentional or not. Right now, he has to be wondering, in the deeps of the night, if being Emperor—which he knows he's going to loathe—is really worth losing *you*. I presented the alternate exile plan because I thought it was a good plan, one that should be looked at as an alternative. It was Julian and the sergeant major who pointed out, afterwards, the *consequences* of the plan. Do you *want* Prince Jackson on the throne? Or a six-way war, more likely?"

"No," Despreaux said in a low voice. "God, what that would do to Midgard!"

"Exactly," Kosutic said. "And to half a hundred other worlds. If Adoula takes the Throne, all the out-worlds are going to be nothing but sources of material and manpower—cannon fodder—he and his cronies will bleed dry. If they don't get nuked in passing during the wars."

"So he has the weight of the Empire on his shoulders," Eleanora repeated, "and he's losing you. And there's a bolt-hole that he can go to that gets both of those problems off his back. It happens that that bolt-hole would mean very bad things for the Empire, but men aren't rational about women."

"That's another thing I can lay out in black and white," Kosutic said. "Lots of studies about it. Long-term rational planning drops off the chart when men are thinking about women. It's how they're wired. Of course, *we're* not all that rational about *them* sometimes, either."

"Now, let's talk about what happens if we succeed," Eleanora went on gently and calmly. "Roger is going to end up Emperor—probably sooner than he expects. I don't know how bad the residual effects of whatever drugs they're using on his mother are going to be, but I do know they're not going to be good. And after what's going on right now gets out, the public's confidence in her fitness to rule is bound to drop. If the drugs' effects are noticeable, it will drop even more. Nimashet, Roger could well find himself on the Throne within a year or less, if we pull this thing off."

"Oh, God," Despreaux said quietly. Her arms were no longer crossed, and her fingers twisted about one another in her lap. "God, he'll really hate that."

"Yes, he will. But there's much worse," Eleanora said. "People are neither fully products of their genetics, nor of their experiences, but . . . traumatic experiences can . . . adjust their personalities in various ways. And especially when they're still fairly young and unformed. Fairly young. Roger is *fairly* young, and, quite frankly, he was also fairly *unformed* when we landed on Marduk. I don't think anyone would be stupid enough to call him 'unformed' now, but the mold in which he's been shaped was our march halfway around Marduk. Effectively, Roger MacClintock's done virtually all of his 'growing up' in the course of *eight months* of constant, brutal combat ops without relief. Think about that.

"More than once, he's ended serious political negotiations by simply shooting the people he was negotiating with. Of course they were negotiating in bad faith when he did it. He never had a choice. But it's become . . . something of a habit. So has destroying any obstacle that got in his path. Again, because he didn't have a choice. Because they were obstacles he couldn't deal with any other way, and because so much depended on their being dealt with effectively . . . and permanently. But what that means is that he has . . . very few experiential reasons to *not* use every available scrap of firepower to remove any problems that arise. And if we succeed, this young man is going to be Emperor.

"There will probably be a civil war, no matter what we do. In fact, I'll virtually guarantee that there'll be one. The pressures were right for one—building nicely to one, anyway—when we left Old Earth, and things obviously haven't gotten any better. What with the problems at home, I'd be surprised if a rather large war doesn't break out—soon—and if it does, a man who has vast experience in killing people to accomplish what he considers are necessary goals is going to be sitting on the Throne of Man. I want you to think about *that* for a moment, too."

"Not good," Despreaux said, licking her lips.

"Not good at all," Eleanora agreed. "His advisers," she added, touching her own chest, "can mitigate his tendency to violence, to a degree. But only if he's amenable. The bottom line is that the Emperor can usually get what he wants, one way or another. If he doesn't like our advice, for example, he could simply fire us."

"Roger . . . wouldn't do that," Despreaux said positively. "No one who was on the March is ever going to be anyone he would fire. Or not listen to. He might not take the advice, though."

"And the armed forces swear an oath to the Constitution *and* the Emperor. He's their commander-in-chief. He can do quite a bit of fighting even without any declaration of war, and if we manage to succeed in this . . . this—"

"This forlorn hope," Kosutic supplied.

"Yes." The chief of staff smiled thinly, recognizing the ancient military term for a small body of troops sent out with even smaller hope of success. "If we succeed in this *forlorn hope,* there's automatically going to be a state of emergency. If a civil war breaks out, the Constitution equally automatically restricts citizens' rights and increases the power of the sitting head of state. We could end up with . . . Roger, in his present mental incarnation, holding as much power as any other person in the history of the human race."

"You sound like he's some bloody-handed murderer!" Despreaux shook her head. "He's not. He's a *good* man. You make him sound like one of the Dagger Lords!"

"He's not that," Kosutic said. "But what he is is damned near a reincarnation of Miranda MacClintock. She happened to be a political philosopher with a strongly developed sense of responsibility and duty, which, I agree, Roger also has. But if you remember your history, she also took *down* the Dagger Lords by being a bloody-minded bitch at least as ruthless as *they* were."

"What he is, effectively," Eleanora continued in that same gentle voice, "is a neobarbarian tyrant. A 'good' tyrant, perhaps, and as charismatic as hell—maybe even on the order of an Alexander the Great—but still a tyrant. And if he can't break out of the mold, putting him on the Throne will be as bad for the Empire as disintegration."

"What's your point?" Despreaux demanded harshly.

"You," Kosutic said. "When you joined the Regiment, when I was interviewing you on in-process, I damned near blackballed you."

"You never told me that." Despreaux frowned at the sergeant major. "Why?"

"You'd passed all the psychological tests," Kosutic replied with a shrug. "You'd passed RIP, although not with flying colors. We knew you were loyal. We knew you were a good guard. But there was something missing, something I couldn't quite put a finger on. I called it 'hardness,' at the time, but that's not it. You're damned hard."

"No," Despreaux said. "I'm not. You were right."

"Maybe. But hardness was still the wrong word." Kosutic frowned. "You've always done your job. Even when you lost the edge and couldn't fight anymore, you contributed and sweated right along with the rest of us. You're just not . . ."

"Vicious," Despreaux said. "I'm not a killer."

"No." Kosutic nodded in acknowledgment. "And I sensed that. That was what made me want to blackball you. But in the end, I didn't."

"Maybe you should have."

"Bullshit. You did your job—more than your job. You made it, and you're the key to what we need. So quit whining, soldier."

"Yes, Sergeant Major." Despreaux managed a fleeting smile, though it was plain her heart wasn't in it. "On the other hand, if you *had* blackballed me, I would have avoided our little plea-sure stroll."

"And you could never be Empress," Eleanora said.

Despreaux's new indigo eyes snapped back to the chief of staff, dark with dread, and Eleanora put a hand on her knee.

"Listen to me, Nimashet. What you are is something the opposite of vicious. I'd call it 'nurturing,' but that's not really right, either. You're as tough-minded and obstinate—most ways—as anyone, even Roger. Or can you think of anyone else in our happy little band who could argue him to a standstill once he gets the bit truly between his teeth?"

Eleanora looked into her eyes until Despreaux's innate honesty forced her to shake her head, then continued.

"But whatever it is we ought to be calling you, the *point* is that with you by Roger's side, he's calmer. Less prone to simply lash out and much more prone to think things through. And that's *important*—important to the Empire."

"I don't *want* to be Empress," Despreaux said desperately.

"Satan, girl," Kosutic laughed. "I *understand*, but listen to what you just said!"

"I'm a country girl," Despreaux protested. "A sod-buster from Midgard! I'm no good, never have been, at the sort of petty, backbiting infighting that goes on at Court." She shook her head. "I don't have the right mindset for it."

"So? How many people do, to start with?" Kosutic demanded.

"A hell of a lot more of them at Court than there are of me!" Despreaux shot back, then shook her head again, almost convulsively. "I don't know how to be a noblewoman, much less a fucking *Empress*, and if I try, I'll fuck it up. Don't you understand?" She looked back and forth between them, her eyes darker than ever. "If I try to do the job, I'll blow it. I'll be out of my league. I'll do the wrong thing, *say* the wrong thing at the wrong time, give Roger the wrong piece of advice—something! And when I do, the entire Empire will get screwed because of *me*!"

"You think Roger isn't thinking exactly the same thing?" Kosutic challenged more gently. "Satan, Nimashet! He has to wake up every single morning with the piss scared out of him just *thinking* about the job in front of him."

"But at least he grew up knowing it was coming. He's got the background, the training for it. I don't!"

"Training?" Eleanora flicked one hand in a dismissive gesture. "To be *Emperor*?" She snorted. "Until Jin told us what's been happening on Old Earth, it never even crossed his mind once that *he* might ever be Emperor, Nimashet! And, frankly, his mother's distrust of him meant that everyone, myself included, was always very careful to never, ever suggest the possibility to him. To be honest, it's only recently occurred to me how much that may have contributed to his refusal—or failure—to recognize the fact that he truly did stand close to the succession."

She shook her head again, her eyes sad as she thought of how dreadfully her one-time charge's life had changed, then looked back at Despreaux.

"Admittedly, he grew up in Court circles, and he may have more training for that than you do, but trust me, he didn't begin to have enough of it before our little jaunt. I know; *I* was the one who was supposed to be giving him that training, and I wasn't having a lot of success.

"But he's been much more strongly ... motivated in that regard recently, and you can be, too. You've seen how much he's grown in the last half-year, probably better than anyone else besides me and Armand Pahner. But nobody's *born* with that 'mindset'; they learn it, just like Roger has, and you've already pretty conclusively demonstrated your ability to master combat techniques. This is just one more set of combat skills. And, remember, if we succeed, you're going to be *Empress*. It's going to take either a very stupid individual, or a very dangerous one, to cross you."

"Our kids would be raised in a cage!"

"All children are," Eleanora countered. "It's why no sane adult would ever really want to be a child again. But your kids' cage would be the best protected one in the galaxy."

"Tell that to John's kids!" Despreaux exploded. "When I think about—"

"When you think about the kids who just up and disappear every year," Kosutic said. "Or end up a body in a ditch. Or raped by their uncle, or their dad's best friend. Think about that, instead. That's one thing you'll never have to worry about, not with three thousand hard bastards watching anyone that comes near them like rottweilers. Every parent worries about her child; that comes with the job. But *your* kids are going to have three thousand of the most dangerous baby-sitters—and you know that's what we are—in the known galaxy.

"Sure, they got to John and his kids. But they did it by killing the *entire* Empress' Own, Nimashet. Every mother-loving one of them. In case you hadn't noticed, there are exactly *twelve* of us left in the entire frigging Galaxy, because the *only* way they could get to the kids, or John, or the Empress was over *us*—over our dead bodies, stacked in front of the goddamned door! And there's been one—count 'em, *one*—successful attack on the Imperial Family in five hundred fucking years! Don't tell me your kids wouldn't be '*safe*'!"

The sergeant major glared at her, and, after a moment, Despreaux's gaze fell.

"I don't want to be Empress," she repeated, quietly but stubbornly. "I swore to him that I wouldn't marry him if he was going to be Emperor. What would I be if I took that back?"

"A woman." Kosutic grinned. "Didn't you know we're allowed to change our minds at random? It comes with the tits."

"Thanks very much," Despreaux said bitingly, and folded her arms again. Her shoulders hunched. "I don't want to be Empress."

"Maybe not," Eleanora said. "But you do want to marry Roger. You want to have his children. You want to keep a bloody-minded tyrant off the Throne, and he'll be far less bloody-minded if he wants to keep your approval in mind. The *only* thing you don't want is to be Empress."

"That's a pretty big 'only,'" Despreaux pointed out.

"What you want is really beside the point," Kosutic said. "The only thing that matters is what's good for the Empire. I don't care if you consider every day of the rest of your life a living sacrifice to the Empire. You swore the oath; you took the pay."

"And this was *never* part of the job specs!" Despreaux shot back angrily.

"Then consider it very unusual duties, if you have to!" Kosutic said, just as angrily.

"Calm down—both of you!" Eleanora said sharply. She looked back and forth between them, then focused on Despreaux. "Nimashet, just think about it. You don't have to say yes now. But for God's sake, think about what refusing to marry Roger will mean. To all of us. To the Empire. To your home planet. Hell, to every polity in the galaxy."

"A person's conscience is her own," Despreaux said stubbornly.

"Heaven's bells, if it is," Kosutic said caustically. "We spend most of our lives doing things because we know they're the right things to do in other people's eyes. Especially the eyes of people we care about. It's what makes us human. If he loses you, he'll do anything he pleases. He knows most of *us* won't give a damn. If he told us to round up every left-handed red-head and put them in ovens, I would, because he's Roger. If he told Julian to go nuke a planet, Julian would. Because he's *Roger*. And even if we wouldn't, he'd find someone else who would—for power, or because he has the legal authority to order them to, or because they *want* to do the deed. The only person who could have kept him under control was Pahner, and Pahner's dead, girl. The only one *left* that he's going to look to for . . . conscience is you.

"I'm not saying he's a *bad* man, Nimashet—we're all agreed on that. I'm just telling you that he's in one Heaven of a spot, with nothing anywhere he can look but more boots coming down on the people the Emperor is responsible for protecting. Just like he was responsible for *us* on Marduk. And do you think for one moment that he wouldn't have killed every other living thing on that planet to keep us alive?"

She half-glared into Despreaux's eyes, daring her to look away, and finally, after a small, tense eternity, the younger woman shook her head slowly.

"Eleanora's spelled it out," Kosutic continued in a softer voice. "He's learned a set of responses that *work*. And he's learned about responsibility, learned the hard way. He'll do *anything* to discharge that responsibility, and once he starts down the slope of expediency, each additional step will get easier and easier to take. Unless someone gets in the way. Someone who prevents him from taking those steps, because his responsibility to her—to be the person *she* demands he be—is as powerful a motivator as his responsibility to all the rest of the universe combined. And that person is you. You're it, girlie. You leave, and there's nothing between him and the universe but the mind of a wolf."

Despreaux bowed her head into her hands and shook it from side to side.

"I *really* don't want to be Empress," she said. "And what about dynastic marriages?" she added from behind her hands.

"On a scale of one to ten, with your stabilizing effect on him at ten, the importance of holding out for a dynastic marriage rates about a minus sixty," Eleanora said dryly. "Externally, it's a moot point. Most of the other human polities don't have our system, or else they're so minor that they're not going to get married to the Emperor, anyway. Internally, pretty much the same. There are a few members of the Court who might think otherwise, but most of them are going to be shuffled out along with Adoula. I have a list, and they never will be missed."

"But that does bring up another point you might want to consider," Kosutic said.

Despreaux raised her head to look at the sergeant major once more, eyes wary, and the Armaghan smiled crookedly.

"Let's grant that with the shit storm coming down on the galaxy, or at least the Empire, there might even be some advantages to having a wolf on the Throne. Somebody the historians will tag 'the Terrible.' At least we know damned well that he'll do whatever needs doing, and I think we're all pretty much agreed he'll do it for the right reasons, however terrible it is. But someday, one of his *children* is going to inherit the Throne. Just who's going to raise that kid, Sergeant? One of those backbiting, infighting Court bitches you don't want to tangle with? What's the *kid's* judgment going to be like, growing up with a daddy smashing anything that gets in his way and a mommy who's only interested in power and its perks?"

"A point," Eleanora seconded, "albeit a more long-ranged one." It was her turn to gaze into Despreaux's eyes for a moment, then she shrugged. "Still, it's one you want to add to the list when you start thinking about it."

"All right." Despreaux raised a hand to forestall anything more from Kosutic. "I'll think about it. I'll *think* about it," she repeated. "Just that."

"Fine," Eleanora said. "I'll add just one more thing."

"What now?" Despreaux asked tiredly.

"Do you love Roger?"

The soft question hovered in Kosutic's stateroom, and Despreaux looked down at the hands which had somehow clasped themselves back together in her lap.

"Yes," she replied, after a long moment. "Yes, I do."

"Then think about this. The pressure of being Emperor is *enormous*. It's driven more than one person mad, and if you leave, you'll be leaving a man you love to face that pressure, all alone. As his wife, you can help. Yes, he'll have counselors, but at the end of the day it will be *you* who'll keep that strain from becoming unbearable."

"And what about the pressure on the Empress?" Despreaux asked. "His prosthetic conscience?"

"Roger's sacrifice is his entire life." Kosutic told her softly. "And yours? Yours is watching the man you love *make* that sacrifice . . . and marching every meter of the way right alongside him. That's *your* true sacrifice, Nimashet Despreaux. Just as surely as you would have been sacrificed on that altar in Krath, if Roger hadn't prevented it."

"This takes some getting used to."

Julian fingered his chin. His hair was light brown, instead of black, and his chin was much more rounded. Other than that, he had generally European features, instead of the slightly Mediterranean ones he'd been born with.

"Every day," Roger agreed, looking over at Temu Jin, the only human aboard *Dawn* who hadn't been modified. The IBI agent had perfectly legitimate papers showing that he'd been discharged from his post on Marduk, with good references, and now was taking a somewhat roundabout route back to Old Earth.

"Where are we?" Roger asked.

"One more jump, and we'll be at Torallo," Jin said. "That's the waypoint the Saints normally use. The customs there have an understanding with them."

"That's pretty unusual for the Alphanes," Roger observed.

"One of the things we're going to point out to them," Julian replied. "It's not the only point where they've got some border security issues, either. Not nearly as bad as the Empire's problems, maybe, but they're going to be surprised to find out that they have *any*."

"Is the 'understanding' with humans?" Roger asked.

"Some humans, yes," Jin said. "But the post commander and others who have to be aware are Althari."

"I thought they were incorruptible," Roger said with a frown.

"So, apparently, do the Altharis," Jin replied. "They're not, and neither are Phaenurs. Trust me, I've seen the classified reports. I'm going to have to avoid that particular point, and thank Ghu I don't have any names of our agents. But we *have* agents among both the Altharis and the Phaenurs. Let's not go around making that obvious, though."

"I won't," Roger said. "But while we go around not making that obvious, what else happens?"

"Our initial cover is that we're entertainers, a traveling circus, to explain all the critters in the holds," Julian said. "We'll travel to Althar Four and then make contact. How we do that is going to have to wait until we arrive."

"Aren't the Phaenurs there going to . . . sense that we're lying?"

"Yes, they will," Jin said. "Which is going to be what has to wait. We have no contacts. We have to play this entirely by ear."

The Alphanes were everything they'd been described as being.

The Althari security officer at the transfer station—a male— wasn't as tall as a Mardukan, but he was at least twice as broad, not to mention being covered in long fur that was silky looking and striped along the sides. The Phaenur standing beside him was much smaller, so small it looked like some sort of pet that should be sitting on the Althari's shoulder. But it was the senior of the two.

The entry into Alphane space had been smooth. Although *Emerald Dawn* had visited Torallo several times, the Saint-friendly customs officials at Torallo had scarcely glanced at her papers, despite the fact that they now identified her as the Imperial freighter *Sheridan's Pride.* They'd simply taken their customary cut, and the ship had proceeded onward with nothing but a cursory inspection that didn't even note the obvious combat damage.

Two jumps later, at the capital system of the Alphane Alliance, the same could not be said. Docking had been smooth, and they'd presented their quarantine and entry passes to the official, a human, sent aboard to collect them. But after that, they'd been confined to the ship for two nerve-wracking hours until "Mr. Chung" was summoned to speak to some "senior customs officials."

They were meeting in the loading bay of the transfer station, a space station set out near the Tsukayama Limit of the
G-class star of Althar. It looked like just about every other
loading bay Roger had ever seen, scuffed along the sides and
floor, marked with warning signs in multiple languages. The big
difference was the reception committee which, besides the two
"senior customs officials" included a group of Althari guards
in combat armor.

"Mr. Chung," the Althari said. "You do not know much of the
Althari, do you?"

"I know quite a lot, in fact," Roger replied.

"One of the things you apparently don't know is that we take
our security very seriously," the Althari continued, ignoring his
response. "And that we do not let people lie to us. Your name is
not Augustus Chung."

"No, it's not. Nor is this ship the *Sheridan's Pride*."

"Who are you?" the Althari demanded dangerously.

"I can't tell you." Roger raised a hand to forestall any reply.
"You don't have the need to know. But I need—*you* need—for
me to speak to someone in your government on a policy level,
and you need for that conversation to be very secure."

"Truth," the Phaenur said in a sibilant hiss. "Absolute belief."

"Why?" the Althari asked, attention still focused on Roger.

"Again, you don't have the need to know," Roger replied. "We
shouldn't even be having this conversation in front of your troops,
because one of the things I *can* tell you is that you have security
penetrations. And time is very short. Well, it's important to me
for us to get to the next level quickly, and it's of some importance
to the Alphane Alliance. How much is up to someone well above
your pay grade. Sorry."

The Althari looked at the Phaenur, who made an odd head
jab.

"Truth again," the lizardlike alien said to its partner, then
looked back at Roger. "We need to contact our supervisors," it
said. "Please return to your ship for the time being. Do you have
any immediate needs?"

"Not really," Roger said. "Except for some repairs. And they're
not that important; we're not planning on leaving in this ship."

✧   ✧   ✧

"Mr. Chung," Despreaux said, cutting her image into the hologram of the Imperial Palace Roger and Eleanora O'Casey had been studying. "Phaenur Srall wishes to speak to you."

The hologram dissolved into the face of a Phaenur. Roger wasn't certain if it was the same one he'd been speaking to. They hadn't been introduced, and they all looked the same to him.

"Mr. Chung," the Phaenur said, "your ship is cleared to move to Station Five. You will proceed there by the marked route. Any deviation from the prescribed course will cause your vessel to be fired upon by system defense units. You mentioned a need for repairs; is your vessel capable of making that trip without them?"

"Yes," Roger said, smiling. "We'd just have a hard time getting out of the system."

"Any attempt to approach the Tsukayama Limit will also cause your vessel to be fired upon," the Phaenur warned. "You will be met by senior representatives of my government."

The screen cut off.

"Not much given to pleasantries, are they?" Roger said.

"Not if they don't like you," Eleanora replied. "They know it ticks us off. They can be very unsubtle about things like that."

"Well, we'll just have to see how subtle we can convince them to be."

Roger stood at the head of the wardroom table as the Alphane delegation filed in. There was a Phaenur who, again, was in charge, two Altharis, and a human. One of the Altharis was a guard—a hulking brute in unpowered combat armor who took up a position against the rear bulkhead. The other wore an officer's undress harness with the four planetary clusters of a fleet admiral.

Roger's staff was gathered around the table, and as the visiting threesome sat, he waved the others to their chairs. This time Honal was missing; his out-sized seat was taken by the Althari admiral.

"I am Sreeetoth," the Phaenur said. "I am head of customs enforcement for the Alphane Alliance, which is just below a Cabinet position. As such, I am as close to a 'policymaker' as you are going to see without more information. My companions are Admiral Tchock Ral, commander of the Althari Home Fleet, and Mr. Mordas Dren, chief of engineering for the Althar System. Now, who are you? Truthfully."

"I am Prince Roger Ramius Sergei Alexander Chiang Mac-Clintock," Roger answered formally. "For the last ten months, I have been on the planet Marduk or in transit to this star system, and I had nothing to do with any coup. My mother is being held captive, and I've come to you for help."

The human rocked back in his chair, staring around at the group in wild surmise. The Althari looked ... unreadable. Sreee-toth cocked its head in an oddly insectlike fashion and looked around the compartment.

"Truth. All of it is truth," the Phaenur said after a moment. "Apprehension, fear so thick you could cut it with a blade ... except off the Mardukans and the Prince. And great need. Great need."

"And why, in your wildest dreams, do you believe we might put our necks on the block for you?" the Althari rumbled in a subterranean-deep voice.

"For several reasons," Roger said. "First, we have information you need. Second, if we succeed in throwing out the usurpers who are using my mother as a puppet, your Alliance will be owed a debt by my House that it can draw upon to the limit. And third, the Alphane require truth. We will give you the truth. You'll find it hard to get one gram of it from anyone associated with Adoula."

"Again, truth," the Phaenur said. "Some quibbling about the debt, but I expect that's a simple matter of recognizing that the needs of his empire may overrule his own desires. But I'm still not sure we'll choose to aid you, Prince Roger. You seek to over-throw your government?"

"No. To restore it; it's already been overthrown ... to an extent. As things stand at this moment, Adoula is still constrained by our laws and Constitution. For the time being ... but not for long. We believe we have until the birth of the child being gestated to save my mother; after that, she'll be an impediment to Adoula's plans. So she'll undoubtedly name him Prime Minister and he or the Earl of New Madrid—" Roger's voice never wavered, despite the hardness in his eyes as he spoke his father's title "—will be named Regent for the child. And then she'll die . . . and Adoula's coup will be complete."

"That is *all* surmise," Sreeetoth said.

"Yes," Roger acknowledged. "But it's valid surmise. Mother would never ally herself with Adoula, and I was *definitely* not involved in the coup. In fact, I was totally incommunicado when it occurred. She also hates and reviles my biological father . . . who's now at her side at all times, and who is the biological father of her unborn child, as well. Given all that, psychological control is the only reasonable answer. Agreed?"

"You believe it to be," the Phaenur said. "And I agree that the logic is internally valid. That doesn't prove it, but—"

"It is true," Tchock Ral rumbled. "We are aware of it."

"I'm in way over my head," Mordas Dren said fervently. "I know you guys thought you needed a human in the room, but this is so far out of my league I wish I could have a brain scrub and wash it out. Jesus!" His face worked for a moment, and he squeezed his eyes shut. "Adoula is a snake. His fingers are in every corporation that's trying to kick in our doors. Him as Emperor . . . That's what you're talking about, right?"

"Eventually," Roger said. "What's worse, we don't think it will work. More likely, the Empire will break up into competing factions. And without the Empress to stabilize it . . ."

"And this would be bad how?" the Althari admiral asked. Then she twitched her massive head in a human-style shake. "No. I agree, it would be bad. The Saints would snap up territory, increasing their already formidable resource base. If they managed to get some of your Navy, as well, we'd be looking at heavy defense commitments on *another* border. And it's my professional opinion that the Empire would indeed break up. In which case, chaos is too small a word."

"The effect on trade would be . . . suboptimal," Sreeetoth said. "But if you try to place your mother back upon the Throne and fail, the results will be the same. Or possibly even worse."

"Not . . . exactly." Roger looked back and forth between the three Alphane representatives. "If we try and fail, and are discovered to be who we are, then Adoula's tracks are fully covered. Obviously, it was me all along, in which case, he'd be much more likely to be able to hold things together. The reputation of House MacClintock would be severely damaged, and that reputation would have been one of the things that stood against him. If I'm formally saddled with responsibility for everything, he'll actually be in a better position to supplant my House in terms of legitimacy and public support."

"Only if no word of where you *really* were at the time of the initial coup attempt ever gets out," the Phaenur pointed out.

"Yes."

Tchock Ral leaned forward and looked at Roger for a long time.

"You are telling us that if you fail, you intend to cover up the fact that you are *not* guilty of staging the first coup?" the Althari said. "That you would stain the reputation of your House for all time, rather than let that information be exposed."

"Yes," Roger repeated. "Letting it out would shatter the Empire. I would rather that my House, with a thousand years of honorable service to mankind, be remembered only for my infamy, than allow that to happen. Furthermore, your Alliance—you three individuals, and whoever else is let in on the secret—will have to hold it, if not forever, then for a very long time. Otherwise..."

"Chaos on the border," Dren said. "Jesus Christ, Your Highness."

"I asked for senior policymakers," Roger said, shrugging at the engineer. "Welcome to the jungle."

"How will you conceal the truth?" Sreeetoth asked. "If you're captured? Some of you, no matter what happens, *will* be captured if you fail."

"It would require a concerted effort to get the information out in any form that would be believed, past the security screen Adoula will throw up if we fail," Roger captured. "We'll simply avoid the concerted effort."

"And your people?" the Althari asked, gesturing at the staff. "You actually trust them to follow this insane order?"

Roger flexed a jaw muscle, and was rewarded by a heel landing on either foot. Despreaux's came down quite a bit harder than O'Casey's, but they landed virtually simultaneously. He closed his eyes and breathed for a moment, then reached back and pulled every strand of hair into line.

"Admiral Tchock Ral," he said, looking the Althari in the eye. "You are a warrior, yes?"

Eleanora was too experienced a diplomat to wince; Despreaux and Julian weren't.

"Yes," the admiral growled. "Be aware, human, that even asking that question is an insult."

"Admiral," Roger said levelly, meeting her anger glare for glare, "compared to the lowest ranking Marine I've got, you don't know the meaning of the word."

The enormous Althari came up out of her chair with a snarl like crumbling granite boulders, and the guard in the corner straightened. But Roger just pointed a finger at Sreeetoth.

"Tell her!" he snapped, and the Phaenur jabbed one hand in an abrupt, imperative gesture that cut off the Althari's furious response like a guillotine.

"Truth," it hissed. "Truth, and a belief in that truth so strong it is like a fire in the room."

The lizardlike being turned fully to the bearlike Althari and waved the same small hand at its far larger companion.

"Sit, Tchock Ral. Sit. The Prince burns with the truth. His —soldiers—even the woman who hates to be one—all of them burn with the truth of that statement." It looked back at Roger. "You tread a dangerous path, human. Altharis have been known to go what you call berserk at that sort of insult."

"It wasn't an insult," Roger said. He looked at the trio of visitors steadily. "Would you like to know why it wasn't?"

"Yes," the Phaenur said. "And I think that Tchock Ral's desire to know burns even more strongly than my own."

"It's going to take a while."

In fact, it took a bit over four hours.

Roger had never really sat down and told the story, even to himself, until they'd worked out the presentation, and he'd been amazed when he truly realized for the first time all they'd done. He'd *known*, in an intellectual way, all along. But he'd been so submerged in the doing, so focused on every terrible step of the March as they actually took it, that he'd truly never considered its entirety. Not until they'd sat down to put it all together.

Even at four hours, it was the bare-bones, only the highlights—or low-lights, as Julian put it—of the entire trip.

There was data from the toombie attack on the *DeGlopper*;

downloaded sensor data from the transport's ferocious, sacrificial battle with the Saint cruisers and her final self-destruction after she'd been boarded, to take the second cruiser with her. There were recorded helmet views of battles and screaming waves of barbarians, of Mardukan carnivores and swamps and mud and eternal, torrential rain until the delicate helmet systems succumbed to the rot of the jungle. There were maps of battles, descriptions of weapons, analyses of tactics, data on the battle for the *Emerald Dawn* from the Saints' tactical systems, enemy body counts ... and the soul-crushing roll call of their own dead.

It was the after-action report from Hell.

And when it was done, they showed the Alphane delegation around the ship. The admiral and her guard noted the combat damage and fingered Patty's scars. The engineer clucked at the damage, stuck his head in holes which still hadn't been patched over, and exclaimed at the fact that the ship ran at all. The admiral nearly had a hand taken off by a *civan*—which she apparently thought was delightful—and they were shown the *atul* and the *basik* in cages. Afterward, Rastar, stony-faced as only a Mardukan could be, showed them the battle-stained flag of the *Basik's* Own. The admiral and her guard thought it was a grand flag, and, having seen an actual *basik*, got the joke immediately.

Finally, they ended up back in the wardroom. Everyone in the command group had had a part in the presentation, just as every one of them had had a part in their survival. But there was one last recorded visual sequence to show.

The Althari admiral leaned back in the big station chair and made a clucking sound and a weird atonal croon that sent a shiver through every listener as Roger ran the file footage from the bridge's internal visual pickups and they watched the final actions of Armand Pahner. The Prince watched it with them, and his brown eyes were dark, like barriers guarding his soul, as the last embers of life flickered out of the shattered, armored body clasped in his arms.

And then it was done. All of it.

Silence hovered for endless seconds that felt like hours. And then Tchock Ral's face and palms were lifted upward.

"They will march beyond the Crystal Mountains," she said in low, almost musical tones. "They will be lifted up upon the shoulders of giants. Their songs will be sung in their homesteads, and they shall rest in peace, served by the tally of their slain. Tchrorr Kai Herself will stand beside them in battle for all eternity, for they have entered the realm of the Warrior, indeed."

She lowered her face and looked at Roger, swinging her head in a circle which was neither nod nor headshake, but something else, something purely Althari.

"I wipe the stain of insult from our relationship. You have been given a great honor to have known such warriors, and to have led them. They are most worthy. I would gladly have them as foes."

"Yes," Roger said, looking at the freeze-frame in the hologram. Himself, holding his father-mentor's body in his arms, the armored arms which, for all their strength, had been unable to hold life within that mangled flesh. "Yes, but I'd give it all for one more chewing out from the Old Man. I'd give it all for one more chance to watch Gronningen being used as a straight man. To see Dokkum grin in the morning light, with the air of the mountains around us. To hear Ima's weird laugh."

"Ima didn't laugh, much," Julian pointed out quietly. The retelling had put all the humans in a somber mood.

"She did that first time I fell off Patty," Roger reminded him.

"Yes. Yes, she did," Julian agreed.

"Prince, I do not know what the actions of my government will be," Tchock Ral said. "What you ask would place the Alphane Alliance in no little jeopardy, and the good of the clan must be balanced against that. But you and your soldiers may rest in my halls until such time as a decision is made. In my halls, we can hide you, even under your true-name, for my people are trustworthy. And if the decision goes against you, you may rest in them for all eternity, if you choose. To shelter the doers of such deeds would bring honor upon my House forever," she ended, placing both paws on her chest and bowing low across them.

"I thank you," Roger said. "Not for myself, but for the honor you do my dead."

"You'll probably have to make this presentation again," Sreeeetoth said with another head bob. "I'll need copies of all your raw data. And if you stay at Tchock Ral's house, you'll be forced to tell your stories all day and night, so be warned."

"And whatever happens, you're not taking this ship to Sol," Mordas Dren put in. The engineer shook his head. "It won't make it through the Empire's scans, for sure and certain. And even if it would, I wouldn't want to trust that TD drive for *one* jump. For one thing, I saw a place where some feeble-minded primitive had been *beating* on one of the capacitors."

"No," Roger agreed. "For this to work, we're going to need another freighter—a clean one—some crew, and quite a bit of money. Also, access to current intelligence," he added. He'd been fascinated by the fact that the admiral *knew* his mother was being controlled.

"If we choose to support you, all of that can be arranged," the Phaenur hissed. "But for the time being, we must report this to our superiors. That is, to *some* of our superiors," he added, looking at the engineer.

"The Minister's going to want to know what it's all about," Dren said uncomfortably.

"This is now bound by security," the admiral replied. "Tell her that. And only that. No outside technicians in the ship until the determination is made, either! And any who finally do get aboard her will be from the Navy Design Bureau. I think, Mordas, that you're going to be left to idle speculation."

"No," the Phaenur said. "Other arrangements will be made. Such conditions are difficult for humans, and more so for one like Mordas. Mordas, would you go to the Navy?"

"I'm in charge of maintenance for the entire star system, Sreeetoth," Dren pointed out, "and I'm a bit too old to hold a wrench. I *enjoy* holding a wrench, you understand, but I'm sure not going to take the cut in pay."

"We'll arrange things," the admiral said, standing up. "Young Prince, *Mr. Chung*, I hope to see you soon in my House. I will send your chief of staff the invitation as soon as determinations are made."

"I look forward to it," Roger said, and realized it was the truth.

"And, by all means, bring your sword," Tchock Ral said, with the low hum Roger had learned was Althari laughter.

Humans are descended from an essentially arboreal species. As a consequence, human homes, whenever it's economically possible, tend to have trees near them, and growing plants. They also tend to rise up a bit, but not very far—just about the height of a tree.

The Altharis, for all that they looked like koala bears, were anything *but* arboreal-descended. That much became abundantly evident to Roger when he first saw the admiral's "halls."

Althari homes were almost entirely underground, and when economics permitted, they were grouped in quantities related to kinship. The admiral's "halls" were a series of low mounds, each about a kilometer across and topped with a small blockhouse of locally quarried limestone . . . and with clear fields of fire stretching out over a four-kilometer radius. There were paved roads for ground cars between them, and several landing areas, including one nearly two hundred meters long, for aircars and shuttles. But the big surprise came when they entered their first blockhouse.

Ramps sloped downward into high-ceilinged rooms. And then downward, and downward . . . and downward. Among Althari, rank was indicated by the depth of one's personal quarters, and Roger found himself ushered into a room about twenty meters across and six meters high, buried under nearly three hundred meters of earth.

He was glad he didn't have a trace of claustrophobia.

Below the surface, all of the standard homes were linked through a system of tunnels. There were stores in the warren, escape routes, weapons—it was a vast underground *fortress,* and the Altharis living in it were a highly trained militia. And it was only one of thousands on the planet. Altharis who didn't live in their own clan homes lived in similar local communities, some of which, from what the visiting Imperials had been told, were far more extensive, virtually underground cities. No wonder the Altharis were considered unconquerable.

The Imperials had arrived the night before, more or less sur- reptitiously, and been shown to their quarters. Those quarters had been modified to some extent for humans, so there were at least human lavatory facilities, built to human sizes. But the bed had been Althari, and Roger had been forced to actually *jump* to get into it. All in all, they weren't bad quarters—as long as you ignored the weight of rock, concrete, and dirt sitting overhead.

Nonetheless, Roger still preferred being up on the surface, as they were now.

The sky above was a blue so deep it was right on the edge of violet. Althar IV's atmosphere was a bit thinner than Old Earth's, although its higher partial pressure of oxygen made for a slightly heady feeling, and the humidity was very low. At the moment, there were no clouds, and after the eternal cloud cover of Marduk, Roger found himself drinking in the clear sky greedily.

Tchock Ral's halls were placed in the approximate center of a long, wide valley on a bit of a plateau. To the east, north, and south, high mountains sparkled with snow; to the west, it opened out. The majority of the valley was given over to other warrens, farms, and a small, primarily Althari city. The city could be seen right on the western horizon, where a few slightly higher bumps marked low multistory buildings.

About a thousand Altharis, all the Marines, and half the Mardukans were either watching the competitions the admiral had decreed in honor of her visitors, preparing an outdoor feast, or just roaming around talking.

The day had started with a simple breakfast of prepared, dried human foods. Since then, for the last couple of hours, they'd been watching Althari sparring matches—mostly, Roger suspected, so that the humans and Mardukans could see the traditional Althari fighting methods. After the sparring matches were done, it had been time for the humans and Mardukans to show their stuff.

Rastar was sparring with a young Althari female. They were of about the same age, and similarly armed. Instead of whetted steel, each was armed with weighted training blades with blunted edges. The Althari held two, one in either bearlike paw, while Rastar held four of them. Rastar was the only Mardukan Roger had met who was truly quaddexterous. Whereas most Mardukans settled for fighting with two hands on only one side, if not a single hand, Rastar could fight with all four hands simultaneously. At the moment, each of his hands held a knife which would have been a short broadsword to a human, and they flickered in and out like lightning.

Each contestant wore a harness which noted strikes and managed scoring. In addition, Rastar wore an environmental suit that left only his face exposed, for Marduk was an intensely hot world, whereas Althar IV was on the cool side of the temperature range even humans would have found acceptable. It was the equivalent of an ice-planet for the cold-blooded Mardukans, and they found it necessary to wear the environment suits everywhere, except in the specially heated rooms set aside for them.

Climatological considerations didn't seem to be slowing him down, however, as all four arms licked in and out. The Althari was good, no question, but Rastar was able to block with both upper hands while his lower hands—the much more powerful pair—flicked in to strike, and he was outscoring her handily.

"Score!" Tchock Ral called as Rastar's lower left-hand blade tapped the Althari's midsection yet again. "*Adain!*"

Adain was the command to separate and prepare for the next round, but instead of lowering her weapons and stepping back, the Althari female let out a hoarse bellow and charged, just as Rastar *was* stepping back. Roger had seen the same Althari win two other fights hands down, so he could imagine why she was so chagrined, and as Sreeetoth has warned him aboard the *Dawn*, no Althari had ever been noted for her calm disposition.

Rastar was taken slightly off-balance, backing away from his opponent as the command required, but he spun nimbly to the side and let her charge past. All four of his blades flickered in and out in flashes of silver, painting the Althari's combat harness with purple holograms at each successful strike. The Althari roared in fury, wheeling and charging furiously after him. But Rastar faded away from her attack like smoke, his own blades flick, flick, flicking with a merciless precision that painted violet blotches across her sides, back, and neck.

"*Adain!*" Ral shouted, and at the second bellow, Rastar's opponent stopped, quivering.

"I apologize for that breach of protocol, Prince Rastar," the admiral said. "Toshok, go to the side and contemplate the dishonor you just brought upon our House!"

"Perhaps it would be better for her to contemplate what real blades would have meant," Rastar suggested. The Mardukan spoke excellent Imperial by now, and the Althari, with their own equivalents of the Empire's implanted toots, understood him perfectly. Not that it made things much better.

"If you wish to face me with live blades—" Toshok ground out in the same language.

"You would be a bleeding wreck on the ground," Ral said. "Look at the markers, you young fool!"

Toshok clamped her mouth shut and glanced angrily at the holographic scoreboard beside the sparring area. Her eyes widened as she saw the numbers under her name and Rastar's, and then she rolled her ursine head from side to side, looking down at the glaring swatches of purple decorating her scoring harness.

"These are nothing!" she snapped angrily. "He barely *touched* me!"

"That's because in a knife fight, the object is to bleed your opponent out, not to get your knife stuck in his meat," Rastar told her. "Would you care to go another round with padding and use these—" he twitched all four blades simultaneously "—as *swords*, instead?"

"I think not," Ral said before Toshok could reply. "I don't want bones broken." The admiral gave a hum of laughter, then beckoned to another Althari. "Tshar! You're up."

The Althari who rolled forward at Ral's summons was a massive juggernaut of muscle and fur, enormous even by Althari standards, and the admiral looked at Roger.

"This is the daughter of my sister's cousin by marriage, Lieutenant Tshar Krot. She is our champion at weaponless combat. Choose your champion, Prince Roger."

Roger shook his head as he contemplated the sheer size of the Althari, but he didn't hesitate. There was only one choice.

"Sergeant Pol," he said.

Erkum stepped forward at the sound of his name. Seeing that the Althari was naked, he removed his harness and kilt, but kept on his environment suit and stood waiting patiently.

"What are the rules?" Roger asked.

"There are *rules* in weaponless combat?" Ral replied with another hum of laughter.

"No gouging, at least?"

"Well, of course not," the admiral said.

"I think we need to make sure Erkum knows that," Roger commented dryly, looking up at Krindi Fain's towering shadow. "Erkum," he said sternly in Diaspran, "no gouging."

"No, Your Highness," the Diaspran said, pounding all four fists together as he sized up his opponent. The Althari was nearly as tall as he was, and even broader. "I'll try not to break any bones, either," Erkum promised.

"*Gatan!*" the admiral barked, beginning the match, and all the Marines and Mardukans started shouting encouragement.

"Break bones, Erkum! Break bones!"

"Turn her into bear paste!"

The two combatants circled each other for a moment, and then Tshar darted forward, grasping an upper wrist and rolling in for a hip-throw. But Erkum dropped his weight, and both of his lower hands grabbed the Althari by the thighs and picked her up. It was a massive lift, even for the big Mardukan, since the Althari must have weighed five hundred kilos, and she got one hand on the environment suit. But Erkum still managed to turn her upside down, then straightened explosively and sent her spinning through the air.

Tshar hit on her back, rolled lithely, and dodged aside as the Mardukan stamped down. Then she was back on her feet. She charged forward again, this time lifting *Erkum* into the air, and threw him down in turn. But he got one hand on one of her knees as he fell, and twisted her off her feet.

Both of them sprang back up, as if they were made of rubber, and, as if they'd planned it ahead of time, charged simultaneously. There was a strange, unpleasant sound as the Mardukan's horns met the Althari's forehead, and then Tshar was on her back, shaking her head dazedly. There was a trickle of blood from her muzzle.

"*Adain,*" the admiral said, just a bit unnecessarily, then moved her head in another complex gesture Roger's toot's analysis of Althari body language read as indicating wry amusement. "Important safety lesson, there," she observed. "Never try to head-butt a Mardukan."

Erkum had a hand around the base of each horn, and was shaking his own head from side to side.

"She got a hard head," he muttered, and sat down with a thump.

"I suggest we call that a draw, then," Roger suggested as Doc Dobrescu and a male Althari darted forward.

The Althari ran a scanner over Tshar and gave her an injection, then came over to the admiral.

"Nothing broken, and no major hematoma," he said. "But she's got a slight concussion. No more fighting for at least two days."

"And the Mardukan?" Ral asked.

"He's got a headache, but that's about it," Doc Dobrescu said, and slapped the still-seated Pol on the upper shoulder as he stood. "They've got a spongy padding under the horns that absorbs blows like that. Still hurts, but he's fine."

"In that case, Your Highness, I don't think we can call that a draw in honor," the admiral pointed out.

"By all means, score it as you prefer," Roger replied.

The admiral waved her right hand at Pol, formally granting him the victory, then turned back to Roger.

"Your companions say you're deft with the sword," she noted.

"I'm okay. It's kept me alive a couple of times."

"Your Mardukans have been competing against my clan," the admiral said in an offhand manner. "Would you care to try?"

"I don't have a practice blade," Roger pointed out.

"Your sword was remotely measured," Ral said and gestured to one of the hovering Althari. The male brought forward a sword that looked very much like Roger's, except that the blade was blunted and seemed to be made of carbon fiber.

Roger stood up and weighed it in his hand. The balance was right, and so was the shape—about a meter and a half long, slightly curved with a thin but strong blade. The weight felt very close, as well, although it might be a tad heavier.

While he was examining the blade, a young Althari female appeared, bearing padding and a sword. The weapon she carried would have been a two-handed blade for a human, something like a claymore in design, but with a straight blade and broad cross guard. The Althari was a bit older than the two previous competitors, fully mature with a broad band of black running up and over her shoulders. She carried the sword with a measure of assurance Roger found somewhat intimidating. Most of his fighting had been in harum-scarum battles, where formal ability counted less than simply making sure the other guy died.

"This is Commander Tomohlk Sharl, my husband's sister's husband's cousin," the admiral said. The relationship was one word in Althari, but Roger's toot translated ably. "She has some knowledge of *tshoon*, our traditional sword art."

"I'll give it my best shot," Roger said, shaking his head when the padding was offered. "That won't help me much," he observed dryly, looking up at his outsized opponent. He did, however, take the helmet after a murderous glance from Despreaux. It was something like a zero-G ball helmet, carbon fiber, padded, with a slotted mask. And he donned the scoring harness, mentally noting that if the monstrous Althari *did* score, it was going to be pretty obvious.

There were two marks, about four meters apart, and Roger moved to one of them, taking the carbon fiber sword in a two-handed grip and settling his shoulders.

"*Gatan*," the admiral said, and sat back down in her chair.

Roger and the Althari approached one another cautiously, reaching out to touch blades, and then backing off. Then the Althari started the match by springing forward, striking quickly from *quarte* towards Roger's chest.

Roger parried on his foible and stepped to the side, measuring his opponent's speed. The Althari followed up quickly, pressing him, and he turned to the side again, rolling her blade off of his and springing to his left and back.

She spun again, bringing her blade down in a forehand strike. But this time he took it on his sword, rolling it off in a neat parry and moving inside the blade, driving past her with a snake-quick slice towards her unprotected stomach. He ended up behind her, and cut down at the hamstring. Both strikes scored in less than a second.

"*Adain*," the admiral said, and Roger returned smoothly to a guard position. The commander was rubbing her leg and shaking her head.

"That's not a legal blow in *tshoon*," she said.

"I'm sorry. I didn't know that," Roger admitted. "I haven't been in any encounters where the term 'legal blow' had meaning."

"I think you're lucky in that," the Althari said. "I've never had the opportunity to battle with the sword in truth. Or, for that matter, to battle more than the occasional pirate with any weapon. Wars are few these days." She made a sound Roger's toot interpreted as a sigh of envy, then produced an Althari chuckle. "You're quick. Very quick."

"I have to be." Roger grinned. "You're huge. But, then again, so are most Mardukans. I've had to learn to be quick."

They resumed their places, and the admiral gave the signal to reengage. This time, the Althari worked to keep Roger outside, using her superior reach against his speed. Time and time again Roger tried to break through the spinning blade, but he couldn't. Finally, the Althari scored on his arm. He partially blocked the blow, but she'd closed slightly, and the leverage was enough to break down his defense. The score was relatively light, but it hurt like hell.

"*Adain*," the admiral said. "One score apiece."

She beckoned them back to their marks.

"*Gatan.*"

They closed again, with the Althari pushing Roger this time. He had to back away, spinning to stay inside the fighting circle. They worked back to the center, and then the commander feinted a stroke, stopped it in mid-blow, and sprang forward in a lunging strike with the point, instead.

The feint fooled Roger completely. He'd been set to block the stroke and found himself abruptly forced to fumble up a parry against the unanticipated thrust, instead. He fell backwards, then bounced back up like a spring, using the weight of his sword for balance. It was a desperation move, but it placed him inside the Althari's defense. He came up to one knee, then struck up and across. The move left a bold purple slash across the commander's stomach.

"*Adain*," the admiral said. "Very nice."

"Hell with nice," Roger responded, rubbing his back. He'd pulled something there. "On the battlefield, I'd have been dead if I didn't have someone at my back."

"You're quite fortunate in that regard," Ral noted, waving at the *Basik*'s Own.

"I've got a lot of friends, that's true," Roger admitted.

"Which is due to your leadership," the admiral pointed out. "Do not discount yourself."

"A good bit of it had to do with Captain Pahner," Roger replied sadly. Then he turned his head. Three groundcars were approaching from the far side of the warren. Roger had already noticed a large shuttle landing, but there'd been a fair amount of comings and goings during the morning, so he'd thought little of it. This caravan seemed pointed towards them, however.

"We seem to have company," he observed.

"Sreeetoth," the admiral agreed, standing up. "And others."

Roger just nodded his head and looked over at Eleanora. The chief of staff shrugged.

The party was still going on overhead, but the meeting had been moved to one of the underground conference rooms. It had the indefinable look of a secure room. Admittedly, getting a bug into any of the Althari rooms would have been difficult, but this one looked as if the walls were encased in a Faraday cage, and the door had sealed like an airlock.

The surface of the table within was adjustable to three different levels, and the chairs about it were also of different heights, with contours which reconfigured at the touch of a control, obviously designed to provide for humans, Althari, and Phaenurs. Another Althari, not the admiral, took the chair at its head, while a Phaenur Roger had not yet met took an elevated, padlike "chair" at the far end. Sreeetoth was seated beside the new Phaenur, with Tchock Ral to the left of the new Althari.

"I am Sroonday, Minister of External Security," the Phaenur at the foot of the table said. "Sreeetoth, Chief of Customs, you know. My coleader is Tsron Edock, Minister of War. We apologize for the . . . informal fashion in which you have been greeted, Your Highness, but . . ."

Roger held up a hand and shook his head.

"There can be nothing formal in my greeting, Minister, given the circumstances," he said. "And I thank you for the indulgence of this meeting."

"It is more than indulgence," Tsron Edock said, leaning forward. "The Empire of Man has been a competitor for the Alphane Alliance's entire existence. But it has been a *friendly* competitor. We do not have to station war fleets on its border with us, which makes it the *only* border we do not have to defend. We maintain fair and equitable trading relations with it. All of this will pass if it breaks up into internecine warfare, or if the Saints are able to establish large inroads into its territory. We have always looked to it as an ally against the Saints, but under current circumstances . . ."

She looked at the Phaenur, and made a head gesture.

"Everyone has sources of information," the Phaenur said sibilantly. "Yes?"

"Yes," Roger replied. "Although the Alphanes are notoriously hard to penetrate."

"This is so," Sroonday admitted. "And Imperial internal security is also quite good. But we do have sources of information . . . including sources in the Adoula faction."

"Ah." Eleanora nodded. "And you don't like what you're hearing from there."

"No," the External Security Minister said. "We do not. Our source is very good. We knew, long before you arrived, that the supposed coup was Prince Jackson's doing. And, yes, your mother is being held under duress, Your Highness. A combination of control of her implants and psychometric drugs. Other things as well . . ."

Sroonday's voice trailed off uncomfortably. Roger simply sat there, brown eyes like stones, and after a moment, the Phaenur continued.

"Opinion among the plotters over the long-term disposition of the Empress is divided. Most, yes, wish her to have a terminal event as soon as the Heir is born. New Madrid wishes to keep her alive, but our analysts believe that is because she is his only hold on power. Furthermore, our source tells us that Adoula intends to . . . change the relationship between the Empire and the Alphane Alliance. Specifically, he intends to invade the Alliance."

"Is he *nuts*?" Roger blurted.

"We have a fine fleet," the War Minister said, glancing at Admiral Ral. "The Empire, however, has *six* rather fine fleets, the smallest of which is the size of our *entire* fleet. We could go down fighting, but we will probably be offered some sort of local autonomy, as a separate satrapy of the Empire."

"And how will that sit with the Althari?" Roger asked.

"Not well," Tchock Ral said angrily. "I did not know this. My clan will not be slaves to the Empire. Not as long as one Tshrow remains alive."

"None of us will allow it," Edock said. "The Altharis can be destroyed, but not conquered."

"The Phaenurs have a somewhat more philosophical approach," Sroonday hissed. "But given that the bulk of our armed forces are Althari, and that we and our dwellings are intermingled with them, our philosophical approach will be of little use. Taking one of our worlds will require sufficient firepower to ensure that the survivors will be so few in number that—"

"Adoula has to understand that," Eleanora interjected. "I mean, that's a known fact in any intelligence estimate about the Alphane Alliance. You can destroy it, but you can't simply absorb it. All he'd get in a war is a bunch of battle casualties and twelve destroyed planets."

"Prince Jackson is fully aware of the estimates," the Phaenur said. "And disbelieves them."

"That's insane," Roger said flatly.

"Perhaps," Sroonday replied. "It is possible that his understanding of us suffers from his own lack of a multispecies outlook. Whereas all three of the Alliance's member species have been forced to come to comprehend the strengths, weaknesses, and fundamental differences which make all of us what we are, Prince Jackson has not. More importantly, he is a creature of the deal. He believes that after our orbitals are taken, he can 'cut a deal' with us, thereby adding our not inconsiderable economic base to the Empire, and placing the Caravazan Empire between two enemies. His long-term goal is to force the Caravazans to . . . retreat. To become less threatening. He believes he can accomplish this by creating a balance of force which is overwhelmingly weighted against them.

"But to accomplish this, he must conquer us, and that will not happen until the entire Alphane Alliance lies in smoking ruin. It brings one of your own folk tales—about a golden avian, I believe—rather forcibly to mind. Unfortunately, he would appear to be unfamiliar with that particular tale's moral. And thus, Prince Roger," the Phaenur concluded, "we have an immense vested interest in considering support for your endeavor. *If* you can convince us it is even remotely likely to succeed."

"We need access to current intelligence," Roger said. "As current as available. And we'll need a ship, and quite a bit of cash. We also need some read on the . . . reliability of Navy units. Our plan relies, perhaps too much, upon the . . . irregularity of the Sixth Fleet. Do you have any current information on it?"

"A replacement for Admiral Helmut was sent out a month ago," Edock said with an odd roll of her shoulders. "The carrier transporting him apparently had severe mechanical problems and had to pull into dock in the Sirtus System. It remains docked there, having twice had major faults detected in its tunnel drive. Absolutely valid faults, as it happens, which apparently appeared quite suddenly and unpleasantly. In one case, it would seem, due to a couple of kilos of well-placed explosives. Helmut's replacement, Admiral Garrity, unfortunately, is no longer concerned about the delays. According to our reports, the good admiral's shuttle suffered a major malfunction entering the atmosphere of Sirtus III shortly after the second tunnel drive malfunction. There were no survivors."

"You don't pock with the Dark Lord of the Sixth," Julian said.

"This has got to stop," Despreaux protested. "I mean, I know why it's going on, but killing fleet commanders—legally appointed fleet commanders . . ."

"Some question about the legality of the appointment," Kosutic replied grimly. "But I have to agree with the general sentiment."

"Unfortunately, it's part and parcel of the way the Empire has been trending for a long time," Eleanora said with a shrug. "The fact that Admiral Helmut probably doesn't think twice about going to these lengths—certainly not under the circumstances—and that other segments of the Navy are supporting Adoula in this coup, is a symptom, not the disease. The disease is called factionalism, and the level of internal strife is reaching the point of outright civil war. That disease is what your mother was trying to head off, Roger. Unsuccessfully, as it turns out."

"It's not *that* bad," Despreaux said. "There's a lot of political infighting, sure, but—"

"It *is* that bad," Eleanora replied firmly. "Largely due to Roger's grandfather, in fact.

"The Empire is going through a very rough period right now, Nimashet, and unfortunately, that's not sufficiently apparent for most people to be worried about doing something to prevent it.

"We've settled out fully from the psychological, economic, and physical results of the Dagger Wars. It's been five hundred and ninety years since Miranda the Great kicked their asses, and we haven't had a real *war* with anyone else since, despite our periodic bouts of . . . unpleasantness with the Saints. And even those have all been out among the out-worlds. So there's no one alive in the core-worlds who remembers a time of actual danger. We had our last serious economic crisis over a generation ago, too, and politics in the core-worlds have revolved around the strife between the industrialists and the socialists for over seventy years.

"The industrialists, by and large, are truly in it purely for the power. There've been times when corporations were unfairly held up as great, evil empires of greed by individuals who were simply deluded, or else intentionally using them as strawmen—as manufactured ogres, created for their own propaganda purposes. But Adoula's cadre truly *is* in the business of seeking personal power and wealth at any cost to anyone else. Oh, Adoula has the additional worry that his home sector is right on the Saint border. That's why he concentrates on what used to be called the 'military-industrial complex.' But while he might be trying to build military power, the way he goes about it is counterproductive in the extreme. The way the power packs blew up on your plasma guns, Your Highness, is a prime example, and he and his crowd are too far gone to realize that making money by cutting costs at every turn, even if it means a suicide bomb in the hands of a soldier, actually *decreases* their own security, right along with that of the rest of the Empire.

"The socialists are trying to counter the industrialists, but, again, their chosen methods are counterproductive. They're buying votes among the poor of the core-worlds by promising more and more social luxuries, but the tax base is never going to be there to support uniform social luxury. They get the taxes which have kept the system propped up so far by squeezing the outer worlds, because the industrialists have sufficient control in Parliament and the core-world economies to work tax breaks that allow them to avoid paying anything like the taxes they might incur if the lunatics weren't running the asylum. At the same time, if the socialists ever did manage to impose all the taxes *they* think the corporations should cough up in order to pay for their social benefits and all the other worker benefits—like increased paid holidays and decreased workweeks—it really would cripple the economy.

"The ones getting squeezed are the out-worlds, and they're also where most of the new economic and productive blood of the Empire is coming from. All the new devices and arts are coming from there. By the same token, they supply the bulk of the military forces, sites for all the newer military bases and research centers, and more and more manufacturing capability. That shift has been underway for decades now, and it's accelerated steadily as local marginal business taxes in the core-worlds build up and up.

"But the out-worlds still don't have the population base to elect sufficient members of Parliament to prevent themselves from being raped by the inner-worlds. Nor do they have the degree of educational infrastructure found in the core-worlds, which is why the core is still supplying the elite research and business brains. The out-worlds are growing—fast, but not fast enough—and to add to all of their other problems, they're the ones most at risk from surrounding empires, especially the Saints and Raiden-Winterhowe.

"It would be an unstable situation under the best of circumstances, and we don't have those. The members of Parliament elected from the core-worlds are, more and more, from the very rich or hereditary political families. By now, the Commons representation from the core is almost indistinguishable from the membership of the House of Lords. They have a lot of commonality of viewpoint, and as the out-worlds' representation in the Commons grows, the politicians of the inner-worlds see an ever-growing threat to the cozy little power arrangements they've worked out. To prevent that from happening, they use various devices, like the referendum on Contine's elevation to full member-world status, to prevent loss of their power. The politics have become more and more brutal, more and more parochial, and less and less focused on the good of the Empire. In fact, the only people you see walking the walk of the 'good of the Empire' are a few of the MPs from the out-worlds. Adoula *talks* about the good of the Empire, but what he's *saying* is all about the good of Adoula.

"And the real irony of it is that if any of them were capable of truly enlightened self-interest, they'd realize just how stupid their cutthroat tactics really are. The inner-worlds, the out-worlds, the socialists, the industrialists, and the traditionalists all *need* each other, but they're too busy ripping at one another's throats to see that. We're in a bit of a pickle, Your Highness, and, frankly, we're ripe for a really nasty civil war. Symptom, not disease."

"So what do we do about it?" Roger asked.

"You mean, if we rescue your mother and survive?" Eleanora smiled. "We work hard on getting all sides to see themselves as members of the Empire first, and political enemies as a distant second. Your grandfather decided that the problem was too many people in the inner-worlds with too little to gain. So, besides siding with the socialists and starting the trend toward heavy taxation of the out-worlds, he tried to set up colonization programs. It didn't work very well. For one thing, the conditions on the core worlds, even for the very poor, are too comfortable, and woe betide the politician who tries to dial back on any of the privileges that have already been enacted.

"Your grandfather was unwilling to cut back there, but he had this romantic notion that he could engender some kind of 'frontier spirit' if he just threw enough funding at the Bureau of Colonization and wasted enough of it on colonization incentives. But the way he paid for simultaneously maintaining the existing social support programs while pouring money into colonization schemes that didn't work was to cut all other spending—like for the Navy—and turn the screws on the out-worlds. And to get the support in Parliament that his colonization fantasies needed, he made deals with the industrialists and the aristocracy which only enhanced their power and made things even worse.

"He never seemed to realize that even if he'd been able to convince people to *want* to relocate from the core-worlds to howling wildernesses in the out-worlds, there simply aren't enough ships to move enough of them to make a significant dent in the population of the core-worlds. And then, when he had his moment of disillusionment with the Saints' promises to 'peacefully coexist' and started trying to build the Navy back up to something like its authorized strength, it made the Throne's fiscal position even worse. Which, of course, created even more tensions. To be perfectly honest, some of the people who're supporting Adoula right now probably wandered into treason's way in no small part because they could see what was coming. A lot of them, obviously, wanted to fish in troubled waters, but others were seeking any port in a storm. And at least some of them, before the Old Emperor's death, probably thought even someone like Adoula would have been an improvement.

"Your mother watched all that happening, Your Highness. I hope you'll forgive me for saying this, but one of the greater tragedies of your grandfather's reign was how long he lived. He had so much time to do damage that, by the time your mother took the Throne, the situation had snowballed pretty horrifically.

"She decided that the only solution was to break the stranglehold of *both* the industrialists *and* the vote-buyers. If you do that, you can start to make things 'bad' enough in the core-worlds that at least the most motivated will move out-system. And you can start reducing the taxation rape of the out-worlds and shifting some of the financial burden onto the core-world industries which haven't been paying their own share for so long. And once the out-world populations begin growing, you can bring in more member worlds as associate worlds, which will bring new blood into the entire political system at all levels. But with the socialists and the industrialists locked together in their determination to maintain the *existing* system while they duel to the death over who controls it, that's pretty hard."

"It won't be when I stand half of them up against the wall," Roger growled.

"That . . . could be counterproductive," Eleanora said cautiously.

"Anyone associated with this . . . damnable plot," Roger said flatly, "whether by omission or commission, is going to face rather *partial* justice. So is anyone I find decided that the best way to make a credit was to cut corners on military gear. Anyone. I owe that debt to too many Bronze Barbarians to ever forget it, Eleanora."

"We'll . . . discuss it," she said, looking over at the Phaenur.

"It's your Empire, but I agree with the Prince," Tchock Ral said. "The penalty for such things in our Alliance is death. To settle for any lesser penalty would be to betray the souls of our dead."

"But a reign of terror has its own unpleasant consequences," Eleanora pointed out. "Right now, the penalty for failure, at the highest level, is already so great that desperate chances are being taken. Or, what's worse, the best and the brightest simply avoid reaching that level. They ... opt out rather than subject themselves and their families to the current virulent version of Imperial politics. Only the most unscrupulous strive for high office as it is; enact a reign of terror, and that trend will only be enhanced."

She shook her head, looking for an argument Roger might accept.

"Look, think of it as something like guerrilla warfare," she said.

"I think you're reaching," Roger replied. "It's not to *that* level yet."

"*Yet*," she said. "Not yet. But there's a saying about counter-guerrilla operations; it's like eating soup with a knife. If you try to simply *break* the political alliances, by cutting up the obvious bits, then you're going to lose, and lose hard. You've got to not simply break the *old* alliances; you have to establish *new* ones, and for that you need an intact political template and people to make it work. You've got to convince the people running the system to make the changes you recognize are necessary, and you're not going to convince the people whose support you need that they should cooperate with you if they think you'll have them shot if they don't do exactly what you want. Not unless you're willing to enact a full reign of terror, turn the IBI into a secret police to watch everyone's actions and suppress *anyone* who disagrees with you. Turn us into the Saints."

"The IBI would be ... resistant to that," Temu Jin said. "Most of it, anyway; I suppose you could always find a few people who always secretly hankered to play storm trooper," he added reluctantly.

"And if you did find them, and you could impose your reign of terror, the Empire you're fighting for—the Empire they *died* for—" she gestured at the Marines, "would be gone. There'd be something there with the same name, but it wouldn't be the Empire that Armand Pahner served."

"I see the point you're trying to make," Roger said with manifest reluctance. "And I'll bear it in mind. But I reiterate; *anyone* associated with this plot, by omission or commission, and *anyone* associated with accepting, creating, or supporting defective military gear—with knowledge, and for profit—is going up against the wall. Understand that, Eleanora. I will not enact a reign of terror, but the point will be made, and made hard. I *will* put paid to this . . . evil rot. We may have to do it by eating soup with a knife, but we *will* eat the entire bowl. To the dregs, Eleanora. To the *dregs*."

Those eyes of polished brown stone swept the beings seated around the conference table like targeting radar, and silence hovered for a handful of fragile seconds.

"We will if we win," Julian said after a moment, breaking the silence.

"*When* we win," Roger corrected flatly. "I haven't come this far to lose."

"So how, exactly, do you propose to go about not losing?" Sroonday asked.

The meeting had gone on well into the afternoon, with a brief break for food served at the table by members of the admiral's family. The "External Security Minister" was the Alphane equivalent of the head of their external intelligence operations, and it had brought a wealth of information with it. The most important, from Roger's perspective, was the nature of the newly reformed "Empress' Own."

"Household troops?" Roger asked, aghast.

"Well, that's what the Empress' Own always have been, after all," Eleanora said.

"But these are Adoula's paid bully-boys," Kosutic pointed out. "They're from his industrial security branches, or else outright hired mercenaries." She shook her head. "I expected a whole hell of a lot better than this out of someone in Adoula's position. Most of them have no real military training at all. For all intents and purposes, they're highly trained rent-a-cops—used to keeping workers in line, breaking up labor riots, and preventing break-ins. The Empress' Own *was* composed of the best fighters we could find from throughout the entire Marine Corps. Troops trained to fight pitched battles, and *then* trained to think in security force terms and given a bit of polish and a pretty uniform."

"Agreed," Admiral Ral said with the Althari equivalent of a nod.

"Either we've been overestimating his military judgment," Eleanora said, "or else his hold on the military is even weaker than we'd dared hope."

"Reasoning?" Roger asked. She looked at him, and he shrugged. "I don't say I disagree. I just want to see if we're thinking along the same lines."

"Probably." The chief of staff tipped her chair back slightly and swung it in a gentle side-to-side arc. "If Adoula actually thinks the force he's assembled is remotely as capable as the *real* Empress' Own, then he's a certifiable lunatic," she said succinctly. "Admittedly, *I* didn't really know the difference between a soldier and a rent-a-cop before we hit Marduk, but I certainly do now. And someone with his background ought to have that knowledge already. But if he does, and if he's chosen to build the force he has anyway, it strongly suggests to me that he doesn't believe he can turn up sufficient troops willing to be loyal to him—or to close their eyes to the irregularities of what's going on in the Palace—from the regular military. Which, in turn, means that his control of what you might call the grass roots of the military, at least, is decidedly weak."

"About what I was thinking," Roger agreed.

"And either way, the first *good* news we've had," Ral said.

"True. But the Palace is still a fortress," Eleanora pointed out. "The automated defenses alone could hold off a regiment."

"Then we don't let the automated defenses come on line," Roger said.

"And how do we stop them?" Eleanora challenged.

"I have no idea," Roger replied, then tapped the face of a hardcopy hologram from one of the data packets the minister had brought. "But I bet anything he does."

"Catrone?" Kosutic said, looking over his shoulder. "Yeah. If we can get him on our side. The thing to understand is that the Palace's defenses aren't one layer. There are sections of the security arrangements I never knew, because I was in Bronze Battalion. You're a senior member of Bronze, you learn the defenses Bronze needs to know. Steel knew more, Silver more than Steel. The core defenses were only authorized to Gold, and Catrone was the Gold sergeant major for over a decade. Not quite the longest run in history, but the longest in *recent* history. If anyone knows a way to penetrate the Palace, it's Catrone."

"Putting all your faith in one person, with whom you have no significant contact, is unwise," Sroonday pointed out. "One does not build a successful strategy around a plan in which *everything* must go right."

"If we can't get Catrone's help, we'll find another way," Roger said. "I don't care how paranoid the Palace's designers were, there'll be a way in. And we'll find it."

"And your Home Fleet?" Edock asked.

"Strike fast enough, and they'll be left with a *fait accompli*," Roger pointed out. "They're not going to want to escalate to the point of nuking the Palace with Mother inside, and if they don't act immediately, we'll have news media and reasonably honest politicians all over it before they can do anything else. Home Fleet doesn't *have* a sizable Marine contingent, and there's a reason for that. They *could* nuke the Palace—assuming they could get through the surface-to-space defenses—but I'd be interested to see the reactions among the officers who heard the order. And that assumes we can't checkmate them, somehow."

"Take out Greenberg, for starters," Julian said. "And Gianetto. We'll have to get control of the Defense Headquarters, anyway."

"And a base?" the Phaenur asked.

"We've got one," Kosutic replied. Sroonday looked at her, and her mouth twitched in a tight grin.

"We've been talking about the Palace's security systems, but security for the Imperial Family isn't about individual structures, no matter how intimidating they may be. It's an entire edifice, an incredibly baroque and compartmentalized infrastructure which, for all intents and purposes, was directly designed by Miranda the First."

"With all due respect, Sergeant Major," War Minister Edock said, "Miranda the First has been dead for five hundred and sixty of your years."

"I realize that, Minister," Kosutic said. "And I don't mean to say that anything she personally designed is still part of the system. Mind you, it wouldn't really surprise me if that were the case. Miranda MacClintock was a bloody dangerous woman to get pissed off, and the terms 'incredibly devious' and 'long-term thinking' could have been invented expressly for the way her mind worked. But what I meant was that she was the one who created the entire concept of the Empress' Own, and established the philosophy and basic planning parameters for the Imperial Family's security. That's why things are so compartmentalized."

"Compartmentalized in what sense, Sergeant Major?" Edock asked.

"The same way the Palace's security systems are," she said. "There are facilities—facilities outside the Palace, outside the entire normal chain of command—dedicated solely to the Imperial Family's security. Each battalion of the Empress's Own has its own set of secure facilities, known only to the battalion's senior members, to be used in case of an emergency. This is the first coup attempt to even come close to success in over half a millennium, Minister. There's a reason for that."

"Are you saying that no one from Steel, Silver, or Gold would know about these 'facilities,' Eva?" Temu Jin asked. "They're *that* secure?"

"Probably not," she conceded. "Most of the senior members of those battalions came up the ladder, starting with Bronze. So it's likely at least someone from the more senior outfits knows where just about everything assigned to Bronze is located. But they're not going to be talking about it, and even if they wanted to, our toots are equipped with security protocols which would make that an ... unpleasant experience even after we retire. Which means there's no way anyone working for Adoula could have that information. So once we get to the Sol System, we'll use one of the Bronze facilities."

"I think, then, that we are as far along as we can get today," Sroonday said sibilantly. "Fleshing out the bones we have already put in place is a matter of details best left to staff. It will take some time, a few days at least, to acquire the materials you need. A freighter and a ... discreet crew. And a captain."

"We have a captain," Roger said. "I'll get a list of the positions we'll need filled on the freighter. An old freighter, or one that *looks* old."

"Done," Sroonday said, rising. "I will not be directly involved in this further. It was hard enough to find a time when I could conveniently disappear as it is. Sreeetoth will be your liaison with me, and Admiral Ral will liaise with the War Minister."

"We thank you for your support, Minister Sroonday," Roger said, rising in turn and bowing across the table.

"As I pointed out, it is in our mutual interest," the Minister replied. "Alliances are always based upon mutual interest."

"So I've learned," Roger said with a thin smile.

Despreaux frowned and looked up from the list of stores she'd been accessing when the door beeped at her.

"Enter," she said, and frowned harder when she saw that it was the sergeant major and Eleanora O'Casey.

"Girl talk time again?" she asked more than a little caustically, swinging her station chair around to face them.

"You see what we meant," Eleanora said bluntly, without pre-amble, as she sat down in one of the room's float chairs and moved it closer to the desk. "I noticed you were really quiet in the meeting, Nimashet," she continued.

"I didn't have any contribution to make," Despreaux replied uncomfortably. "I'm already in way over my pay grade."

"Bullshit you didn't have a contribution," Kosutic said, even more bluntly than O'Casey. "And you know just what that con-tribution would be."

"Except that in this case, I halfway agree with him!" Despreaux replied angrily. "I think standing Adoula and his cronies, and everyone else associated with this plot, up against a nice, bead-pocked wall is a dandy idea!"

"And their families, too?" Eleanora asked. "Or are you going to let their relatives continue to have the positions of power their families held before the coup and also a blood feud with the Emperor? The point of courts and laws is to distance the individual from the act. If Roger has Adoula and everyone else summarily executed, everyone who disagrees with the decision will be after his scalp. And let's not even think about how the news media would play it! If he stands them all up against a wall and has a company of Mardukans shoot them, we *will* have a civil war on our hands. And a guerrilla war, and every other kind of war you can imagine."

"So we let them *walk*?" Despreaux demanded in exasperation.

"Just like they always do? Or maybe they should get some quality time in a country-club prison, and then come out to make more minor mischief?"

"No," Kosutic said. "We arrest them, charge them with treason, and put them in jail. Then the IBI gathers the evidence, the courts do their work, and the guilty get quietly put to death. No passion. No fury. Calmly, efficiently, legally, and *justly.*"

"And you think they won't walk with a passel of high-priced Imperial City lawyers?" Despreaux half-sneered. "With as much money as they have to throw at the problem?"

"Roger . . . didn't see all the data Sroonday had," Eleanora said uncomfortably. "With the things the Empress will have to say about . . . what's going on, I'd be very surprised if anyone were *willing* to be their lawyer, no matter what the fee. The difficulty will be keeping Adoula and New Madrid from being torn limb from limb."

"And just what," Despreaux asked carefully, "didn't Roger see?"

"I think that, for now, that will be kept to the Sergeant Major and myself," Eleanora said sternly. "You just focus on how to keep Roger from turning into another Dagger Lord. When he finds out, I think you'll have all you can handle keeping him from gutting New Madrid on the Palace steps."

"Welcome, Your Highness, to my home," Sreeetoth said, bowing to the prince as Roger stepped through the door.

"It's beautiful," Despreaux said in a hushed voice.

The home was a large plant—not exactly a tree, but more of a very *large* root. The top of the root-bole towered nearly twenty meters in the air and covered a roughly oval base which measured about thirty meters in its long dimension. Narrow branches clothed in long, fernlike purple leaves extended from the tops and sides, and the brown and gray moss which covered the surface of the root itself formed intricate patterns, something like a Celtic brooch.

It was placed against the slope of a low hill in a forest. Apparently, it had been positioned directly in the path of what had been a waterfall, for water moved among the twisting branches of the root, pouring out of the front of the "house" in a thousand small brightly sparkling streams. The interior, however, was snug and dry. There were some human chairs, but scattered around the main room were pillows and rugs made of some sort of deep-pile fabric.

"I was fortunate to acquire it while I was still a young officer," Sreeetoth said. "It is nearly two hundred of your years old. It takes only a decade or so for a *po'al* root to grow to maximum size, but they...improve with age. And this one is remarkably well-placed. May I offer drinks? I have human tea and coffee, beer, wine, and spirits."

"I'll take a glass of wine," Roger said, and Despreaux nodded in agreement.

"Thank you for joining me," the Phaenur said, reclining on one of the pillows, then widened its eyes as Roger and Despreaux sank down on others.

"Most humans use the chairs," it noted.

"We've been on Marduk for so long that chairs seem strange," Roger said, taking a sip of the wine. It was excellent. "Very nice," he complimented.

"A friend keeps a small winery," Sreeetoth said, bobbing its head in one of the abrupt, lizardlike gestures of its species. "*Tool* fruit wine is a valuable, though small, export of the Alphane Alliance. Most of it," it added dryly, "is consumed internally, however. Your health."

"Thank you," Roger said, raising his own glass in response.

"You are uneasy about being asked to join me in my home," the Phaenur said, taking a sip of its own wine. "Especially when I specifically invited the young Sergeant to accompany you, and no others."

"Yes," Roger said, simply. "In a human, that would be a guess. In your case, it's as plain as if I'd said it out loud, right?"

"Correct," it replied. "The reason for my invitation is simple enough, however. Much of the success of this operation depends upon you—upon your strength and steadiness. I wanted to meet with you in a situation uncluttered by other emotions."

"Then why not invite me to come alone?" Roger asked, tilting his head to the side.

"Because your own emotions are less cluttered when the Sergeant is near you," the Phaenur said simply. "When she leaves your side, for even a moment, you become uneasy. Less . . . centered. If you were Phaenur, I would say she was a *tsrooto*, an anchor. It translates badly. It means . . . one part of a linked pair."

"Oh." Roger looked at Despreaux. "We . . . are not so linked."

"Not in any official form or way," Sreeetoth agreed. "But you *are* so linked. The Sergeant, too, is uneasy when away from you. Her agitation does not show on her surface, but it is there. Not the same as yours. You become . . . sharp, edgy. In some circumstances, dangerous. She becomes . . . less focused, unhappy, worried."

"Are we here for couples counseling, then?" Despreaux asked dryly.

"No, you are here because your Prince is happier when you are around," it replied, taking another sip of wine. "On the other hand, if this *were* a matter for counseling, I would point out to both of you that there is nothing whatsoever wrong in requiring—or being—a *tsrooto*. The fact that the Prince is calmer, more centered, in your presence does not mean that he is weak or ineffectual without you, Sergeant. It simply indicates that he is in some ways still stronger and more effective *with* you. That the two of you have much strength to give one another, that together you become still more formidable. It is a reminder that—as I believe you humans put it—the whole can be greater than the sum of its two parts, not that either of you becomes somehow weak, or diminished, in the other's absence.

"But that is not why you are here. The Prince is here because I wanted to taste him, to know what we are wagering our trust upon. You are an odd human, Prince. Did you know that?"

"No," Roger said. "I mean, I'm quick—probably neural enhancements I didn't know I had—but . . ."

"I did not refer to any physical oddity," Sreeetoth said. "I have seen the reports, of course. Your agility and physical good looks, for a human, were noted in the reports we had from before your supposed death. As was your . . . untried but clearly capable mind. *Athroo* reports, samplings of your emotions, were few, but said that you were childish, disinterested in anything but play. Now we have this . . . other Prince. Before, you were normal; now we have someone who radiates more like an Althari than a human. There is no dissembling in you, none of the constant desire to hide your purpose we find among most humans. Fear of revealing your hidden faults, that overarching miasma of guilt that humans seem to run around in all the time. For the most part, you are as clear and clean as a sword. It is refreshing, but so odd that I was told to sample it fully and make a report."

It cocked its head to the side as if doing just that.

"There's no point in lying," Roger said. "Not with the Phaenur. I'll admit that was a pleasant change."

"Yet the Imperial Court is no place for a truly honest man," the Phaenur suggested.

"Maybe I can change that." Roger shrugged. "And if I can't, I have some truly dishonest advisers."

The Phaenur cocked its head to the side and then bobbed it.

"I sense that was a joke," it said. "Human and Phaenur concepts of humor are often at odds, alas."

"One thing I would be interested in," Roger noted, "to try to make the Court a more . . . honest place, is some Phaenur advisers. Not immediately, but soon after we retake the Palace."

"That could be arranged," Sreeetoth said, "but I strongly recommend that you contract with independent counselors. We like and trust the Empire, and you like and trust us. But having representatives of our government in your highest councils would be . . . awkward."

"I suppose." Roger sighed. "I'd like to do as much as possible in the open, though. The Court hasn't *been* a place for an honest man, and one way to change that might be to make sure that what's said in Court is honest. Among other things, it would place me in a position where I could work to my strengths, not my weaknesses. I've never understood the importance that's placed upon dishonesty in business and politics."

"I do," Despreaux said with a shrug. "I don't like it, but I understand it."

"Oh?" the Phaenur said. "There is a point to dishonesty?"

"Certainly. Even the Phaenurs and the Althari don't wear their thoughts on their sleeves. For example, Roger in command of the Empire will be a very restless neighbor. You have to know that. Surely there are others you'd prefer?"

"Well, yes," Sreeetoth admitted.

"But you don't bring it up, don't emphasize it. In it's own way, that's dishonest—or at least dissembling. And I have no doubt that you're capable of lying by omission, Mr. Minister." She looked directly into the Phaenur's eyes. "That there are things you have no intention of revealing, because to do so might evoke reactions which would run counter to the outcomes you're after."

"No doubt," Sreetoth conceded, bobbing its head respectfully at her. "And you are correct. Roger's personality, the style of ruler-ship we anticipate out of him, will not be ... restful under the best of circumstances."

It made a soft sound their toots interpreted as quiet laughter.

"That may not be so bad a thing, however," it continued. "His grandfather, for example, was quite soothing. Also an honest man, but surrounded by deceit and virtually unaware of it. His lack of competence precluded the Empire's becoming a threat to us, which was restful, yet it also created the preconditions for the crisis we all face today.

"Still, that does not mean a restless human ruler is necessarily in our best interests. Roger's mother, unlike her father, is a very deceitful person, but not at all, as you put it, restless. She was solely concentrated on the internal workings of the Empire and left us essentially alone. From our reports, it is unlikely she will continue very long as Empress. That will leave this ... restless young man as Emperor. We could prefer someone *less* restless, but he is the best by far of the choices actually available to us."

"How badly has Mother been injured?" Roger asked angrily.

"Quite badly, unfortunately," the Phaenur replied. "Calm yourself, please. Your emotions are distressing in the extreme. It is why we have not brought up the full measure of damage before."

"I'll ... try," Roger said, as calmly as he could, and inhaled deeply. Then he looked directly at his host. "How damaged?"

"The nature of the reports on her condition we have received— their very existence—means that maintaining security to protect our source is ... difficult," Sreeetoth replied. "We have been able to clear only one specialist in human psychology and physiology to take a look at them, but she is among the best the Alliance can offer in her speciality, and I have read her analysis. It would appear that the ... methods being used are likely to cause irrepa-rable long-term damage. It will not kill her, but she will no longer be ... at the top of her form. A form of senility is likely."

Roger closed his eyes, and one jaw muscle worked furiously.

"I apologize for my current . . . feelings," he said after a moment in a voice like hammered steel.

"They are quite bloody," Sreeetoth told him.

"We'll handle it," Despreaux said, laying a hand on his arm. "We'll *handle* it, Roger."

"Yes." Roger let out a long, hissing breath. "We'll handle it."

He touched the hand on his arm very lightly for just an instant, then returned his attention to Sreeetoth.

"Let's talk about something else. I love your house. You don't have neighbors?"

"Phaenurs tend to separate their dwellings," his host said. "It is quite impossible to fully shield one's feelings and thoughts. We learn, early on, to control them to a degree, but being in crowds is something like being at a large party for a human. All the thoughts of other Phaenurs are like a gabble of speech from dozens of people at once. All the emotions of others are like the constant roar of the sea."

"Must be interesting working in customs," Despreaux observed.

"It is one of the reasons so much of the direct contact work is handled by humans and Althari males," Sreeetoth agreed. "Alas, that has been somewhat less successful than we had hoped. Your reports on Caravazan penetration have caused a rather unpleasant stir, with some serious political and social implications."

"Why?" Roger asked. "I mean, you're an honest society, but *everyone* has a few bad apples."

"Humans have been a part of the Alphane Alliance since its inception," Sreeetoth explained. "But they have generally been—not a lower class, but something of the sort. Few of them reach the highest levels of Alphane government, which has not sat well with many of them. They know that Altharis and Phaenurs are simply more trustworthy than their own species, but that is not a pleasant admission for them, and whatever the cause, or whatever the justification, for their exclusion, the fact remains that they do not enjoy the full range of rights and opportunity available to Altharis or Phaenurs.

"Althari males, however, most definitely *are* a lower class. Althari females, until recently, considered them almost subsentient, useful only for breeding and as servants."

"Barefoot and . . . well, I guess not pregnant," Despreaux said dryly, and grimaced. "Great."

"It is humans who have pushed for more rights for Althari males, and over the last few generations they have attained most of those rights. But it was humans and Althari males, and a single Phaenur who was supposed to be keeping an eye on them, who were corrupted by the Saints. I have already seen the level of distrust of the males growing in the females who work with them, those who know of their betrayal. Such a betrayal on the part of a *female* Althari would be considered even worse, and might shake their world view . . . and their prejudices. But, alas, only males were involved. And humans."

"So now both groups are under a cloud," Roger said. "Yes, I can see the problem."

"It is damaging work which has taken a generation to take hold," Sreeetoth said. "Most distressing. Admiral Ral has reinstituted communications restrictions on the males in her household, since you are staying there. That, in itself, is a measure of the degree of distrust which has arisen. She has lost faith in the honor of the males of her own household."

"Lots of fun," Roger said, and grimaced. "I almost wish we hadn't given you the information."

"Well, I cannot wish that," the Phaenur said. "But we have had to increase the level of counseling and increase the number of counseling inspectors. It is a difficult process, since they need to move about so that the counselors are unavailable for corruption. It is, in fact, something I had pressed for previously, but prior to your information the funds were unavailable. They are becoming available. Quickly."

"Sorry," Roger said with a frown.

"I am not," Sreeetoth said. "It helps me to ensure that the affairs of my department are in order. But you do seem to bring chaos wherever you go, young Prince. It is something to beware of."

"I don't mean to," Roger protested, thinking of the trail of bodies, Mardukan and human, the company had left behind on Marduk.

"You appear simply to be responding to your surroundings and the threats you encounter," Sreeetoth said, "not *seeking* to become a force of destruction. But be careful. However justified your responses, you *thrive* on chaos. That is not an insult; I do the same. To be in customs, it is a necessity."

"I think that was a joke," Roger said.

"You humans would consider it so, yes—an ironic reality," it replied. "There are those who manage chaos well. You are one; I am another. There are others who cannot handle chaos at all, and fold in its face, and they are much more numerous. The job of a ruler, or any policymaker, is to reduce the chaos in life, so that those who simply wish tomorrow to be more or less the same as today, possibly a bit better, can get on with their lives.

"The danger for those who manage chaos well, though, is that they seek what they thrive upon. And if they do not have it in their environment, they may seek to create it. I have found such tendencies in myself; they were pointed out to me early on, by one of my superiors. Since then I have striven, against my nature, to create placidness in my department. To find those who thrive on *eliminating* chaos. I have many subordinates, humans, Altharis, and Phaenurs, who also thrive on chaos—but those who cannot create order out of it, I remove. Their ability to manage the chaos is unimportant in the face of the additional chaos they create. So which will you do, young Prince? Create the chaos? Or eliminate it?"

"Hopefully eliminate it," Roger said.

"That is to be desired."

They ate, then, from a smorgasbordlike selection of the Phaenur foods that were consumable by humans, with several small servings of multiple dishes rather than one main entrée. Conversation concentrated on their travels on Marduk, the things they'd seen, the foods they'd eaten. Roger couldn't entirely avoid reminiscing about the dead—there were too many of them. And whenever he had a fine repast, and this was one such, it brought back memories of Kostas and the remarkable meals he had produced from such scanty, unpromising material.

When the meal was done, they departed, walking out of the grove to the waiting shuttle. It was the Phaenur custom, not a case of "eating and running." Phaenur dinner parties ended at the conclusion of the meal. In fact, the original Phaenur custom had been to conclude any gathering by the giving of foods to be eaten afterwards. That custom had been modified only after the Phaenur culture's collision with human and Althari customs.

Roger thought it was rather a good custom. There was never the human problem of figuring out when the party was over.

He and Despreaux boarded the shuttle in silence, and they were halfway through the flight back to the admiral's warren before Roger shook his head.

"Do think it's right?" Roger asked. "Sreeetoth? That I create chaos wherever I go?"

"I think it's hard to say," Despreaux replied. "Certainly there *is* chaos wherever we go. But there's usually some peace, when we're done."

"The peace of the grave," Roger said somberly.

"More than just that," Despreaux said. "Some chaos, to be sure. But an active and growing chaos, not just some sort of vortex of destruction. You . . . shake things up."

"But Sreeetoth is right," Roger noted. "There's only room for a certain amount of shaking up in any society that's going to be stable in the long-term."

"Oh, you generally leave well enough alone, if it isn't broken," Despreaux argued. "You didn't shake things up much in Ran Tai. For the rest, they were places that desperately needed some shaking. Even K'Vaern's Cove, where you just showed them they needed to get off their butts, and how to do it. It's not easy being around you, but it *is* interesting."

"Interesting enough for you to stay?" Roger asked softly, looking over at her for the first time.

There was a long silence, and then she nodded.

"Yes," she said. "I'll stay. If it's the right thing to do. If there's no serious objection to it, I'll stay even as your wife. Even as—ick!—the Empress. I do love you, and I want to be with you. Sreeetoth was right about that, too. I don't feel . . . whole when I'm not around you. I mean, I need my space from time to time, but . . ."

"I know what you mean," Roger said. "Thank you. But what about your absolute pronouncement that you'd never be Empress?"

"I'm a woman. I've got the right to change my mind. Write that on your hand."

"Okay. Gotcha."

"I'm not going to be quiet," Despreaux warned him. "I'm not going to be the meek little farm girl over in the corner. If you're going off the deep end, I'm going to make that really, really plain."

"Good."

"And I don't do windows."

"There are people for that around the Palace."

"And I'm not going to every damned ribbon-cutting ceremony."

"Agreed."

"And keep the press away from me."

"I'll try."

"And I want to get laid."

"*What?*"

"Look, Roger, this is silly," Despreaux said angrily. "I haven't been in bed with a guy—or with a female, for that matter—in nearly ten months, and I have needs, too. I've been waiting and waiting. I'm *not* going to wait for some damned matrimonial ceremony, if and when. And it's not healthy for you, either. Parts start to suffer."

"Nimashet—"

"We've discussed this," she said, holding up her hand. "If you're going to have a farm-girl as your wife, then you're going to have to be willing to have one that's clearly no virgin, if for no other reason than that she's been sleeping with *you*. And we're not on Marduk anymore. Yes, I'm one of your guards, technically, but we both know that's just a job description anymore. I guess I'm one of your staff, but mostly I'm there to keep the peace. There's no ethical reason, or moral one, come to think of it, why we can't have . . . relations. And we're *going* to have relations, if for no other reason than to take the edge off *you*. You're like a live wire all the time, and I *will* ground you."

"You always have grounded me," Roger said, patting her hand. "We'll discuss it."

"We already have," Despreaux said, taking the patting hand and putting it in her lap. "Any *further* discussion will take place in bed. Say 'Yes, Dear.'"

"Yes, Dear."

"And these tits are new, so they're still a bit sore. Be careful with them."

"Yes, Dear," Roger said with a grin.

"My, Your Highness," Julian said, looking up as a whistling Roger walked into the office he'd set up. "You're looking chipper today."

"Oh, shut up, Julian," Roger said, trying unsuccessfully not to grin.

"Is that a hickey I see on your neck?"

"Probably. And that's all we're going to discuss about the evening's events, Sergeant. Now, what did you want to tell me?"

"I've been looking into the information the Alphanes provided on our Navy dispositions." Julian was still grinning, but he spoke in his getting-down-to-business voice.

"And?" Roger prompted.

"Fleets can't survive indefinitely without supplies," Julian said. "Normally, they get resupplied by Navy colliers and general supply ships sent out from Navy bases. But Sixth Fleet is right on the edge of being defined as operating in a state of mutiny, with everything that's going on. So Navy bases have been ordered *not* to resupply its units."

"So where are they getting their supplies?" Roger asked, eyes narrowing in interest as he leaned his shoulders against the office wall and folded his arms.

"At the moment, from three planets and a station in the Halliwell Cluster."

"Food and fuel, you mean?" Roger asked. "I don't see them getting resupply on missiles. And what are they doing for spares?"

"Fuel isn't really that big a problem...yet," Julian replied. "Each numbered fleet has its own assigned fleet train service squadron, including tankers, and Sixth Fleet hasn't been pulling a lot of training maneuvers since the balloon went up. They haven't been burning a lot of reactor mass, and even if they had been, feeding a fusion plant's pretty much dirt cheap. I don't think Helmut would hesitate for a minute when it came to 'requisitioning' reactor mass from civilian sources, for that matter.

"Food, on the other hand, probably is a problem, or becoming one. Missile resupply, no sweat, so far—they haven't expended any of their precoup allotment. But spare parts, now. *Those* are definitely going to be something he's worrying about. On the other hand, you and I both know how inventive you can get when you're desperate."

"'Inventive' doesn't help if a capacitor goes out," Roger pointed out. "Okay, so they're getting resupplied by friendly local planets. What's that do for us?"

"According to the Alphanes, Helmut's supplies are being picked up by three of his service squadron's colliers: *Capodista*, *Ozaki*, and *Adebayo*. I was looking at the intel they have on Sixth Fleet's officers—"

"Got to love their intel on us," Roger said dryly.

"No shit. I think they know more about our fleets than the Navy does," Julian agreed. "But the point is, the captain of the *Capodista* is one Marciel Poertena."

"Any relation to . . . ?"

"Second cousin. Or once removed, or something. His dad's cousin. The point is, they know each other; I checked."

"And *you* know Helmut."

"Not . . . exactly. I was one of the Marines on his ship, once upon a time, but there were fifty of us. We met. He might remember me. Then again, given that the one time we really *met* met it was for disciplinary action . . ."

"Great," Roger said.

"Who the messenger is isn't really that important," Julian pointed out. "We just need to get him the message—that the Empress is in trouble, that the source of the trouble is provably not you, and that you're going to fix it."

"And that if we *can't* fix it, he has to disappear," Roger said. "That we're not going to crack the Empire over this. Anything is better than that, and I don't want him coming in after the fact, all guns blazing, if we screw the pooch."

"We're going to have a civil war whatever happens," Julian countered.

"But we're not going to Balkanize the Empire," Roger said sternly. "He has to understand that and *agree*. Otherwise, no deal. On the other hand, if he supports us, and if we win, he has his choice: continue in Sixth Fleet until he's senile, or Home Fleet, or Chief of Naval Operations. His call."

"Jesus, Roger! There's a reason those are all two-year appointments!"

"I know, and I don't really care. He's loyal to the Empire first—*that* I care about. Tell him I'd *prefer* CNO or Home Fleet."

"I tell him?"

"You. Turn over your intel-gathering to Nimashet and Eleanora. Then get Poertena. You're on the next ship headed towards the Halliwell System." Roger stuck out his hand. "Make a really *good* presentation, Julian."

"I will," the sergeant said, standing up. "I will."

"Good luck, Captain," Roger added.

"Captain?"

"It's not official till its official. But from now on, that's what you are from my point of view. There are going to be quite a few promotions going on."

"I don't want to be a colonel."

"And Nimashet doesn't want to be Empress," Roger replied. "Face facts, Eva. I'm going to need people I can trust, and they're going to have to have the rank to go with the trust. For that matter, you're going to be a general pretty damned quick. I know you think about the Empire first."

"That's . . . not precisely true," the Armaghan said. "Or, not the way it used to be." She looked him straight in the eye. "I'm one of *your* people now, Roger. I agree with your reasoning about the Empire, but the fact that I agree with it is less important than the fact that it's *your* reasoning. You need to be clear on that distinction. Call me a fellow traveler, in that regard."

"Noted," Roger said. "But in either case, you know what I'm trying to do. So if you think I'm doing something harmful to the Empire, for whatever reason, you tell me."

"Well, all right," she said, then chuckled. "But if that's what you really want me to do, maybe I should start now."

"Now?"

"Yeah. I'm just wondering, have you really *thought* about the consequences of making Poertena a lieutenant?"

"Pocking nuts, t'at's what t'ey are," Poertena muttered, looking at the rank tabs sitting on the bed. "Modderpocking nuts."

Poertena had spent most of his life as a short, swarthy, broad individual with lanky black hair. Now he was a short, broad, fair-skinned individual, with a shock of curly *red* hair. If anything, the new look fitted his personality better. If not his accent.

"How bad can it be?" Denat asked.

The Mardukan was D'Nal Cord's nephew. Unlike his uncle, he was under no honor obligation to wander along with the humans, but he did suffer from a severe case of horizon fever. He'd accompanied them to the first city—what he'd considered a city at the time—Q'Nkok, to help his uncle in negotiations with the local rulers. But when Cord followed Roger and his band off into the Kranolta-haunted wilderness, Denat (for reasons he couldn't even define at the time) had followed along, despite the fact that everyone *knew* it was suicide.

In the ensuing third of a Mardukan year, he'd been enthralled, horrified, and terrified by turns, each beyond belief. He'd very rarely been bored, however. He'd also discovered a hidden gift for languages and an ability to "blend in" with a local population—both of which abilities had been pretty well hidden among a tribe of bone-grinding savages—which had proved highly useful to the humans.

And in Marshad, he had acquired a wife as remarkable, in her own way, as Pedi Karuse. T'Leen Sena was as brilliant a covert operator as any race had ever produced, and although she was small—petite, actually—for a Mardukan, and a "sheltered city girl," to boot, she was also a very, very dangerous person. The fact that she'd seen fit to marry a wandering warrior from a tribe of stone-using barbarians might have shocked her family and friends; it did not shock anyone who knew Denat.

In addition to gaining adventure, wealth, fame, and a wife he doted upon, he and Poertena had become friends. Representatives of two dissimilar species, from wildly divergent backgrounds, somehow they clicked. Part of that was a shared love of gambling, at least if the stakes were right. The two of them had introduced various card games to unsuspecting Mardukans across half a planet, and done rather well financially in the process. To a Mardukan, cheating was just part of the game.

"Ask me if I trus' him," Poertena griped as he packed his valise. "He's a *Poertena*! I gotta say yes, but t'ey got no *idea* what an insult t'at would be. *Of course* you can' trus' him."

"I trust *you*," Denat said. "I mean, not with cards or anything, but I'd take you at my back. I'd trust you with my knife."

"Well, sure," Poertena said. "But . . . damn, you don' have to make a big t'ing about it. An' it ain't t'e same t'ing, anways. If Julian goes in all 'good of t'e Empire,' Marciel's gonna *preak*."

"Well, at least you're getting off this damned planet," Denat grumped. "It's a pocking ice ball, playing cards with these damned bears is *boring*, and the sky is overhead *all the time*. Doesn't it ever *rain*?"

Rain and overcast skies were constant companions on Marduk, one of the reasons the locals had evolved with slime-covered skin.

"You wanna come along, come along," Poertena said, looking up from his packing.

"Don't tempt me," Denat said wistfully. "Sena would kill me if I ran off without her."

"So?" Portena snorted. "She also one of t'e bes' pockin' 'spooks' I know. Might be she come in handy in somet'ing like t'is."

"You really think Roger would agree to let both of us come?" Denat perked up noticeably, and Portena chuckled.

"Hey, got's to prove somehow where t'e pock we been for t'e las' year, don' we? I t'ink a pair of Markduans migh' be abou' t'e bes' pockin' proof we gonna find." He shrugged. "We can get more tickets. I don' know wha' we do por t'e passports, but we pigure out somet'ing. Ones we got are pretty good por complete pakes."

"Ask, please," Denat said. "I'm going crazy here."

"Well, we're moving." Roger pulled out a strand of hair, then tucked it behind his ear. "We can get an abort message to Julian, if it reaches him in time. But for all practical purposes, the die is cast."

"Second thoughts?" Despreaux asked. They were in Roger's quarters eating a quiet meal, just the two of them.

"Some," he admitted. "You don't know how good the 'government-in-exile' plan's looked to me from time to time."

"Oh, I think I do. But it was never really an option, was it?"

"No, not really." Roger sighed. "I just hate putting everyone in harm's way, again. When does it end?"

"I don't know." Despreaux shrugged. "When we win?"

"If we capture Mother, and New Madrid," he never called New Madrid "father," "and Adoula. Maybe everything will hold together. Oh, and capture the replicator, too. And if Helmut can checkmate Home Fleet. And if none of Adoula's cabal grabs a portion of the Navy and flees back to the Sagittarius Sector. If, if, if."

"You need to stop fretting about it," Despreaux said, and then smiled crookedly at the look he gave her. "I know—I know! Easier to say than to do. That doesn't keep it from being good advice."

"Probably not, he agreed. "But there's not much point giving someone advice you *know* he can't follow."

"True. So let's at least worry about something we might be able to do something about. Any news on the freighter?"

"Sreeetoth said maybe two more days," Roger replied with a shrug of his own. "They didn't have one that was quite right in-system. It's coming from Seranos. Everything else is ready to go, so all we can do is wait."

"Whatever will we do with the time?" Despreaux smiled again, not at all crookedly.

None of the crew recruited for the freighter were aware of the true identities of their passengers. They'd been recruited in spaceport bars around the Seranos System, one of the fringe systems of the Alphane Alliance which bordered on Raiden-Winterhowe, and they knew *something* was fishy. Nobody, no matter how rich and eccentric, charters a freighter, picks up a crew, and loads the freighter with barbarians, live animals of particularly nasty dispositions, and food that can't possibly recoup the cost of the voyage for reasons that weren't "fishy." But the crew, most of whom had some questionable moments tucked away in their own backgrounds, assumed it was a standard illegal venture. Smuggling, probably, although smuggling *what* was a question. But they knew they were getting paid smuggler's wages, and that was good enough for them.

It was twelve days to the edge of Imperial space, and their first stop was Customs in the Carsta System, Baron Sandhurt's region.

They intended to stop only long enough to clear customs, but it was a nerve-wracking time. This was "insertion," the most dangerous moment of any covert operation. Anything could go wrong. The Mardukans were all briefed with their cover stories. The Earther had hired them to go to Old Earth to work in restaurants. Some of them were soldiers from their home world, yes; but wars were getting short, which was leaving them unemployed, and unemployable. Some of them were cooks, yes. Would you like to try some roast *atul?*

Roger waited at the docking port as the shuttle came alongside, standing with his hands folded behind him and his feet shoulder width apart. Not entirely calm; total calm would have been a dead giveaway. Everyone was always uncomfortable at customs. You never knew when something could go wrong—some crewman with contraband, a change in some obscure regulation that meant a portion of your cargo impounded.

Beach appeared much calmer, as befitted her role. She was only a hired hand, right? Of course she was, and she'd been through customs repeatedly. And if anything was amiss, well, it wasn't her money, was it? The worst that could happen was a black mark against her and, well, that had happened before, hadn't it? She'd still be a captain on some vessel or another. It was just customs.

The airlock's inner hatch slid aside to reveal a medium-height young man with brown hair and slight epicanthic folds to his eyes. He wore a skin-tight environment suit and carried his helmet under his arm.

"Lieutenant Weller?" Roger said, holding out his hand. "Augustus Chung. I'm the charterer for the ship. And this is Captain Beach, her skipper."

Weller was followed by four more customs inspectors—about right for a ship this size. Most of them were older than Weller, seasoned customs inspectors, but not ones who were ever going to be promoted to high rank. Like Weller, they racked their helmets on the bulkhead, then stood waiting.

"Pleased to meet you, Mr. Chung," Weller said.

"Ship's documents," Beach said, extending a pad. "And identity documents on all the passengers and crew. Some of the passengers are . . . a little irregular. Mardukans. They've got IDs from the planetary governor's office, but . . . well, Mardukans don't have birth certificates, you know?"

"I understand," Weller said, taking the pad and transferring the data to his own. "I'll look this over while my team does its survey."

"I've detailed crew to show you around," Beach said, gesturing to the group behind her. It consisted of Macek, Mark St. John, Corporal Bebi, and Despreaux. "Go for it," she continued, looking at Weller's assistants. "I'll be available by com if you need me, but where I'll *be* is down in Engineering." She transferred her glance to Roger. "I'm going to make sure the damned TD capacitors aren't overheating this time, Mr. Chung."

She nodded to the customs party generally, then walked briskly away, and Weller looked up from the data on his pad to cock his head at Roger.

"Trouble with your ship, sir?"

"Just old," Roger replied. "Chartering any tunnel drive ship's bloody expensive, pardon my Chinee. There's little enough margin in this business at all."

"Restaurants?" Weller said, looking back down at the data displayed on his pad. "Most of this appears to be foodstuffs and live cargo."

"It was all checked for contamination," Roger said hurriedly. "There's not much on Marduk that's infectious and transferable. But, yes, I'm starting a restaurant on Old Earth—authentic Mardukan food. Should do well, if it catches on; it's quite tasty. But you know how things are. And the capitalization is horrible. To be successful in the restaurant business, you have to be capitalized for at least eighteen months, so—"

"I'm sure," Weller said, nodding. "Bit of an interesting group of passengers, Mr. Chung. A rather . . . diverse group."

"I've been in the brokering business for years," "Chung" said. "Like my investors, the people I picked to assist me in this venture are friends I've made over the years. It may look like a bit of a pickup crew, but they're not. Good people. The best."

"I can see what your captain meant about the Mardukans." Weller was frowning at the data entries on the Mardukans.

"They're all citizens of the Empire," Roger pointed out. "That's one of the points I've kept in mind—free passage between planets, and all that. No requirement for work visas, among other things."

"It all looks right," Weller said, holstering his pad. "I'll just go tag along with my inspectors."

"If there's nothing else, I'll leave you to your duties. I need to catch up on my paperwork," Roger said.

"Just one more thing," Weller said, taking a device from the left side of his utility belt. "Gene scan. Got to confirm you're who you say you are," he added, smiling thinly.

"Not a problem," Roger replied, and held out his hand with an appearance of assurance he didn't quite feel. They'd tested the bod-mods using Alphane devices, but this was the moment of truth. If the scanner picked up who he really was . . .

Weller ran the device over the back of his hand, then looked at the readout.

"Thank you, Mr. Chung," the lieutenant said. "I'll just get on with my work."

"Of course."

"We're cleared," Beach said as she came into the office.

"Good," Roger replied, then sighed. "This is nerve-wracking."

"Yes, it is," Beach agreed with a grin. "Covert ops are bloody nerve-wracking. I don't know why I don't give it up, but for now, things are looking good. A day more to charge, and we're on our way to Sol."

"Three weeks?" Roger asked.

"Just about—twenty and a half days."

"Time, time, time . . ." Roger muttered. "Ask me for anything but time."

"That damned inspector!" Despreaux groused.

"Problems?" Roger asked. As far as he'd been able to determine, the only trouble the inspectors had found was one of the pickup crew who'd had a stash of illegal drugs. The crewman had been escorted off the ship, and a small fine had been paid.

"No, he just kept trying to pinch my butt," Despreaux said angrily. "*And* asking me to reach up and get things from over-head bins."

"Oh." Roger smiled.

"It's not funny," Despreaux said, glaring at him exasperatedly. "I'll bet you wouldn't have enjoyed it if it'd been *your* butt, either!

And I kept expecting him to say something like: 'Aha! You are the notorious Nimashet Despreaux, known companion of the dangerous Prince Roger MacClintock!'"

"I really doubt they'd put it like that, but I know what you mean."

"And I'm worried about Julian."

"So am I."

"If I never see another pocking ship, it be too soon," Poertena muttered as they stepped off the shuttle.

"Sorry to hear you feel that way, Poertena," Julian replied, "since with any luck, we'll see a few more. And try like hell not to talk, okay? Your damned passport says you're from Armagh, and that is *not* an Armaghan accident."

"How do we find this guy?" Denat asked. "I don't see anything that looks like a Navy shuttle."

Halliwell II was a temperate but arid world, right on the edge of Imperial space, near the border with Raiden-Winterhowe. Raiden had tried to "annex" it twice, once since the Halliwell System had joined the Empire. It was an associate world, a nonvoting member of the Empire, with a low population which consisted mostly of miners and scattered farmers.

Sogotown, the capital of Halliwell II and the administrative center for the surrounding Halliwell Cluster, boasted a rather mixed architecture. The majority of the buildings, including the row of godowns around the spaceport, were low rammed-earth structures, but there were a few multistory buildings near the center of town. The entire modest city was placed on the banks of one of the main continent's few navigable rivers, and the newly arrived visitors could see barges being offloaded along the riverfront.

Several ships were scattered around the spaceport—mostly large cargo shuttles, but including a few air-cargo ships, and even one large lighter-than-air ship. None of them had Imperial Navy markings.

"They might be using civilian shuttles," Julian said, "but it's more likely they're not here right now. We'll ask around. Come on, we'll try the bars."

Entry was informal. They'd asked about a customs inspector, but the shack where he should have been was empty. Julian left a data chip with their information on the desk, and then they walked into town.

The main road into town was stabilized earth, a hard surface that was cracked and rutted by wheeled traffic. There were a few electric-powered ground cars around, but much of the traffic (what of it there was) seemed to be tractor, horse, and even ox-drawn carts. It was midday, and hot (by human standards; Denat and Sena had their environment suits cranked considerably higher), and most of the population seemed to be sheltering indoors.

They walked through the godowns ringing the port and past a couple of hock-shops, then stopped outside the first bar they came to. Its garish neon sign advertised Koun beer and featured a badly done picture of a horse's head.

The memory-plastic door dilated as Julian walked up to it. The interior was dim, but he could see four or five men slouched around the bar, and the room smelled of smoke, stale beer, and urine. A corner jukebox played a whining song about whiskey, women, and why they didn't go well together.

"God," Julian whispered. "I'm home."

Denat pulled the membrane mask off his face and looked around, sniffing the air.

"Yeah," he said. "Guess some things are universal."

"So I've noticed," Sena said dryly, true-hands flicking in a body language gesture which expressed semiamused distaste. "And among them are the fact that males are all little boys at heart. Spoiled little boys. Try not to get falling down drunk, Denat."

"You just talk that way because you love me," Denat told her with a deep chuckle, then looked back at Julian. "First round's on you."

"Speaking of universal," Julian muttered, but he led the way to the bar.

The drinkers were all male, all of them rather old, with the weathered faces and hands of men who'd worked outside most of their lives and now had nothing better to do than to be drinking whiskey in the early morning. The bartender was a woman, younger than the drinkers, but not by much, with a look that said she'd been rode hard and put up wet and was going to keep right on riding. Blonde hair, probably from a bottle, with gray and dark brown at the roots. A face that had been pretty once, but a nice smile and a quizzical look at the Mardukans.

"What you drinkin'?" she asked, stepping over from where she'd been talking with the regulars.

"What's on tap?" Julian asked, looking around for a menu. All that decorated the room were signs for beer and whiskey and a few pinups with dart holes in them.

"Koun, Chika, and Alojzy," the woman recited. "I've got Koun, Chika, Alojzy, Zedin, and Jairntorn in bulbs. And if you're a limp-wrist wine drinker, there's red, white, and violet. Whiskey you can see for yourself," she added, jerking a thumb over her shoulder at the racked bulbs and plastic bottles. Most of them were pretty low-cost whiskey, but one caught Julian's eye.

"Two double shots of MacManus, and a full highball," he said, then glanced at Sena and raised an eyebrow. She flicked one hand in a gesture of assent, and he smiled. "Make that two highballs. And then, two glasses of Koun, and a pitcher."

"You know your whiskey, son," the woman said approvingly. "But those highballs're gonna cost you."

"I'll live," Julian told her.

"Who're your big friends?" the bartender asked when she came back with the drinks.

"Denat and Sena. They're Mardukan."

"Scummies?" The woman's eyes widened. "I've heard of them, but I've never seen one. Well, I guess you get all kinds. Long way from home, though."

"Yes, it is," Denat said in broken Imperial. He picked up one of the highballs and passed the second to Sena. Then both of them clinked glasses with Julian and Poertena. "Death to the Kranolta!" He tossed off the drink. "Ahhhh," he gargled. "Smooooth."

Sena sipped more sedately, then twisted both false-hands in a complicated gesture of pleasure.

"It actually is," she said in Mashadan, looking across at Julian. "Amazing. I hadn't expected such a discerning palette out of you, Julian."

"Smart ass," the Marine retorted in the same language, and she gave the coughing grunt of a Mardukan chuckle.

"What'd he say?" the barkeep asked, glancing back and forth between Sena and Julian.

"He was just observing that you should be glad Denat's past his heat, or there'd be blood on the walls," Julian said with a chuckle, grinning at both Mardukans. He took a more judicious sip of his own drink, and had to admit that it was smooth. "God, it's been a long time since I've had a MacManus."

"What are you doing in this godforsaken place?" she asked.

"Looking for a lovely bartender," Julian said with a smile. "And I got lucky."

"Heard it," the woman said, but she smiled back.

"Actually, we've been traveling," Julian replied. "Bit of this here and that there. Picked up Denat and Sena on Marduk, when I had a bit of a problem and they helped me out with it. I heard the Navy's been landing here, and that they've got some civilian crews in their service squadrons. I've got a clean discharge, and so does Magee here," he said, gesturing to Poertena. "Looking to see if there's any work."

"Doubt it." The woman shook her head. "Only thing that lands is cargo shuttles. They pick up supplies and take off again. Sometimes, the crews come in for a drink, but they don't stay long. And they're the only ones who land. Others've asked about work, but they're not hiring. You know what they're doing, right?"

"No," Julian said.

"They're waiting to see who wins in Imperial City. Seems there's a chunk of Parliament that's really gotten ugly about what's happening with the Empress."

"What *is* happening?" Poertena asked, with only the slightest trace of an accent.

"Yeah, the news is saying everything's peachy," Julian noted.

"Yeah, well, they would, wouldn't they?" The bartender shook her head.

"Only one seeing the Empress these days is that snake's asshole Adoula," one of the regulars said, sliding down a stool. "Won't even let the Prime Minister in to see her. They say they've tombied her. She's not in control anymore."

"Shit," Julian said, shaking his head. "Bastards. Calling Adoula a snake's asshole's insulting to snakes."

"Yeah, but he's got the power, don't he?" the regular replied. "Got the Navy on his side. Most of it, anyway. And he's got friends in the Lords, and all."

"I didn't swear my oath to Prince Jackson and his buddies when I was in," Julian said. "I swore it to the Constitution and the Empress. Maybe the admirals will remember that."

"*Sure* they will," one of the other drinkers said mockingly. "In your dreams! The officers're all for Adoula. He's bought them, and they know it. I heard he stepped on a *sierdo* once, and it didn't bite him because of professional courtesy."

There was a chuckle from the group, but it sounded weary.

"Well, just because others have asked, it doesn't mean we shouldn't," Julian said with a sigh. "If they're not hiring, somebody else will be. Any place to sleep around here?"

"Hotel up the road a few blocks," the bartender said. "Tuesday, Friday, and Saturday nights, we've got live entertainment. Strippers on Saturday. Don't be a stranger."

"We'll be back," Julian said, finishing his beer in one long pull. "Let's go look around, guys."

"You'll be back," the regular who'd slid over said. "Isn't much to see."

"And a round for your friends," Julian added, sliding a credit chip onto the scarred bar top. "See you later."

"So what do you think?" the bartender asked after the quartet had left.

"They're not spacers," the regular replied, sipping the cheap whiskey. "Don't move right. Hair's too short. If that guy's *got* discharge papers, they're from the Marines, not Navy. Probably casual muscle. Think they're planning on muscling in on Julio?"

"Doubt it," the bartender said with a frown. "But Julio's generally hiring. And even if he's not, he'll want to know about them. I'd better give him a call.

"You wanna gamble, there's a cut to the house," the bartender said. "Gotta have it to pay the local squeeze."

Poertena glanced up from his hand and shrugged.

"How much?"

"Quarter-credit a hand," she replied. "And here's why," she

added as a short, pale-skinned man stepped through the door to the bar.

The newcomer was apparently about thirty standard years old, with slick black hair and a thin mustache. He was dressed in the height of local fashion—acid-silk red shirt, black trousers, bolero, and a cravat. The line of the bolero was slightly spoiled by a bulge which might have been a needler or a small bead pistol. He was followed by three others, all larger, one of them massive. The short jackets they wore all bulged on the right hip.

"Hey, Julio," the bartender said.

"Clarissa," the man replied with a nod. "I hope you're doing well?"

"Well enough. You want your usual?"

"And a round for the boys," he said, walking over to the table where Poertena, Denat, and one of the regulars were playing. Sena sat nearby, reading what looked like a cheap novel but was actually a Mardukan translation of an Imperial Marines field manual on infiltration tactics and nursing a Mardukan-sized stein of beer.

"Mind if I take a seat?"

"Go ahead," Poertena replied. "Call."

"Two kings," the local said.

"Beats my pocking pair of eights," Poertena said, and the local scooped in the pot.

"New man deals," the "Armaghan" continued, and passed the deck to Julio.

"Seven card stud," the pale-skinned man said, riffling the cards expertly.

Just before he started to deal, Denat reached out one massive hand and placed it over the cards.

"On Marduk," he said solemnly, "cheating is considered part of the game."

"Take your hand off of me unless you want to eat it," Julio said dangerously.

"I wish to know if this is the case here," Denat said, not lifting his hand. "I have been told it isn't, so I haven't palmed any cards. Besides, it's difficult in an environment suit. I simply wish to know, is it the local custom to cheat?"

"You saying I'm cheating?" Julio asked as the most massive guard stepped forward. His move put Sena behind him, and she glanced up casually from her manual, then went back to her reading.

"I'm simply wondering out loud," Denat replied, ignoring the guard. "If it *isn't* the custom, perhaps you would like to remove that card you stuck up your sleeve and shuffle again."

Julio raised one hand to the guard, and then slipped the ace of diamonds from the cuff of the same wrist.

"Just checking," he said, sliding it back into the deck. "Julio Montego."

"Denat Cord," Denat said as the bar regular slid back from the card table.

"I'm just gonna—" the old man said.

"Yeah, why don't you?" Julio agreed without even glancing away from the Mardukan to look at him.

"As I said, on Marduk we have a saying: if you aren't cheating, you aren't trying," Denat explained. "I have no personal reservations about anything along those lines. Humans are so . . . picky about it, though. I was pleased to see you weren't."

"You wanna give it a try?" Julio asked, sliding the cards over. "Just a friendly hand? No money, that is."

"Doesn't seem much point," Denat muttered, "but if you wish."

He'd pulled off the environment suit's gloves and flexed his hands, then shuffled. He moved the cards so quickly they seemed to blur, then slid the deck over for a cut. After Julio had carefully cut the cards, he picked them back up and tossed out a three-way hand.

"Straight stud. No draw."

Julio picked up his cards and shook his head.

"What are the odds of getting a royal flush on the deal?" he asked. "Wow, am I lucky, or what?"

"Yes, very," Denat said. "Yours in diamonds would even have beaten mine, in spades."

"I t'ink maybe we don't play cards," Poertena said. "It's times like t'is I regret teaching t'at modderpocker poker."

"Or maybe, instead of playing, we just put the cards on the table," Julian said, sliding into the chair the regular had vacated. "What can we do for you, Mr. Montego?"

"I dunno," Julio replied. "What *can* you do for me?"

"We're not muscling in on your turf," Julian said delicately. "We're just looking for work with the Navy. If that's not available, we're just going to slide out. No muss, no fuss. No trouble."

"You aren't spacers."

"I've got a data chip says different," Julian pointed out.

"I can pick them up for a credit a pop," Julio scoffed. "And I've got local responsibilities to maintain."

"We're not going to cause any trouble with the locals," Julian said. "Just call us the invisible foursome."

"You've got two scummy bodyguards and a guy says he's from Armagh that's probably never even seen the planet," Julio said. "You're not exactly invisible. What's your angle?"

"Nothing that concerns you, Mr. Montego," Julian replied smoothly. "As I said, it would be better all around if you just ignored us and pretended we were never here. It's not something you want to stick your nose into."

"This is my turf," Julio said flatly. "Everything that goes on here concerns me."

"Not this. It has nothing to do with Halliwell or your turf."

"So what's the angle? You a drug contact for the Navy? Porno? Babes?"

"You're not going to let this lie, are you?" Julian said, shaking his head.

"No."

"Mr. Montego, do you have someone who you . . . deal with? Not a boss, not that. But someone to whom you, perhaps, forward a portion of your local income? For services rendered?"

"Maybe," Montego said cautiously.

"Well, that gentleman probably has someone with whom he deals in turn. And so on, and so forth. And at some level, Mr. Montego, well above what a friend of mine would refer to as our pay grade, there's a gentleman who probably should have mentioned that some of his associates were going to be sliding through your turf. We're not dealers, we're not mules. We're . . . associates. Conveyors of information. And before you ask, Mr. Montego, no. You're not going to find out what information. If you choose to get busy about that, Mr. Montego, things will get very ugly, very quickly. Not only in this bar, but at a level you don't even want to think about. The sort of level where people don't hire spaceport bouncers, but professional gentlemen who are familiar with the use of powered armor and plasma cannon, Mr. Montego."

All of this was said with a thin smile while Julian's eyes were locked on the local's.

"He's not pocking kidding," Poertena said, and rolled up his sleeve to reveal a thin scar line where an arm had been regrown. "Pocking trust me on t'at."

"I would, if I were you," Sena said in perfect Imperial from behind the mobster.

It was the first time she'd spoken anything but Mardukan, and Julio's head turned in her direction. She looked back at him with the closest thing to a smile a Mardukan's limited facial muscles could produce, and his eyes narrowed as he observed the heavy, military-grade bead pistol which had somehow magically appeared in her lap. She made no move to touch it, only went back to her book.

"One such professional gentleman, in his own way," Julian observed dryly, never so much as glancing in Sena's direction.

"You're correct," Julio said. "There should have been some word passed. But there wasn't. And there's a price for doing business on my turf; two thousand credits, and this meeting never happened."

"T'at's pocking—"

"Pay him," Julian said. He stood up. "Nice doing business with you, Mr. Montego."

He held out his hand.

"Yes," Montego replied. "And the name was?"

"Pay the man," was all Julian said, and walked over to the bar.

Poertena pulled out two large-denomination credits chips and slid them across the tabletop.

"I don' suppose you'd care por a priendly game of poker?"

"I don't think so," Montego said, standing up. "And it would probably be better if you kept your mouth shut."

"Story of my pocking life," Poertena muttered.

The stripper turned out to be a rather tired looking woman in her forties, and the live band was louder than it was capable.

Sena and Denat, whose species' sexuality was rather different from that of humans, found the entire production bizarre, to say the very least, but they'd turned out to be quite popular with the regulars. Eight Mardukan-sized hands could set and maintain a beat for bumps and grinds that not even *this* band could completely screw up. And whatever else, the noise and crowd made for a decent place for a secure conversation.

Julian slid into the vacant seat beside the Navy warrant officer and nodded.

"Buy you a drink?" he asked. "Seems right for our boys in black."

"Sure," the pilot said. He was young, probably not too long out of flight school. "I'll take an alcodote before I lift, but, Christ, a guy's got to have some downtime."

"I've only seen shuttle crews come down," Julian said over the noise of the band and the Mardukans' enthusiastic clapping. Nobody in the bar had to know that Denat and Sena's contribution was the body-language equivalent of semihysterical laughter among their people.

"Fleet orders!" the pilot shouted back as the drummers started an inexpert riff. "No contact with the planet. Hell, even *this* is better," he said, pointing at the tired-looking stripper. "We've about run through the pornography available on the ship, and my right forearm is getting sort of overdeveloped."

"That bad?" Julian laughed.

"That bad," the warrant replied.

"You're from Captain Poertena's ship, right?" Julian said, leaning closer.

"Who wants to know?" The warrant took a sip of his drink.

"Yes or no?"

"Okay, yes," the warrant said. "Man, I know I've had too much to drink. She's starting to look good."

"In that case, I need you to pass a message to your captain."

"What?" The warrant officer really looked at Julian for the first time.

"I need you to pass a message to your captain," Julian repeated. "Do it in person, and do it alone. Message is: The boy who stole the fish is sorry. Just that. And everything he's heard lately is a lie. Got it?"

"What's this all about?" the warrant asked as Julian stood up.

"If your captain wants you to know, he'll tell you," Julian replied. "In person, alone. Got it? Repeat it, Warrant." The last was clearly an order.

"The boy who stole the fish is sorry," the warrant officer repeated.

"Do it, on your honor," Julian said, and walked into the crowd.

"How was the run?" Captain Poertena asked. He was looking at data on a holo display and eating a banana. Fresh fruit was a precious rarity in Sixth Fleet these days, even in one of the supply haulers, like *Capodista*, and he was breaking it into small bites to enjoy it properly.

"Went fine, Sir," Warrant Officer Sims replied. "We got a full load this time, and I spoke with one of the Governor's representatives. They've been trying to fill our parts list, so far with no luck."

"Not surprising," Poertena said. "Well, maybe better luck next week. Sooner or later Admiral Helmut is going to have to fish or cut bait. Any new news from the capital?"

"No, Sir," Sims said. "But I had a very strange conversation on-planet. A guy came up to me and asked me to pass you a message. In person, and alone."

"Oh?" Poertena looked up from the holo display, one cheek bulging with banana while another piece rose towards his mouth.

"The boy who stole the fish is sorry," Sims said.

The hand stopped rising, then began to drop as Poertena's swarthy face went gray.

"What did you say?" the captain snapped, his mouth half-full.

"The boy who stole the fish is sorry," Sims repeated.

The piece of banana was crushed between two fingers, and then flung onto the desk.

"What did he look—No. Did this guy have an accent?"

"No, Sir," the warrant said, coming halfway to attention.

"Did he say anything else?"

"Just something about everything being a lie," Sims said. "Sir, what's this all about?"

"Sims, you do not have the need to know," Poertena said, swallowing and shaking his head. "Modderpocker. *I* don't have the need to pocking know." The captain had worked hard on his accent, and it only tended to show in times of stress. "I did not pocking *need* t'is. Where was t'is guy?"

"Well . . ." Sims hesitated. "In a bar, Captain. I know they're off limits—"

"Forget t'at," Poertena said. "Modderpocker. I've got to t'ink. Sims, you don't tell *anyone* about t'is, clear?"

"Clear, Sir." It was Sims' turn to swallow hard.

"I'll probably need you in a while. Get some chow and crew rest if you need. I t'ink we're going back to Halliwell."

"Sir, regulations state—"

"Yeah. Well, I t'ink t'e pocking regulations jus' wen' out t'e pocking airlock."

Julian looked up as a sizable shadow loomed over the restaurant table.

"Guy that looks a lot like a Poertena just walked into the bar," Denat said. "He's with that shuttle pilot. Sena's keeping an eye on them."

Julian had gone over to one of the local restaurants that served a really *good* bitok. He'd missed them on Marduk, and this place did them right—thick, cooked to a light pink in the middle, and with really good barbecue sauce. It was infinitely preferable to the "snacks" served in the bar, and Denat and Sena had remained behind to keep an eye on things while he ate it.

Now he set down the bitok and took a sip of cola.

"Okay, showtime," he said. "Where's Magee?"

"Dunno," the Mardukan said.

"Find him," Julian replied, and tried very hard not to be irritated by the little Pinopan's absence. After all, Julian hadn't expected Captain Poertena to show up this fast, either, and it was late at night by local time. *Capodista*'s skipper must have gotten the message and taken the first available shuttle back.

Julian dropped enough credits on the table to pay for the bitok and a tip and walked out. He glanced around as he stepped out of the restaurant's door. The street was somewhat more animated at night, with groups moving from bar to bar, and he felt mildly uneasy without backup. But there was nothing he could do about that.

He went to the bar and looked around. Despite the hour, the party was still in full roar, and the band had gotten, if anything, worse. At least the stripper was gone.

He moved along the edge of the crowd around the bar until he spotted Sena. She was by the bar, one lower elbow propped nonchalantly on its surface while a true-hand nursed a beer, where she could keep an unobtrusive eye on the two Navy officers who'd taken one of the tables at the back. Lousy trade craft. It was like signaling "Look over here! *We're* having a Secret Conversation!"

He chose a spot of his own at the bar, out of sight of them but where Sena could flash him a signal if they tried to leave. About ten minutes later, Denat loomed through the door, followed by Poertena.

"Where were you?"

"Taking care of some pocking personal business."

"You know that human who was taking off her clothes?" Denat asked.

"God*damn* it, P . . . Magee!"

"Hey, a guy's got pocking needs!"

"Well, you're not gonna have the equipment to do anything about them if you just wander off that way again," Julian said ominously, then sighed and shook his head at Poertena's unrepentant look.

"C'mon," he said, and led the way through the crowd towards the Navy officers' table.

"Captain Poertena," he said, sitting down and shifting his chair to a spot from which he could keep an eye on the bar.

"Well, I know *he's* not Julio," the captain said, pointing at the Mardukan. "And neither is he," he added dryly as Sena wandered over to join them. "And you're too tall," he continued, looking at Julian.

"Hey, Uncle Marciel," Poertena said with a slight catch in his voice. "Long pocking time."

"Goddamn it, Julio," the captain said, shaking his head. "What have you gotten yourself into? I should have had a team of Marines standing by, you know that? I'm putting my balls on the line here for you."

"They're not on the line for him," Julian said. "They're on the line for the Empire."

"Which one are you?" the captain snapped.

"Adib Julian."

"I don't recognize the name," the captain said, regarding him intently.

"You wouldn't. I was just a sergeant in one of the line companies. But get this straight, we've been on Marduk," Julian gestured with a thumb at Denat and Sena, "for the last ten months. *Marduk*. We can prove that a dozen different ways. We had *nothing* to do with it."

"This is about the coup!" the pilot blurted. "Holy shit."

"Sergeant—well, Captain, sort of, Adib Julian," Julian said, nodding. "Bronze Battalion of the Empress' Own. Currently, S-2 to Prince Roger Ramius Sergei Alexander Chiang MacClintock. Heir Primus to the Throne of Man."

Despite the racket all around them, a brief bubble of intense silence seemed to surround the barroom table.

"So," Captain Poertena said after a moment, "what's the plan?"

"I need to talk to Helmut," Julian said. "I've got encrypted data chips that prove beyond any reasonable doubt that we were on Marduk when the coup occurred, not Old Earth. This is *Adoula's* plot, not the Prince's. Helmut needs to know that."

"What's *he* going to do with it?" Sims asked.

"Warrant, that's between the Admiral and myself," Julian said. "You realize, of course, that you're going to spend the next few weeks, at least, in solitary lockdown. Right?"

"Shit, this is what I get for talking to strangers in bars," the warrant said. "Let me get this straight. The Prince was on *Marduk*. Which means the whole line about him being behind the attempted coup so much bullshit. Right?"

"Right," Julian ground out. "Trust me on that one. I was there the whole time. Poertena and I are two of only twelve survivors from an entire Marine *company* that went in with him. We had to *walk* across that hot, miserable, rain-filled ball of jungle and swamp. It's a long story. But we didn't even know there'd *been* a coup until a month, month and a half ago. And *Adoula* is in charge, not the Empress."

"We'd sort of figured that out," the captain said dryly. "Which is why we're stooging around in the back of beyond out here. You're either a godsend or a goddammed menace, and I can't decide which." He sighed and shrugged. "You'll have to meet the Admiral. Sims, you and these other four go in solitary when we get to the ship. When we make rendezvous with the Fleet, I'll send them over in your shuttle to the *Zetian*. Why you four, by the way?"

"Julio to convince you," Julian said. "Me, because I've met Admiral Helmut before. And Denat and Sena because they're a counterpoint to proving we were on Marduk. And because Denat's a buddy of Julio's."

"Taught me everything I know," Denat said, shrugging all four shoulders.

"In that case, remind me not to play poker with you."

Admiral Angus Helmut, Third Baron Flechelle, was short, almost a dwarf. Well under regulation height, his feet dangled off the deck in a standard station chair, which was why the one in which he now sat was lower than standard. He had a gray, lined face, high cheekbones, thinning gray hair, and gray eyes. His black uniform was two uniform changes old—the pattern he'd worn as an ensign, and quite possibly the *same* uniform Ensign Helmut had worn, judging by the smoothness of the fabric. He wore his admiral's pips on one collar point, and the crossed cloak and daggers of his original position in Naval Intelligence on the other, and his eyes were slightly bloodshot from lack of sleep as he stared at Julian as if the Marine were something a cat had left on his doorstep.

"Adib Julian," he said. "I should have known. I noticed your name on the seizure orders and thought that treason would be about your *métier*."

"I've never committed treason," Julian shot back. "No more than you have by keeping your fleet out of contact. The traitors are Adoula and Gianetto and Greenberg."

"Perhaps. But what I see before me is a jumped-up sergeant—one I last met standing charges for falsifying a readiness report."

"There've been changes," Julian replied.

"So you tell me." The admiral considered him with basilisk eyes for several seconds, then tipped his chair very slightly back. "So, the wastrel prince returns as pretender to the Throne, and you want *my* help?"

"Let's just say . . . there have been changes," Julian repeated. "Calling Master Rog a wastrel would be . . . incorrect at this point. And not a pretender to the Throne; he just wants his mother back on it, and that bastard Adoula's head. Although his balls would do in a pinch."

"So what's the non-wastrel's plan?"

"I have to get some assurances that you're going to back us," Julian pointed out. "Not simply use the information to carry favor with Adoula, *Admiral.*"

The admiral's jaw muscles flexed at that, and he shrugged angrily.

"Well, that's the problem in these little plots that run around the Palace," he said. "Trust. I can give you all the assurances in the universe. Prepare the fleet for battle, head for Sol. And then, when we get there, clap you in irons and send you to Adoula as a trophy, along with all your plans. By the same token, there could be Marines standing right outside my cabin, waiting for me to reveal my disloyalty to the Throne. In which case, when I say 'Oh, yes, Sergeant Julian, we'll help your little plot,' they come busting in and arrest me."

"Not if Sergeant Major Steinberg is still in charge," Julian said with a slight grin.

"There is that," Helmut admitted. He and the sergeant major had been close throughout their respective (and lengthy) careers. Which was one reason Steinberg had been Sergeant Major of Sixth Fleet as long as Helmut had commanded it. "Nonetheless."

"The Prince intends to capture his mother, and the Palace, and then to bring in independents to show that she's been held in duress, and that he had nothing to do with it."

"Well, that much is obvious," Helmut snapped. "How?"

"Are you going to back us?"

The admiral leaned further back and steepled his fingers, staring at the sergeant.

"Falsifying a weapons room readiness report," he said, changing the subject. "It wasn't actually your doing, was it?"

"I took the blame. It was my *responsibility.*"

"But you didn't do the shoddy work, did you?"

"No," Julian admitted. "I trusted someone else's statement that it had been done, and signed off on it. The *last* time I made that particular mistake."

"And what did you do to the person who was actually responsible for losing you your stripes?"

"Beat the crap out of him, Sir," Julian replied after a short pause.

"Yes, I saw the surgeon's report," Helmut said with a trace of satisfaction. Then— "What happened to Pahner?" he rapped suddenly.

"Killed, Sir," Julian said, and swallowed. "Taking the ship we captured to get off that mudball."

"Hard man to kill," Helmut mused.

"It was a Saint covert commando ship," Julian said. "We didn't know until we were in too deep to back out. He died to save the Prince."

"That was his responsibility," Helmut said. "And what was his position on this . . . countercoup?"

"We developed the original plan's framework before the attack on the ship, Sir. It had his full backing."

"It would," the admiral said. "He was a rather all-or-nothing person. Very well, Julian. *Yes*, you have my backing. No Marines at the last minute, no double crosses."

"You haven't asked what you get for it," Julian noted. "The Prince will owe you a rather large favor."

"I get the safety of the Empire," Helmut growled. "If I asked for anything else, would you trust me?"

"No," Julian admitted. "Not in this. But the Prince authorized me to tell you that, as far as he's concerned, you can have Sixth Fleet or Home Fleet or CNO 'until you die or go senile.' That last is a direct quote."

"And what are *you* getting, Sergeant?" the admiral asked, ignoring the offer.

"As a *quid pro quo*? Nada. Hell, Sir, I haven't even been *paid* in over ten months. He told me before we left that I'm a captain, but I didn't ask for it."

Julian paused and shrugged.

"The safety of the Empire? Admiral, I'm sworn to serve the Empire, we both are, but *I* serve Master Rog. We all do. You'd have to have been there to understand. He's not . . . who he was. None of us are. We're Prince Roger's Own. Period. They call aides 'dog-robbers' because they'll rob a dog of its bone, if that's what the admiral wants. We're … we're *pig*-robbers. We'll steal slop, if that's what Roger wants. Or conquer the Caravazan Empire. Or set him up as a pirate king. Maybe Pahner wasn't that way, maybe he fought for the Empire, even to the last. But the rest of us are, we few who survive. We're Roger's dogs. And if he wants to save the Empire, well, we'll save the Empire. And if he'd told me to come in here and assassinate you, well, Admiral, you'd be dead."

"Household troops," the admiral said distastefully.

"Yes, Sir, that's us. And the nastiest group thereof you're ever likely to see. And that doesn't even count the Mardukans. Don't judge them by Denat; he just follows us around to see what mischief we get into. Rastar or Fain or Honal would nuke a world without blinking if Roger told them to."

"Interesting that he can command such loyalty," Helmut mused. "That doesn't … fit his profile from before his disappearance. In fact, that was one factor in my disbelief that he had anything to do with the coup."

"Well, things change," Julian said. "They change fast on Marduk. Admiral, I've got a presentation on what we went through and what our plans are. If you'd like to see it."

"I would," Helmut admitted. "I'd like to see what could change a clothes horse into—"

"Just say a MacClintock."

"Well, well—Harvard Mansul." Etienne Thorwell, Editor in Chief of *Imperial Astrographic*, shook his head with an expression which tried, not entirely successfully, to be more of a scowl than a grin. "Late as usual—*way* past deadline! And don't you dare tell me you want *per diem* for the extra time, you little weasel!"

"Good to see you again, too, Etienne," Mansul said with a smile of his own. He walked across the office, and Thorwell stood to shake his hand. Then the editor gave a "what-the-hell" shrug and wrapped both arms around the smaller man in a bear hug.

"Thought we'd lost you for sure this time, Harvard," he said after a moment, stepping back and holding the reporter at arm's length. "You were supposed to be back months ago!"

"I know." Mansul shrugged, and his smile was more than a little crooked. "Seems our information on the societal setup was a bit, um, out of date. The Krath have undergone a religious conversion with some really nasty side effects. They almost decided to eat me."

"*Eat* you?" Thorwell blinked, then regarded Mansul skeptically. "Ritualistic cannibalism of 'great white hunters' by any sort of established city-building society is for bad novelists and holo-drama, Harvard."

"Usually." Mansul nodded in agreement. "This time around, though—" He shrugged. "Look, I've got the video to back it up. But even more important, I got caught in a shooting war between the 'civilized' cannibals and a bunch of 'barbarian tribesmen' who objected to being eaten . . . and did something about it. It's pretty damned spectacular stuff, Etienne."

That much, he reflected, was certainly true. Of course, he'd had to do some pretty careful editing to keep any of the humans (or their weapons) from appearing in the aforesaid video. A few carefully scripted interviews with Pedi Karuse's father had also been added to the mix, making it quite plain that the entire war—and the desperate battle which had concluded it—had been the result of purely Mardukan efforts. The fact that it made the Gastan look like a military genius had tickled the Shin monarch's sense of humor, but he'd covered admirably for the human involvement.

"Actual combat footage?" Thorwell's nose almost twitched, and Mansul hid a smile. He'd told Roger and O'Casey how his boss would react to that. The official *IAS* charter was to report seriously on alien worlds and societies, with substantive analysis and exploration, not cater to core-world stereotypes of "barbarian behavior," but the editorial staff couldn't afford to ignore the realities of viewership demographics.

"Actual combat footage," he confirmed. "Pikes, axes, and black powder and the decisive defeat of the 'civilized' side by the barbarians who *don't* eat people. And who happen to have saved my own personal ass in the process."

"Hot damn," Thorwell said. "'Fearless reporter rescued by valiant barbarian ruler.' That kind of stuff?"

"That was how I figured on playing it," Mansul agreed. "With suitably modest commentary from myself, of course."

They looked at each other and chuckled almost in unison. Harvard Mansul had already won the coveted Interstellar Correspondents Society's Stimson-Yamaguchi Medal twice. If this footage was as good as Thorwell suspected it was, he might be about to win it a third time.

Mansul knew exactly what the chief editor was thinking. But what made *him* chuckle was the knowledge that he had the SYM absolutely sewed up once he was able to actually release the documentary he'd done of Roger's adventures on Marduk. Especially with the inside track he'd been promised on coverage of the countercoup after it came off, as well.

"I've got a lot of other stuff, too," the reporter went on after a few moments. "In-depth societal analysis of both sides, some pretty good stuff on their basic tech capabilities, and an update on the original geological survey. It really underestimated the planet's vulcanism, Etienne, and I think that probably played a big part in how some of the social developments played out. And a lot on basic culture, including their arts and crafts and their cuisine." He shook his head and rolled his eyes appreciatively. "And I've gotta tell you, while I don't think I'd care a bit for Krath dietary staples, the rest of these people can *cook*.

"Just before the wheels came off for the Krath, they made contact with these people from the other side of the local ocean—from a place called K'Vaern's Cove, sort of a local maritime trading empire—and I got some good footage on *them*, too. And the *food* those people turned out!"

He shook his head, and Thorwell chuckled again.

"Food, Harvard? That was never your big thing before."

"Well, yeah," Mansul agreed with a smile, "but that was when *I* wasn't likely to be winding up on anyone's menu. What I was thinking was, we play off the cuisine of the noncannibals when we start reporting on the Krath. Use it as a contrast and compare sort of thing."

"Um." Thorwell frowned thoughtfully, scratching his chin, then nodded. Slowly, at first, and then more enthusiastically. "I like it!" he agreed.

"I thought you might," Mansul said. Indeed, he'd counted on it. And it fitted in with the traditional *IAS* position—a way to use the shuddery-shivery concept of cannibalism by simply mentioning it in the midst of a scholarly analysis and comparison of the rest of the planet's cooking.

"All right," he said, leaning forward and setting his small, portable holo player on Thorwell's coffee table, "I thought we might start with this bit. . . ."

"Helmut's moving," General Gianetto said as Prince Jackson's secretary closed the prince's office door behind him.

The office was on the top occupied level of the Imperial Tower, a megascraper that rose almost a kilometer into the air to the west of Imperial city. Adoula's view was to the east, moreover, where he could keep an eye on what he was more and more coming to consider his personal fiefdom.

Jackson Adoula was man in late middle age, just passing his hundred and twelfth birthday, with black hair that was graying at the temples. He had a lean, ascetic face and was dressed in the height of current Court fashion. His brocade-fronted tunic was of pearl-gray natural silk, a tastefully neutral background for the deep, jewel-toned purples, greens, and crimson of the embroidery. His round, stand-up collar was, perhaps, just a tiny bit lower-cut than a true fashion stickler might have demanded, but that was his sole concession to comfort. The jeweled pins of several orders of nobility gleamed on his left breast, and his natural-leather boots glistened like shiny black mirrors below his fashionably baggy dark-blue trousers.

Now he looked up at his fellow conspirator and raised one aristocratic eyebrow.

"Moving where?" he asked.

"No idea," Gianetto said, taking a chair. The general was taller than the prince, fit and trim-looking with a shock of gray hair cut short enough to show his scalp. He was also the first Chief of Naval Operations—effectively, the Empire's uniformed commander in chief—who was a general and not an admiral. "The carrier I had watching him said Sixth Fleet just tunneled out, all at once. I've pushed out sensor ships. If they come back in anywhere within four light-days of Sol, we'll know about it."

"They can sit out eighteen light-*years* and tunnel in in six hours," Adoula said.

"Tell me something I don't know," Gianetto replied.

"All right," Adoula said, "I will. One of Helmut's shuttles picked up four people from Halliwell Two before he departed. Two humans and a pair of Mardukans."

"Mardukans?" The general frowned. "You don't see many of those around."

"The word from our informants is that they were heavies for an underworld organization. One of the humans had a UOW passport; the other one an Imperial. They're both fakes, obviously, but the Imperial one is in the database. He's supposedly from Armagh, but his accent was Pinopan."

"Criminals?" Gianetto rubbed his right index and thumb together while he considered that. "That makes a certain amount of sense. Helmut has got to be hurting for spares; they're trying to get their ships refurbed off the black market."

"Possibly. But we don't want to assume that."

"No," the general agreed, but he was clearly already thinking about something else. "What about this bill to force an independent evaluation of the Empress?" he asked.

"Oh, I'm supporting it," Adoula replied. "Of course."

"Are you *nuts?*" Gianetto snarled. "If a doctor gets one look at her—"

"It won't come to that," Adoula assured him. "*I'm* supporting it, but every vote I can beg, bribe, cajole, or blackmail is against it. It won't even get out of committee."

"Let's hope," Gianetto said, and frowned. "I'm less than enthused by the . . . methods you're using." His frown turned into a grimace of distaste. "Bad enough to keep the Empress on a string, but . . ."

"The defenses built into the Empress are extraordinary," Adoula said sternly. "Since she proved unwilling to be reasonable, extraordinary measures were necessary. All we have to do is sit tight for five more months. Let me handle that end. You just keep your eye on the Navy."

"That's under control," Gianetto assured him. "With the exception of that bastard, Helmut. And as long as we don't get any 'independent evaluation' of Her Majesty. If what you're doing to the Empress gets out, they won't just kill us; they'll cut us into pieces and feed us to dogs."

✦   ✦   ✦

"Now I'm a real estate agent," Dobrescu grumped.

"Broker," Macek said. "Facilitator. Lessor's representative. Something."

The neighborhood was a light industrial park on the slope of what had once been called the "Blue Ridge." On a clear day, you could see just about to the Palace. Or you would have been able to, if it weren't for all the skyscrapers and megascrapers in the way.

It had once been a rather nice industrial park, but time and shifting trade had left it behind. Its structures would long ago have been demolished to clear space for larger, more useful buildings, but for various entailments that prevented change. Most of the buildings were vacant, a result of the boom and bust cycle in commercial real estate. Fortunately, the one they were looking for was one such. They were supposed to be meeting the owner's representative, but she was late.

And, inevitably, it was a miserable day. The weather generators *had* to let an occasional cold front through, and this was the day that had been scheduled for it. So they sat in the aircar, watching the rain sheet off the windscreen, and watched the empty building with a big "For Lease" sign on the front.

Finally, a nine-passenger utility aircar sat down, and a rather attractive blonde in her thirties got out, set up a rain shield, and then hurried over to the building's covered portico.

Dobrescu and Macek got out, ignoring the rain and cold, and walked over to join her.

"Mr. Ritchie?" The woman held out her hand. "Angie Beringer. Pleased to meet you. Sorry I'm late."

"Not a problem," Dobrescu said, shaking the offered hand.

"Let me get this unlocked," she said, and set her pad against the door.

The personnel door led into a small reception area. More locked doors led into the warehouse itself.

"Just over three thousand square meters," the real estate lady said. "The last company that had it was a printing outfit." She pointed to the rear of the big warehouse and a line of heavy plasteel doors. "Those are secure rooms for ink, from what I was told. Apparently it's pretty hazardous stuff. The building has a clear bill of environmental health, though."

"Figures," Macek said, picking up a dust-covered flyer from a box—one of many—against one of the walls. "Escort advertisements. Hey, this one looks just like Shara!"

"Can it," Dobrescu said, and looked at Beringer. "It looks good. It'll do anyway."

"First and last month's deposit, minimum lease of two years," the woman said diffidently. "Mr. Chung's credit checked out just fine, but the owners insist."

"That's fine. How do we do the paperwork?"

"Thumb print here," the real estate agent said, holding out her pad. "And send us a transfer."

"Can I get the keys now?" Dobrescu asked as he pressed the pad to give his wholly false thumb print.

"Yes," Beringer said. "But if we don't get the transfer, the locks will be changed, and you'll be billed for it."

"You'll get the money," Dobrescu promised, holding his pad up to hers. He checked to make sure the key codes had transferred and made a mental note to change them. "We're going to take a look around," he said then.

"Go ahead," she replied. "If you don't need me?"

"Thanks for meeting us in this mess," Macek replied.

"What are you going to use it for, again?" she asked curiously.

"My boss wants to start a chain of restaurants," Dobrescu answered. "Authentic off-planet food. We need some place to store it, other than the ship it's coming in on."

"Well, maybe I'll get a chance to try it out," Beringer said.

"I'll make sure you get an invite."

Once the woman was gone, they went back out to the aircar and got the power pack, some tools, and a grav-belt.

"I hope like hell the modifications haven't covered it up," Macek said.

"Yeah," Dobrescu agreed. He took out a laser measuring device, checked the readout, and pointed to the center plasteel door. "There."

The room beyond was dimly lit, but what were clearly power lines stuck out of one wall near the ceiling.

"Nobody ever wondered about those?"

"Buildings like this go through so many changes and owners," Dobrescu said, putting on the belt, "that stuff gets rewired all the time. As long as it's not currently hot, nobody cares what it used to power."

He touched a stud on the belt and lifted up to the wiring, where he cautiously applied a heavy-gauge voltage meter. There were smaller wires for controls beside the power cables, and he hooked a box to them and took a reading.

"Yeah, there's something back there," he said. "Toss me the power line."

He caught the coil of heavy-duty cable on the second toss, and wired it into the power leads. Then he hooked up the control wires and lowered himself back down to the ground.

"Now to see if we're on a fool's errand," he muttered, and keyed a sequence into the control box.

There was a heavy grinding noise. The walls of the warehouse were set into the side of the hill and made of large, precast slabs of plascrete, with thin lines separating them for expansion and contraction. Now the center slab began to move backward, apparently into the solid hill. It cleared the slabs on either side, then began to slide sideways, revealing a tunnel into the hill. It moved surprisingly smoothly . . . until it abruptly stopped part way with a metallic twang.

"We need a lamp," Dobrescu said.

Macek went back out to the aircar for a hand light, and, with its aid, they found the chunk of fallen plascrete that blocked the door's track, levered it out of the way, and got the door fully open and operating. The air in the tunnel had the musty smell of long disuse, and they both put on air masks before they followed it into the hill.

The walls were concrete—real, old-fashioned concrete—dripping with water and cracked and pitted with extreme age. The door that sealed the far end of the tunnel was made of heavy steel, with a locking bar. Both had been covered in protective sealant, and when they got the sealant off, the portal opened at a touch.

The room beyond was large, and, unlike the approach tunnel, its air was bone-dry. More corridors stretched into the distance, and there was a small fusion generator on the floor of the main room. It was a very old model, also sealed against the elements.

Dobrescu and Macek cut the sealant away and, after studying the instructions, got it into operation.

Lights came on in the room. Fans began to move. In the distance, a gurgling of pumps started up.

"Looks like we're in business," Dobrescu said.

"What's the name of this place?"

"It used to be called Greenbriar."

"This one's not nearly as pretty as the last one," Macek said.

"Get what you're given," Dobrescu replied as they climbed out of the aircar. He'd been keeping a careful eye on a group of young men lounging on the corner. When the real estate agent landed and got out, they straightened up and one of them whistled.

The young woman—this one a short woman in her twenties, with faintly African features—ignored the whistle and strode over to the two waiting "businessmen."

"Mr. Ritchie?" she asked, looking at both of them.

"Me," Dobrescu said.

"Pleased to meet you," she said, shaking his hand, then gestured at the building. "There it is."

This area had once been a small town, before it was absorbed by the burgeoning Imperial City megalopolis. The town, for historical reasons, had managed to maintain its "traditional" buildings, however. This specific building had predated even the ancient United States . . . which had predated the Empire by over a thousand years. The home of an early politician of the unified states, it had a pleasant view of the small river that ran through the town. It had been maintained, literally, for millennia.

Yet shifting trade, again, had finally ruined it. The plaster walls were cracked and peeling, the roof sunken in. Windows had been broken out. The massive oaks which had once shaded the beautiful house of an early president were long gone, victims of the narrow band of sunlight available in a town surrounded by skyscrapers. The small town was now a drug and crime haven.

There were, however, signs of improvement. The pressure of real estate values this near the center of Imperial City had sent the outriders of a "gentrification" wave washing gently through it. Many of the ancient buildings were cloaked in scaffolding, and there were coffee shops and small grocers scattered along the narrow streets. The quaint old houses of what had once been Fredericksburg, Virginia, had become a haven for the Bohemians who survived in the urban jungle.

And they were about to get a new restaurant.

Dobrescu poked through the building, avoiding holes in the wood floors and shaking his head at the plaster fallen from the ceiling.

"This is going to take one helluva lot of renovation," he said, again shaking his head.

"I have some other buildings I can show you," the real estate agent offered.

"None of them meet the specifications," Dobrescu said. "This is the only one in the area that will do. We'll just have to get it fixed up. Fast." He consulted his toot and frowned. "In . . . fourteen days."

"That's going to be . . . tough," the young woman said.

"That's why the boss sent me." Dobrescu sighed.

Roger rolled over carefully, trying not to disturb Despreaux, and pressed the acceptance key on the flashing intercom.

"Mr. Chung," Beach said. "We've exited tunnel-space in the Sol System, and we're currently on course for the Mars Three checkpoint. We've gotten an updated download, including messages for you from your advance party on Old Earth."

"Great," Roger said quietly, keeping his voice down. "How long to orbit?"

"About thirteen hours, with the routing they gave us," Beach replied with a frown. "We're in a third-tier parking orbit, not far from L-3 position. Best I could get."

"That doesn't matter," Roger lied, thinking about how long that meant with Patty on a shuttle. "I'll go check the messages now."

"Yes, Sir," Beach said, and cut the connection.

"We're there?" Despreaux asked, rolling over.

"In the system," Roger replied. "Ten hours to parking orbit. I'm going to go see what Ritchie and . . ." He trailed off.

"Peterka," Despreaux prompted.

"Peterka have to say." He got to his feet and slipped on a robe.

"Well, I'm going back to sleep," Despreaux said, rolling back over. "I have to be insane to marry an insomniac."

"But a very cute insomniac," Roger said as he turned on his console.

"And getting better in bed," Despreaux said sleepily.

Roger looked at the messages and nodded in satisfaction.

"We got both buildings," he said.

"Mm . . ."

"Good prices, too."

"Mmmm . . ."

"The warehouse looks like it's in pretty good shape."

"Mmmmmmm!"

"The restaurant needs a lot of work, but he thinks it can be ready in time."

"MMMMMMMMMM!"

"Sorry. Are you trying to sleep?"

"Yes!"

Roger smiled and looked at the rest of the messages in silence. There were codes embedded in them, and he nodded in satisfaction as he scanned them. Things were going well. If anything, too well. But it was early in the game.

He checked out some other information sources, including a list of personal ads on sites dedicated to the male-friendly segment of society. His eyes lit at one, but then he read the signature and mail address and shook his head. Right message, wrong person.

He pulled out the schematic of the Palace again and frowned. All the surviving Marines, Eleanora, and his own memories had contributed to it, but he'd never realized how little of the Palace he actually *knew*. And the Marines, apparently deliberately, had never been shown certain areas. He knew of at least three semisecret passages in the warren of buildings, the Marines knew a couple of others, and he suspected that it was laced with them.

The original design had been started by Miranda MacClintock, and she'd been a terribly paranoid person. Successive designers had tried to outdo her, and what they'd created was something like the ancient Mycenaean labyrinth. He doubted that *anyone* knew all the secret passages, storerooms, armories, closets, and sewers. It covered in area which had once been home to a country's executive mansion, capital buildings, a major park, two major war memorials, and various museums and government buildings. All of that area—nearly six square kilometers—was now simply "the Palace." Including the circular park around it, grass only, with clear fields of fire. And there was talk of expanding it even further. Wouldn't that be lovely? Homelike.

Finally, realizing he was working himself into a fret, he went back to bed and lay looking at the overhead. After several minutes, he nudged Despreaux.

"What do you mean I'm getting better?"

"*Mwuff?* You woke me up to ask me that and you expect me to *answer?*"

"Yeah. I'm your Prince, you've got to answer questions like that."

"This whole plan is going to fail," Despreaux said, never opening her eyes, "in about thirty seconds. When I strangle you with my bare hands."

"What do you mean, 'getting better'?"

"Look, good sex requires practice," Despreaux said, shaking her head and still not turning over. "You haven't had a lot of practice. You're learning. That takes time."

"So I need more practice?" Roger grinned. "No time like the present."

"Roger, go to sleep."

"Well, you said I needed practice—"

"Roger, if you ever want to be able to practice again, go to sleep."

"You're sure?"

"I'm very sure."

"Okay."

"If you wake me up again, I'm going to kill you, Roger. Understand that."

"I understand."

"I'm serious."

"I believe you."

"Good."

"So, there's no chance—?"

"One . . ."

"I'll be good." Roger crossed his arms behind his head and smiled at the overhead. "Going to sleep now."

"Two . . ."

"Grawwwkkkkkk."

"*Roger!?*"

"What? Is it *my* fault I can't sleep without snoring?" he asked innocently. "It's not like I'm doing it on *purpose.*"

"God, why me?"

"You asked for it."

"Did not!" Despreaux sat up and hit him with a pillow. "*Liar!*"

"God, you're beautiful when you're angry. I don't suppose—?"

"If that's what it takes for me to get some *sleep,*" Despreaux said half-desperately.

"I'm sorry." Roger shook his head. "I'm sorry. I'll leave you alone."

"Roger, if you really are serious—"

"I'll leave you alone," he promised. "Get some sleep. I'll be good. I need to think anyway. And I can't think with that lovely nipple staring at me."

"Okay," Despreaux said, and rolled over.

Roger lay back, looking at the overhead. After a while, as he listened to Despreaux's breathing *not* changing to the regular rhythm of sleep, he began counting in his head.

"I can't sleep," Despreaux announced, sitting up abruptly just before he reached seventy-one.

"I said I was sorry," he replied.

"I know, but you're going to lie there, not sleeping, aren't you?"

"Yes. I don't need much sleep. It doesn't bother me. I'll get up and leave you alone, if you want."

"No," Despreaux said. "Maybe it's time for the next practice session. If you've learned anything, at least *I'll* get some sleep."

"If you're sure . . ."

"Roger, Your Highness, my Prince, my darling?"

"Yes?"

"Shut up."

✧   ✧   ✧

Roger pulled out the long, curved blade, its metal worked into the wavery marks of watered steel.

"Pedi," he said. "Demonstration."

Cord's wife—who, as always, was following *him* about—picked up one of the metal rods being used for reinforcement of the new foundation work. She held it out, and Roger took the sword in his left hand and, without looking at the bar, cut off a meter-long section with a single metallic "twang."

"The local cops are right down on guns," Roger said, handing the sword back to Cord. "Sensors everywhere to detect them. You use guns much, Mr. Tenku?"

"It's just Tenku," the gang leader said, his face hard. He didn't answer the question, but he didn't have to. What his answer would have been was plain on his face, and in the glance he cast at the environment-suited Cord, who'd closed the case once more and gone back to leaning on the long pole that might, in certain circles, have been called a three-meter quarterstaff.

"You see them?" Roger pointed at the Diasprans who were picking up the yard. "Those guys are Diaspran infantry. They're born with a pike in their hands. For your information, that's a long spear. The Vasin cavalry who will be joining us shortly are born with *swords* in their hands. All *four* hands. Swords and spears aren't well-liked by the cops, but we're going to have them as 'cultural artifacts' to go with the theme of the restaurant. Mr. Tenku, if we 'get it stuck in' as you put it, then you are—literally—going to be chopped to pieces. I wouldn't even need the Mardukans. *I* could go through your entire gang like croton oil; I've done it before. Or, alternatively, you and your fellows could do a small community service and get paid for it. Handsomely, I might add."

"I thought this was a restaurant?" the gang leader said suspiciously.

"And I thought you were the welcome wagon." Roger snorted in exasperation. "Open your *eyes*, Tenku. I'm not muscling your turf. So don't try to muscle mine. Among other things, I've got more muscle." *And more brains*, Roger didn't add.

"How handsomely?" Tenku asked, still suspicious.

"Five hundred credits a week."

"No way!" Tenku retorted. "Five *thousand*, maybe."

"Impossible," Roger snapped. "I have to make a profit out of this place. Seven hundred, max."

"Why don't I believe that? Forty-five hundred."

They settled on eighteen hundred a week.

"If one of my guests gets so much as panhandled..."

"It'll be taken care of," Tenku replied. "And if you're late..."

"Then come on by for a meal," Roger said, "and we'll square up. And wear a tie."

Thomas Catrone, Sergeant Major, IMC, retired, president and chief bottle washer of Firecat, LLC, was clearing off his mail—deleting all the junk, in other words—when his communicator chimed.

Catrone was a tall man, with gray hair in a conservative cut and blue eyes, who weighed just a few kilos over what he'd weighed when he joined the Imperial Marines lo these many eons ago. He was well over a hundred and twenty, and not nearly the hulking brute he'd once been. But he was still in pretty decent shape. Pretty decent.

He flicked on the com hologram and nodded at the talking head that popped out. Nice blonde. Good face. Just enough showing to see she was pretty well stacked. Probably an avatar.

"Mr. Thomas Catrone?"

"Speaking."

"Mr. Catrone, have you been checking your mail?"

"Yes."

"Then are you aware that you and your wife have won an all-expenses-paid trip to Imperial City?"

"I don't like the Capital," Catrone said, reaching for the disconnect button.

"Mr. Catrone," the blonde said, half-desperately. "You're scheduled to stay at the Lloyd-Pope Hotel. It's the best hotel in the City. There are three plays scheduled, and an opera at the Imperial Civic Center, plus dinner every night at the Marduk House! You're just going to turn that down?"

"Yes."

"Have you asked your *wife* if you should turn it down?" the blonde asked acerbically.

Tomcat's hand hovered over the button, index finger waving in the air. Then it clenched into a fist and withdrew. He rattled his fingers on the desktop and frowned at the hologram.

"Why me?" he asked suspiciously.

"You were entered in a drawing at the last Imperial Special Operations Association meeting. Don't you remember?"

"No. They've generally got all sorts of drawings ... but this one is pretty odd for them."

"The Association uses the Ching-Wrongly Travel Agency for all its bookings," the blonde said. "Part of that was the lottery for this trip."

"And I won it?" He raised one eyebrow and peered at her suspiciously again.

"Yes."

"This isn't a scam?"

"No, sir," she said earnestly. "We're not selling anything."

"Well ..." Catrone scratched his chin. "I guess I'd better schedule—"

"There is one small ... issue," the blonde said uncomfortably. "It's ... prescheduled. For next week."

"Next week?" Catrone stared at her incredulously. "Who's going to take care of the horses?"

"Sorry?" The blonde wrinkled her brow prettily. "You've sort of lost me, there."

"Horses," Catrone repeated, speaking slowly and distinctly. "Four-legged mammals. Manes? Hooves? You ride them. Or, in my case raise them."

"Oh."

"So you just want me to drop everything and go to the Capital?"

"Unless you want to miss out on this one-of-a-kind personalized adventure," the woman said brightly.

"And if I do, Ching-Wrongly doesn't have to pay out?"

"Errrr ..." The woman hesitated.

"Hah! Now I know what the scam is!" Tomcat pointed one finger at the screen and shook it. "You're not getting me that easily! What about travel arrangements? I can't make it in my aircar in less than a couple of days."

"Suborbital flight from Ulan-Batorr Spaceport is part of the package," the blonde said.

"Okay, let's work out the details," Catrone said, tilting back in his desk chair. "My wife loves the opera; I hate it. But you can gargle peanut butter for three hours if you have to, so what the hell . . ."

"What a horribly suspicious man," Despreaux said, closing the connection.

"He has reason to be," Roger pointed out. "He's got to be under some sort of surveillance. Contacting him directly at all was a bit of a risk, but no more than anything else we considered."

The bunker behind the warehouse had the capability to artfully spoof the planetary communications network. Anyone backtracking the call would find it coming from the Ching-Wrongly offices, where a highly paid source was more than willing to back up the story.

"You think this is really going to work?" Despreaux asked.

"O ye of little faith," Roger replied with a grin. "I just wonder what our opposition is up to."

"And how is the Empress?" Adoula asked.

"Docile," New Madrid said, sitting down and crossing his long legs at the ankle. "As she should be."

Lazar Fillipo, Earl of New Madrid, was the source of most of Roger's good looks. Just short of two meters tall, long, lean, and athletically trim, he had a classically cut face and shoulder length blond hair he'd recently had modded to prevent graying. He also had a thin mustache that Adoula privately thought looked like a yellow caterpillar devouring his upper lip.

"I could wish we'd been able to find out what got dumped in her toot," Adoula said.

"And in John's," New Madrid replied with a nod. "But it was flushed, whatever it was, before we could stop it. Pity. I'd expected the drugs to hold back the dead man's switch longer than they did. Long enough for our . . . physical persuasion to properly motivate him to tell us what we wanted to know, at least."

"Always assuming it was the 'dead man's switch,'" Adoula pointed out a bit acidly. "The suicide protocols can also be deliberately activated, you know." *And*, he thought, *given what you were doing to him—in front of his mother—that's a hell of a lot more likely than any "Dead Man's Switch," isn't it, Lazar? I wonder what you'd have done to Alexandra herself by now . . . if you didn't need her alive even more than I do?*

"Always possible, I suppose." New Madrid pursed his lips poutingly for several seconds, then shrugged. "Well, I imagine it was inevitable, actually. And he had to go in the end, anyway, didn't he? It was worth a try, and Alexandra might always have volunteered the information herself, given that he was all she had left by that point. On the other hand, I've sometimes wondered if she could have told us even if she'd wanted to. The security protocols on their toots were quite extraordinary, after all."

"True. True." New Madrid pursed his lips poutingly for several seconds, then shrugged. "I suppose it was inevitable, actually. The security protocols on their toots *were* quite extraordinary, after all."

The Earl, Adoula reflected, had an absolutely astonishing talent for stating—and *re*stating—the obvious.

"You wanted to see me?" the prince asked.

"Thomas Catrone is taking a trip to the capital."

"Oh?" Adoula leaned back in his float chair.

"Oh," New Madrid said. "He's supposedly won some sort of all-expenses-paid trip. I checked, and there was such a lottery from the Special Operations Association. Admittedly, *anyone* who won it would be worth being suspicious of. But I'm particularly worried about Catrone. You should have let me take him out."

"First of all," Adoula said, "taking Catrone out would *not* have been child's play. He hardly ever leaves that bunker of his. Second, if the Empress' Own start dying off—and there are others, just as dangerous in their own ways as Catrone—then the survivors are going to start getting suspicious. More suspicious than they already are. And we *don't* want those overpaid retired bodyguards getting out of hand."

"Be that as it may, I'm putting one of my people on him," New Madrid said. "And if he becomes a problem . . ."

"Then *I'll* deal with it," Adoula said. "You concentrate on keeping the Empress in line."

"With pleasure," the Earl said, and smirked.

✦   ✦   ✦

"Indian country," Catrone said as he looked the neighborhood over.

"Not a very nice area for an upscale restaurant," Sheila replied nervously.

"It's not so bad," the airtaxi-driver, an otterlike Seglur, said. "I've dropped other fares here. Those Mardukans that work in the place? *Nobody* wants to mess with them. You'll be fine. Beam down my card and call me when you want to be picked up."

"Thanks," Catrone said, getting the driver's information and paying the fare—and a small tip—as they landed.

Two of the big Mardukans stood by the entrance, bearing pikes—fully functional ones, Catrone noticed—and wearing some sort of blue harness over what were obviously environment suits. A young human woman, blonde and stocky, with something of a wrestler's build, opened the door.

"Welcome to Marduk House," the blonde said. "Do you have reservations?"

"Catrone, Thomas," Tomcat said.

"Ah, Mr. and Mrs. Catrone," she replied. "Your table is waiting. Right this way."

She led them through the entrance, into the entry room, and on to the dining room. Catrone noticed that there were several people, much better dressed than Sheila and he but having the look of local Imperial staff-pukes, apparently waiting for tables.

A skinny, red-headed woman held down the reception desk, but most of the staff seemed to be Mardukans. The restaurant area had a long bar at one side, on which slabs of some sort of meat were laid out. As they walked through the area, one of the Mardukans took a pair of cleavers—they would have been swords for a human—and began chopping a long section of meat, his hands moving in a blur. The sounds of the blades thunking into flesh and wood brought back unpleasant memories for Catrone, but there was a small ripple of applause as the Mardukan bowed and started throwing the chunks of meat, in another blur, onto a big iron dome. They hit in a star pattern and started sizzling, filling the room with the cooking noise and an odd smell. Not like pork or beef or chicken, or even human. Catrone had smelled them all in his time. Cooking human smelled pretty much like pork, anyway.

The table they were led to was already partially occupied. A big, vaguely Eurasian guy, and the blonde from the call. When he saw her, Tomcat almost stopped, but recovered with only the briefest of pauses.

"There seems to be someone at our table," he said instead to the hostess.

"That's Mr. Chung," she replied quietly. "The owner. He wanted to welcome you as a special guest."

Riiiight, Tomcat thought, then nodded at the two of them as if he'd never seen the blonde in his life.

"Mr. and Mrs. Catrone," the big guy said. "I'm Augustus Chung, the proprietor of these premises, and this is my friend, Ms. Shara Stewart. Welcome to Marduk House."

"It's lovely," Sheila said as he pulled out her chair.

"It was . . . somewhat less lovely when we acquired it," Chung replied. "Like this fine neighborhood, it had fallen into disrepair. We were able to snap it up quite cheaply. I was glad we could; this is a house with a lot of history."

"Washington," Catrone said with a nod. "This is the old Kenmore House, right?"

"Correct, Mr. Catrone," Chung replied. "It wasn't George Washington's home, but it belonged to one of his family. And he apparently spent considerable time here."

"Good general," Catrone said. "Probably one of the best guerrilla fighters of his day."

"And an honorable man," Chung said. "A patriot."

"Not many of them left," Catrone probed.

"There are a few," Chung said. Then, "I took the liberty of ordering wine. It's a vintage from Marduk; I hope you like it."

"I'm a beer drinker myself."

"What the Mardukans call beer, you would not care for," Chung said definitely. "There are times when you have to trust, and this is one of them. I can get you a Koun?"

"No, wine's fine. Tipple is tipple." Catrone looked at the blonde seated beside his host. "Ms. Stewart, I haven't said how lovely you look tonight."

"Please, call me Shara," the blonde said, dimpling prettily.

"In that case, it's Sheila and Tomcat," Catrone replied.

"Watch him," Sheila added with a grin. "He got the nickname for a reason."

"Oh, I will," Shara said. "Sheila, I need to powder my nose. Care to come along?"

"Absolutely," Sheila said, standing up. "We can trade our war stories while they trade theirs."

"Nice girl," Tomcat said as the two walked toward the powder room.

"Yes, she is," Chung replied, then looked Catrone in the eyes. "And a fine soldier. I'd say Captain Pahner sends his regards, but he is, very unfortunately, dead."

"You're him," Catrone said.

"Yes."

"Which one is she?"

"Nimashet Despreaux. My aide and fiancée."

"Oh great!"

"Look, Sergeant Major," Roger said, correctly interpreting the response. "We were on Marduk for *eight months*. Completely cut off. Stranded. You don't maintain garrison conditions for eight months. Fraternization? Hell, Kosutic—that's the hostess who led you over here—was carrying on for most of the time with Julian, who's now my S-2. And don't even get me *started* on the story of Gunny Jin. Nimashet and I at least waited until we were off-planet. And, yes, I'm going to marry her."

"You got any idea how easy it is to monitor in a restaurant?" Catrone asked, changing the subject.

"Yes. Which is why everyone entering and leaving is scanned for any sort of surveillance device. And this table, in particular, is placed by the fire pit for a reason. That sizzling really does a number on audio."

"Shit. Why the hell did you have to get my wife involved in this?"

"Because we're on a very thin margin," Roger pointed out. "Inviting just you would have been truly obvious."

"Well, I'm not getting involved in treason, whatever your reasoning," Catrone said. "You go your way, I'll go mine."

"This is not treason. I wasn't *there*. I was on *Marduk*, okay? I've got all the proof of that you could ask for. *Marduk*. This is all Adoula. He's holding my mother captive, and I *am* going to free her."

"Fine, you go right ahead." Catrone took a hard pull on the

wine; his host was right, it was good. "Look, I did my time. And extra. Now I raise horses, do a little consulting, and watch the grass grow. What there is of it in the Gobi. I'm out of the Empire-saving business. Been there, done that, got *really* sick and tired of it. You're wrong; there are no patriots any more. Just more and less evil fatcats."

"Including my mother?" Roger demanded angrily.

"Keep your voice down," Catrone said. "No, not including your mother. But it's not about your mother, is it? It's about a throne for Roger. Sure, I believe you weren't in on the coup in the first place. But blood calls to blood, and you're New Madrid's boy. Bad seed. You think we don't talk to each other in the Association? I *know* you, you little shit. You're not worth a pimple on your brother's ass. You think, even if it were possible, I'm going to walk in and give the Throne to *you?*"

"You *knew* me," Roger grated. "Yeah, you're right. I was a little shit. But this *isn't* about me; it's about Mother. Look, I've got some intel. What they're doing to her is *killing* her. And as soon as the can is popped, Mom dies. Bingo. Gone."

"Maybe, maybe not," Catrone said, then looked up. "Ladies, you're looking even better than when you left, if that's possible."

"Isn't he a lech?" Sheila said with a grin.

"He's sweet," Despreaux said.

"I'm not." Catrone winked. "I'm a very bad boy. I understand you can be a right handful, too."

"Sometimes," Despreaux said warily.

"Very dangerous when cornered," Tomcat continued. "A right bad cat."

"Not anymore." Despreaux looked over at Roger. "I . . . gave it up."

"Really?" Catrone's tone softened. "It happens . . . even to the best partyers."

"I . . . got very tired," Despreaux said. "All the partying gets to you after a while. Got to me, anyway. R—Augustus, well, I've never seen him turn down a party. He doesn't start many, but he's always the last man standing."

"Really?" Catrone repeated in rather a different tone.

"Really." Despreaux took Roger's hand and looked at him sadly. "I've seen him at . . . too many parties. Big ones, small ones. Some . . . very personal ones. Sometimes I think he lives a little too much for partying."

"Ah," Roger said. "Rastar's chopping up another joint. You have to watch this. He's a master with a blade."

"We saw it on the way in," Sheila said. "He's incredibly fast."

"Augustus," Despreaux said, "why don't you show Sheila a real master?"

"You think?"

"Go ahead," she said, catching Rastar's eye.

Roger nodded, then stood up and walked to the far side of the bar. Rastar bowed to him and stepped back as Roger reached under the bar and pulled out two slightly smaller cleavers. He set them down, put a long apron on over his expensive clothes, and stepped up on the raised platform even the tallest human required to work at a cutting surface designed for Mardukans.

The cleavers were more like curved swords, about as long as a human forearm. Roger slid them into sheaths on a belt and buckled the belt around his waist, then bowed to the audience, which was watching the demonstration with interest.

He drew a deep breath and crossed his arms, placing a hand on either sword. Then he drew.

The blades blurred, catching the firelight as they twirled around his body, close enough from time to time that his long hair rippled in the breeze. They whirled suddenly upward in free flight, then dropped, only to be caught by the tips of the blades between either hand's thumb and forefinger. He held them out at full extension by the same grips, and then they blurred again. Suddenly there was the sound of the blades hitting flesh, and perfectly sliced chunks of meat flew through the air to land on the dome in a complex dodecahedron.

The last slice flashed through the air, and Roger bowed to the applause as he cleaned the blades, then put all the tools away. He walked back to his table and gave another bow to the three diners.

"Very impressive," Catrone said dryly.

"I learned in a hard school."

"I'll bet."

"Would you like to see an example of the school?" Roger asked. "It's a . . . special demonstration we perform. You see, we slaughter our own meat animals here. That way everything's fresh. Caused a bit of a stink with the local animal lovers, until we showed them the meat animals in question."

"You probably don't want to watch this one, Sheila," Despreaux said.

"I'm a farm girl," Sheila replied. "I've seen slaughtering before."

"Not like this," Despreaux said. "Don't say I didn't warn you."

"If you're trying to impress me, Augustus . . ." Catrone said.

"I just think you should learn a little about the school," Roger replied. "See some of the . . . faculty I studied under, as it were. It won't take long. If Ms. Catrone wishes to sit it out . . . ?"

"Wouldn't miss it for worlds," Sheila declared, standing up. "Now?"

"Of course," Roger said, standing in turn and offering her his arm.

Catrone trailed along behind, wondering what the young idiot might think would impress him about killing some Mardukan cow. A few other diners, who'd heard about the slaughtering demonstration, attached themselves and followed "Mr. Chung" through a corridor and out into the back of the restaurant.

Behind the restaurant, there were a series of heavy-mesh plasteel cages, emitting a chorus of hissing. Three Mardukans stood by one of the cages, beside a door which led from it into an enclosed circular run, wearing heavy leather armor and carrying spears, two of them long, one short.

"There are several meat animals on Marduk," Roger said, walking over to a Mardukan who looked old for some reason and held a long case. "But for various reasons, we tend to serve one called *atul*. Humans on Marduk call them damnbeasts."

He opened the case and withdrew a really beautiful sword, fine folded steel, looking something like a thicker bladed *katana*.

"There's a local ordinance against firearms," Roger said, "so we have to take a more personal approach to slaughtering. In the jungle, and here, they use spears—rather long ones. Or a sword, for the more . . . adventurous. And there's a reason they're called damnbeasts."

What entered the run when one of the Mardukans opened the gate was the nastiest animal Catrone had ever seen. Three meters of teeth and claws, rippling in black-and-green stripes. It was low-slung and wide, six-legged, with a heavily armored head and shoulders. It darted into the light and looked at the humans on the other side of the run's mesh. Catrone could *see* the logic running through its head, and wondered just how smart the thing was.

One of the Mardukans with one of the long spears stabbed downward, but the thing moved aside like a cobra and caught at the Mardukan with the other long spear. Its jaws slammed shut on the Mardukan's leg with a clearly audible clop, and it tossed the three-meter-tall ET aside as if he were no heavier than a feather. It whipped around the circular run, watching the two remaining spearmen with the same feral intelligence, then turned and leapt at the fence.

The plasteel held it for a moment, then the half-ton-plus beast was up and onto the sagging fence, facing the ring of former diners, who suddenly looked likely to become dinner, instead.

"Okay, this is just not on," Roger said. "Higher fences are clearly in order."

He sprang forward as Catrone wondered what in hell the young idiot was about. The ex-Marine was torn between training, which told him to put himself between the prince and the threat, and simple logic, which said he'd last barely an instant and do no damned good at all. Not to mention making people wonder why he'd risked his life for a businessman. Instead, he moved in front of Sheila, noting that Despreaux had taken a combat stance and was shaking her head at the prince's action as well. But she also wasn't blocking him, which was interesting.

The beast scrambled higher, rolling the fence over with its weight until the plasteel collapsed almost completely. Then it was outside the run, turned to the diners, and charged.

What happened was almost too fast for even Tomcat's trained eyes to follow, but he caught it. The prince slashed downwards with the sword, striking the beast on the tip of the nose and turning it ever so slightly. A quick flash back, and the sword ran across its eyes, blinding it. Now sightless, it continued straight ahead, just past the prince's leg, and the last slash—full forehand—caught it under the neck, where it was partially unprotected. The blade sliced up and outward, neatly severing its neck, and the thing slid to a stop in the dirt of the slaughter yard, its shoulder just brushing the prince's leg.

The prince had never moved from his spot. He'd taken one step for the final slash, but that was it.

Bloody hell.

The crowd which had followed them was applauding politely— probably thinking it was all part of the demonstration—as the prince flicked the sword to clear it of blood. The movement, Catrone noticed, was an unthinking one, a reflex, as if the prince had done it so many times it was as natural as breathing. He began an automatic sheathing maneuver, just as obviously an old habit, then stopped and walked across to the old Mardukan, who handed him a cloth to complete the cleaning of the blade. He said something quietly and put the clean sword back in the case while the headless monster lashed its tail in reflex, still twitching and clawing. Catrone sincerely doubted that Roger had learned that technique working on those things in a run.

Bloody *damned* hell.

"Is that what we're having for supper?" one of the audience asked as the two uninjured Mardukans dragged the thing away. The injured one was already on his feet, saying something in Mardukan that had to be swearing. The questioner was a woman, and she looked pretty green.

"Oh, we don't serve only *atul*," Roger said, "although the liver analog is quite good with *kolo* beans—rather like fava beans—and a nice light chianti. There's also *coll* fish. We serve the smaller, coastal variety, but it turns out they grow up to fifty meters in length in open waters."

"That's huge," a man said.

"Yes, rather. Then there's *basik*. That's what the Mardukans call humans, as well, because they're small, pinkish bipedal creatures that look just a bit like humans. They're basically Mardukan rabbits. My Mardukans refer to themselves as the *Basik*'s Own—bit of a joke, really. Then there's roast suckling damnbeast. Admittedly, it's the most expensive item on the menu, but it's quite good."

"Why is it so expensive?" Sheila asked.

"Well, that's because of how it's gathered," Roger said, smiling at her in a kindly fashion. "You see, the damnbeasts—that's those—" he added, jerking his thumb at the head which was still lying on the ground, "they lair in rocky areas in the jungle. They dig dens with long tunnels to get to them, low and wide, like they are. They dig them, by the way, because they, in turn, are preyed upon by the *atul-grack*."

"The what?" Sheila asked.

"*Atul-grack*," Roger repeated. "Looks pretty much like an *atul*, but about the size of an elephant."

"Oh, my . . ." the first woman whispered.

"Obviously, *atul-grack* are one of the hazards of hunting on Marduk," Roger continued. "But to return to the damnbeasts. One of the parents, usually the female—the larger of the two—always stays in the lair. So to get to the suckling damnbeast, someone has to crawl into the lair after it. It's very dark, and there's always an elbow in the tunnel near the den, where water gathers. So, generally, right after you crawl through the water, holding your breath, Momma," he gestured towards the pens again, "is waiting for you. You have, oh, about half a second to do something about that. One of my hunters suggests long, wildly uncontrolled bursts from a very heavy bead pistol, that being the only thing you can get into the den. You might have noticed they're armored on the front, however. Sometimes the bead pistol doesn't stop them. *Atul* hunters cannot get life insurance.

"And even if you do manage to kill Momma, there's a problem. The *atul* dig their tunnels about as wide and high as they are. So you have to . . . get past the defending *atul*. Generally using a vibroknife. But you're not done yet. Suckling *atul* range in size from about the size of a housecat to the size of a bobcat, and they trend towards the upper end of that range. There are usually six to eight of them, and they're generally hungry and look at the hunter as just more food. And, just as a final minor additional problem, you have to bring them out *alive*." Roger grinned at the group and shook his head. "So, please, when you look at the price for roast suckling damnbeast, keep all of that in mind. I don't pay my hunters enough as it is."

"Have *you* ever done that?" Sheila asked quietly as they were walking back to the table.

"No," Roger admitted. "I've never hunted suckling *atul*. I'm rather large to fit into the tunnel."

"Oh."

"The only time I've ever hunted suckling, it was an *atul-grack*."

After dinner, "Shara" took Sheila to show her some of the interesting exhibits they'd brought back from Marduk, leaving Roger and Catrone over coffee.

"I missed this," Roger said.

"I still say this is a lousy spot for a private conversation," Tomcat countered.

"It is, it is. It's also the best place I've got, though. What do I have to do to convince you to side with us?"

"You can't," Catrone sighed. "And demonstrations of bravado aren't going to help. Yes, you have some people—some good people—who apparently think you've changed. Maybe you have. You were certainly more than willing to put yourself in harm's way. Too willing, really. If that thing had gotten you, your plan would have been all over."

"It was ... reflex," Roger said, and made an almost wistful face. Tomcat had had a rather serious drink of wine after the "demonstration," but he'd noticed that Roger hadn't even appeared to have the shakes.

"Reflex," the prince repeated, "learned in a hard school, as I mentioned. I'm having to ride a fine line. On the one hand, I know I'm the indispensable man, but some chances—such as meeting with you—have to be taken. As to the *atul* ... I was the only person there who was armed *and* knew how to take one out. Even if it had gotten to me, I'd probably have survived. And ... it's not the first time I've faced an *atul* with nothing but a sword. A very hard school, Sergeant Major. One that also taught me that you can't do everything by yourself. I need you, Sergeant Major. The Empire needs you. Desperately."

"I said it once, and I repeat: I'm out of the Empire-saving business."

"That's *it*? Just that?" Roger demanded, and not even his formidable self-control could quite hide his amazement.

"That's it. And don't go around trying to recruit my boys and girls. We've discussed this—in much more secure facilities than you have here. We're out of this little dynastic squabble."

"It's going to end up as more than a dynastic squabble," Roger ground out.

"Prove it," Catrone scoffed.

"Not if you're not with us." Roger wiped his lips and stood. "It was very nice meeting you, Mr. Catrone."

"It was . . . interesting meeting you, Mr. Chung." Catrone rose and held out his hand. "Good luck in your new business. I hope it prospers."

When treason prospers, then none dare call it treason, Roger thought. *I wonder if that was an intentional quote.*

He shook Catrone's hand and left the table.

"Where's Mr. Chung?" Shelia asked when they got back to the table.

"He had some business to take care of," Tomcat replied, looking at "Shara." "I told him I hope it prospers."

"Just that?" Despreaux asked incredulously.

"Just that," Catrone said. "Time to leave, Sheila."

"Yes," Despreaux said. "Maybe it is. Sheila," she said, turning to Ms. Catrone, "this has been lovely. I hope we meet again."

"Well, we'll be back for supper tomorrow," Sheila said.

"Maybe," Catrone qualified.

"The *basik* was wonderful," Sheila said, glancing at her husband. "But it's been a long day. We'll be going."

Catrone nodded to the blonde hostess as they were leaving.

"Hell send, Mistress," he said.

"Heaven go with you, Mr. Catrone," the hostess replied, her nostrils flaring.

"What was that all about?" Sheila asked as they waited for the airtaxi.

"Don't ask," Tomcat answered. "We're in Indian country until we get home."

Tomcat didn't do anything that night except fool around with his wife a bit, courtesy of the bottle of champagne from the management. The all-expenses-paid trip he'd "won" had them in a very nice suite. Suites had not been high on his list of previous accommodations, and this one was really classy, more like a two-story apartment on the top floor of the hotel. He could see Imperial Park and a corner of the Palace from it, and when Sheila was asleep, he stood by the unlighted window for a while, looking at the place where he'd lived for almost three decades. He could see a few of the guards near the night entrances. Adoula's bully-boys—not real Empress' Own. And sure as hell not guarding the Empress, except against her friends.

The next day, their third in the city, they took in the Imperial Museums. Plural. It was a pain in the ass, but he'd married Sheila, his third wife, after he left the Service, and she'd never been to the Capital. They'd met while he was buying horses, shortly after he got out. He'd grown up on a farm, in an area in the central plains that was now chockablock with houses. He'd wanted to go back to a farm, but the only land he could afford was in Central Asia. So after gathering a small string, he'd set up the Farm. And along the way, he'd picked up another wife.

This one was a keeper, though. Not much to look at, compared to his first wife, especially, but a real keeper. As they walked through the Art Museum, with Sheila gawking at the ancient paintings and sculpture, he looked over at her and thought of what failure would mean. To her, not to him. He'd put it on the line too many times, for far less reason, to worry about himself. But if everything went down, they weren't going to target just him.

That evening, they ate in a small restaurant in the hotel. He made the excuse that they didn't have time to go over to Marduk house, not if they were going to make it to the opera.

They dressed for the evening, a classically simple black low-cut suit for her, and one of those damned brocaded court-monkey suits for him. The management had arranged the aircar for them, and everything was laid on. He added a stylish evening pouch to his ensemble, mentally swearing at the aforementioned monkey suit with its high collar and purple chemise.

As the second intermission was ending, he took Sheila's arm when they headed back to the box.

"Honey, I can't take much more of this," he said. "You stay. You like it. I'm going to go for a walk."

"Okay." She frowned. "Be careful."

"I'm always careful," he grinned.

Once out of the Opera House, with its ornate façade, he

turned down the street and headed for one of the nearby multi-level malls. It was still open, still doing a fair business, and he wandered through, poking into a couple of clothing stores and one outdoor equipment store. Then he saw what he was looking for, and followed a gentleman down a corridor to the bathrooms.

The bathroom, thankfully, was deserted except for them. The guy headed over to the urinal, and Tomcat palmed an injector, stepped up behind him, and laid the air gun against the base of his neck.

The target dropped without a word, and Tomcat grabbed him under the shoulders, muttering at his weight, and dragged him into one of the stalls. He quickly stripped off his monkey suit and started pulling things out of the evening pouch.

There was a light, thin jumpsuit with dialable coloration. He set it to the same shade as the garments the target had been wearing. The target had also worn a floppy beret and a jacket, and Tomcat took those, as well as his pad and spare credit chips. He squirted alcohol on the target's shirt, then extracted the facial prosthetic from the pouch and slipped it on. It didn't look like the target, but anyone looking for Thomas Catrone wouldn't recognize him. There were thin gloves, as well, ones that disappeared into the flesh but would camouflage DNA and fingerprints.

He turned the pouch inside-out, so that it looked like a normal butt-pack, and stuck it up under the jacket for concealment, since the target hadn't been wearing one. Satisfied, he made one more sweep to ensure the site was clean, then stepped out of the bathroom. On the way out, he dumped the monkey suit into the incinerator chute. In one way, it was a damned shame—the thing had cost an arm and a leg. On the other hand, he was glad to see it gone.

He spotted the tail as soon as he left the dead-end corridor—a young male, Caucasian, with a holo jacket and a nose ring. The shadow paid no attention to the blond man in the jacket, his beret pulled down stylishly over one eye. The tail appeared to be enjoying a coffee and reading his pad, standing at the edge of the store with one leg propped up against the storefront.

Catrone walked on down the mall, slowly, strolling and shopping, searching for a certain look. He found it not far from a store which sold lingerie. Most women avoid eye contact with men they don't know; this young lady was smiling faintly at most of the passing men between glances at the pad she held in her lap.

"Hi, there," Catrone said, sitting down next to her. "You look like a woman who enjoys a good time. Whatever are you doing sitting around this boring old mall?"

"Looking for you," the girl said, smiling and turning off her pad.

"Well, I'm just a little busy at the moment. But if you'd like to really help me out in a little practical joke, I'd appreciate it."

"How much would you appreciate it?" the hooker asked sharply.

"Two hundred credits worth," Tomcat replied.

"Well, in *that* case . . ."

"My friend is waiting for me, but . . . I had another offer. I don't want him to feel dumped or anything, so . . . why don't you go take my place for a while?"

"I take it he goes both ways?"

"Very," Tomcat replied. "Dark hair, light skin, standing outside the Timson Emporium reading a pad and drinking coffee. Show him a *really* good time," he finished, handing her two hundred-credit chips.

"A lot of money for a practical joke," the hooker said, taking the chips.

"Call it avoiding the end of a wonderful relationship," Tomcat replied. "He can't know it was from me, understand?"

"Not a problem," the woman said. "And, you know, if you're ever in the mood for company . . ."

"Not my type." Tomcat sighed. "You're a lovely girl, but . . ."

"I understand." She stood up. "Light skin, dark hair, standing in front of the Emporium."

"Wearing a holo jacket. Drinking coffee—Blue Galaxy-coffee bulb."

"Got it."

The target was taking a long damned time on the toilet. Too long. Long enough that Gao Ikpeme was getting worried. But Catrone was wearing a damned evening suit; there was no way Ikpeme could have missed seeing *that* come out of the can.

He slid one leg down and lifted the other to rest it—then damned near jumped out of his own skin as a tongue flickered into his ear.

"Hi, handsome," a sultry voice said.

He whipped around and found himself face-to-face with a pretty well set up redhead. Keeping in fashion, she wore damned near nothing—a halter top and a miniskirt so low on her hips and so high cut that it was more of a thin band of fabric to cover her pubic hair and butt.

"Look," the redhead said, leaning into him and quivering, "I just took some Joy, and I'm, you know, *really* horny. And you are *just* my type. I don't care if it's in one of the restrooms, or in a changing stall, or right here on the damned floor—I just *want* you."

"Look, I'm sorry," Gao said, trying to keep an eye on the corridor door and failing. "I'm meeting somebody, you know?"

"Bring her along," the woman said, breathing hard. "Hell, we'll be *done* by the time she gets here. Or he. I don't *care*. I want you *now*!"

"I said—"

"I want you, I want you, *I want you*," the woman crooned, sliding around in front of him and up and down, her belly pressing against the world's worst erection. "And you want *me*."

"Geez, buddy, get a room," one of the shoppers said in passing. "There're *kids* here, okay?"

"Quit this!" Gao hissed. "I can't go with you right now!"

"Fine!" The woman raised one leg up along his body and rocked up and down. "I'll just . . . I'll just . . ." she panted hoarsely.

"Oh, Christ!" Gao grabbed her by the arm, darted into the store, and managed to find a more or less deserted aisle for what turned out to take about six seconds.

"Oh, that was good," the girl said, pulling her panties back into place and licking her lips. She ran her hands up and down his jacket and smiled. "We need to get together again and spend a little more time together."

"Yeah," Gao gasped, rearranging his clothes. "Christ! I've got to get back out there!"

"Later," the hooker said, waving fingers at him as he practically ran to the front of the store. There. She didn't even have to feel bad about the two hundred credits. Quickest trick she'd ever turned, too.

Gao looked up and down the mall corridors, but the target was nowhere in sight. He *could* have come out while he was off-post, but ... Damn. Nothing for it.

Gao walked across the mall and down the corridor into the bathroom. There was nobody in sight inside. Feet in one of the stalls, though.

He pushed on the door, which slid open. There was a drunk sprawled all over the toilet; it wasn't the target.

Oh, shit.

He walked back out into the main passageway, hoping that maybe the target had just stepped into a store or something. But, no, there was nobody in sight.

He frowned for a moment, then shrugged and pulled out his pad. He keyed a combination, and shook his head at the person who appeared on the screen.

"Lost him."

Catrone tapped at his pad as if scrolling something and leaned into his earbug.

"I dunno, he went into the can. I watched it the whole time ... No, I don't think it was a deliberate slip, I just lost him ... Yeah, okay. I'll try to pick him up at the hotel."

Catrone consulted a directory, but the number the tail had called was unlisted. He could countertail him, and see what turned up, but that was probably useless. He'd have at least a couple of cutouts. Besides, Thomas Catrone had things to do.

Tomcat walked to a landing stage and caught an airtaxi across town. The taxi was driven by a maniac who seemed to be high on something. At least he cackled occasionally as they slid under and over slower cars. Finally, the cab reached Catrone's destination—a randomly chosen intersection. He paid in chips, some of them from the unfortunate citizen in the mall bathroom, and walked two blocks to a public access terminal.

He keyed the terminal for personal ads, and then placed one.

"WGM seeks SBrGM for fun lovin and serious crack romp. Thermi. *ThermiteBomb@toosweetfortreats.im*."

He did a quick check and confirmed that there were no identical ads on that site.

"Please pay three credits," the terminal requested, and he slid in three credit chips.

"Your ad in *Imperial Singles Daily* is confirmed. Thank you for using Adoula Info Terminals."

"Yeah," Catrone muttered. "What a treat."

He took the public grav-tube back to the hotel and sat by the window, watching the city go by. Even at this time of night, all the air-lanes were full, with idiots like that taxi driver weaving up and down and in and out of the lanes. The tubecars moved between the lanes, drawing their power from inductive current and surrounded by clear glassteel tubes, rounding the buildings three hundred meters in the air. You could see into windows, those that weren't polarized or curtained. People sitting down to a late dinner. People watching holovid. A couple arguing. Millions of people stacked in boxes, and the boxes stretching to the horizon. What would they think if they knew he was going past, with what was in his head? Did they care that Adoula was in control of the Throne? Did they want the Empress restored? Or were they so checked out that they didn't even know who the Empress was?

He thought about something someone had told him one time. Something like most men aren't good for anything but turning food into shit. But the Empire wasn't the Empress, it was all those people turning food into shit. They had a stake, whether they knew it or not. So what would *they* think? Anyone who tried to rescue Alexandra was risking a kinetic strike on the Palace, but just the civil disorder which would follow a *successful* countercoup would make all of those millions of lives about him a living hell. Air-lanes jammed, tubes grounded, traffic control shut down . . .

He got out of the tube at a station a few blocks from the hotel and let himself in the back way. He'd dumped all the remaining credits from the target, along with the jacket and beret, in a public incinerator chute.

Sheila was sitting up in bed watching a holomovie when he walked into the suite. She raised one eyebrow at the way he was dressed, but he shook his head and took off the clothes. They, too, went into the incinerator. It was a room incinerator, moreover. This was a classy place that probably normally had staff-pukes and their bosses staying in its suites. It was as secure as anything he was going to find, and there probably wasn't anything incriminating on the clothes, anyway. But better safe than sorry.

He climbed into bed with his wife and laid an arm over her shoulder.

"How was the opera?"

"Great."

"I don't see how anything can be great that's all in a foreign language."

"That's because you're a barbarian."

"Once a barbarian, always a barbarian," Tomcat Catrone replied. "Always."

"Catrone was as clear as he could be that he won't help," Roger said. "And that the senior members of the Association aren't going to help, either. They're sitting this one out."

"That is so totally . . . bogus," Kosutic said angrily.

They'd come to the warehouse to "check on resupply." The restaurant was doing even better than Roger had hoped, almost to the point of worry. Even an interstellar freighter could carry only so much Mardukan food, and they were running through it nearly twenty-five percent faster than he'd anticipated. If he sent a ship back, *now*, for more goods, it might get back in time, but he doubted it. Fortunately, the Mardukans and their beasts could eat terrestrial food, and he'd been substituting that for the last few days. It didn't have all the essential nutrients they needed, though. The Mardukans were suddenly on the reverse side of what the Marines had faced on Marduk, but without Marine nanites which could convert some materials to essential vitamins.

It wasn't exactly what he would have called a "good" situation under any circumstances, but at least it gave them a convenient excuse to use the secure rooms in the underground bunker.

"The good news is that the first of our 'machine tools' have arrived from our friends," Rastar said. He was handling the warehouse and restaurant while Honal worked on another project.

"Good," Roger said. "Where?"

Rastar led them out of the meeting room and down a series of corridors to a storeroom which was stacked with large—some of them very large—plasteel boxes. Rastar keyed a code into the pad on one of them and opened it up, revealing a suit of powered armor plated in ChromSten.

"Now is when we need Julian and Poertena," Despreaux observed unhappily.

"These're Alphane suits," Roger pointed out, coming over to examine the armor carefully. "They'd be as much a mystery to Julian as they are to us. But we're going to have to get them fitted anyway."

"And they came through on the rest of it, too," Rastar said, making a Mardukan hand gesture which indicated amusement. He opened up one of the larger boxes and waved both left hands.

"Damn," Roger breathed. "They did."

This suit was much larger than the human-sized one in the first box, with four arms and a high helmet to accommodate a Mardukan's horns. The upper portion had even been formed to *resemble* horns.

"And this." Rastar opened up another long, narrow box.

"What in the hell is that?" Krindi Fain asked, looking down at the weapon nestled in the box.

"It's a hovertank plasma cannon," Despreaux said in an awed tone. "*Cruisers* carry them as antifighter weapons."

"It's the Mardukan powered armor's primary weapon," Rastar said smugly. "The extra size of the suit adds significant power."

"It had better," Fain grunted, hoisting the weapon out with all four hands. "I can barely lift this!"

"Now you over-muscled louts know how humans feel about plasma cannon," Roger said dryly. Then he looked around the human and Mardukan faces surrounding him.

"The Imperial Festival is in four weeks. It's the best chance we're going to have on the mission, and if Catrone and his fence-sitters aren't going to lift a lily-white finger, there's no reason to waste time trying for some sort of fancy coordination. Send the codeword to Julian, for Festival Day. We won't tell the Alphanes we don't need the additional suits—better we have more than we need than come up short. Start getting all the Marines fitted to them, and as many Mardukans as we have suits for. Training in close combat in *this* place is going to be easy enough. We'll plan around the details of the Palace that we know. It will have to be a surface assault; there's no other way in. At least the exterior guards are in dress uniform to look pretty. I know the Empress' Own's 'dress uniforms' are kinetic-reactive, but however good they may be against bead fire, they're not armor, which should let us kick the door open if we manage to hit them with the element of surprise.

"We'll initiate with the Vasin . . ."

Catrone sat at his desk, looking out the window at the brown grass where three horses grazed. He wasn't actually seeing the scene as he sat tapping the balls of his fingers together in front of him. What he did see were memories, many of them bloody.

His communicator chimed, and he consulted his toot for the time. Bang on.

"Hey, Tom," Bob Rosenberg said.

"Hey, Bob," Tomcat replied, grinning in apparent surprise. *Stay smooth, stay natural.* "Long time."

There was a slight signal delay as the reply bounced around from satellite to satellite. Any or all of which could be, and probably were, beaming the conversation to Adoula.

"I'm in-system for a bit. Thought you might be up for a party." Rosenberg had taken a job as a shuttle pilot on a freighter after resigning from the Corps.

"Absolutely," Tomcat said. "I'll call a couple of the boys and girls. We'll do it up right—roast the fatted calf."

"Works for me," Rosenberg replied after a slightly longer pause than signal delay alone could have accounted for. "Wednesday?"

"Plenty of time," Tomcat said. "Turn up whenever. Beer's always cold and free."

"I'll do about anything for free beer." Rosenberg grinned. "See you then."

"Catrone is throwing a party," New Madrid said with a frown.

"He's done it before," Adoula sighed. "Twice since we assumed our rightful position." As usual, he was up to his neck in paperwork—

why couldn't people decide things on their own?—and in no mood for New Madrid's paranoia.

"Not right after a trip to Imperial City, he hasn't," New Madrid pointed out. "He's invited ten people, eight from the Empress' Own Association and two from the Raider Association, of which he's also a member. All senior NCOs except Robert Rosenberg, who was the commander of Gold Battalion's stinger squadron."

"And your point is?"

"They're *planning* something," New Madrid said angrily. "First Helmut moves—"

"Where did you hear that?"

"I was talking to Gianetto. I do that from time to time, since *you're* ignoring me."

"I'm not ignoring *you*, Lazar." Adoula was beginning to get angry himself. "I've considered the threat of the Empress' Own, and I'm ignoring *it*."

"But—"

"But *what*? Are they coordinating with Home Fleet? Not as far as we can see. Do they have heavy weapons? Most assuredly not. Some bead rifles, maybe a few crew-served weapons they've squirreled away like the paranoid little freaks they are. And what are they going to do? Attack the Palace?"

The prince shoved back in his chair and glowered at his taller, golden-haired coconspirator exasperatedly.

"You're putting two and two together and getting seven," he said. "Take Helmut's decision to move and Catrone's meeting. Helmut could *not* have gotten word to them, unless he did it by telepathy. We've been watching him like a hawk. Sure, we don't know where he is *now*, but he hasn't communicated with anyone in the Sol System. He hasn't even linked to a beacon. For them to have made prior contact and coordinated any sort of planning between Sixth Fleet and Catrone after we moved, they would have required an elaborate communications chain we couldn't possibly have missed. And there was no reason for them to have set up any sort of plan in advance. So the two events are *unrelated*, and without Sixth Fleet to offset Home Fleet, anything Catrone and his friends could come up with would be doomed. They have *no* focal point—the heirs are *dead*,

Her Majesty is damned near dead, and *will* be, just as soon as the new Heir is born."

"That's not necessary," New Madrid said peevishly.

"We've discussed this," Adoula replied in a tight, icy voice. "As soon as the Heir is born—which will be as soon as possible for guaranteed survival in a neonatal care ward—she goes. Period. Now, I'm extremely busy. Do quit bothering me with ghosts. Understand?"

"Yes," New Madrid grated. He got up and stalked out of the office, his spine rigid. Adoula watched him leave, and then sighed and tapped an icon on his pad.

The young man who entered was pleasant faced, well-dressed, and entirely unnoticeable. His genes could have been assembled from any mixture of nationalities, and he had slightly tanned skin, brown hair, and brown eyes.

"Yes, Your Highness?"

"Ensure that everything is in place to remove the Earl when his utility is at an end."

"It will be done, Your Highness."

Adoula nodded, the young man withdrew, and the prince returned his attention to his paperwork.

Loose ends everywhere. It was maddening.

"Hey, Bob," Tomcat said, shaking hands as his guests arrived. "Lufrano, how's the leg? Marinau, Jo, glad you could make it. Everybody grab a beer, then let's head for the rec room and get seriously stinko."

He led them into the basement of the house, through a heavy steel door, and down a corridor. Getting hold of the amount of land the Farm had needed to do things right had meant buying it in Central Asia, where prices had not yet skyrocketed the way they had in the heartland of North America. There was, of course, a reason prices were so much lower here, but even in Central Asia, there was land, and then there was *land*. In this case, he'd gotten the chunk he'd bought directly from the office of the Interior for a steal, given that it had "facilities" already on it.

The house sat on top of a command-and-control bunker for an old antiballistic missile system. "Old" in this case meant way before the Empire, but still in nearly mint condition, thanks to the dry desert air. There was a command center, bunk rooms, individual rooms for officers, kitchen, storerooms, and magazines.

When he'd gotten the place, those spaces were all sitting empty, except for the ones which had been half-filled with the fine sand for which the region was famous. He'd spent a couple of years, working in the time available, to fix a few of them up. Now the command center was his "rec room," a comfortable room with some float chairs and, most importantly, a bar. He used one of the bunk rooms as an indoor range. The kitchen had been fitted up to be a kitchen again, he'd fitted out a couple of bedrooms, and the storerooms—lo and behold—held stores. Lots of stores.

People joked that he could hold off an army. He knew they were wrong. He'd have a tough time dealing with more than a platoon or so.

And, ritually, once a week, he swept all the rooms for bugs. Just an old habit. He'd never found one.

"Hey, Lufrano," Rosenberg said as the rest filed into the rec room. He had a long metal wand, and he ran it over the visitors as he talked. "Been a long time."

"Yep," Lufrano Toutain, late Sergeant Major of Steel Battalion, agreed. "How's the shipping business?"

"Same old same old," Rosenberg replied. He ran the entire group, then nodded. "Clear."

"Fatted calf," Toutain, said in an entirely different voice, grabbing a beer. "Son of a—"

"Empress," Tomcat finished for him. "And a pretty impressive one. Boy's grown both ears and a tail."

"Now that would take some doing," Youngwen Marinau said, catching the brew Tomcat tossed him. Marinau had been first sergeant in Bronze Battalion for eighteen miserable months. He popped the bulb open and took a long drink, swilling it as if to wash the taste of something else out of his mouth. "He was a punk when I knew him."

"There's a reason Pahner got Bravo Company," Rosenberg pointed out. "Nobody better for bringing on a young punk. Where in the *hell* have they been, though? The ship never made it to Leviathan; no sign of them."

"Marduk," Catrone answered. "I didn't get the whole story, but they were there a long time—I can tell that. And Pahner bought it there. I took a look at what there is in the database about it." He shook his head. "Lots of carnivores, lots of barbs. I don't know exactly what happened, but the Prince has got about a company-plus of the barbs following him around. They're masquerading as waiters, but they're soldiers, you can tell. And they had some trouble with one of the carnivores they use as food. And that Roger . . ."

He shook his head again.

"Tell," Marinau said. "I'd love to hear that there's something in that pretty head besides clothes and fashion sense."

Catrone ran through the entire story, ending with the killing of the *atul*.

"Look, I don't shake, and I don't run," Catrone ended. "But that damned thing shook me. It was just a mass of claws and fangs, and Roger didn't even blink—just took it out. Whap, slash, gone. Every move was choreographed, like he'd done it two, three thousand times. Perfect muscle memory movement. Lots of practice, and there's only one way he could have gotten it. And fast. Just about the fastest human I've ever seen."

"So he can fight." Marinau shrugged. "Glad he had at least some MacClintock in him after all."

"More than that," Catrone said. "He's *fast*. Fast enough he could have left us all standing and let us take the fall. The thing probably would have savaged one of us, and then either fed or left. *He* could have gotten away while it was munching, but he didn't. He stood the ground."

"That's not his job," Rosenberg pointed out.

"No, but he was the one with the weapon and the training," Toutain said, nodding. "Right?"

"Right," Catrone said.

"Any chance it was a setup?" Marinau asked.

"Maybe," Catrone conceded with a shrug. "But if so, what does that tell us about the Mardukans?"

"What do you mean?" Rosenberg said.

"If it was a setup, one of them took a heavy hit for him," Catrone pointed out. "It didn't kill him, but I bet it was touch and go. If they set it up, they did so *knowing* the thing could kill them. Think about it. Would *you* do that if Alexandra asked you to?"

"Which one?" Marinau asked, his voice suddenly harsher with

old memories and pain. He'd retired out of Princess Alexandra's Steel Battalion less than two years before her murder.

"Either," Catrone said. "The point's the same. But I don't think it was a setup. And Despreaux was interesting, too."

"She usually is." Rosenberg chuckled. "I remember when she joined the Regiment. Damn, that girl's a looker. I'm not surprised the Prince fell for her."

"Yeah, but she's trained the same way we are. Protect the primary. And all she did was get ready to back him up. What does *that* tell you?"

"That she's out of training," Marinau said. "You said she'd implied she'd lost it."

"She didn't 'lose it' in the classical sense," Catrone argued. "She stood her ground, unarmed, but she *knew* the best person to face the thing was Roger. And she *trusted* him. She didn't run, and she didn't go into a funk, but she also didn't move to protect the primary. She let *him* handle it."

"Just because he's brave," Marinau said, "and, okay, can handle a sword—which is a pretty archaic damned weapon—that doesn't mean he's suited to be Emperor. And that's what we're talking about. We're talking about being a Praetorian Guard, just what we're not supposed to be. Choosing the Emperor is *not* our job. And if I did have a choice, Roger wouldn't be it."

"You prefer Adoula?" Catrone demanded angrily.

"No," Marinau admitted unhappily.

"The point is, he *didn't* do the deed. We already knew that." Catrone said. "And he's the *legitimate* heir, not this baby they're fast-cooking. And if somebody doesn't act, Alexandra's going to be as dead as John and Alex." His face worked for a moment, and then he shook his head, snarling. "You're going to let Adoula get *away* with that?"

"You're impressed," Rosenberg said. "I can tell that."

"Yeah, I'm impressed," Catrone replied. "I didn't know it was going to be him, just that something was fishy. And I wasn't impressed when I met him. But . . . he's got that MacClintock *thing* you know? He didn't before—"

"Not hardly," Marinau muttered grumpily.

"—but he sure as hell does now," Catrone finished.

"Does he want the Throne?" Joceline Raoux asked. She was a

former sergeant major of the Raiders, the elite insertion commandos who skirmished with the Saint Greenpeace Corps along the borders.

"We didn't get into that, Jo," Catrone admitted. "I put them off. I wasn't going to give him an okay without a consult. But he was more focused on getting the Empress safe. That might have been a negotiating ploy—he's got to know where our interests and loyalties lie—but that's what we talked about. Obviously, though, if we secure the Throne, he's the Heir."

"And from our reports, he'll be Emperor almost immediately," Rosenberg pointed out gloomily.

"Maybe," Catrone said. "I'm not going to believe it until I've seen Alexandra. She's strong—I can't believe she won't get over it."

"I want her safe," Toutain said suddenly, his voice hard. "And I want that bastard Adoula's head for what he did to John and the kids. The damned *kids* . . ." His face worked, and he shook his head fiercely. "I want that bastard *dead*. I want to do him with a knife. Slow."

"No more than I want New Madrid," Catrone pointed out. "I *am* going to take that bastard, if it's the last thing I do. But Roger can give us more than just revenge—he can give us the Empire back. And that's important."

Rosenberg looked around at the group of senior NCOs, taking a mental headcount, based upon body language. It didn't take long.

"Catrone, Marinau, and . . . Raoux," he said. "Arrange to meet. Tell him we'll back him if he's got a real plan. And find out what it is."

"It won't include what we know," Catrone said. "It won't even include the Miranda Protocols."

"How do we meet him?" Marinau asked.

"Slipping our tethers will be harder than finding him." Catrone shrugged. "I know I'm being monitored. But finding him won't be hard; there's only a couple of places he can be."

"Meet him, again. Get a reading on him," Rosenberg said. "If you're all in agreement, we'll initiate the Miranda Protocols and gather the clans."

✧   ✧   ✧

"Honal," Roger smiled tightly, controlling his gorge through sheer force of will, "the idea is to *survive* flying in a light-flyer."

The sleek, razor-edged aircar, a Mainly Fantom, was the only sports model large enough to squeeze a Mardukan into. It was also the fastest, and reportedly the most maneuverable, light-flyer on the market.

At the moment, Honal was proving that both those claims were justified, weaving in and out of the Western Range at dangerously high speeds. He had his lower, less dexterous, hands on the controls, and his upper arms crossed nonchalantly. There were some tricky air currents, and Roger closed his eyes as one of them caught the flyer and brought it down towards an upthrust chunk of rock. The flyer banked, putting the passenger side down, and Roger opened his eyes a crack to see the rocks of the mountainside flashing by less than a meter from the tip of the aircar's wing.

The car suddenly flipped back in the other direction, banking again, and stood up on its tail. Roger crunched his stomach, feeling himself beginning to gray out, as Honal left out a bellow.

"I *love* this thing!" the Mardukan shouted, rolling the car over on its back. "Look at what it can *do*!"

"Honal," Roger shook his head to clear it, "if I die, this plan goes to shit. Could we land, please?"

"Oh, sure. But you wanted to make sure we knew what we were doing, right?"

"You have successfully demonstrated that you can fly an aircar," Roger said carefully. "Most successfully. Thank you. The question of whether or not you can fly a stingship still remains; they're *not* the same."

"We've been working with the simulators." Honal shrugged all four shoulders. "They're faster than this, but a bit less maneuverable. We can fly stingships, Roger."

"Targeting is—"

"The targeting system is mostly automatic." Honal banked around another mountain, this time slower and further away from the rocks, and landed the car beside the more plebeian vehicle Roger had flown out to the site. "It's a matter of *choosing* the targets. Human pilots use mainly their toots, with the manual controls primarily for backup, but obviously, we can't do that.

On the other hand—you should pardon the expression—humans only have one set of hands. *We're* training to fly with the lower hands ... and control the targeting with the upper. I've 'fought' on the net with a few humans, including some military stingship pilots. They're good, I give you that. But one-on-one, I can take any one of them, and a couple of the rest of the team are nearly as good. Where they kick our ass is in group tactics. We're just getting a feel for those; it's not the same thing as riding a *civan* against the Boman. Go in against them wing-to-wing, and we just get shot out of the sky. The good news is that the squadron at the Palace isn't trained in group tactics, either. But they've got some pretty serious ground-based air defenses, and taking those out is another thing we're not great at, yet."

"Anything to do about it?" Roger asked.

"I've been reading up on everything I can get translated on stingship doctrine. But we've got a lot of studying to do, and I'm not sure what's relevant and what's not. We're not as far along as I'd hoped. Sorry."

"Keep working on it," Roger said. "That's all we can do for now."

"They're using Greenbriar," Raoux said. The sergeant major no longer looked like herself. Like the Saint commandos, Raiders often had to modify their looks, and she'd gotten a crash retraining in old skills since the coup. "He's on his way there at the moment."

"Why Greenbriar?" Marinau asked. "It's just about the smallest of the dispersal facilities."

"Probably the only one Kosutic knew about," Catrone said. "Pahner would've known more, but—" He shrugged. "We'll shift the base to Cheyenne quick enough if it goes well."

"You ready?" Raoux asked.

"Let's get our mission faces on."

"All right," Roger said, looking at the hologram of the Palace. "Plasma cannon here, here, here, and here. Armored and embedded. ChromSten pillboxes."

"Won't take them out with a one-shot," Kosutic said. "But they can only be activated by remote command from the security bunker."

"Autocannon here and here," Roger continued.

"Ditto," Kosutic replied. "Both of them are heavy enough to take out armor, which we can't get into the area in the first assault anyway, because the sensors all over the City would start screaming, and the Palace would go on lock-down."

"Air defenses," Roger said.

"The minute stingers get near the Capital," Kosutic said, "air defenses all over the place go live. Civilian traffic's grounded, and the air becomes a free-fire zone. Police have IFF; we might be able to emulate that to spoof *some* of the defenses. It's going to be ugly, though. And that ignores the fact that we don't *have* stingships. We might have to mount weaponry on those aircars Honal is using for training."

"Wouldn't *that* be lovely." Roger grimaced and shook his head. "A formation of Mainly Fantoms going in over the parade..."

"We make the assault in the middle of the parade, and we're going to cause enormous secondary casualties," Despreaux pointed out unhappily.

"It's still the best chance we have of getting close to the Palace," Roger replied.

"And every scenario we've run shows us losing," Kosutic said.

"And if you ran a scenario of our making it across Marduk?" Roger asked.

"Different situation, Your Highness," Kosutic replied firmly. "There, we had zip for advance information on the tactical environment. Here we know the relative abilities, the mission parameters, and most of the variables, and, I repeat, *every single model we've run* ends up having us lose."

"I guess you need a new plan, then," Catrone said from the doorway. Heads snapped around, and his lips curled sardonically as he stripped off the mask he'd been wearing. The two people with him were doing the same.

"And how did *you* get in here?" Roger asked calmly, almost conversationally, then glanced at Kosutic. "Son of a *bitch*, Kosutic!"

"I'd like to know that, too," the sergeant major said tightly.

"We got in the through a well-shielded secret passage...the same way we're getting into the Palace," Catrone told her. "*If* you can convince us we should back you."

"Sergeant Major Marinau," Roger said with an extremely thin smile. "What a *pleasant* surprise."

"Hey, dork." The sergeant major waved casually.

"That's Your Highness the Dork, to you, Sergeant Major," Roger replied.

"Glad to see you've a gotten a sense of humor." The sergeant major sat at the table. "What happened to Pahner?" he continued, coming right to the point.

"Killed by Saint commandos," Kosutic answered as Roger worked his jaw.

"Now that hasn't been part of the brief," Raoux said. "Greenpeace?"

"Yeah," Roger said. "The tramp freighter we were jacking turned out to be one of their damned insertion ships . . . and we weren't exactly at full strength, anymore. Thirty remaining marines. They all got pinned down in the first few minutes. We didn't know who *they* were; they didn't know who *we* were. It was a pocking mess."

"*You* were there?" Marinau's eyes narrowed.

"No," Roger said flatly. "I was in the assault shuttles, with the Mardukans. Arm—Captain Pahner had pointed out that if I bought it, the whole plan was through. So I was sitting it out with the reserve. But when they found out it was commandos, I had to come in. So, by the end, yeah, I was there."

"You took Mardukans in against Greenpeace?" Raoux asked. "How many did you lose?"

"Fourteen or fifteen," Roger replied. "It helped that they were all carrying bead and plasma cannon."

"Ouch." Marinau shook his head. "They can handle them? I wouldn't put them much over being able to use rocks and sticks."

"Do *not* underestimate my companions," Roger said slowly, each word distinct and hard-edged. "All of you are veteran soldiers of the Empire, but the bottom line is that the Empire hasn't fought a major war in a century. I don't know you." He jabbed a finger at Raoux.

"Joceline Raoux," Kosutic told him. "Raiders."

"You're Eva?" Raoux asked. "Long time, Sergeant."

"Sergeant Major, Sergeant Major," Kosutic said with a grin. "Colonel, according to His Highness, but we'll let that slide."

"The point," Roger said, "is—"

He paused, then looked at Kosutic.

"Eva, how many actions did you have, prior to Marduk?"

"Fifteen."

"Sergeant Major Catrone?" Roger asked.

"A bit more," the sergeant major said. "Twenty something."

"Any pitched battles?" Roger asked. "A battle being defined as continuous or near continuous combat that lasts for more than a full day?"

"No, except one hostage negotiation. But that wasn't a battle, by any stretch. Your point?"

"My point," Roger said, "is that during our time on Marduk we had, by careful count, *ninety-seven* skirmishes and *seven* major battles, one of which had us in the field, in contact, for three days. We also had over two hundred attacks by *atul, atul-grack,* damncrocs, or other hostile animals which penetrated the perimeter."

He paused and looked at the three NCOs for a long, hard moment, and then bared his teeth.

"You may think you're the shit, Sergeants Major, but you aren't worth the price of a *pistol bead* compared to one of *my* troops, is that *clear?*"

"Easy, Roger," Eleanora said.

"No, I won't be easy. Because we need to be clear on this from the beginning. *Eleanora* has been in the middle of more battles than all three of you put together. From the point of view of combat time, I've got everyone in this *room*—except Eva—beat. Yes, we took on a Saint commando *company*. In *their* ship. And we smashed their ass. They didn't have enough people left to bury their dead. And compared to a couple of things we did on Marduk, it was a pocking *picnic. Don't* try to treat us like cherries, Sergeants Major. Don't."

"You'd used that sword before on those damnbeasts," Catrone said evenly.

"We had to *walk* across a *planet,*" Despreaux said angrily. "You can't carry enough ammunition. The plasma guns blew up. And the damned *atul* just kept *coming!*" She shook her head. "And the Kranolta, and the Boman. The Krath. Marshad . . ."

"Sindi, Ran Tai, and the *flar-ke,*" Roger said. "That damned *coll* fish . . . We have a little presentation, Sergeants Major. It's sort of the bare-bones of what happened, call it an after-action report.

It takes about four hours, since it covers eight months. Would you care to view it?"

"Yeah," Marinau said after a moment. "I guess maybe we'd better see what could take a clotheshorse jackass and . . . make him something else."

Roger left after the first thirty minutes. He'd been there the first time, and he'd watched the presentation once already. Adventures are only fun if they happen to someone else a long way away. Someday he might be able to just kick back and tell the stories. But not yet.

Despreaux followed him out, shaking her head.

"How did we do it, Roger?" she said softly. "How did we survive?"

"We didn't." Roger put his arm around her. "The people who went into that cauldron didn't come out. Some bodies came out, but their souls stayed there." He looked at her and kissed the top of her head, inhaling the sweet scent of her hair. "You know, I keep saying we need to do this for the Empire. And every time I do, I lie."

"Roger—"

"No, listen to me. I'm not doing this because I want the Throne. I'm doing this because I owe a debt. To you, to Kostas, to Armand, to Ima Hooker."

He frowned and tried to find the words.

"I know I need to protect myself, that it's all on my shoulders. But I don't want to. I feel like I need to protect *you*." His arm tightened around her. "Not just you, Nimashet Despreaux, but Eva, and Julian, and Poertena. We few who remain. We few who saw what we saw, and did what we did. You're *all* . . . special to me. But to do that, I have to do the rest. Rescue Mother—and, yes, I want to do that. I want Mother to be well. But I need to do the rest so *you* can be safe. So that you don't wake up every morning wondering if today they're going to come for you. To do that, I have to protect the Empire. Not a fragment, not a piece, not a remnant—the *Empire*. So that it's wrapped around you few like a blanket. And to do that, yes, I have to survive. I have to safeguard myself. But I think *first* about . . . we few."

"That's . . . crazy," Despreaux said, tears in her eyes.

"So I'm crazy." Roger shrugged. "Like I said, none of us survived."

"Well, that's enough of that," Raoux said, stepping into the corridor. She paused. "Oh, sorry."

"We were just discussing motivations," Roger said.

"Must have been a pretty intense discussion," Raoux said, looking at Despreaux.

"My motivation is pretty intense," he replied.

"I can see why," Raoux said. "I left when that . . . thing melted one of the troops."

"Talbert." Roger nodded. "Killerpillar. We figured out how to avoid them, and the poisons turned out to be useful." He shrugged. "You should have stuck around. You didn't even get to the Mohinga."

"The Mohinga?" Raoux's eyebrows rose. "That's a training area in Centralia Province. One nasty-assed swamp."

"We had one of our own." Roger looked at Despreaux. "Before Voitan, remember?"

"Yes," Despreaux said. "I thought it was bad. Until Voitan gave a whole new perspective to the word 'bad.'"

"Hey, you got to save my life. I still remember that really clear view of your butt. I thought I liked you before, but all I could think about all the time was what that butt looked like."

"Hell of a time to think of that!" Despreaux said angrily.

"Well, it was a very nice-looking butt." Roger smiled. "Still is, even if it's a bit . . . rounder."

"Fatter."

"No, not *fatter*, very nice . . ."

"Excuse me." Raoux folded her arms. "You guys want to get a room?"

"So, are we going to get your support?" Roger asked sharply. His smile disappeared, and he turned his head, locking onto her eyes. "From the Association?"

"Associations," Raoux said, turning slightly aside. "Plural."

The prince's expression, the way he moved and looked at her, reminded her uncomfortably of a bird of prey. Not an eagle, which had a certain majesty to it. More like a falcon—something that was no more than a swift, predatory shape wrapped around a mind like a buzz saw.

"We just call ourselves the clans," she continued. "Raider Association. Special Operations Association. Empress' Own Association. Lots of intermingling, what with people like Tomcat."

"All of them?" Roger asked.

"Why do you think I'm here?" Raoux countered. "I was never in the Pretty-Boy Club."

"And are we going to get the support?" Roger pressed.

"Probably. Marinau was a holdout, probably because he knew you. But if he can sit through that . . . briefing from Hell, I don't think he'll hold out for long. People change."

"That's what we were talking about," Roger said quietly. "I was just explaining to Nimashet that none of us got off Marduk alive, not really. Not the people that landed. We've all changed."

"Some for the worse," Despreaux said in a low voice.

"No," Roger said sternly. "You're my conscience, my anchor. You can't be my conscience *and* my sword. I've got people who can hold guns and pull triggers, and I can find more of them, if I have to. But there's only one you, Nimashet Despreaux."

"He's got a point," Raoux said. "And don't sweat combat fatigue—not after what I just watched. Anyone ever got hammered big time, it was you people. You've earned a change of duty assignments, and you've got your part to play."

"I suppose," Despreaux said.

"So what, exactly, are you bringing to the table?" Roger asked.

"Wait for the others," Raoux replied.

It didn't take long for Marinau to leave the room, as well, and Catrone followed shortly thereafter. Of the three NCOs, only Catrone was smiling.

"Christ," he said. "I wish I'd been there!"

"You would." Raoux shook her head. "You like nightmares."

"Okay, I'm convinced," Marinau said. "I kept looking for the special effects. There weren't any; that was real."

"As real as it gets," Roger said, his face hard.

Marinau cleared his throat, shook his head, and finally looked at the prince.

"I'm in," he said, still shaking his head. "But do you think you could have shown just a *little* bit of that when *I* was in charge?" he asked plaintively. "It would have made my job . . . well, not easier. More *satisfying*, I guess."

"Maybe I shouldn't have always shucked my guards when I went hunting," Roger said with a shrug. "But you all sounded like *flar-ta* in the woods."

"I'll tell you a secret," Marinau said, shame-faced. "We all figured it was your guides doing the hunting, and that you were just showing off and bringing back the heads. Shows how wrong I can be. And I'm man enough to admit it. I'm in."

"Raiders are in," Raoux said.

"Special Ops is in," Catrone said. "But only if we get a chance to get stuck in with some of those Mardukans. And I want the Earl of New Madrid. I'm going to spend the rest of my natural life torturing him to death. There's this thing you can do with a steel-wire waistcoat and a rock—"

"We'll discuss it," Roger said sternly. "Okay, back to the conference room."

"Here's the thing," Catrone said, when the playback had been turned down. Roger left the video playing, though, as a less than subtle point. "You know who the Strelza were, Your Highness?"

"No," Roger said.

"Yes," Despreaux, Kosutic, and Eleanora replied.

"What am I missing?" Roger asked.

"We got it on our in-brief to the Regiment," Despreaux told him, frowning at a distant memory. "Russian troops."

"Okay, ever heard of the Praetorian Guard?" Catrone asked.

"Sort of." Roger nodded. "Roman."

"Both the same thing," Catrone said.

"Not *exactly*," Eleanora said. "The Praetorians were originally Caesar's Tenth Legion, and—"

"For my point, they are," Catrone said, annoyed. "Both of them were guard forces for their respective Emperors. The equivalent of the Empress' Own. Okay?"

"Okay," Roger said.

"And both of them ended up deciding that *they* got to choose who was Emperor."

"I begin to see your point," Roger said.

"The Empress' Own is weeded *really* hard," Marinau said. "You can't just be able, you have to be . . . right."

"Pretty boys," Raoux said with a smile.

"That, too," Marinau agreed with a shrug. "But pretty boys that aren't going to be kingmakers. In a lot of ways, we're deliberately . . . limited. Limited in size—"

"And never up to full strength," Catrone interjected.

"And limited in firepower," Marinau continued. "Home Fleet can take us out anytime."

"If they want to kill the Empress," Roger said.

"True. But the point is that we *can* be taken down," Marinau said. "For that matter, garrison troops from outside NorthAm could do it the hard way, if they were prepared to lose enough bodies. As that bastard Adoula demonstrated."

"Some of this was deliberately set up by Miranda MacClintock," Catrone said.

"Who was one seriously paranoid individual," Marinau added.

"And a scholar," Eleanora pointed out. "One who knew the dangers of a Praetorian Guard. And while it's true you can be taken out, you're also the *only* significant Imperial ground force allowed on this entire continent. The brigade that attacked the Palace was a clear violation of Imperial regulations."

"But Miranda set up other things, too," Catrone said, waving that away. "This, for example." He gestured around himself at the facility. "You notice we're surrounded by skyscrapers, but none of them are here?"

"I did notice that," Roger agreed.

"Deliberate and very subtle zoning," Catrone told him. "To prevent this facility from ever being discovered. And you don't find out about some things until you've *left* the Regiment."

"Ah," Kosutic said. "Tricky."

"Some stuff has gotten passed down," Catrone said. "In the Association. Keywords. Secrets. Passed *from* former commanders and sergeants major *to* former commanders and sergeants major. Some of it's probably been lost that way, but it's been . . . pretty secure. You're out, maybe you've got some gripes with the current Emperor, but you've got this sacred trust. And you keep it. And you're no longer in a position to play kingmaker."

"Until now," Eleanora said, leaning forward. "Right?"

"Asseen," Catrone said, ignoring her and looking at Roger. "Are you Prince Roger Ramius Sergei Alexander Chiang Mac-Clintock, son of Alexandra Harriet Katryn Griselda Tian Mac-Clintock?"

Roger brushed his forehead, like a man brushing away a mosquito, and frowned in puzzlement.

"What are you doing?" he asked suspiciously.

"Answer yes or no," Catrone said. "Are you Prince Roger Ramius Sergei Alexander Chiang MacClintock, son of Alexandra Harriet Katryn Griselda Tian MacClintock?"

"Yes," Roger said firmly.

"Is there a usurper upon the Throne?"

"Yes," Roger said, after a moment. He could *feel* something searching his thoughts, looking for falsehood. It was an odd and terrifying experience.

"Do you attempt to take your rightful place for the good of the Empire?"

"Yes," Roger said after another pause. His quibbles about motivation didn't matter; it *was* for the good of the Empire.

"Will you keep Our Empire safe, hold Our people in your hands, protect them as you would your children, and ensure the continuity of Our line?" Catrone's voice had taken on a peculiar timbre.

"Yes," Roger whispered.

"Then We give unto you Our sword," Catrone said, his voice now distinctively female. "Bear it under God, to defend the right, to protect Our people from their enemies, to safeguard Our people's liberties, and to preserve Our House."

Roger dropped his head, holding it in his hands, his elbows on the table.

"Roger?" Despreaux said, putting her hand on his shoulder.

"It's okay," Roger gasped. "*Shit.*"

"It doesn't *look* okay," she said anxiously.

"God," Roger groaned. "Oh, God. It's all there . . ."

"*What's* there?" Despreaux turned on Catrone, her expression furious. "What did you *do* to him?!"

"I didn't do anything to him," Catrone said, his voice now normal. "Miranda MacClintock did."

"Secret routes here, here, here, here," Roger said, updating the map of the Palace through his toot. "This one is an old subway line. The control bunker is in the basement of an old *rail* station!"

"This was all in your head?" Eleanora asked in an almost awed tone as she gazed into the holo.

"Yes. Which—much as I hate to even think about it—makes me wonder if *they* could have gotten it from Mother."

"I won't say it's impossible," Catrone replied, "but it's set to dump if the subject is under any form of duress. Even harsh questioning would do it. I happen to know that *you* got updated, twice, after conversations with your mother."

"That figures," Roger said. "She always was one for ... harsh questions. 'Why don't you cut your hair?' 'What do you *do* all day on those hunting trips?'" he added in a falsetto.

"The setup is incredibly paranoid," Catrone continued. "The doctors who handle the toot updates don't even know about it. It's a hack that's arranged by the Regiment, and the only thing *they* know is that it's an old mod. Hell, for that matter the hack that gave *me* the activation codes is handled the same way. Except—" his smile was crooked "—*our* toots don't just dump. They still have their active-duty suicide circuits on-line in case anyone tries to sweat us for what we know about the Protocols. As for the Imperial Family and the full packet, it's just one of the traditions of the Regiment. That's all most of us who know about it at all know. And the subjects aren't aware of it at all. None of them."

"You could slip anything in," Roger said angrily.

"So maybe we are kingmakers," Catrone admitted. "I dunno. But we don't even know what's in it. It's just a data packet. We get the data packet from the IBI. I think they're in charge of keeping the current intelligence info side of it updated, but even *they* don't know what it's *for.*"

"It's more than just a data packet," Roger said flatly. "It's like having the old biddy in your head. God, it's weird. No, not having her in your head, but the way the data's arranged ..."

His voice trailed off.

"What?" Despreaux finally asked.

"Well, first of all, the data's nonextractable." Roger was looking at the tabletop, but clearly not actually seeing it as his eyes tracked back and forth. "That is, I can't just dump it out. It's in a compartmented memory segment. And there's a lot more than just the Palace data. Assassination techniques, toombie hacks, poisons—method and application of, including analyses and after-action reports. Hacking programs. Back doors to Imperial and IBI datanets. Whoever caretakers this thing for the IBI's been earning his pay updating it with current tech and passwords. And there's more in here than I thought a toot had room for."

"Is there a way *in?*" Kosutic asked pointedly.

"I can see several. All of them have problems, but they're all better than what we'd been—" He held up his hand and shook his head. "Hang on."

He closed his eyes and leaned back in his float chair, swinging it from side to side. The group watched him in silence, wondering what he was seeing. Then he leaned suddenly forward and opened his eyes, crossing his arms and grinning.

Despreaux felt faintly uneasy as she studied that grin. It wasn't cold, by any stretch of the imagination. Quite the contrary, in fact. It was almost . . . mad. Evil. Then it passed, and he laughed and looked up at them.

"Now I know what Aladdin felt like," he said, still grinning.

"What are you talking about?" Kosutic sounded as uneasy as Despreaux had felt.

"Let's take a walk," Roger replied, and led them out of the room and down a series of corridors to the back of the south end of the complex. They ended up facing a blank wall.

"We swept this," Kosutic pointed out.

"And if it had been a normal door, you would've found it." Roger drew a knife out of his pocket and rapped on the solid concrete. "Asseen, asseen, Protocol Miranda MacClintock One-Three-Niner-Beta. Open Sesame!"

He slapped the wall and then stood back.

"Paranoid *and* with a sense of humor," Catrone said dryly as the wall started to slide backwards into the hill. The movement revealed that the "wall" was a half meter of concrete slab, pinned to the bed-rock of the mountain ridge. The plug that had filled the corridor was nearly four meters deep, yet it slid backwards smoothly, easily. Then it moved sideways, revealing a large, domed room whose walls and ceilings reflected the silver of ChromSten armoring.

Ranked against the left wall were five stingships—a model Roger didn't recognize, with short, stubby wings, and a wide body—and a pair of shuttles. Opposite them were three light skimmer tanks, and both sets of vehicles were wrapped in protective covers.

"Wait." Roger held out his hand as Catrone started to step past him. "Nitrogen atmosphere," the prince continued as lights came on and fans started to turn in the distance. "You go in there now, and you'll keel over in a second."

"That up there, too?" Catrone asked, gesturing with his chin at Roger's head.

"Yep."

"Is there one of these at each dispersal facility?" Catrone asked.

"Yep. And a bigger set at the Cheyenne facility. You were the Gold sergeant major; you know about that one, right?"

"Yes. How many others?"

"Four, five total," Roger replied. "Greenbrier, Cheyenne, Weather Mountain, Cold Mountain, and Wasatch."

"Thirty stingships?" Rosenberg asked.

"Fifty," Roger told him. "There are ten each at Weather Mountain, Cold Mountain, and Wasatch, and fifteen at Cheyenne."

"I *knew* it didn't look right!" Catrone snapped. "That one's designated for the Empress, and I checked it out one time. The dome's too flat!"

"That's because the entire lower section is missing," Roger said. "All the stuff in there is *under* the known facilities. And this isn't part of the original facility; it was a later add-on." He glanced at a readout on the side of the tunnel and nodded. "That's long enough."

"I don't recognize those." Despreaux pointed at the stingships, as they crossed the chamber towards them. "Or the tanks, for that matter."

"That's because they're antiques," Rosenberg said, running his hand lovingly over the needlelike nose of the nearest. "I've only ever seen them in air shows. They date back more than a hundred years. Densoni Shadow Wolves—forty megawatt fusion bottle, nine thousand kilos of thrust, Mach Three-Point-Five or thereabouts." He touched the leading edge of one wing and sighed. "Bastards to fly. They used more aero-lift than modern ships—let them get away from you, and they went all over the sky, then hit the ground. Hard. They called them Widow-Makers."

"Not much good against Raptors, then," Roger sighed. "I thought we'd hit the jackpot."

"Oh, I dunno." Rosenberg pursed his lips. "It'll take good pilots, and I don't have fifty of those I can get in on this and be sure of security. It'd help if they're crazy, too. But basic stingship design just hasn't changed a lot over the last hundred years or so. Shadow Wolves are actually *faster* than Raptors, and, maybe, a tad more maneuverable because of the aero-surfaces. Certainly more maneuverable at high speeds; they'll pull something like thirty gees in a bank, before damping. But they sacrifice direct lift and gravity control, and the damping only brings it down to about sixteen gees at max evolution. The big difference is modern high-density fusion plants, which equates to more brute acceleration—better grav damping—and a considerably more powerful weapons fit. And, like I said, their out-of-control maneuvers are a bitch. No neural interfaces, either." He looked over at Roger and cocked an eyebrow. "Ammo?"

"Magazine." Roger pointed to the exit corridor. "And an armory. No powered armor. Soft-suits and exoskeletons."

"They didn't have the power-tech a hundred years ago that we have now," Catrone said, striding down the corridor. "Powering ChromSten armor took too much juice. Weapons?"

"Old—*really* old—plasma guns," Roger replied. "Forty-kilowatt range."

"That won't do it against powered armor," Kosutic said.

"And I'm not too happy about the idea of old plasma guns," Despreaux pointed out. "Not after what happened on Marduk."

"Everything's going to have to be checked out," Roger said. "Most of it should be pretty good; no oxygen, so there shouldn't have been any degradation. And the guns may be old, Nimashet, but they weren't built by Adoula and his assholes. On the other hand, some of the stuff was stashed by Miranda herself, people—it's damned near *six* hundred years old. Most of the other bits and pieces were emplaced later."

"So somebody's been collecting the stuff," Catrone said. "The Association?"

"Sometimes," Roger said. "And others. But usually the Family took care of it directly. Which left the entire process with some kinks Miranda couldn't really allow for. There are some . . . time bombs in this thing. Like I say, some of this stuff was put up by Great Gran, using the IBI, and some of the Family have followed up over the years with more modern equipment. Like your Shadow Wolves," he said, looking at Rosenberg. "But I think . . ."

Roger frowned and looked up at the ceiling, clearly considering schedules.

"Yeah," he said after a moment. "Mother should already have done some upgrades. I wonder why—" He paused. "Oh, that's why. God, this woman was paranoid."

"What?" Despreaux said.

"Bitch!" Roger snapped.

"*What!?*"

"Oh, not you," Roger said quickly, soothingly. "Miranda. Mother, for that matter. There are . . . familial security protocols, I guess you'd call them, in here. God, no wonder some of the emperors've gone just a touch insane." He closed his eyes again and shook his head. "Imagine, for a moment, a thought coming out of nowhere . . ."

"Oh, Christ," Catrone said. "'Do you trust your family? Really, *really* trust them?"

"Bingo." Roger opened his eyes and looked around. "The protocols only opened up if the Emperor or Empress of the time fully trusted the people he or she was going to use to upgrade the facilities. And the people they were upgrading the facilities *for*. If they didn't trust them, from time to time they'd be . . . probed again. According to the timetable, Mother probably was being asked as often as monthly if she really trusted, well, *me*."

"And she didn't," Catrone said.

"Apparently not," Roger replied, tightly. "As if I didn't know that before."

"We pull this off, and she will," Marinau said. "Keep that in mind."

"Yeah," Roger said. "Yeah. And it wasn't just Mother, either. Grandfather's head just didn't work the way Miranda's—or Mom's—did. He didn't want to think about this kind of crap . . . so he didn't, and the Protocols jumped over him completely. That's why the stingships we've got here date clear back to before he took the Throne, although the ones at Cheyenne are more modern."

His mouth twisted. "Probably because these were the ones *I* was most likely to get my hands on if it turned out Mom was right about me."

"But at least they're here," Despreaux pointed out.

"And because they are, we've got a chance," Rosenberg put in. "Maybe even a good one."

"We can't use the Cheyenne stingships," Roger pointed out. "Not in any sort of first wave; they're too far away. For that matter, they'd have to run a gauntlet even after the first attack. *Especially* after the first attack."

"And I've only got one other pilot I'd bring in on this," Rosenberg said.

"Pilots . . . aren't a problem," Roger replied evenly. "But we're going to have to get techs in to work on this stuff. It *should* be in good shape, but there's bound to be problems. There are spares here, as well."

"And we're gonna need more armor," Catrone said.

"Well, that's not a problem, either," Roger said. "Or modern weapons. The plasma guns here are ancient as hell, but they're fine for general antipersonnel work, and there are some heavy weapons the Mardukans can handle, for that matter. And we've got another source of supply. We've got over twenty heavy plasma and bead guns, and some armor, as well."

"Oh?" Catrone eyed him speculatively.

"Oh." Roger seemed unaware that the older man was looking at him. "But the big problem is, we're going to have to *rehearse* this, and this op's just gotten a lot bigger than we can squeeze into Greenbrier here. Somehow, we've got to bring everyone together in one place, and how the *hell* are we going to do that without opping every security flag Adoula has?"

"Tell you what," Catrone said suspiciously. "If you'll ante up your suppliers, we'll ante up how to rehearse. And where the techs are going to come from."

"Okay," Catrone said when he and Roger were back in the meeting room. Despreaux, Kosutic, and Marinau were going over weaponry, while Rosenberg was doing an in initial survey of the stingships and shuttles. "We need to get one thing out of the way."

"What?"

"No matter what, we're not going to oppose you, and we're not going to burn you," Catrone said. "But there are still some elements that don't think too highly of Prince Roger MacClintock."

"I'm not surprised," Roger said evenly. "I was my own worst enemy."

"They do, however, support *Alexandra*," Catrone continued, shaking his head. "Which could create a not-so-tiny problem, since when we take the Palace, *you're* going to be in control."

"Not if the Association is against me," Roger pointed out.

"We don't want a factional fight in the Palace itself," Catrone said tightly. "That would be the worst of all possible outcomes. But—get it straight. We're not fighting for Prince Roger; we're fighting for Empress Alexandra."

"I understand. There's just one problem."

"Your mother may not be fully functional," Catrone said. "Mentally."

"Correct." Roger considered his next words carefully. "Again," he said, "we have . . . reports which indicate that. The people who provided the analysis in those reports believe there will be significant impairment. Look, Tom, I don't *want* the Throne. What sort of lunatic *would* want it in a situation like this one? But from all reports, Mother isn't going to be sufficiently functional to continue as Empress."

"We don't know that," Catrone argued mulishly, his face set. "All we have are rumors and fifth-hand information. Your mother is a *very* strong woman."

Roger leaned back and cocked his head to the side, examining the old soldier as if he'd never seen him before.

"You love her," the prince said.

"What?" Catrone snapped, and glared at him. "What does that have to do with it? She's my Empress. I was sworn to protect her before *you* were a gleam in New Madrid's eye. I was Silver's battalion sergeant major when she was *Heir Primus*. Of course I love her! She's my *Empress*, you young idiot!"

"No." Roger leaned forward, resting his forearms on the table, and stared Catrone in the eye. "Being in that pressure cooker taught me more than just how to swing a sword, Tomcat. It made me a pretty fair judge of human nature, too. And I mean you *love* her. Not as a primary, not as the Empress—as a woman. Tell me I lie."

Catrone leaned back and crossed his own arms. He looked away from Roger's modded brown eyes, then looked back.

"What if I do?" he asked. "What business is that of yours?"

"Just this." Roger leaned back in turn. "Which do you love more—her, or the Empire?" He watched the sergeant major's face for a moment, then nodded. "Ah, there's the rub, isn't it? If it comes down to a choice between Alexandra MacClintock and the Empire, can you decide?"

"That's hypothetical," Catrone argued. "And it's impossible to judge—"

"It's an *important* hypothetical," Roger interrupted. "Face it, if we succeed, we *will* be the kingmakers. And people—everyone on Old Earth, in the Navy, in the Corps, the Lords, the Commons, *all* of them—are going to want to know, *right away*, who's in charge." He made a cutting motion with his hand in emphasis. "Right then. Who's giving the orders. Who holds the reins. Not to mention the planetary defense control codes. *My* information is that Mother's in no condition to assume that responsibility. What do *your* sources say?"

"That she's . . . impaired." Catrone's face was obsidian-hard. "That they're using psychotropic drugs, toot controls, and . . . sexual controls to keep her in line."

"What?" Roger said very, very softly.

"They're using psychotropic—"

"No. That last part."

"That's why the Earl is involved," Catrone said, and paused, looking at the prince. "You didn't know," he said quietly after a moment.

"No." Roger's fists bunched. His arms quivered, and his face went set and hard. For the first time, Thomas Catrone felt an actual trickle of fear as he looked at the young man across the table from him.

"I did not know," Prince Roger MacClintock said.

"It's a . . . refinement." Catrone's own jaw worked. "Keeping Alex in line is apparently pretty hard. New Madrid figured out how." He paused and took a deep breath, getting himself under control. "It's his . . . style."

Roger had his head down, hands together, nose and lips resting on the ends of his fingers, as if he were praying. He was still quivering.

"If you go in now, guns blazing, Prince Roger," Catrone said softly, "we're all going to die. And it won't help your mother."

Roger nodded his head, ever so slightly.

"I've had some time to get over it," Catrone said, gazing at something only he could see, his voice distant, almost detached. "Marinau brought me the word. All of it. He brought it in person, along with a couple of the other guys."

"They have to hold you down?" Roger asked quietly. His head was still bent, but he'd managed to stop the whole-body quivers.

"I nearly broke his arm," Catrone said, speaking each word carefully, in a sort of high, soft voice of memory. He licked his lips and shook his head. "It catches me, sometimes. I've been wracking my brain over what to do, other than getting myself killed. I don't have a problem with that, but it wouldn't have helped Alex one bit. Which is why I didn't hesitate, except long enough for some tradecraft, when you turned up. I want those bastards, Your Highness. I want them so bad I can taste it. I've never wanted to kill anyone like I want to kill New Madrid. I want a new meaning of pain for him."

"Until this moment," Roger said quietly, calmly, "we've been in very different places, Sergeant Major."

"Explain," Catrone said, shaking himself like a dog, shaking off the cold, drenching hatred of memory to refocus on the prince.

"I knew rescuing Mother was a necessity." Roger looked up at last, and the retired NCO saw tears running down his cheeks. "But frankly, if the mission would have worked better, if it would have been safer, ignoring Mother, I would have been more than willing to ignore her."

"What?" Catrone said angrily.

"Don't get on your high horse, Sergeant Major," Roger snapped. "First of all, let's keep in mind the safety of the Empire. If keeping the Empire together meant playing my mother as a pawn, that would be the right course. *Mother* would insist it was the right course. Agreed?"

Catrone's lips were pinched and white with anger, but he nodded.

"Agreed," he said tightly.

"Now we get into the personal side," Roger continued. "My mother spent as little time with me as she possibly could. Yes, she was Empress, and she was very busy. It was a hard job, I know that. But I also know I was raised by nannies and tutors and my goddammed *valet*. Mother, quite frankly, generally only appeared in my life to explain to me what a little shit I was. Which, I submit, didn't do a great deal to motivate me to be anything *else*, Sergeant Major. And then, when it was all coming apart, she didn't trust me enough to keep me at her side. Instead, she sent me off to Leviathan. Instead of landing on Leviathan, which is a shithole of a planet, I ended up on Marduk—which is worse. Not exactly *her* fault, but let's just say that she and her distrust figure prominently in why almost two hundred men and women who were very close and important to me *died*."

"Don't care for Alexandra, do you?" Catrone said menacingly.

"I just found out that blood is much, much thicker than water," Roger replied, cheek muscles bunching. "If you'd asked me, and if I'd been willing to answer honestly, five minutes ago if I cared if Mother lived or died, the *honest* answer would have been: no." He paused and stared at the sergeant major, then shook his head. "In which case, I would have been lying to myself at the same time I was trying to be honest with *you*." He twisted his hands together and his arms shook. "I really, *really* feel the need to kill something."

"There's always those *atul*," Catrone pointed out, watching him work through it.

Frankly, the prince was handling it better than he had. Maybe he didn't care as much, but Catrone suspected that it was simply a very clear manifestation of how controlled Roger could be. Catrone understood control. You didn't get to be sergeant major of Gold Battalion by being a nonaggressive nonentity, and he could recognize when a person was exercising enormous control. Well, enough to prevent an outright explosion, at least. He wondered—for the first time, really, despite having seen the "presentation" from Marduk—just how volcanic Roger could be when pushed. Based on the degree of control he was seeing at this moment, he suspected the answer was *very* volcanic. Like, Krakatoa volcanic.

"Putting myself in the way of an *atul* right now would be

stupid," Roger said. "If I die, the whole plan dies. Mom dies, and she . . . shit!" He shook his head again. "Besides, I've killed so many of them that it just wouldn't be *satisfying* enough, you know?" he added, looking at the sergeant major.

"Oh, yeah. I know."

"God, that hit me." Roger closed his eyes again. "At so many levels. Christ, I don't want her to die. I want to strangle her myself!"

"Don't joke about that," Catrone said sharply.

"Sorry." Roger sat motionless for another moment, then reopened his eyes. "We've got to get her out of there, Sergeant Major."

"We will," Catrone said. "Sir."

"I learned, a long time ago," Roger said, smiling faintly, his cheeks still wet with tears, "all of eleven months or so ago, the difference between being called 'Your Highness' and 'Sir.' I'm glad you're fully on board."

"Nobody is that good an actor," Catrone told him. "You didn't know. Your . . . sources didn't know?"

"I . . . think they did," Roger replied. "In which case, certain cryptic glances between members of my staff are now explained."

"Wouldn't be the first time staff held back something they didn't want their boss to know. Be glad it wasn't something more important."

"Actually, *this* is rather important. But I take your meaning," Roger said. "On the other hand, I think I'll just explain to them the difference between personal and important." He looked at the sergeant major, his face hard. "Don't get down on me, by the way, for considering Mother as a pawn. I saw too many friends die . . ."

"I watched," Catrone said, nodding to where the hologram had played.

"Yes, but even for someone who's been on the sharp end, you can't know," Roger replied. "You can't know what it's like to have to keep going every day, watching your soldiers being picked off, one by one, losing men and women that you . . . love, and the journey seems to never end. Seeing them dying to protect you, and nothing—*nothing*—you can do to help them that won't make it worse. So, I did. I did make it worse. I kept throwing myself out there. And getting them killed while they were trying to keep me alive. Until I got good enough that I was keeping *them* alive. Good enough that they were watching my back instead of getting between me and whatever was trying to kill us, because they knew I was, by God, the nastiest, most cold-blooded, *vicious* bastard on that entire fucking planet.

"I wasn't fighting this battle for Mother, Sergeant Major; I was fighting it for *them*. To get that damned Imperial Warrant off their heads. To make sure they could go to bed at night in reasonable certainty that they'd wake up in the morning. So that the *dead* could be honored in memory, their bodies brought home to lie beside the fallen heroes of the Empire, instead of being remembered only as losers in a failed coup. As incompetent traitors. That was no way to remember Armand Pahner. I'd use anyone—you, the Association, Mother, *anyone*—to keep them from—"

He shrugged angrily, and his nostrils flared as he drew a deep breath.

"But, yeah, I just found out that blood is thicker than water. Before, I only wanted Adoula . . . moved aside. He was another obstacle to be removed, period. Now . . . ?"

"New Madrid is the real bastard," Catrone ground out. "He's the one—"

"Yes, he is." Roger flexed his jaw. "I agree with that. But I'll tell you something else, Sergeant Major. You're not getting your wire waistcoat."

"Like hell," Catrone said uncomfortably. "You're not going to let him *walk*?"

"Of course not. And if the timing is right, you can shoot the bastard, father of mine though he is—genetically speaking, at least. Or I'll hand you my sword, and you can cut his pretty head off. But in all likelihood, if he doesn't get accidentally terminated during the operation, or if he's not in a position where early termination is the best course, we're going to turn him over to the courts and slip a nice little poison into his veins after a full and fair trial."

"Like hell!" Catrone repeated, angrily, this time.

"That's what's going to happen," Roger said sternly. "Because one of the things I learned in that little walk is the difference between the good guys and the bad guys. The good guys don't *torture* people just because they want vengeance, Sergeant Major.

No matter what the reasoning. I didn't torture that damned Saint bastard who killed Armand Pahner after he'd 'surrendered.' I *shot* him before I left Marduk, and given the Saints' violation of Imperial territory and the operations those Greenpeace commandos carried out under his orders—not to mention killing so many Imperial Marines right there in Marduk orbit—it was completely, legally justified. I won't pretend for a moment that I didn't take a certain savage satisfaction out of it; as Armand himself once pointed out to me, I *am* a bit of a savage—a barbarian—myself. But I didn't torture even the sons of bitches who killed him and tried to kill me, and I never tortured a damncroc for killing Kostas. Killed quite a few, but they all went out quick. If there's a reason to terminate New Madrid as part of this operation, he'll be terminated. Cleanly and quickly. If not, he faces Imperial justice. Ditto for Adoula. Because we're the good guys, whatever the *bad guys* may have done."

"Christ, you *have* grown up," Catrone muttered. "Bastard."

"That I am," Roger agreed. "I was born out of wedlock, but I'm my *mother's* son, not my father's. And not even he can turn me into him. Is that clear?"

"Clear," Catrone muttered.

"I can't *hear* you, Sergeant Major," Roger said without a hint of playfulness.

"Clear," Catrone said flatly. "Damn it."

"Good," Roger said. "And now that that little *UNPLEASANTNESS*—" he shouted "—is out of the way, I'll give you one more thing, Sergeant Major."

"Oh?" Catrone regarded him warily.

"I've taken a shine to you, Sergeant Major. I didn't understand why, at first, but you remind me of someone. Not as smooth, not quite as wise, I think, but pretty similar in a lot of ways."

"Who?" Catrone asked.

"Armand Pahner." Roger swallowed. "Like I said, none of that trip would have worked without Armand. He wasn't perfect. He had a tendency to believe his own estimates that damned near killed us a couple of times. But . . . he was very much like a father to me. I learned to trust him more than I trust ChromSten. You with me, Sergeant Major?"

"Pahner was a hell of a man," Catrone said. "A bit of a punk, when I first met him. No, not a punk—never a punk. He was good, even then. But, yeah, cocky as hell. And I watched him grow for a bit. I agree, he was more trustworthy than armor. Your point?"

"My point, Tom, is that I've come to trust you. Maybe more than I should, but . . . I've gotten to be a fair judge of character. And I know you don't want to play kingmaker . . . which is why that's exactly what you're going to do."

"Explain," Catrone said, wary again.

"When we take the Palace," Roger said, then shrugged. "Okay, *if* we take the Palace. And we rescue Mother. *You* are going to decide—right then, right there."

"Decide who gets the reins?"

"Yes, who gets the reins. If Mother is even semifunctional, I'll step back. Give her time to get her bearings, time to find out how damaged she is. But you, Thomas Catrone, are going to make the evaluation."

"Shit."

"Do you think Adoula has this?"

Buseh Subianto had been in the IBI for going on forty years. She'd started out as a street agent, working organized crime, and she'd done it well. There'd been something about her fresh face and dark-green eyes that had gotten men, often men who were normally close-mouthed, to talk to her. Such conversations had frequently resulted in their incarceration—frequently enough, as a matter of fact, that she'd been quickly promoted, and then transferred to counterintelligence.

She'd been in the counter-intel business for more than twenty-five years, now, during which she'd slowly worked her way up the ladder of the bureaucracy. The face wasn't so fresh any more. Fine lines had appeared in her skin, and there was a crease on her brow from years of concentrated thought. But the green eyes were still dark and piercing. Almost hypnotic.

Fritz Tebic had worked for his boss long enough to know when to avoid the hypnotism. So he swallowed, then shrugged, looking away.

"He may have it," he replied. "He's seen the report on the

Mardukans who met with Helmut's courier. And New Madrid was definitely having Catrone followed. Catrone went to the Mardukan restaurant here in Imperial city, and a week later, he's meeting with the hard-core members of the Associations. But . . . there are a lot of threads. Adoula's people might not have connected them. Might not."

"If they had, we'd already have an Imperial arrest warrant for treason for Catrone and . . ." she looked at the data, frowning, the thin crease getting deeper, "this Augustus Chung. What gets me is that the players don't make any *sense*. And where are the materials Chung's been receiving *coming* from?"

"I don't know," Tebic said. "OrgCrime Division's already looking at this Marduk House pretty closely—they think Chung is laundering money. But they don't have the information on the shipments. I haven't put any of this into the datanet. The original report on the meeting with Helmut's officers is in there, but none of the connections. And . . . there are a few Mardukans running around. They don't have any skills, so they tend to end up as heavies of one sort or another. Some *do* work for orgcrime, so basically, the Sixth Fleet link looks like a false-positive unless you also have the information on the equipment Chung's been receiving. Ma'am, what are we going to do?"

It was difficult to hide much from the Imperial Bureau of Investigation. Most money was transferred electronically, as were most messages, and everything electronic went past the IBI eventually. And the IBI had enormous computing power at its disposal, power that sifted through that enormous mass of data, looking for apparently unconnected bits. Over the years, the programs had become more and more sophisticated, with fewer and fewer false hits. Despite draconian privacy limitations which were—almost always—rigorously observed, the IBI had eyes everywhere.

Including inside the Imperial Palace. Which meant the two of them knew very well the actual condition of the Empress.

Tebic remembered a class from early in his Academy days. The class had been on the history of cryptography and information security, and one of the examples of successful code-breaking operations had been called Verona, a program from the earliest days of computers—even before transistors. The code-breakers had successfully penetrated an enemy spy network, only to find out that the other side had agents so high in their own government that reporting the information was tantamount to committing suicide. At the time of the class, Tebic's sympathy for them had been purely intellectual; these days, he connected with them on a far more profound level.

A few key people in the IBI knew that Adoula and the Earl of New Madrid had the Empress under their complete control. They even knew how. The problem was, they had no one to tell. The IBI's director had been replaced, charged as an accessory to the "coup." Kyoko Pedza, Director of Counterintelligence, had disappeared within a day afterwards, just before his own arrest on the same charges. It was five-to-one odds in their internal pool that he'd been assassinated by Adoula; Pedza had been a serious threat to Adoula's power base.

But the problem was that the IBI wasn't the Empress' Own. It wasn't even the Navy, sworn to defend the Constitution *and* the Empress. The IBI's first and only mission was the security of the *Empire*. Yes, Adoula had effectively usurped the Throne. Yes, he'd committed a list of offenses a kilometer long in doing so. Perjury, murder, kidnapping, and physical and psychological torture. Technically, they should lay out the data, slap a set of restraints on him, and lead him away to durance vile.

But realistically, he was too powerful. He had a major base in the Lords and the Commons, *de facto* control of the Empress, and control of most of the Navy, and Prime Minister Yang had obviously decided it wasn't time to challenge him too openly. Whether that was because of the chaos Yang feared would overwhelm the Empire if he did so, or because he was more concerned about his own power than he was about the Empress and the Constitution was impossible to say, although Subianto had her own suspicions in that regard.

But whatever the Prime Minister's thinking, as Navy Minister, Prince Jackson was effectively in control of all of the Empire's external and *internal* security organs, especially after he'd replaced Tebic and Subianto's superiors with his own handpicked nominees. If they wanted to arrest Adoula, they'd need to present a list of charges to a magistrate. And even if they found one stupid enough to sign a warrant, they'd never live to process it. Besides, Adoula had already done too much damage. He'd managed to *destroy* the Imperial Family, and Subianto and Tebic, unlike all too many citizens of the Empire, knew precisely how vital to its stability House MacClintock had been. Without it, there was only Adoula, however corrupt, however "evil," to hold things together. Without him, what did the Empire have? An Empress who was severely damaged. Probably civil war. And no clear heir to the Throne.

And now they had this. Smuggling of illegal and highly dangerous materials. Collusion with a foreign power—they were pretty sure about that one, although which foreign power was less clear. Conspiracy to commit treason—sort of; that one depended on the definition and whether or not it was technically possible to commit treason against someone who had treasonously seized power in the first place. Illegal monetary transfers—definitely. Falsification of identity without a doubt. Assault. Theft.

But . . .

"No chance of getting eyes and ears into the building?" Subianto asked.

"No," Tebic replied unhesitatingly. "Security is pretty unobtrusive, but very tight. Good electronics—very good, very professional. And those Mardukans literally sleep at the warehouse and the restaurant. The restaurant has countersurveillance devices—two agents have been asked to leave for trying to get floaters and directional mikes inside—but plenty of restaurants in Imperial City would've done exactly the same thing. Too many conversations nobody wants overheard."

"Who *are* they?" Subianto whispered to herself. "They're not the Associations. They're not with Adoula. They're not those idiots in the Supremacy Party."

"They're acting like they're going to counter Adoula," Tebic said. "But the Associations *have* to know the Empress isn't in the best condition, and there's no clear alternate Regent, much less a clear Heir, other than this fetus Adoula and New Madrid are growing." He paused and shrugged. "We've got three choices."

"I know." Subianto's face was hard and cold. "We can turn the data over to Adoula, and they disappear—or, maybe, get tried. We can do nothing, and see what happens. Or we can contact them."

"Yes, Ma'am," Tebic said, and waited.

His superior's face could have belonged to a statue—one of

the old Persian emperors, the omnipotent semideities, often more than just a little insane, who had gifted humanity with such enduring phrases as "killing the messenger" and "maybe the horse will sing" and "the Sword of Damocles." *This* was a Sword of Damocles over both their heads, hanging by a thread. And the way those omnipotent emperors had wandered into the borderlands of sanity, Tebic knew, was from making decisions which would determine the fate of far more than just their own empire . . . and when they'd known their own lives, and their families', were on the line.

"I think," Subianto said, then paused. "I think, I'm in the mood to try some new food."

"When were you planning on doing this?" Catrone's voice was still cold, but he was focused again, had his mission face on once more.

"During the Imperial Festival," Roger replied. "We were going to have to do the attack fully on the surface—frontal assault. We were going to be in the parade that passes the Imperial Park. Mardukans in all their finery, *civan*, *flar-ta*, the works. We knew we could take down the outer perimeter guards with the Mardukans, but we couldn't get any further than that."

"Adoula's rarely at the Palace," Catrone pointed out. "He's either at the Lords, or in his offices in the Imperial Tower."

"I'll be honest," Roger said. "I've got a hard-on for Adoula, more than ever now, and I know we have to keep him from getting away. But mostly, I've been concentrated on getting to Mother and the replicator. Capture the queen and bring in impartial witnesses, and Adoula's out of power. Maybe he can make it off-planet, especially with his control of Home Fleet, but he's not going to be holding the Empire."

"True, but we have to take him out as well. We don't want him breaking off his own section of the Empire. And he's got a good many of the Navy's commanders in his pocket. For that matter, he's got *Greenberg* in his pocket. Taking the Palace isn't going to do us much good if Home Fleet drops a kinetic weapon on our heads. Or drops all their Marines on us, for that matter. The most we're going to be able to field is a very short battalion of guys who are mostly out of practice. We do *not* want to take on the Home Fleet Marine contingent supported by the ships."

"Okay," Roger sighed. "Cards on the table time. We're in contact with the Alphanes, and they have solid intelligence that Adoula intends to try to bring them into the Empire as soon as Mother is out of the picture."

"Is he *nuts*?" Catrone demanded. "No, he's not nuts; are *you* nuts? You're *sure*?"

"The Alphanes are—sure enough that if we don't get this working, they're going to jump Third Fleet. Adoula hasn't completely filled the command and staff there with his cronies, yet, but he's positively, according to them, planning on using Third and Fourth Fleets against them. Fourth is already his, but he can't divert too much of it from watching the Saints, or they may jump him from behind, so he needs Third, too. But once he's been able to make sure he has it, all the evidence says he's going after them. He doesn't believe they can't be conquered, and although they've got a sizable fleet, as Admiral Ral pointed out, the Empire has *six* fleets their size."

"Of course we do, but they won't back down," Catrone argued. "Not even if you take the orbitals. The bears are *nuts* about honor. They'll all die fighting, to the last cub."

"I know that," Roger said, shaking his head. "You know that. Adoula's *advisers* know that. But Adoula doesn't believe it. So if the command and staff of Third Fleet changes, the Alphanes are going active. That's something we have to keep an eye on."

"And they're your source of supply?"

"They're our source of supply," Roger confirmed. "Armor and weapons. Even armor for the Mardukans, which you'll have to see to believe. But nothing heavier than that, and it's been hard enough to hide even that much."

"I can believe that. Security on this is going to be a bitch. Somebody is *going* to notice, sooner or later. You do realize that, right?"

"We'll just have to hope it's later." Roger shrugged. "If the IBI starts sniffing around Marduk House, they'll discover what's pretty obviously a cover for money laundering."

"Show them what they expect to see?"

"Right. The only problem is, there *is* more money going out than coming in. But the money coming in is clean, too. So they're looking for a negative if they try to build a case. It's not exactly *clean*—it's from the Alphanes. But it's not anything they can tie to anything illegal."

"All right," Catrone said. Not because he was happy about it, but because he recognized that all they could do was the best they could do.

"Home Fleet," he continued, continuing his methodical examination of Roger's plans. "Any ideas there?"

"Well, how about a complete replacement of command and staff?" Roger replied lightly. Then his expression sobered. "The current plan is to take Greenberg out, simultaneous with the attack."

"Assassination?" Catrone said levelly.

"Yes," Roger replied unflinchingly. "There's no way to ensure we can simply grab him and move him out of the loop. And there are officers who will follow Greenberg just because he *is* the designated Home Fleet commander. Take him out of the loop, and they're going to have to make up their minds who to back. To be honest, if they're willing not to shoot at us, I don't care if they just sit the whole thing out. But I do *not* want Greenberg in charge, and the only way to ensure that, distasteful as it may be, is to kill him. There's already a team in place."

Catrone's face worked for a moment, and then he shrugged angrily.

"You're right, and I don't like it."

"Do you have a better solution?" Roger asked calmly.

"No," Catrone admitted. "And I agree it's necessary. But I still don't like it."

"We do a lot of things we don't like, because they're necessary. That's the nature of our business. Isn't it, Sergeant Major?"

"Yes," Catrone admitted again. "So . . . where are we?"

"Taking out Greenberg ought to put Wallenstein in command, as his exec," Roger continued, "but our intel says that whole thing's not as clear as it ought to be. Apparently, Captain Wallenstein . . . is not well thought of in the Navy. Something to do with his career track and the fact that he's never commanded anything bigger than a single cruiser.

"So with Greenberg gone, and Wallenstein labeled a paper-pusher in Adoula's pocket, that leaves Kjerulf with a damned good chance of taking over command . . . if he has a reason to try. And if we can prime him just a bit, I think he *will* try, which should at least muddle the hell out of Home Fleet's command structure. The other staff and commanders loyal to Adoula will want to intervene, but Kjerulf is going to wait and see what's going on. I'd expect some response from Home Fleet, but without Greenberg, it'll be uncoordinated."

"Even an uncoordinated response will be bad," Catrone pointed out. "Maybe worse. Desperate men will try desperate measures."

"Well, we've also got a fleet of our own," Roger said.

"Who?" Catrone asked, then nodded. "Dark Helmut, right?"

"Yes. We sent a team to contact him. They reported having made contact with one of his ship commanders, who'd arranged to transport them to meet with him, and Sixth Fleet's moved since then. It *might* be coming to warn Adoula, but if so, the warning should already have been here. If Helmut were working Adoula's side—which I doubt strongly—we'd already be in custody."

"So how do you get word to Sixth Fleet to coordinate things?"

"If they're on schedule, they'll pick up a standard data dump from the Wolf Cluster in—" Roger thought about it and ran some calculations on his toot, then shrugged. "In three days or so. They'll get a message that we're in place and preparing the assault, and they'll send a message telling us whether Helmut's on our side or not. But we won't know one way or the other until just before the assault. Time lag."

"Got it." Catrone looked unhappy, then grimaced. "Ever think how nice it must have been to be a general or admiral back in the good old days, when everyone was stuck on one planet and you didn't have to worry about messages taking days, or even weeks, to get to their destinations?"

"I'm sure they had their own problems," Roger replied dryly.

"Yeah, but a man can dream, right?"

"We'll have to send out our message giving the timing for the assault before we know whether or not Sixth Fleet is going to be available," Roger continued, ignoring Catrone's chuckle. "Impossible to avoid."

"Security on that?" Catrone asked more seriously.

"Personal ads," Roger said with a shrug. "What else?"

"You ever wondered how many of those personals are covert messages?" Catrone asked with another grin.

"Not until recently. A lot, I'd guess."

"I'm beginning to think they're the majority." Catrone's grin faded into a frown. "Security on covert ops gives me ulcers. There's a reason my hair is gray."

"Yeah," Roger agreed, then reached out through his toot to reactivate the updated hologram.

"We've been looking at the best schematic of the Palace we could put together before you and Great Gran Miranda came along, trying to come up with a plan that isn't suicide." He loaded the simulation of the best plan they had so far, and the two of them watched it in fast-forward as the attackers' blue icons evaporated. None of them even made it into the Palace.

"So far, we haven't found one," Roger observed dryly.

"Obviously," Catrone said with a wince. He sat back, scratching his nose, and frowned thoughtfully.

"There's a rhythm to taking the Palace," he said after a moment. "There are uniformed guards at these locations," he continued, highlighting the positions. Most of them had been filled in already, but he put in a few more that were in "Gold" and "Silver" sectors Kosutic hadn't known about. "But the real problems are the armored reaction squad you've got *here*," he highlighted the position, "the automated defenses, and the bulk of the guards, who are in the barracks."

He highlighted the other two threat locations briefly.

"I was in charge of the Palace's security for a long time," he said sourly, "and one of my background thoughts was always how *I* might take the place. I decided that, based on some of my own changes—well, the various *commanders'* changes which I sort of suggested—it would be a bitch. But I also knew that no matter what I could do, there was a weakness. The key is Number Three Gate and the North Courtyard," he said, highlighting them.

"Why?"

"The North Courtyard has two manned defense posts." Catrone pointed them out, "but it's accessible via Gate Three. This assumes that the automated defenses are down, you understand that?"

"Yes."

"The courtyard is also the parade ground for the Empress' Own. It more or less severs the barracks and the outer servants' wing from the Palace proper. There are connecting corridors, but they're all covered by the courtyard. Take the courtyard, and you can use it as a landing zone for support forces. The only thing stopping them would be the defensive positions, but they're lightly manned, normally. Even upgraded security doesn't increase those guards, because they aren't guarding the principles directly, understand?"

"Yes." Roger was studying the schematic intently. "Take the gate, pin most of the garrison down in barracks, and seize the courtyard as an LZ. Then bring in your troops, use most of your support to reduce the bulk of the guards still in their barracks, and punch a group into the Palace. What about air support for the guards?"

"Stingship squadron." Catrone highlighted the hangar embedded in the sprawling Palace. "Only half strength, according to my information; it took a beating in the first coup, and finding more people for it is harder than finding the sort of grunts Adoula's been willing to settle for. It takes them at least fifteen minutes to go active. The reaction squad, if it's fully trained, can be armored up in three minutes, and react anywhere in the Palace within ten. Guards are full up in less than an hour. Completely down and surprised, when I was in charge, everyone was in armor and countering an assault in forty minutes, but an hour is the standard."

"Their communications will be dislocated," Roger said. "I can turn those off, scramble their internal communications, with the Protocols. Leave Temu Jin in place to keep them scrambled."

"Which means taking the command post *first*." Catrone highlighted one of the new, hopefully secure routes. "You'll have to do it. You're the man with the codes, and most of them will only respond to you."

"Agreed."

"Send the first-wave Mardukans in to take the gate," Catrone continued, and Roger nodded.

"They can scale the wall if they have to. They've done it before. And I have codes for opening the gate, too."

"However they do it, they get in," Catrone said, "and take the courtyard away from the duty company before the rest of them get organized."

"With swords and pikes against bead guns." Roger winced. "But they can do it."

"Once they have the courtyard, the shuttles come in," Catrone continued. "Can they use human weapons? There'll be some lying around."

"Like pistols," Roger said. "Again, something they've done."

"This takes, say, five minutes," Catrone said. "More. They've got to cross the Park just to reach the gate."

"A thousand meters." Roger pursed his lips. "Two minutes for *civan* at a run; not much longer for the Diasprans. Say seven to ten minutes to take the courtyard."

"Which means the reaction team is up."

"Yeah, but they're busy dealing with an armored force that's already well into the Palace," Roger countered, highlighting the route from the command center to his mother's quarters.

"You're important," Catrone said warily. "Which means you're in the command post, right?"

"Wrong. Because *I* have to open doors here, here—lots of doors," he said, highlighting them. "That's why there will be fifteen armored troops—to protect *me*."

"Okay, okay." Catrone obviously didn't like it, but he recognized both necessity and intransigence when he saw them. "So *probably* the reaction squad is off chasing you when our forces land and punch into Adoula's mercenaries. One group detaches to take the Palace proper."

"The automated defenses will go to local control when the command post is compromised," Roger pointed out. "I can keep the secondary CP from going on-line, but I can't keep the automatics from going local."

"We'll deal with it," Catrone said, and stood back from the hologram. He and the prince studied it together for several silent seconds, then Roger tossed his head.

"I think we got us a plan," he said.

"Yeah," Catrone mused, still looking at the schematic. "You really trust the Mardukans that much? If they don't get that courtyard, we're going to have over a thousand heavily armed mercs swarming over us."

"I trust them with my life. More—I trust them with the Empire. They'll take the gate."

"Did you know that the Empress' Own Association's annual meeting is scheduled during the Imperial Festival?" New Madrid demanded as he strode into Jackson Adoula's office.

"Yes." Adoula didn't look up from the hologram on his desk.

"And so is the Raider Association's . . . and the Special Operations Association's," New Madrid continued angrily.

"Yes," Adoula replied calmly.

"You don't think there might be some minor problems stemming out of all that?" New Madrid asked, throwing up his hands.

"My dear Earl," Adoula said, still looking at his hologram, "we have the Saints poking around on the border in fleet strength. We have the Alphanes massing for what looks very much like an attack. There's another bill in Parliament for an evaluation of the Empress—this time pressed by my *opponents*, and thus much less easy to quash—and even that gutless trimmer Yang has stated that his last meeting with the Empress was less than satisfactory. Apparently our good Prime Minister considers that having her simpering at you during the meeting was . . . odd. As was the fashion in which she kept constantly referring all questions to your judgment."

"That bitch has got a mind like steel," New Madrid said tightly, "and her natural resistance to the drugs is high, and getting higher. And I can't afford to leave any noticeable bruises. So even with the . . . other controls in place, we've got to keep her dialed down to the level of an amiable *moron* if we want to be sure she doesn't say something we can't spin the right way. She can't even remember how many *planets* we have, much less what sort of infrastructure is best where. And she certainly can't keep track of whose districts they're in."

"Neither," Adoula said angrily, looking up from the hologram at last, "can you, apparently. I gave very clear instructions on what she was supposed to say during the negotiations. We both know why *she* couldn't follow them; the question is why *you* couldn't either."

"Your 'instructions' covered sixty separate star systems!" New Madrid snapped.

"Then you should have brought *notes!*"

"You said nothing *written!*" New Madrid shouted.

"In this case, apparently," Adoula's cold, level tone cut through the earl's bluster like a scalpel, "we have to make an exception. And the point which apparently escaped you was that nothing that could be tied to *me* was to be written down. For the *next* meeting, however, I will ensure you have precise, written instructions as to what is to be spent, and where. I'll even ensure that they're written in very small words. In the meantime, your worries about those idiot Associations are duly noted. I'll have my guards on high alert in case they come over to make faces at the Palace. A Palace with walls, ChromSten gates, automated defenses, a squadron of stingships, and hundreds of armed guards. Is there anything else on your mind?"

"No." New Madrid thrust himself angrily to his feet.

"In that case, I have real work to do." Adoula waved at the door. "Good day."

He didn't bother to watch New Madrid flounce—that really was the only verb for it—out of his office. It was a pity, he thought, that the powered door couldn't be slammed properly.

He keyed up the next list and shook his head. There were far too many MacClintock loyalists in the IBI, but his supply of people loyal to *him* was finite. Getting reliable people into all of the necessary spots was going to take time.

Who was it who'd said "Ask me for anything but time"? He couldn't remember off the top of his head, but he knew he was asking himself for it.

Just a little time.

"You seem pretty tense," Despreaux said as she slid onto Roger's arm and rested her head on his shoulder.

"Uh-huh."

"It's going well," she added. "The Association, the supplies. This is as good as its looked in a long time."

"Uh-huh."

"So why in hell are you answering me in monosyllables? Something I don't know?"

"More like something I think you do know and didn't tell me," Roger said, jaw muscles clenching. "Something about my mother?"

"Shit." Despreaux sat up and eyed him warily. "The Association knew?"

"Catrone, at least. He assumed my so-capable sources had already informed me. I think he was wondering why I was so . . . calm about it."

"Why *are* you so calm about it?" she asked.

"I'm not," he replied. "I'm what you might call livid about what's been happening to my mother. And I'm almost as livid about the discovery that nobody told me about it. It wasn't like I wasn't going to find out. And if I'd first found out when New Madrid or Adoula were in reach—" He shook his head. "I don't want to think about what I might have done."

"I know," she said unhappily. "We've been discussing it."

"Yeah? Well, you were discussing it with the wrong person." He looked at her finally, and his eyes were hard. "You were *supposed* to discuss it with *me*. Remember me? The Prince? Boss-man? The Heir? The guy who's killed people for a whole hell of a lot less than torturing and raping his mother for months at a time? The guy who really needs to *not* start his reign by chopping off the heads of major political players out-of-hand? Roger? Me? Remember *me*, Nimashet?!"

"Okay, we pocked up!" She threw her arms up. "Maybe we're not as strong morally as we are physically! Do you really think we *wanted* to tell you? The Phaenurs were quite clear that they did *not* want to be around you when you found out. Neither did *I*, okay?"

"No, it's not 'okay.' The purpose of a staff is to manage the information so that the boss gets the information he or she *needs*. I *needed* that information. I needed to *not* be blindsided by it—not when we finally got my mother out, nor in negotiations with a still not particularly trustworthy ally!"

"You don't trust the *Association*?"

"I don't trust anyone but us and the Mardukans. And now I'm wondering if I should trust you."

"That's not fair!" she said angrily.

"Why is it not fair? Hello! You kind of forgot to tell me something *very* important about the operation, about postoperation conditions, about my responses . . . Why is it not fair?"

Her face worked, and it was obvious she was fighting not to cry.

"Damn it, Roger," she said quietly. "Don't do this. Don't *pound* me for this. Okay, we pocked up. We should have told you. But do *not* pound on *me* to get your mad out."

"Shit." He slid down and wrapped his head in a pillow. "Shit." He paused and shook his head, voice still muffled. "I'm sorry."

"I am, too," she said, openly crying.

"You're right," he said, still with his face in the pillow. "I did need to bring it up, but this wasn't the time or the place. I'm sorry. How the hell do you put up with me?"

"Well," she said lightly, even while tears still choked her voice, "you're good-looking. And you're rich . . ."

"God."

"Why didn't you bring this up earlier today?" she asked after a moment.

"The time wasn't right." Roger shrugged. "Too much going on. We sure as hell didn't need a big internal fight in front of the Association guys. But I couldn't keep it in once we got to bed. And I'm still angry, but now I'm angry at myself, too. Christ."

"Roger," Despreaux said quietly, "this is what's called a pillow-fight. There are rules for those."

"One of them being don't bring up business to beat up on your girlfriend?" he asked, finally pulling his head out of the pillow.

"No, the rules don't work that way. Not about what we fight about, so much as how we fight about it. And this is the rule you need to keep in mind—either we work it out while we're still awake, or you go sleep on a couch."

"Why do *I* have to sleep on the couch? I'm the prince. For that matter, this is *my* room."

"You sleep on the couch because you're the guy," she said, batting her eyelashes at him. "Those are the rules. It doesn't matter if this is your room or my room—this is my *bed*. And you can't use one of the other bedrooms. You have to sleep on a couch. With a blanket."

"Do I get a pillow?" he asked plaintively.

"Only if you're good. Otherwise, I get all of them."

"I . . . I don't *like* these rules."

"Too bad. Them's the rules."

"When I'm Emperor, I'm going to *change* them," Roger said, then shook his head. "God, that brings it up again."

"And so on, and so forth," she said. "Until one of us gets tired enough for you to go to the couch."

"Don't hide important things from me," Roger said quietly, "and I'll *try* not to use business to beat up on you. Okay?"

"Fair." Despreaux lay back down and leaned her head on his arm once more. "We'll discuss the more advanced techniques for quarreling another time. What's allowed, what's not, what works, what just makes things worse."

She yawned and snuggled closer.

"I get to sleep here?"

"Are we done?"

"I guess so," he said. "I'll take out the rest of the mad on Adoula."

"Do that."

"Hey, we just had a lovers' quarrel, right?"

"Don't go there . . ." she muttered, then yawned again. "So, other than that, is it *working*?"

"Too soon to tell. Too many things that can go wrong." It was his turn to yawn, and he pulled her closer to him. "For now, all we can do is keep to the path and hope nobody notices."

"Ms. Subianto," Roger said, stopping by the woman's table. "A pleasure to have you in Marduk House. I hope you're enjoying the *basik*."

"Lovely," Subianto replied, touching her lips with a napkin. "A truly new taste sensation. That's so rare these days."

"And this *atul* is great," Tebic said, cutting off another bite. "I can't believe it's so tender."

"We use a special tenderizer," Roger said with a quiet smile. "The rarest ingredients. Marinated for thirty-six hours."

Said ingredients consisted of killerpillar flesh-dissolving enzymes, diluted a hundred-to-one. One of Kostas' discoveries on the long march. The prince forbore to elaborate, however.

"You certainly got this restaurant up and running very quickly," Subianto said. "And in such a . . . prime location."

"Hardly prime," Roger demurred. "But the neighborhood does seem to be improving. Probably by example."

"Yes," she said dryly. "The physicians at Imperial General have noticed some of the . . . examples."

"I hope that's not an official complaint?" Roger raised one eyebrow. "Surely a lonely extraterrestrial has the right to self-defense?"

"It was not, in fact, a complaint at all," Subianto said. "The local PD's gang team thinks you're the best thing since . . . roast *basik*." She smiled. "And many of Parliament's staffers appreciate a restaurant with such . . . elaborate, if quiet, electronic security."

"The privacy of my guests is important," Roger said, smiling in turn. "As much a part of Marduk House's services as anything on the menu, as a matter of fact After all, this is a town with many secrets. Many of them are ones that you're supposed to protect, right?"

"Of course," she said smoothly, "others are ones we're supposed to penetrate. Such as who Augustus Chung really is? Why certain of his associates are meeting with an admiral who's been . . . remiss about responding to orders from central command? Why one Augustus Chung has been receiving heavy weaponry and armor from an off-planet source? What Mardukans are doing training in stingship operations? Why Mr. Chung has been meeting with representatives from the Empress' Own Association? Why, in fact, such representatives—who are notoriously loyal to the Empress—are meeting with him at all?"

"I suppose I could say I have no idea what you're talking about," Roger replied, still smiling faintly. "But that would be a rather transparent, and pointless, lie. I guess the only answer is another question. Why haven't you reported this to Prince Jackson? Or, more to the point, to your superiors, which we both know would be the same thing."

"Because, whatever his current unusual position," Subianto said, "the IBI is in the service of the *Empire*, not Prince Jackson or his cronies. The evidence we have all points in one direction, Mr. Chung. So I'm here, sampling your excellent *basik*, and wondering what in the hell you think you're doing. And who you really are. Because simply capturing the Palace isn't going to help the Empire one bit, and if you have nothing more in your head than that—rescuing Her Majesty from her current admittedly horrible conditions—then . . . other arrangements will have to be made. For the Empire."

She smiled brightly at him.

"The IBI is a department of the executive branch of government, correct?" Roger asked carefully.

"Correct." Subianto eyed her host warily. She'd already noted that her normal charms seemed to slide right off of him. He'd noticed her as a woman, and she was sure he wasn't gay, but beyond that he seemed totally immune.

"And the Empress is the head of the executive branch, your ultimate boss, also correct?"

"Yes."

"And we might as well drop the pretense that the Empress is not under duress," Roger pointed out. "Which means the control of the executive branch goes to . . . whom?"

"The Heir," Tebic said with a frown. "Except that there isn't one. John and Alexandra, and John's children, are all dead, and Roger is reported to be at large and to have been instrumental in the supposed coup. But he's not. Adoula had him killed. The ship was sabotaged and lost in deep space. We know that."

"I hope like hell you found out *after* it happened," "Chung" said, showing signs of emotion for the first time.

"Afterward." Subianto frowned at the intensity of the reaction. "We found out through information received after Adoula took control, but we have three confirmations."

"In that case, Ms. Subianto, I will leave you," Roger said, smiling again, if somewhat tightly. "But in parting, I wish you would join Mr. Tebic in trying the *atul*. It really is as tender as . . . a fatted calf. Please ponder that. Silently." He smiled again. "Have a nice meal."

As their host walked away, Tebic looked at his boss and frowned.

"Fat—" he began. He could recognize a code phrase when he heard it, but this one made no sense to him.

"Don't," Subianto said, picking at the remaining bits of *basik* on her plate. "Don't say it."

"What . . . ?"

"Not here. I'm not sure where. I don't trust our secure rooms to not be monitored by *us*. You're a Christian, aren't you, Tebic?"

"Um." Tebic shrugged at the apparently total *non sequitur.* "Sort of. I was raised Armenian Orthodox. My dad was Reform Islam, but he never went to mosque, and I haven't been to church since I was a kid."

"I'm not sure it's translated into Armenian the same way," Subianto said, "and I'm Zoroastrian. But I recognize it. It's a phrase from the Bible—Emperor Talbot version, I think. That's still the most common Imperial translation."

"I can run a data search—" Tebic started to say, looking inward to activate his toot.

"Don't!" Subianto said, more sharply than she'd intended. Panicked might have been a better word. "Don't even think about it. Don't write it down, don't put it on the net, don't say it in public. Nothing. Understand?"

"No," Tebic said, going gray. "But if you say so ..."

"I do," Subianto said. "Get the check."

The next day, late in the morning, Subianto walked into Tebic's office with a book in her hand. An actual, honest-to-God paper *book.* Tebic couldn't remember seeing more than half a dozen of them in his life. She set it on the desk and opened it to a marked page, pointing to a line of text.

"And bring hither the fatted calf, and kill it;
and let us eat, and be merry:
For this my son was dead, and is alive again;
he was lost, and is found."

At the top of the page was the title: "The Parable of the Prodigal Son."

"Holy ..." Tebic's voice trailed off as his eyes widened.

"Yes." Subianto picked up the book, took out the marker, and closed it. "All that's holy. Let's hope it stays holy. And very, *very* quiet."

"You *told* her?" Catrone yelled.

"There wasn't much she didn't already know." Roger shrugged. "If they'd wanted to arrest us, we'd already be taken down or in a firefight."

"The Bureau won't be monolithic in these circumstances," Temu Jin said with a frown. The IBI agent had been managing the electronic and physical security aspects of the mission, keeping out of sight in the Greenbrier bunker. Of them all, he was the only one who hadn't had a body-mod. No one could possibly discover his connection to Roger without actually going to Marduk and piecing things together, and any attempt to do that would run into major resistance from the locals who were the prince's partisans. Those who'd been his enemies were no longer around to be interviewed.

There wasn't even much danger of Jin being noticed as "out of cover" by the IBI if that organization should happen to spot him. He was openly listed as a communications technician on the staff of the restaurant, and if the IBI used the right protocols, they *might* spot him as one of their own and realize they already had an agent in place. In which case he was in position to file a wholly false report on a minor money-trafficking operation, with no clue as to where the money was coming from.

Then again, he'd been a Counterintelligence and Imperial Security operative, and the head of that division had vanished under mysterious circumstances. He'd also sent out codes telling "his" agents they were in the cold, which meant, in all probability, that the records of one Temu Jin had been electronically flushed. So as long as no one who might recognize him by sight actually *saw* him, he was probably clean. But Buseh Subianto—who'd been in the same department, if not in his chain of command—might just possibly have been able to do exactly that. *He'd* certainly recognized the video of her and her companion, Tebic.

"Subianto is one of the really straight players," he continued. "Apolitical as anyone in Counter-Intel can get. It's why she's been in her current position so long; go higher, and you're dealing with policy, and policy *means* politics."

"She's playing policy now," Catrone muttered. "If she'd filed a report, we'd have Marines or IBI tac-teams swarming all over us. But that doesn't mean she's on our side, Roger."

"She was going to keep pushing," Roger said calmly. "She's an IBI agent, even if she doesn't work the streets anymore, and curiosity is what they're all about. But if I'm the Heir, then any decision she makes *is* policy. My estimate, based on her questions and the manner in which they were presented, was that she'd just keep her head down if she knew who I was. And I was the person handling it; I had to decide *how* I was going to handle it right then. It was my decision to handle it in that way."

"There's another aspect to consider," Eleanora said. "One of our big weaknesses is current intelligence. Up to date intel, especially on Adoula's actions and movements. If we had a contact in the IBI—"

"Too risky." Catrone shook his head. "She might be willing to keep her head down and ignore us. For that matter, I think Roger's probably right, that she is. But we can't risk bringing her in, or trying to pump her for information."

"Agreed," Roger said. "And if that's settled, let's move on. Are we agreed on the plan?"

"Home Fleet is still the big question," Catrone said with a frown.

"I know," Roger replied. "Macek and Bebi are in position, but we need a read on Kjerulf."

"Contacting him would tip our hand." Catrone was shaking his head again.

"That depends on Kjerulf," Roger pointed out. "And we're finding friends in the oddest places."

"I know him," Marinau said suddenly. "He was my CO when I was on Tetri." He shrugged. "I'd say he's probably more likely to be a friend than an enemy."

"You can't contact him, though," Catrone objected. "You're needed to arrange the rehearsals. Besides, we can be damned well certain Adoula's keeping an eye on you."

"Eleanora could do it," Roger said. "He's stationed on Moonbase. That's only a six-hour hop."

"Contacting him for a meet would be . . . difficult," Marinau pointed out.

"Is there some code he'd recognize as coming from you?" Roger asked. "Something that's innocuous otherwise?"

"Maybe." Marinau rubbed one ear lobe. "I can think of a couple of things."

"Well, even after everything else I've done, I never thought I'd stoop to this," Roger said, "but we'll send out a spam message, with your code in the header. He'll get at least one of the messages and recognize the header. I hope."

"I can set that up." Catrone grimaced. "The software's out there. Makes me sick, though."

"We've done worse, and we'll do it again," Roger said dryly. "I know that's hard to believe when we're talking about *spam*, but there it is. Are we in agreement otherwise?"

"Yes," Marinau replied. "It looks like the best we can cobble together to me. I'm still not happy about the fact that there's no reserve to speak of, though. You want a reserve for more than just somebody to retreat on."

"Agreed, and if I could provide one, I would," Roger said. "At least there's the Cheyenne stingship and shuttle force. If they can get here in time. And if it runs long, we can probably call on the Sixth Fleet Marines."

"How's the training on your Mardukans coming?" Catrone asked.

"From what I hear," Roger said with a grin, "the biggest problem is shoehorning them into the cockpits."

"This is pocking cramped," Honal complained.

The bay under the main Cheyenne facility was much larger than the one at Greenbrier . . . and even more packed with equipment. There were fifteen of the later and considerably nastier Bearkiller stingships, four Velociraptor assault shuttles, ten light hovertanks, and a series of simulators for all of them. Honal was currently stuffed into one such simulator, trying out the new seat.

"It's not my fault you guys are oversized," Paul McMahon said.

The stingship engineer had been between jobs when Rosenberg shanghaied him—hiring him off the net for "secure work at a remote location without the opportunity for outside contact." The salary offered had been twice his normal pay rate, but when he found out who'd hired him, there'd been a near mutiny, despite the fact that Rosenberg had been his CO before he retired from the Imperial Marines. He'd only agreed to help under duress and after receiving a sworn statement that he was *not* a voluntary participant. Rosenberg's recorded, legally attested statement probably wouldn't keep him out of jail, but it might let him at least keep his head, although he wasn't wildly enthusiastic about his prospects under any circumstances.

Of course, the engineer might have felt even less sanguine if he'd known who he was really working for. So far as he knew, Rosenberg was simply fronting an Association operation to rescue the Empress; he had no clue that he'd actually fallen into the toils of the nefarious Traitor Prince. Rosenberg didn't like to think about how McMahon might have reacted to that little tidbit of information.

At the moment, however, the man's attention was completely focused on his job, and he frowned as Honal popped the hatch and climbed out of the simulator—not without a certain degree of huffing, puffing, and grunting.

"It wasn't easy changing those seats, you know," he continued as Honal shook himself vigorously, "and the panel redesign and legroom extension were even tougher, in some ways. This model was already a bit like a whole-body glove when all they wanted to put in it was *humans*. And forget ejecting. The motivator is *not* designed for your weight, and we don't have time to redesign it. Not to mention the fact that you'd rip your legs off on the way out; they're in what used to be the forward sensor array."

"Hell with my legs—I can barely move my *arms*," Honal pointed out.

"But can you fly it?" Rosenberg asked. "That's the only thing that matters. We can't *hire* pilots for this, and I've only got a few I'd trust for it. We're really laying it all on the line. Can you *fly* it?"

"Maybe." Honal grimaced, lowered himself back into the simulator, and began startup procedures. "This isn't going to be fun," he observed.

"Tell me about it," Rosenberg sighed.

"How's the rest of the training going?" Honal asked.

"Nominal."

The team moved cautiously down the corridor, every sense strainingly alert, each foot placed carefully.

The corridor walls were blue plasteel, with what appeared to be abstract paintings every couple of meters. They'd looked at one of the paintings, and that had been enough. Within the swirling images, mouths screamed silently and demon faces leered. There was a distant dripping of water, and occasional unearthly howls sounded in the distance.

Raoux held up a fist as they reached an intersection. She pointed to two of their point guards and signaled for them to check it out. The first guard rolled a sensor ball into the intersection, bouncing it off the opposite wall, and then sprang forward, covering the intersection as the rest of the team bounded past. The second point moved down the corridor—then checked as a screamer abruptly appeared, apparently out of a solid wall.

The screamer was nearly as tall as a Mardukan, and had similar horns, but red skin and scales that were at least partially resistant to bead rifle fire. Despite that, the point engaged with a burst of low-powered beads which went downrange with a quiet crack and caught the screamer in the chest.

Unfortunately, the screamer lived up to its name and began howling. Alarms began to shrill in the background.

"We're blown," Marinau snarled. "Plan Delta!"

The team began to move faster, but as they passed a corridor, a blast of plasma came down it, and took out the team member who'd been covering the movement element's advance. Flamers— bigger versions of the screamers, with heavier armor that could at least partially resist the team's *heavy* weapons—came down the side corridor, while more flooded in behind them. Then things like flowers started popping out of the walls, throwing liquid fire that burned their armor.

Raoux blinked her eyes as she came out of the VR simulation, then cursed as more of the team members popped into the gray formlessness of "between" with her.

"Well, that didn't go too well," Yatkin observed with truly monumental understatement.

"No, it didn't," Raoux agreed dryly, shaking her head.

"There ought to be a way we can mimic the flamers, Jo," Kaaper mused.

"Paint ourselves red?" Raoux said bitingly.

"You know what I mean," Kaaper replied as two more figures formed.

One of them was a humanoid, tiger-striped tomcat, a bit short of two meters tall, cradling a bead rifle. The other figure was short, overweight, and young, with mussed hair and messy clothing. It was a standard Geek Mod One, the normal first-timer's persona avatar in the Surreal Battle matrix. He wore holstered, pearl-handled bead pistols for weapons.

"Hey, Tomcat," Raoux greeted, and looked over at the other figure. "Who's this?"

"I'm Sabre," the geek said. "Can I play?"

"Great," Yatkin said. "Just what we need. For cannon fodder."

"Can I play? Huh? Huh? Can I?" Sabre bounced up and down.

"Sure." Kaaper waved a hand, and a screamer appeared out of the air and turned towards the capering figure.

A bead pistol appeared, gripped in both of Sabre's hands. Even as he continued to bounce in excitement, the pistol began spitting beads. The screamer was spun in place as beads took off both arms, then the head. The rounds continued long after the magazine should have quit firing, and the head was blown into pulp before it even hit the ground.

"I got it!" Sabre squealed. "I got it!"

"Hacks are *not* going to help!" Yatkin snarled.

"No hacks," the human-sized tomcat said.

"Bullshit," Yatkin replied.

"No hacks," Sabre said, and changed. Again, it was an off-the-shelf mod, one styled to look slightly like Princess Alexandra. It could be used for male or female; Alexandra had been a handsome woman and made a damned handsome man. It looked very unlike Prince Roger, though, except in the eyes. The mod kept Alexandra's long, light brown hair, and now wore a torn, chameleon-cloth battle suit, patched with odds and ends of much less advanced textiles. Beside the bead pistols, which were now standard IMC military models, the figure carried a sword and had a huge chem-powered rifle across its back.

"Not hacks—experience. In a hard school," Sabre added in cold tones, and there was no trace of the excited kid anymore.

"Have to be a pretty damned hard school," Kaaper replied mockingly.

"Death planet, one each," Roger said to the VR system, and the formlessness changed. Now they were standing on a ruined parapet. Low mounds, the vine-covered ruins of a large city, stretched down the hill to a line of jungle. Rank upon rank of screamers were emerging from the jungle, and a voice spoke in the background.

"I'm sorry ... *scriiiitch* ..." the voice said, breaking up in static. "Forget that estimate of five thousand. Make it *fifteen* thousand. ..."

A hot, moist wind carried the smell of jungle rot as the endless lines of screamers lifted their weapons and began a loud chant. They broke into a run, charging up the hill, soaking up the fire of the defenders, climbing the walls with rough ladders, swarming up the sides, pounding on the gate. Spears arced up and transfixed the firers, hands reached up and pulled them off the walls, down into the waiting spears and axes.

Through it all, Sabre left a trail of bodies as the sword flicked in and out, taking attackers in the throat, chest, stomach. Arms fell and heads flew as he carved the howling screamers into ruin, but they came on. The wall's other defenders died around him, leaving him practically alone against the screamer horde, and *still* the sword flashed and bit and killed. ...

The scene changed again. It was dark, but their low-light systems showed a line of ax-wielding screamers, at least a thousand, charging a small group in a trench. Sabre spun in place, a large chemical pistol in one hand, sword in the other. Bullets caught the screamers—generally in the throat, sometimes the head—as the sword spun and took off a reaching arm, the head of an ax, a head. The trench filled with blood, most of the defenders were down, but still Sabre spun in his lethal dance.

A throne room. A screamer king speaking to Sabre, weird intonations, and a voice like a grave. Sabre nodding and reaching back, pulling each strand of his hair into place in a ponytail. He nodded again, his hands ostentatiously away from the bead pistols on his hips, not watching the guards at his back—not really looking at the king. Eyes wide and unfocused.

"You and what army?" he asked as the hands descended, faster than a snake, and the room vanished in blood.

"Lots of fun," Yatkin said after a minute.

"Oodles and oodles," Sabre replied.

"Yeah, but the firing *had* to be a hack," Kaaper pointed out. "Too many rounds. The old infinite-bead gun."

"Oh, please," Sabre said. "Watch." He summoned a target and drew the bead pistol at his right hip. He didn't appear to be trying to impress them with the draw, but it simply *appeared* in his hand. And then he fired, rapidly, but not as rapidly as he had.

"Not particularly hard," Sabre said, lifting his left hand up for a moment to fire with a two-handed grip.

"You just reloaded," Yatkin said, wonderingly. "You'd palmed a magazine, and you reloaded on the fly. I caught it that time. Son of a bitch."

"Don't talk about my mother that way," Sabre said seriously. Then he lowered his arm and shook it, dropping a cascade of magazines onto the gray "floor."

"Sorry," Yatkin replied. "Sir. But can you really . . . ?"

"Really," Sabre replied.

"So . . ." the tomcat said. "He in?"

"I dunno." Raoux rubbed the back of her neck. "Can he handle armor?"

"Wanna death match?" Sabre inquired with a grin.

"No," Raoux said, after a long pause. "No, I don't think I want to death match."

"The VR training on the rest of the teams is going well," Tomcat told Sabre. "Can't bring in your oversized buddies very well, the sets aren't made for them, and they don't have toots, but their job is pretty straightforward, and they'll have trained teams leading them. I think our opponents are going to be remarkably surprised when we go for the big push."

"Gotta love net-gaming," Raoux said with a nasty smile. "And I've always thought Surreal Battle was the best around. How's our support coming?"

"Well, that's sort of hard to know," Tomcat said, frowning and waving a hand. "Sort of hard to know . . ."

"What fun," Helmut said, shaking his head. "During the Imperial Festival? Why not just put up a big sign: 'Coup in progress!' Security is always maxed during the Festival."

He sat behind the desk in his day cabin. Much as he trusted his personal command staff, this was one message he'd had no intention of viewing anywhere outside the security of his personal quarters. Now he looked across his desk at Julian with what could only be described as a glare.

"Roger will have his reasons—good ones," Julian replied. "I don't know what they are, but I'm sure of that. Anyway, that's the signal."

"Very well. Since Sergeant Julian is certain His Highness has good reasons for his timing, I'll prepare to move the Fleet." Helmut frowned as he consulted his toot and routed orders through it, then nodded. "We're on our way to the next rendezvous point."

Julian blinked. Given the movement schedule Roger's message had included, there was no need for quite that much rush. By his estimate, they had at least ten days' leeway, but he reminded himself that interstellar astrogation was definitely not his strong suit.

"What now, Sir?" he asked after a moment.

"Now we ponder what we'll find upon entering the system."

Helmut hopped off his station chair and walked across to the far side of his cabin, where a large section of deck had been cleared. The architect responsible for designing the admiral's flagship had probably intended the space for an intimate chair and sofa arrangement. Now it was simply a well-worn section of rug, and its function became evident as Helmut folded his hands behind him and started striding up and down it, nodding his head in time with his strides while he considered the skeletal plan and the intelligence updates on the Sol System which had accompanied the message.

"I have to admit," he said after several moments, whether to himself or Julian it would have been hard to say, "that Roger—or whoever put this together—isn't a complete idiot. At least he's grasped the importance of the KISS principle and applied it as far as anyone could in an operation this fundamentally insane. I think, however, that we might be able to improve on it just a bit."

"Sir?" Julian's tone was so cautious Helmut grinned tightly at him.

"Don't worry, Sergeant. We'll do exactly what His Highness wants. I simply think it may be possible to do it a bit more effectively than he envisioned. Or do you think he'd object to the exercise of a little initiative?"

"Master Rog generally thinks initiative is a good thing," Julian said. "Within limits."

"Oh, certainly, Sergeant. Certainly." The admiral's grin turned decidedly nasty.

"The key to his current plan," he continued, "is that we're to arrive four hours before the attack on the Palace kicks off, correct? We'll be almost ten hours flight time out from the planet at that point, but the system recon platforms will pick us up, and that should draw Home Fleet out to meet us. At the very least, given the dispositions in the intelligence packet, it will almost require them to concentrate well away from Old Earth, between us and the planet and out of range to interfere with the attack on the Palace when *it* kicks off, or risk letting us run over individual squadrons and mop them up in detail. Right?"

"As I understand it, Sir," Julian agreed, still cautiously, watching in fascination as the diminutive admiral began to pace faster and faster.

"Well, that's sound planning, given how many imponderables your Prince—or his advisers—had to juggle to come up with it. We'll pose a threat the other side *must* honor. But suppose we could find a way to simultaneously pose a threat they don't realize they *need* to honor?"

"Sir?" Julian was confused, and it showed.

"Roger intends to assassinate Greenberg," Helmut said. "Good start. Wallenstein's his XO, but everyone knows he's only there because Adoula owns him as completely as he does Greenberg. And unlike Greenberg, he's a chip-shuffler, never had a serious field command in his entire useless life. So he's not going to have a support base with Greenberg gone, and *that* ought to put Kjerulf in as temporary CO, at least until one of the other squadron commanders can get to Moonbase. Even then, the odds are that Kjerulf isn't going to just cede that command. So! There are—how many squadrons in Home Fleet, Sergeant Julian?" he barked, spinning on one heel to glare at the Marine.

"Six, Sir!" Julian replied.

"Very good." Helmut spun back to his pacing. "Always remember that fleets and squadrons are *not* just machines, Sergeant; they're *human beings!* A regiment is only as good as its officers. Who said that Sergeant Julian?" he asked, spinning again to glower at the noncom.

"I don't . . ." Julian began, then frowned. "Napoleon?"

"You've been learning, Sergeant," Helmut said, and nodded and resumed his pacing.

"The Prince told me that, I think."

"Then he had good tutors." The admiral frowned thoughtfully. "So, six carrier squadrons, effectively without a head. In that situation, they devolve to local command, whatever The Book says. Which means we must read the minds of those local commanders if we want to predict their actions and reactions. Pro-Adoula? Pro-Roger? Sit it out? Neutrality? Informed neutrality? Nervous breakdown?"

His sentences came out in a staccato. Despite the relentless, machine-gun pace of his questions, it was clear they were rhetorical—that his thoughts were already racing far ahead of even his rapidfire questions.

"I don't even know, off the top of my head, who the squadron commanders *are*, Sir," Julian said, "much less anything about their personalities."

"Eleventh Carrier Squadron, Admiral Brettle," Helmut told him. "Recent promotion via Adoula. Impetuous, but not particularly bright. Two hundred and fifteenth out of a class of two hundred and forty at the Academy. Classroom brilliance doesn't necessarily equate to brilliance in the field, of course, but he's done no better since. Unlikely to have made much advancement, for both personality and ability reasons, without pull from higher up. He had such pull, having long ago given his allegiance to Adoula. Owes one of the Prince's banks a bit more than five years' earnings for an admiral. No indications that he's behind on payments, but I'm sure he is. He spends too much not to be."

"Twelfth Carrier Squadron," Helmut continued. "Admiral Prokourov. Good deceptive tactician. Only middling at the Academy, but much better standing at Command and Staff College, and excellent in exercises. One command in a brief skirmish with the Saints—Saints came off a distant last. I know him—as well as anyone does. Hard to say exactly where his loyalty lies, or what contact he had with Adoula pre-coup. I'd've thought he was loyal to the Empire, but he's still in command, so maybe I was as wrong about him as I was about Gianetto. Operationally, he started as a fighter pilot and likes fighters. Always look for his fighter wings to be where you don't want them to be. . . ."

"Sir, are you consulting your toot?" Julian asked quietly.

"If you have to consult records for this sort of thing, you don't deserve a command," Helmut snapped, and his eyes narrowed as he paced faster.

"Larry Gianetto, Larry *Gianetto*, Larry Gianetto," he half-sang, and did a slight skip in his pacing. "Ground force commander. Never particularly liked him, but that's neither here nor there. Good commander, well-liked in the Marines, considered a really honest man. Clearly a bad reading on many people's parts. But he's a *ground* commander, no experience running a space battle. Leaves the work of Home Fleet to Greenberg, by and large. Still a bit of a micromanager, though. Probably passes some orders, to known Adoula squadrons, directly—undoubtedly pissing Greenberg off. Last report has Fourteenth Squadron as the most solidly Adoula, so . . ."

He hummed the tune he'd been singing to himself for a moment, then nodded.

"Admiral Gajelis has the Fourteenth, and it's been reinforced by a third carrier division. Makes it fifty percent stronger than any of the other squadrons, and four of his six carriers have had their COs switched out since the coup. Very heavy-handed fighter. A cruiser officer—uses them for his primary punch. Thinks fighters are purely for defense.

"Gianetto," he sang again. "Gianetto's going to . . . put Fourteenth in somewhere near Mercury orbit. He'll figure they can react from there in any direction. A 'central reserve' to watch the inner system while he deploys the rest of his forces where they can close in behind any attacker. Very much in keeping with ground force tactics—ground-pounders don't think in terms of light-speed lag the way spacers do. He's overlooking the fact that his outer maneuver units won't know to start maneuvering until he *tells* them to. And if the intel's right, he's using Twelfth to sandwich Old Earth from the outside, same distance towards the periphery as Fourteenth to sunward. Which says things we may not like about Prokourov's loyalties."

The admiral went back to his humming, eyes unfocused, then shrugged.

"On the other hand, it probably also means Gianetto doesn't trust Prokourov quite as much as he does Brettle or La Paz, with the Thirteenth. Sure, he's got him in close to cover Old Earth, but by the same token, he's got Fourteenth close enough to cover *him*. So he's got his 'central reserve' either side of the planet and uses Gajelis to keep an eye on Prokourouv at the same time. Then he scatters the rest of Home Fleet out to watch the approaches.

"Greenberg may've squawked about that—he damned well should have!—but probably not. He knows about me, but he doesn't know about the Prince. So he also 'knows' that *I* know I don't have a hope in hell of accomplishing anything while Adoula controls the Palace and the Empress. *I'm* not going to hit Imperial City with KEWs—not when the Empress is the only person who could possibly rally resistance to him—and I don't have enough Marines to take the Palace against its fixed defenses before the entire Home Fleet closes in on me, signal-lag or no. So he's probably content to let Gianetto put Gajelis and Prokorouv wherever makes Gianetto—and Adoula—happy, while he covers the outer arc of the system with Eleventh and Thirteenth, which he can be confident will fight for Adoula if he needs them."

"What about Fifteenth and Sixteenth, Sir?" Julian asked.

"Out on the periphery with Eleventh and Thirteenth," Helmut said positively. "I'm not certain about Admiral Mahmut, with the Fifteenth. *He's* going to be an Adoula loyalist, but his carrier skippers may have other ideas. Hard to say. Admiral Wu, on the other hand, is not going to be one of Adoula's strong supporters."

Julian looked at him, and the admiral shrugged.

"Look, Sergeant, a lot of the officers who aren't actively opposing Adoula right now are sitting it out because they simply don't see a viable alternative. The Prince is dead, as far as they know, and even if they knew differently, his reputation isn't one to engender confidence in him. So they may hate Adoula's guts and still see him as the only alternative to chaos the Empire simply cannot afford. I've taken pains for years—with, I might add, the Empress' explicit private approval—to build a cadre of ship commanders and senior officers here in Sixth Fleet which is prepared to blow hell out of Adoula and his lackeys anyway.

Which is why Sixth Fleet 'just happened' to be stationed way the hell out on the frontier when the ball went up back at Sol. And also the reason Adoula's cronies at Defense HQ finagled ways for years to whittle Sixth down to the smallest carrier strength of the numbered fleets.

"But the point is, Wu's as apolitical as a flag officer can be these days. She's loyal to the Empire, but she's also cold-blooded enough to put the good of the Empire ahead of the good of the *Empress*. But she's also too good, and too popular with her officers and spacers—most of whom are going to follow her lead if the shit hits the fan—to fire without a really good reason. So Gianetto—and Greenberg—are making what they consider to be the best use of her. They figure they can count on her to resist outside attacks on the system, but maybe not to stay out of it if there's some sort of trouble planet-side. So they stick her out with Eleventh and Thirteenth, but covering a less critical section of the Tsukayama Limit."

"That . . . seems like a good idea," Julian said bemusedly.

"The target is *Old Earth*, Sergeant," Helmut snapped. "Yes, our fleet can come in from anywhere on the TD sphere. But if we come in from the other side of the system, or off-ecliptic, we've got a long drive across the system. That gives Gianetto all the time in the world to maneuver *inside* of us. *If* the squadrons are *near* Old Earth. But if they're still distributed the way they were when our last data packet was dropped, everything except Fourteenth and Twelfth is far too widely dispersed, trying to cover too much of the *system's* volume. Not concentrated. They're going to have to be assembled from all over the system from a cold start to defend the *planet* when we turn up. Figure four hours actual transit time to Old Earth orbit for Fourteenth and Twelfth, but over twelve for the farthest out. We'll be *to* Old Earth in less than ten, and they won't even know to begin moving to intercept us till they get light-speed confirmation of our arrival. So we'll have had a lot of time to start building velocity for Old Earth before *they* do. That's precisely the weakness the Prince—or whoever thought this up—picked up on. They'll *have* to begin reshuffling their dispositions when we turn up, because they're so badly out of position to begin with.

"What Gianetto *should* be doing is worrying about covering the planet, and the hell with the outer system. And he should be putting only forces he knows he can *trust* in close. But Gianetto will go the other way, and Greenberg will let him. Instead of parking Fourteenth directly in Old Earth orbit, where it would already be in position, he's got it stationed way the hell in-system. And instead of allowing only forces he knows he can trust in-system, he's got Fourteenth double-tasked to keep an eye on Twelfth. Keep your friends close, and your enemies closer, where you can keep an eye on them—that's what he's thinking . . . when he should be concentrating on the fact that he's got the *rest* of his units so scattered that they'll find it harder than hell to concentrate before we get to Old Earth ourselves."

"What about Moonbase?" Julian asked.

"A point," Helmut conceded. "And to be fair—which I don't much want to be—probably the real reason Greenberg didn't bitch when Gianetto started spreading Home Fleet all over the backside of hell. Moonbase has the firepower of at least two carrier squadrons' ship-to-ship weapons all by itself, so in a way, he *does* have a task group—without cruisers, of course—in position to cover the planet at all times. But if Kjerulf can take over when Greenberg goes down, that gives *him* control of the Moonbase launchers and emplacements. Assuming he has the current release codes for them, at any rate. Best-case is for him to come in on our side and have the codes, but we can live with it if he only manages to deny Adoula's people access to them."

"That's fixed weapons, Sir. What about the Moonbase fighters?"

"They could be a problem. But there are two companies of Fleet Marines on Moonbase, and I've been careful to ensure that all the *worst* rumors I've gotten about the Empress' condition were dumped on the sites where Marines grouse to each other. I don't even have to guess what the response has been, do you?"

"No, Sir," Julian admitted.

"I've kept the Moonbase fighter wing in my thoughts," Helmut told him with a thin smile. "I'm sure the Marines have, as well. And Kjerulf, I know, has access to the same intelligence."

"Yes, Sir."

"Well, then," Helmut folded both hands behind him and frowned as he resumed his pacing. "The point is, Sergeant, that while Home Fleet will almost certainly move to concentrate between us and Old Earth, as predicted, when we arrive, the fleet's options are going to change rather abruptly when the planet goes up in flames behind them. What will they do then?"

"Turn around to go after the planet after all?"

"No," the admiral said firmly. "That's precisely why the Prince—or whoever—specified that we arrive so early. Gajelis is stationed a tad over four hours from Old Earth on a zero/zero intercept profile. That means that if he wants to stop and drop into orbit around the planet, he'll have to go to decel roughly two hours after he begins accelerating towards the planet. But he'll have been accelerating for *three and a half hours*—it'll take about thirty-five minutes for Perimeter Security to pick up our TD footprint and get the word to him—before anything happens on Old Earth. He won't be able to decelerate and insert himself into orbit. In fact, by the time he overran the planet, decelerated to relative zero, and then built a vector back towards it, we'd be running right up his ass."

"So they're screwed, Sir. Right?"

"Assuming—as I do—that Home Fleet's loyalty to Adoula is going to come unraveled in a hurry when Greenberg buys it and the fleet's officers realize someone's mounting an attempt to rescue the Empress, then, yes, Sergeant. Screwed is *exactly* what they'll be. But if they react quickly enough, they'll still be able to cut their losses and run for it. They'll be inside us, Sergeant. They can break for any point on the TD sphere, and the range will still be long enough for them to avoid us without much difficulty. Which means we could face a situation in which quite a lot of Adoula loyalists will get away from us. And if *he* gets away, as well—a distinct possibility, I submit; he's the sort of man who always has a rathole handy to dash down—we're going to be looking at a civil war whatever your Prince wants. In which case, I further submit, it would be nice if he didn't have any more ships on his side than we can help. Yes?"

"Yes, Sir," Julian said fervently.

"I'm so happy you agree, Sergeant," Helmut said in a dust-dry voice, then wheeled to give him another ferret-sharp smile.

"Which is why we're leaving a little *early*, Sergeant Julian. I have a small detour I need to make."

"Who are these guys?"

"I dunno, Mr. Siminov," the gang leader said, standing as close to attention as he could manage.

Alexi Siminov referred to himself as a "businessman," and he had a large number of fully legitimate businesses. Admittedly, he owned only one of them—a restaurant—on paper; the rest he owned through intermediaries as a silent, and senior, partner. But the legitimate businesses of his small empire were quite secondary to its *illegitimate* businesses. He ran most of the organized crime in the south Imperial City district: racketeering, "protection," illegal gambling, data theft, illegal identities, drugs—they all paid Siminov a percentage, or they didn't operate at all.

"I thought they was just a restaurant," the gang leader continued, "but then I had to wonder. They smelled fishy. Then I guessed they was probably your people, and I made real nice to them. Besides, they've got heavy muscle. Heavier than I wanted to take on."

"If they were one of my operations, I'd have let you know," Siminov said, angrily. "They're laundering money. It's not *my* money, and I'm *not* getting my share of the action. That makes me upset."

"I'm sorry, Mr. Siminov." The gang leader swallowed. "I didn't know."

"No, you didn't," Siminov conceded. "I take it you shook them down?"

"We had to come to an agreement," the gang leader said with a slight but audible gulp. "They were pretty . . . unhappy about an . . . arrangement."

"And if they were one of *my* operations, do you think they would have *come* to an agreement?" Siminov's eyes flickered dangerously.

"Uh . . ."

"I suppose that logic was a bit too much for you." Siminov's lips thinned. "After all, you don't hold your position for your brains."

"No, sir," the gang leader said with a wince.

"You did come to an agreement though, right?" Siminov said quietly. "I'd hate to think you're losing your touch."

"Yes, sir. And you got your cut, sir."

"I'm sure. But not a cut of the action. Very well, you can go. I'll handle the rest."

"Thank you, sir." The gang leader backed out of the office, bowing jerkily. "Thank you."

Siminov rubbed his chin in thought after the gang leader's departure. The fool had a point; this group had some serious muscle. Mardukans were few off-planet, and of that few, quite a number of them worked as "muscle" in one organization or another, but always in tiny numbers. He didn't have *any*, and he'd never seen more than one of them at a time, yet this guy, whoever he was, had at least fifty. Maybe more. And they all had that indefinable air of people who could be unpleasantly testy.

Which meant the direct approach to enforcing his rules was out. But all *that* meant was that he'd need to use subtlety, and that was okay with him. Subtle was his middle name.

"Captain Kjerulf," Eleanora O'Casey said as she shook his hand. "Thank you for meeting with me."

They were in a fast-food establishment in the low-grav portion of Moonbase. She noticed that he showed no trace of awkwardness moving in the reduced gravity.

Kjerulf really did look a lot like Gronningen, she thought. Same size, just a shade over two meters, same massive build, same close-cropped blond hair, blue eyes, and square jaw. But he was older and, she could tell by his eyes, wiser. Probably what Gronningen would have been like if he'd had the time to grow up.

"There are people who handle supplemental supplies, Ms. Nejad," the captain observed, shaking his head as he sat down across the table from her. "I'm afraid I can't really help you in that."

His casually apologetic, meeting-you-to-be-polite tone was perfect, but he knew the meeting wasn't about "supplementary supplies." Not with that "roses are red and sauerkraut's yellow" message header.

"I realize that this isn't, strictly speaking, your area of responsibility, Captain," Eleanora said. "But you *are* a very influential individual in Home Fleet, and the Mardukan comestibles we can supply would be a welcome change for your spacers and Marines."

"I don't handle procurement, Ms. Nejad," Kjerulf said in a slightly cooler tone, and frowned.

"Perhaps. But I'm sure you have some influence," she said. "Left. For now."

He'd opened his mouth to reply before she finished speaking. Now he closed it, and his eyes narrowed. With Adoula replacing everyone who hadn't been bought and paid for, she had a point. But not one that a comestibles supplier would make. It might be one that . . . someone else would make, but whether that was good or bad would depend upon who she represented. On the other hand, Marinau had ended up as a sergeant major in the Empress' Own, he knew that. So—

"Perhaps," he said. "A few of the captains might accept a suggestion or two. But that would depend entirely upon the quality of the . . . supplies."

Eleanora considered the captain's background carefully, and hoped like hell that he'd had the same general upbringing as Gronningen.

"Some of our *atul*," she said, quietly, "are as moist as a fatted calf, Captain."

Kjerulf sat there for a moment, his face unchanging. Perhaps too unchanging.

"Impossible," he said finally.

"No, really," Eleanora replied. "They may be predators, but they're just as tasty—tasty enough even an Armaghan satanist would swear by them. I think you'd like one. They're vicious and deadly to their natural enemies, yes, but they provide a very fine . . . main course."

Kjerulf reached forward and picked a handful of fries off of her plate. He stuffed them into his mouth and masticated slowly and thoughtfully.

"I've never had . . . *atul*," he said. "And I've heard it's not very good, to be honest. And rare. To the point of extinction."

He dusted his fingers against each other to get the salt off, and looked at them distastefully. Finally, he wiped the grease off with a napkin.

"Your information is out of date," Eleanora replied. "They're very much alive, trust me."

"And you have them in-system, where they could be delivered promptly?" Kjerulf asked, still wiping his hands.

"Yes," Eleanora said. "And other fleets have added them to their supply list and found the taste quite acceptable. Much better than they'd expected from some other people's reports."

She picked up a fry of her own and squirted ketchup from a bulb down its length. As she bit delicately into the fry, her other hand squirted out the word "O'Casey" on her plate. Then she picked up another fry and wiped out the ketchup with it.

"I take it you're a senior member of this business venture?" Kjerulf said.

"I'm in charge of marketing and sales." Eleanora finished eating the fry which had erased her name. "And policy advising."

"And other fleets have found these supplies satisfactory?"

"Absolutely," Eleanora replied. "I want you to understand, Captain, that those people you can convince to try this new taste sensation will be in on the ground floor. We're planning on being a big name in the business here in the Sol System. Very soon."

"I'm sure you are," Kjerulf said dryly. "There are, however, many competitors in any business. And ..." He shrugged and frowned.

"We realize that," Eleanora replied. "And, of course, there's the question of monopoly markets," she added, having thought long and hard about how *not* to use the words "Empress" and "Palace" in the conversation. "It's never easy to get started when someone else controls access to the critical markets. But we intend to break those monopolies, Captain, and free those markets. It's central to our business plan. Depending upon the quality of the businesses we find participating in the present monopolies, we might be interested in a buyout. That would depend upon the quality of those businesses' management, of course. We've heard they may have some internal problems."

"And your competitors?" Kjerulf said, puzzling over that rather complicated metaphor string.

"Our competitors are going to find out just how deadly to their future marketing prospects our ability to supply genuine *atul* really is."

"How are your projections?" Kjerulf asked after another pause.

"I'll admit that sales to Home Fleet are a big part of our expansion plans. But they're not essential. Especially since other fleets are already in our supply chain. But I'd hate to have any bickering between the various fleets' supply officers, and sales to Home Fleet would be very helpful. With them, our projections are excellent. Without them, they're . . . fair."

"I couldn't guarantee sales to the whole fleet," Kjerulf said. "I could make suggestions to some of the captains, but my boss—" He shrugged.

"During the expansion phase, your boss won't be an issue," Eleanora said coldly. "And if our expansion is successful, he won't become an issue, either. Ever."

"Good," Kjerulf said, and showed her his first smile. It was a little cold and thin, but it was a smile. She'd seen Gronningen smile that same way so many times it made her hurt. But, on the other hand, it also made her fiercely glad. Things were looking up.

Three days had passed since O'Casey's return from Moonbase. And the pace was picking up. Which explained why none of Roger's human companions were on-site when the visitors arrived at Marduk House.

The human in the lead was a pipsqueak, Rastar thought. The two guys following him were pretty big, for humans, but Rastar towered over them, and Fain and Erkum Pol were watching from the back door of the restaurant. One of the Diasprans was ostentatiously pitching live *basik* to the *atul*, for that matter; that usually tended to bring salesmen down a peg. But this guy wasn't backing up. One of his "heavies" looked a little green—glancing over his shoulder as one of the big female *atul* crashed into the side of her cage, ignoring the squealing *basik* as she tried to reach the Diaspran, instead—but the leader didn't even blink.

"It's really quite important that I speak with Mr. Chung," he said. "Important to him, that is."

"Isn't here," Rastar said, thickening his accent. He'd actually gotten quite fluent in Imperial, but the "big dumb barb" routine seemed the way to go.

"Perhaps you could call him?" the man suggested. "He really will wish to speak to me."

"Long way," Rastar replied, crossing all four arms. "Come later."

"Perhaps you could screen him. I'll wait."

Rastar stared at him for a moment, then looked over his shoulder.

"Call Mr. Chung," he said deliberately speaking in High Krath. "See what he wants me to do. Off the top of my horns, I'd say kick their asses and feed them to the *atul*." He turned back in time to see the leader twitch his face. So, they *did* have updated Mardukan language packs, did they? Interesting. He hoped Fain had noticed.

"Roger," Despreaux said, leaning in through the door to his office. "Krindi's on the com. We've got some heavies of some sort who want to see 'Mr. Chung.' They're pretty insistent."

"Crap." Roger glanced at Catrone. "Suggestions?"

They'd been refining the plan for the Palace assault and looking over the reports from VR training. So far, it was looking good. Casualties in the models, especially among the unarmored Vasin and Diasprans who were to make the initial assault, were persistently high, and Roger didn't like that one bit, but the plan should work.

"Play for time," Catrone advised. "Sounds like you're getting shaken down again."

"It's times like this I wish Poertena were around," Roger said. "Nimashet, rustle up Kosutic. Let's go see what they want. And tell Rastar to let them wait inside."

The visitor was dressed in an obviously expensive suit of muted bronze acid-silk, not the sort of garish streetwear Roger had anticipated. The two heavies with him, both smaller than Roger and nothing compared to the Mardukans, were sampling some Mardukan food at a nearby table. Their culinary explorations didn't prevent them from keeping a close eye on their surroundings, where Mardukans—most of them Diaspran infantry—were setting up for the evening. Erkum Pol and another Diaspran, in turn, were keeping an eye on them. Not at all unobtrusively.

"Augustus Chung." Roger held out his hand. He'd found a tailor who was accustomed to handling large customers, and he was dressed less formally, although probably at even greater expense, than his visitor.

"Ezequiel Chubais," the visitor said, standing up to take Roger's hand. "Pleased to meet you, Mr. Chung."

"And what can I do for you, Mr. Chubais?" Roger sat down, waving Despreaux and Kosutic to chairs on either side of his own.

"You've got a nice place here," Chubais said, sitting back down himself. "Very classy. We're both businessman, though, and we're both aware that the restaurant isn't all the business you're conducting."

"And your point, Mr. Chubais?"

"My point—more importantly, my boss's point—is that there's a protocol about these things. You don't just set up a laundering operation in somebody else's territory, Mr. Chung. It's not done."

"We're already paying our squeeze, Mr. Chubais," Roger said coldly. "One shakedown is all you get."

"You're paying your rent for operating a *restaurant*, Mr. Chung," Chubais pointed out. "Not a laundering operation. There's a *percentage* on that; one you neglected to pay. You've heard the term 'penalties and fines,' right?"

"And if we're disinclined to acquiesce to your . . . request for them?"

"Then we will, with great reluctance, have to take appropriate action." Chubais shrugged. "You've got a lots of muscle, Mr. Chung. Enough that it's a big question in our minds if you're just setting up a laundering operation, or if you're contemplating something a bit more . . . acquisitive. My boss doesn't like people horning in on his territory. He can get very unpleasant about it."

"We're not horning in on his territory," Roger said softly. "We've set up a quiet little operation that has so little to do with your boss that you wouldn't believe it."

"Nonetheless," Chubais said. "It looks like you've pushed through right on two million credits. The percentage on that would be two-fifty kay Penalties for failure to associate us with the operation, and failure to pay previously, are five hundred kay."

"Out of the question," Roger snapped. He paused and thought about it, frowning. "We'll ante up the percentage, but the penalties are out of the question."

"The penalties are nonnegotiable." Chubais stood and nodded to his guards. "We'll expect full payment within three days."

"Chubais, tell your boss that he really does *not* want to push this," Roger said very softly as he stood, as well. "It would be a very bad idea. Possibly the last one he ever has. He has no idea who he's pocking with."

"Pocking?" Chubais repeated, and one cheek twitched in a grin. "Well, Mr. Chung, I don't know where you come from, but you're in our territory now, and it's apparent that you have no idea who *you* are . . . pocking with. If you fail to pay, however, you'll find out."

He nodded, then left, trailed by his heavies.

"Roger," Despreaux said quietly, "our next transfer from our . . . friends isn't due until next week. We don't *have* seven hundred and fifty thousand credits available."

"I know." Roger frowned. "Kosutic, I know everyone's already on alert, but pass the word. They'll probably try to hit us either at the restaurant or the warehouse. I'd guess they'll try to stage something at the restaurant, probably when it's operating. Push the perimeter out a little bit."

"Will do," the sergeant major acknowledged. "It's going to play hell with our training schedule, though."

"Needs must." Roger shrugged. "If it was easy, it wouldn't need us, would it?"

"He was remarkably . . . unresponsive," Chubais said.

"Not surprising." Siminov touched his lips with a napkin. He was having dinner in his sole "legitimate" establishment and enjoying a very nice pork dish in wine sauce. "He's got enough muscle that we'd have to bring in every gang we have. And then we'd probably bounce."

"It would cause him a fair bit of trouble," Chubais pointed out. "Cops would be all over it."

"And they'd find a perfectly legitimate restaurant that was having gang problems." Siminov frowned. "Maybe they'd harass him a little bit, but not enough to shut him down. No, I want what's mine. And we're going to get it."

✧   ✧   ✧

"Sergeant Major," Captain Kjerulf said, nodding as the NCO entered the secure room.

"Captain," Sergeant Major Brailowsky said, returning the nod.

"Have a seat," Kjerulf invited, looking around at the four ships' captains already present. "I've had my own people sweep the room. The posted agenda is readiness training and the next cycle of inspections. That is not, in fact, accurate."

No one seemed particularly astonished by his last sentence, and he turned back to Sergeant Major Brailowsky.

"Sergeant Major, do you know Sergeant Major Eva Kosutic?" he asked coldly.

"Yes, Sir," the sergeant major said, his face hard. "She was in my squad back when we were both privates. I've served with her . . . several times."

"So what do you think about the idea of her being involved in a plot against the Empress?" Kjerulf asked.

"She'd cut her own throat first," Brailowsky said without a trace of hesitation, his voice harsh. "Same with Armand Pahner. I knew him, too. Both as one of my senior NCOs and as a company commander. I was first sergeant of Alpha of the Three-Four-Two when he had Bravo Company. Sir, they don't come any more loyal."

"And I would have said the same of Commodore Chan, wouldn't you?" Kjerulf said, looking around at the other captains. One of them was . . . looking a tad shaky. The other three were stone-faced.

"Yes, Sir," Brailowsky said. "Sir, permission to speak?"

"You're not a recruit, Brailowsky," Kjerulf said, smiling faintly.

"I think I am," the sergeant major said. "That's what this is about, right? Recruiting?"

"Yes," Kjerulf said.

"In that case, Sir, I've known half the NCOs in Bravo of Bronze," Brailowsky said, "and I know what they thought of the Prince. And of the Empress. Between the two, there was just no comparison. That Roger was a bad seed, Sir. There was no *way* they were going to help him try to take the Throne."

"What if I told you they'd changed their minds?" Kjerulf asked. "That while you're right about their nonparticipation in the so-called coup attempt, they'd come to think rather better of Roger than you do? That, in fact, they're not all dead...and that he isn't, either?"

"You know that?" Captain (Senior-Grade) Julius Fenrec asked. He was the CO of the carrier *Gloria*, and he'd been listening to the conversation with a closed, set expression.

"I met someone who identified herself as Eleanora O'Casey," Kjerulf admitted with a shrug. "It *could* have been a setup to try to get me to tip my hand, but I don't think so. Can't prove it, of course...yet. But she says Roger is alive, and she used the parable of the prodigal son, which I think has more than one level of meaning. She also slipped to me that Eva Kosutic is alive, as well. And fully in the plan. I don't know about Pahner."

"That's not much to go on," Captain Atilius of the *Minotaur* said nervously.

"No," Kjerulf agreed, his face hard. "but I've seen the confidential reports of what's going on in the Palace, and I don't like it one damned bit."

"Neither do I," Fenrec said, "And I know damned well that Adoula thinks I'm too loyal to the Dynasty to retain my command. I'm going to find myself shuffling chips while some snot-nosed commander who owes Adoula his soul takes my ship. I don't like that one damned bit, either."

"We're all going to be shuffling chips." Captain Chantal Soheile was the CO of HMS *Lancelot*. Now she leaned forward and brushed back her dark hair. "Assuming we're lucky, and we don't have an 'accident.' And the rumors in the Fleet about what's happening to the Empress—I've never seen spacers so angry."

"Marines, too," Brailowsky said. "Sir, if you're going to make a grab for the Empress...Home Fleet Marines are on your side."

"What about Colonel Ricci?" Atilius asked.

"What about him, Sir?" Brailowsky asked, his eyes like flint. "He's a Defense Headquarters pussy shoved down our throats by the bastards who have the Empress. He's never had a command higher than a company, and he did a shitty job at that. You think we're going to follow *him* if it comes to a dynastic fight, Sir?"

He shook his head, facial muscles tight, and looked at Kjerulf.

"Sir, you really think that jerk Roger is alive?"

"Yes." Kjerulf shrugged. "Something in the eyes when O'Casey was dropping her hints. And I don't think O'Casey is the woman who left Old Earth, Sergeant Major. If the Prince has changed as much as she has ... well, I'm going to be interested to meet him. Roast the fatted calf, indeed."

"Are we going to?" Soheile asked. "Meet him?"

"I doubt it," Kjerulf said. "Not before whatever's going down, anyway. I think they're getting ready for something, and since they seem to be planning on its happening soon, I'd say around the Imperial Festival."

"And what are we going to do?" Fenrec asked, leaning forward.

"Nothing. We're going to do *nothing*. Except, of course, to make sure the *rest* of Home Fleet does nothing. Which is going to take some doing."

"Hell, yes, it is," Atilius said, throwing up his hands. "We've got four carriers! We're talking about four carriers from three different squadrons taking on six full *squadrons*!"

"We're liable to get some help," Kjerulf said.

"Helmut," Captain Pavel of the *Holbein* said. He'd been sitting back, quietly observing.

"Probably," Kjerulf agreed. "You know how he is."

"He's nuts for Alexandra," Pavel said.

"So are you—which is why you're here."

"Takes one to know one," Pavel said, his face still closed.

"You in?" Kjerulf asked.

"Hell, yes." Not even the most charitable would have called the expression which finally crossed Pavel's face a smile. "I figure someone else will get Adoula's balls before I get there. But I'm still in."

"I'm in," Fenrec said. "And my officers will follow me. Regular spacers, too. They've heard the rumors."

"In," Soheile said. "If Roger doesn't move—and, frankly, I'd be astonished if he's changed enough to grow the balls for that—I say we do it ourselves. The Empress is better dead than what's going on, if the rumors are true."

"They are," Kjerulf said bleakly, looking at Atilius. "Corvu?"

"I've only got two more years to pension," Atilius said unhappily.

"A desk is looking good about now." He looked miserable for a second, then straightened his shoulders. "But, yeah, I'm in. All the way. What's the line about sacred honor?"

"'Our lives, our fortunes, and our sacred honor,'" Pavel said. "That's what we're putting down for sure. But this had *better* be about restoring the Empress, not putting that pissant Roger on the Throne."

"If any of us survive, we'll see to that," Fenrec said. "But how are we going to signal commencement? I assume the idea is to keep the fleet from getting close enough to support Adoula's forces with kinetics and Marines."

"Ain't one damned Marine going to board a shuttle, Sir," Brailowsky said. "Except to kill Adoula."

"The Marines are going to have another job, Sergeant Major," Kjerulf said. "What the Marines are going to do is put down an attempted mutiny against the Throne by their own ships."

"Damn," the sergeant major said, shaking his head. "I was afraid it would be something like that."

"That, and certain duties on the Moon," Kjerulf said, and looked around at the others' faces, his own grim. "I don't know everything Greenberg and that weasel Wallenstein have been up to. I may be chief of staff for the fleet, but they've cut me out of the loop on a lot of stuff, especially right here on Moonbase. I've got a really bad feeling that Greenberg's changed the release codes on the offensive launchers, for instance, but there's no way to check without his knowing I've done it. If he has, I'll be locked out for at least ten to twelve hours while we break the lock. That's if everything goes well. And it's also why I need you and your ships in close to the planet."

"Speaking of Greenberg..." Soheile murmured, and Kjerulf smiled thinly.

"I have it on the best of authority that he won't be a factor. Ever again," he said.

"Oh, good," she said softly, showing her teeth.

"But for right now, he definitely *is* a factor," Kjerulf continued. "On the other hand, there are a few things *I* can get away with—routine housekeeping sorts of things—without mentioning them to him, either. Which is how the four of you got detached from your squadrons. I picked you because I figured I knew which way you'd jump, sure, but sliding you and Julius both out of CarRon 13 is also going to make a hole in one of the squadrons Greenberg's been counting on, Chantal."

"Umf." Soheile frowned thoughtfully, then nodded. "Probably the right call," she agreed. "I was thinking that having the two of us in the middle of his squadron might make La Paz think twice about jumping in on Adoula's side when he couldn't be sure who we'd fire on, but you're going to need us here worse, especially with the way Gianetto's reinforced Fourteenth."

"And not knowing which way Twelfth's going to jump," Fenrec agreed sourly, and looked at Kjerulf. "Any read on that?"

"No more than you've got," Kjerulf admitted sourly. "The one thing I'm pretty sure of is that Prokourov's captains will back him, whatever he decides. And whatever I may think, *Gianetto* trusted him enough to give him the outer slot covering Old Earth."

"Yeah, but the one thing Gianetto's dispositions prove is that as an admiral he's a freaking wonderful ground pounder," Laj Pavel pointed out.

"That's true enough, and one of the few bright points I see," Kjerulf agreed. "We're still going to get the piss knocked out of us holding on, even if Prokorouv decides to sit it out with Twelfth. If I can get the launchers on line, Moonbase can cover the outer arc while you people fend Gajelis off, but in the end, they'll plow us under no matter what unless Helmut gets here on schedule."

"He will," Fenrec said, then barked a harsh laugh. "Hell! When was the last time any of us ever saw him miss his timing, however complicated the ops schedule was?"

"There's always a first time," Atilius pointed out dryly. "And Murphy always seems to guarantee that it happens at the worst possible time."

"Granted." Kjerulf nodded again. "But if I had to pick one admiral in the entire Navy to depend on to get it right, Helmut's the one, when all's said. No one ever called him a sociable soul, but no one's ever questioned his competence, either. And if he comes in where I expect he will, and if Thirteenth is already down fifty percent..."

"I see your logic," Chantal Soheile said, and gave him a tight smile. "You really are killing as many birds per stone as you can, aren't you?" She grinned at him again, then frowned. "But this is all still way too nebulous to make me what you might call happy. I know a lot of it has to stay that way, under the circumstances, but that brings us back to Julius' point about the signal to start the op. Was O'Casey even able to set up a channel to tell us when to move?"

"No. But I think we'll probably get all the signals from Old Earth we're going to need to know when to start the music. We'll just ignore the orders we don't like. The orders I've already had cut to move all your ships back to the L-5 Starbase, preparatory for overhaul, should be good long enough to get us through the Festival. If nothing actually happens, then we play things by ear. But that'll keep you all semidetached from your squadrons at least through the end of the Festival. Not to mention keeping you inside all the ships that aren't actually in dock. And I'll make sure all the ships in dock *stay* in dock.

"When the ball goes up, you four move to hold the orbital positions, and hold off Gajelis—and Prokourov, if it comes to that. You may have to deal with the Moonbase fighter force, if I can't get them to stand down. God knows I'm going to be trying like hell, as well as trying to get the missile batteries up *and* talking to all the captains that aren't bought and paid for by Adoula. All we have to do is hold the orbital positions, far enough out that they can't get accurate KEW down to the surface, until Helmut gets here. At that point, with Helmut outside and us inside, Adoula's bastards are either going to surrender or be blown to hell."

"If we don't get blown to hell first," Atilius said.

"Our lives, our fortunes . . ." Pavel said.

"I got it the first time," Atilius said.

"They're not going to be at their best, Sir," Brailowsky said. "Leave that to us. And when the time comes, you can bet we're going to be having some serious discussions with the Moonbase fighter force, Sirs." He wasn't grinning, but it was close.

"Glad you're enjoying yourself, Sergeant Major," Soheile said.

"Ma'am, I've been pretty damned mad about what was happening on Old Earth," Brailowsky said soberly. "I'm very happy to have a chance, any chance, to do something about it."

"Vorica, Golden, Kalorifis, and all the rest of CarRon Fourteen are Adoula's," Soheile said, shrugging at the sergeant major's elan. "Eleventh is going to be split, but I think it's going to go three-to-one for Adoula. Thirteenth won't be split anymore—not with me and Julius both here—but there's a good chance Fifteenth will be. Sixteenth . . . I don't know. Wu's been playing her cards as close as Prokourov has. But Brettle, La Paz, and Mahmut are as much Adoula's as Gajelis, and so are their flag captains. So figure all six of Gajelis' carriers, two of La Paz', three—at least—of Brettle's, and probably at least three of Mahmut's, from the Fifteenth. That's fourteen to our four, and all of them are going to fight like hell. That's damned near four-to-one odds. Even *if* the rest sit this one out. If Prokourov gets off the decicred and comes in on Adoula's side, as well, then we are truly screwed if Helmut doesn't get here right on the dot. And, sorry, Sergeant Major, that's going to be despite the Marines. There's only a squad or two on each of those ships."

"I didn't say it was going to be easy," Kjerulf said.

"How's he going to tell the sheep from the goats?" Ferenc asked. "Helmut, that is. Even if he's fast, we're going to be pretty mixed up at that point."

"Simple," Kjerulf said, grinning ferally. "We'll just reset our transponders to identify ourselves as the Fatted Calf Squadron."

Nimashet Despreaux was not, by any stretch of the imagination, a clotheshorse. Certainly not in comparison to her fiancé. She'd grown up on a small farm on one of the border worlds, where hand-me-downs had been the order of the day. A new dress at Yule had been considered a blessing during her childhood, and she'd never really felt any pressure, even after she joined the Marines and had a bit more spending money, to dress up. Uniform took care of any business-related sartorial requirements, and slacks and a ratty sweater were always in style off-duty, in her opinion.

Still, certain appearances had to be maintained under the present circumstances. She had only three "dressy" outfits to wear at the restaurant, and some of the regulars had to have noticed by now that she was cycling through them. So whatever her personal wishes, it was time to get a few more.

She stepped out of the airtaxi on a fifth-story landing stage and paused, frowning, as she considered the mall. She could probably get everything she needed in Sadik's. She hoped so, anyway. She'd never been one of those odd people who actively enjoyed the task of shopping, and she wanted to get this chore done and out of the way as quickly as possible. Thirty-seven seconds would have been her own preference, but this was the real world, so she'd settle for finishing within no more than an hour.

As she started for the mall, an alarm bell rang suddenly in her head. She was a highly trained bodyguard, and something about the too-casual demeanor of two rather hefty males headed in her general direction was causing a bit of adrenaline to leach into her system.

She glanced behind her as an airvan landed on the stage, and then whipped back around as the heavies she'd already spotted abruptly stopped being "casual." They moved towards her with sudden purposefulness, as if the airvan's arrival had been a signal—which it almost certainly *had* been. But they weren't quite as perfectly coordinated as they obviously fondly believed they were, and Despreaux flicked out a foot and buried the sole of her sensible, sturdy shoe in the belly of the one on her left. It was a hard enough snap-kick, augmented by both training and Marine muscle-enhancing nanites, that he was probably going to have serious internal injuries. She spun in place and slammed one elbow towards the attacker on the right. Blocked, she stamped down and crushed his instep, then brought her other elbow up, catching his descending jaw and probably giving herself a bone bruise. But both thugs were down—the second one just might have a broken neck; at the very least he was going to have a strained one—and it was time to run like hell.

She never heard the stunner.

"Has anyone seen Shara?" Roger asked, poking his head into the kitchen.

"She was going shopping." Dobrescu looked up from the reservation list. "She's not back?"

"No." Roger pulled out his pad and keyed her number. It beeped three times, and then Despreaux's new face popped up.

"Shara—" he said.

"Hi, this is Shara Stewart," the message interrupted. "I'm not available right now, so if you'll leave a message, I'll be happy to get back to you."

"Shara, this is Augustus," Roger said. "Forgotten we're working this evening? See you later."

"Maybe you will," Ezequiel Chubais said from the doorway, "and maybe you won't."

Roger turned the pad off and turned slowly towards the visitor.

"Oh?" he said mildly as his stomach dropped.

"Hello, Ms. Stewart," a voice said.

Despreaux opened her eyes, then closed them as the light sent splinters of pain through her eyes and directly into her brain.

"I really hate stunner migraines," she muttered. She moved her arms and sighed. "Okay. I've been kidnapped, and since I have little or no value as myself, you're either planning on rape or using me to get to . . . Augustus." She opened her eyes and blinked, frowning at the pain in her head. "Right?"

"Unfortunately," the speaker agreed. He was sitting behind a desk, smiling at her. "I suppose it might be 'b' and then 'a' if things don't go as we hope. There are certain . . . attractions to that," he added, smiling again, his eyes cold.

"So what are you asking? Penalties and fines?"

"Oh, the penalties and fines have gone up," the man said. "I'm afraid that, what with my costs associated with persuading your gentleman friend, you'd better hope you're worth a million credits to him."

"At least," Despreaux replied lightly. "The problem being that I don't think he has it on hand as spare cash."

"I'm sure he can make . . . arrangements," Siminov said.

"Not *quickly*," Despreaux said angrily. "We're talking about interstellar transit times, and—"

"—and, in case it's not clear to you, the money isn't all *mine* to distribute," Roger said angrily.

"Too bad." Chubais shrugged. "You'll have the money ready in two days, or, I'm sorry, but we'll have to send your little friend back. One small piece at the time."

"I've killed people for less than telling me something like

that," Roger said quietly. "More than one. A great *many* more than one."

"And if I end up as food for your pets," Chubais said, his face hard, "then the *first* piece will be her heart."

"I doubt it." Roger's laugh could have been used to freeze helium. "I suspect she's worth more to me than you are to your boss."

"Chop away," Despreaux said, wiggling her fingers. "I'd prefer anesthetic, but if you'll just hold a stunner on me and toss me a knife, I'll take the first finger off right here. I might as well; we don't *have* a million credits sitting around at the moment!"

"Well, Mr. Chubais," Roger stood and gestured to Cord, "care to tell me where to send whatever remains there are?"

"You wouldn't dare."

Chubais glanced over at his guards, and the two men got up. They reached into their coats . . . and dropped as an oaken table, designed to seat six diners comfortably, came down on their heads. Erkum looked up at Roger and waved one false-hand.

"Was that right?" he asked.

"Just right," Roger said, without even looking at Chubais as he opened the case Cord held out and withdrew the sword. He ran one finger down the edge and turned it to the light. "Cleaning up the mess in here would be a bother. Take him out back."

Erkum picked up the no longer sneeringly confident mobster by the collar of his thousand-credit jacket and carried him through the restaurant, ignoring his steadily more frantic protests.

"Roger," Cord said, in the X'Intai dialect, which couldn't possibly have been loaded to Chubais' toot, "this is, perhaps, unwise."

"Too bad," Roger ground out.

He and his *asi* followed Erkum out into the slaughtering area, and Roger gestured to the *atul* pens. Erkum carried the mobster over and lifted him up against the pen. The *atul* inside it responded by snarling and snapping at what looked very much like dinner.

"Care to tell me where you're holding my friend?" Roger asked in a deadly conversational tone.

"You wouldn't *dare!*" Chubais repeated, desperately, his voice falsetto-high as the *atul* got one claw through the mesh and ripped his jacket. "Siminov will kill her!"

"In which case, I'll have precisely zero reason to restrain my response," Roger said, still in that lethally calm voice. "Gag him. And someone get a tourniquet ready."

When Chubais was gagged and Rastar had produced a length of flexible rubber, Roger took the mobster's wrist in his left hand and extended his arm. Chubais resisted desperately, fighting with all of his strength to wrench away from Roger's grip, but the prince's hand pinned him with apparent effortlessness. He held the arm rock-steady, fully extended, and raised the sword to take it off at the elbow.

But as he did, Cord put his hand on the sword.

"Roger," he said, again in The People's dialect, "you will not do this."

"Damn straight I will," Roger growled.

"You will not," Cord said again. "Your lady would not permit it. The Captain would not permit it. You will *not* do it."

"If he doesn't, *I* will," Pedi Karuse said flatly. "Des—Shara's a friend of mine."

"You will be silent, *asi*," Cord said gravely. "There will be another way. We will take it."

"Ro—Mr. Chung!" Kosutic came barreling through the door from the kitchen, followed by Krindi Fain. "What the *hell* is going on?"

Roger held the sword, still poised for a stroke, and began to tremble in pure, undiluted rage. Silence hovered, broken only by the *atul's* hungry snarls of anticipation and the gangster's ragged breathing. Finally, the prince twisted his sword hand's wrist, and the blade moved until its razor edge just kissed the mobster's throat.

"You have no idea who you are dealing with," he said, deadly calm once more. "No *pocking* idea at all. You and your boss are two slimy little problems which are less than a flea to me, and killing you would have about as much meaning to me. But a Mardukan barbarian just saved your ass, for the time being. He had more control, and more moral compunctions about chopping up a little piece of shit like you, than *I* ever will. Care to tell me where you're keeping my friend while I'm still inclined to listen to you?"

The mobster eyed the sword, obviously terrified, but shook his head convulsively.

"Fine," Roger said calmly. "I'll try another route. If, however, I'm unable to find the information that way, I'll give you to this young lady." He gestured at Pedi. "Have you ever read Kipling?"

Despite his fear, the mobster's eyes widened in surprise, and he produced another spastic headshake.

"There's a line from Kipling which you'll find appropriate if I don't find the information I want very quickly indeed." Roger's almost caressing tone carried an edge of silken menace. "It begins: 'When you're wounded and left on Afghanistan's plain, and the women come out to cut up what remains.'" He showed his teeth in a sharklike smile. "If the approach I'm about to try doesn't work, I'll leave you, as they used to say, 'to the women.' And she won't be cutting off your *arm*."

"Ms. Bordeaux," Roger said, after the three mobsters—one of whom would never again be a problem for anyone, thanks to Erkum's table—had been flown off to the warehouse in a van. "I need you to go see someone for me."

"Mr. Chung—" Kosutic began.

"I'm in no mood to be 'handled,' Ms. Bordeaux," Roger said flatly, "so you *will* shut the hell up and listen to my orders. You need to somehow arrange a meeting with Buseh Subianto. Now."

"Are you *sure* that's a good idea?" she asked, blanching.

"No. But it's the only idea I have short of chopping that silly little shit up into pieces. Would you prefer I do that, Ms. Bordeaux? Make up your mind, because I'd *much* prefer it!"

"No." Kosutic shook her head. "I'd really prefer that you avoided that."

"In that case, get with Jin and *find* her," Roger snapped. "If she knows where Ni—Ms. Stewart is, we'll go from there. If not, that guy is going to be walking and eating with stumps."

"I thought you said the good guys don't torture people?" Catrone said evenly.

"In the end, I didn't," Roger replied coldly. "And I might argue that there's a difference between torturing someone for vengeance and because you need information they won't give you. But I won't, because it would be an artificial distinction."

He looked at Catrone, with absolutely no expression.

"You should have listened more carefully, Tomcat. Especially to the part about Nimashet being my 'prosthetic conscience.' Because I'll tell you the truth—you'd rather have one of my Mardukans on the Throne than me without Nimashet."

Roger's eyes were cold and black as agates.

"Chubais is an operator for a rather larger fish named Alexi Siminov," Fritz Tebic said. His voice cracked at least a little of the tension between Catrone and the prince, and the IBI agent flashed a hologram of a face. "We have a long list of potential offenses to lay against Siminov, but he's rather ... tricky in that regard. Nothing that we can take to court, in other words."

"I've known Siminov professionally for years," Subianto said.

It had been difficult for the two of them to disappear, especially without warning, but Buseh had worked undercover for years, and she hadn't lost her touch. They'd made it to the warehouse before Roger got there, and the two of them were now bemusedly working a sideline to what was apparently a countercoup.

"He was just starting his rise back when I was in OrgCrime," she continued. "Very smooth operator. Worked his way up in a very tough business. Did some strong-arm work to establish his rep, and clawed his way up, over the dead bodies of a couple of competitors, since. Polished on the surface, but more than a bit of a mad-dog underneath. Kidnapping is his style. So—" she glanced sideways at the prince "—is 'disappearing' the kidnap victim to avoid arrest or to punish an adversary."

"He's associated with several operations," Tebic said. "Theoretically, he could be almost anywhere, but he often uses this building for meetings." Another hologram appeared: a four-story building with some rather large men hanging around the front door. "It's a neighborhood association, technically. In fact, it's where he often meets with the groups he controls. We've tried to bug it several times with no success—very tight security. Armed security, by the way, legally authorized to carry weapons."

"What Fritz is saying," Subianto said, "is that because of our interest in Siminov, this particular building is always under electronic surveillance. And a woman matching the height and shape of your 'Shara Stewart' was seen being carried into the building. Since there was no missing persons report on her, it was assumed she was a street prostitute who'd run afoul of Siminov for some reason. The ImpCity PD wanted to do an entry on the basis that what we were seeing was a kidnap, assuming we could get a warrant. But the idea was shot down. If we did the entry and the presumed hooker had either 'disappeared' or refused—as she probably would—to swear out charges, we'd look like fools. Who is she, by the way?"

"Nimashet Despreaux," Roger ground out. "*Sergeant* Nimashet Despreaux. She's also my fiancée, which makes her a rather important person."

"But not an identity we can use," Subianto pointed out sourly. "Somehow I don't think you want me going to a judge to report that Siminov has kidnapped a woman wanted for high treason under an Imperial warrant. Which means we can't use ImpCity tac-teams to spring her."

"I wouldn't trust ImpCity SWAT to walk my dog," Catrone said contemptuously, "much less to do an entry with a principal this important."

"They're very good," Tebic protested.

"No, they're not," Catrone said definitely. "This is my profession. Trust me, they're not very good at all, Mr. Tebic."

"We know where she is," Roger said, "and we don't *have* the ransom. So I'd best go get her."

"Like hell," Catrone said. "Leave it to the professionals."

"Sergeant Major," Roger snapped, "again, get the wax out of your ears. I *am* the professional!"

"And you're *indispensable!*" Eleanora snapped back at him. "You're not going off on a Galahad mission, Roger. Yes, you'd probably be the best for the job, but you're *not* getting in the line of fire. Get that through your head."

"Try to stop me," Roger said coldly.

"We're on a tight schedule, here," Catrone pointed out, "and we don't have the personnel, associated with the main mission, or the time, to go rescue your girlfriend."

"We are *not* going to leave her to be chopped into pieces," Roger said, coming to his feet with dangerous grace.

"No, we're not," Catrone agreed calmly. "But *you* are essential for gaining entry to the Palace, and you can't be in two places at one time. If you walk out of this room, I'm walking out of the mission, and so is everyone I'm bringing to the table. *I* can handle this; you don't have to get any nearer. Do you know what I do for a living?"

"Raise horses," Roger said, "and draw your munificent pension."

"And *train* tac-teams," Catrone said angrily. "You can't get a weapon anywhere near Siminov's offices; *I* can. And he's got legal bodyguards that are *armed*; a sword isn't going to do you a damned bit of good!"

"You might be surprised," Roger said quietly.

"Maybe." Catrone shrugged. "I've seen you operate. But, as I said, let the *professionals* handle this—and I know the professionals."

"Ms. Subianto," Roger said, "I imagine it's pretty clear what's going on here."

"It was clear before our *first* meeting," Subianto said. "I wasn't aware it was this far along, but it was obvious what was going on. To me at least. I'm fairly sure no one else has connected the dots."

"We could use your help. Especially on current intelligence on movements and on details of Imperial City police security."

"I *hate* politics." Subianto shook her head angrily. "Why can't all you damned politicians solve your problems in council?"

"I wish it could be so," Roger said. "But it isn't. And I hate politics, too, probably more than you do. I tried to avoid them as hard as I could, but . . . some are born to them, some force their way into them, and some are forced into them. In your case, the last. In mine, the first and last. Do you *know* what they're doing to my mother?" he finished angrily.

"Yes," she said unhappily. "That was why I decided to ignore what was going on when you slid me that nice little 'fatted calf' code phrase. But that doesn't mean I want to help you. Do *you* know what sort of a nightmare this is going to cause in Imperial City? In the *Empire*?"

"Yes, I do. And I also know some of Adoula's plans that you don't. But I also know what there is of you in the public record, and what Temu said about you—and that you're an honorable person. What's happening is *wrong*. It's *bad* for the Empire, and it's going to get worse, not better, and you know damned well which side you should be on!"

"No, I don't," Subianto said, "because I don't know that what you're doing is *better* for the Empire."

"Here we go again," Kosutic groaned. "Look, forget *everything* you think you know about Master Rog unless you're prepared to puke up your guts for about four hours."

"What does *that* mean?" Tebic asked.

"She's right," Catrone said. "Ms. Subianto, you know something about me?"

"I know quite a bit about you, Sergeant Major," Subianto said dryly. "Counter-Intel considers keeping an eye on the Empress' Own to be just good sense. You hear too many secrets to not be considered a security risk."

"Then trust my judgment," Catrone said. "And Sergeant Major Kosutic's. Roger isn't the worthless shit he was when he left."

"Why, *thank you*, Sergeant Major." Roger actually managed a chuckle. "Nicely . . . put."

"I'm starting to get that impression myself," Subianto said dryly, "although I'm not so sure he hasn't gone too far the other way. Almost cutting a suspect's arm off to get him to talk doesn't make me particularly thrilled about his judgment."

"You're going to need to block out four hours some time, then," Roger said. "After that, you'll understand what I consider 'appropriate'—and why. And that brings us back to Nimashet. Probably the only reason I didn't cut off the bastard's arm was Cord's very cogent point that Nimashet would not approve. Even to save *her*," he added bleakly.

"I need to speak to this IBI agent you have attached to you," Subianto said equivocally. "I don't recognize his name."

"And there's no record of him in the files," Tebic said. "He's a nonperson, as far as we're concerned."

"He's at the restaurant at the moment," Roger said. "We need to get this operation to pull Despreaux worked out, though. I'll get him headed over right away."

"I'll call my people," Catrone said. "Good thing we've got the datanet wired from here."

"This will *not* be a legal operation," Eleanora pointed out.

"I know. I'm not saying they'll be happy to do it; I said they *would* do it. I thought about bringing them in on the main op, but ... Well, I trust them, but not that far. Besides, they're not combat troops—they're tac-teams. There's a fine line, but it's real. For *this*, though, they're perfect."

"Jin," Roger said, as the IBI agent stepped into the meeting room at the warehouse. "You recognize Ms. Subianto, and this is Mr. Tebic."

"Ma'am." Jin came to something like attention.

"Mr. Jin," Subianto replied with a nod.

"There's some question about your ID, Temu," Roger said, raising an eyebrow. "You don't appear to be listed in Mr. Tebic's records. Anything you'd care to tell me?"

"I was deep cover on Marduk," Jin said uneasily. "Kyoko Pedza's department. I got a coded message to go into the cold when this supposed coup occurred. I've sent two counter messages, requesting contact, but no response. Either Assistant Director Pedza has gone to ground, or he's dead. I would estimate the latter."

"So would I," Subianto sighed. "Which angers me. Kyoko and I have been good friends for many years. He was one of my first field supervisors."

"Assistant Director Pedza managed to dump lots of his files before he disappeared," Tebic pointed out. "It's not unlikely that Jin's was one of them."

"And Jin has been ... an extremely loyal agent," Roger said. "He started covering for us long before we ever even met, and he was instrumental in getting us the weapons we needed to take the spaceport on Marduk. Capable, too; he cracked the datanet on the Saint ship in really remarkable time."

"Saint ship?" Subianto asked.

"It would take far too long to explain even a fraction of our story, Ms. Subianto. The point is that Jin has been an extremely loyal aide. Loyal, I think, to the Empire *first*. He's been assisting me because he sees it as his duty to the Empire."

"Yes, Sir," Jin said. "I'm afraid I'm not one of your Companions, Your Highness—only an agent assisting in what I see as a legitimate operation under Imperial law against a conspiracy of traitors."

"But," Subianto said, still frowning, "while I know a great many of our operatives, at least by name, I'm sorry to say that I don't recognize you at all."

"I'm sorry to hear that, Ma'am," Jin said politely.

"What was your mission?"

"Internal security monitoring," Jin replied. "Keeping an eye on what the local governor was doing. I'd been compiling a report I was pretty sure would have landed him in prison, at the very least. But that's not an issue anymore."

"No, it isn't," Roger said. "Based on the evidence against him, I gave him a field court-martial and had him executed."

"That was a little high-handed," Subianto said, arching her eyebrows. "I don't believe even the Heir Primus has the authority to arbitrarily order executions, however justified."

"It wasn't 'arbitrary,'" Roger said a trifle coldly. "You did hear me use the phrase 'court-martial,' didn't you? I'm also a colonel of Marines, who happened to be on detached—very detached—duty. I discovered evidence of treason while operating under field conditions in which reference to headquarters was not, in my estimation, possible. It's covered, Ms. Subianto. Every 'i' dotted and every 't' crossed."

He held Subianto's gaze for perhaps two heartbeats. Then the IBI agent's eyes fell. It wasn't a surrender, so much as an acknowledgment . . . and possibly a decision not to cross swords over a clearly secondary issue.

"Mr. Jin," she said instead, focusing on the other agent, "I'm sorry to say that Marduk is a fairly minor planet. Not exactly a critical, high-priority assignment, whatever the governor may have been up to. So I have to ask this—what is your IS rating?"

Jin cleared his throat and shrugged.

"Twelve," he said.

"TWELVE?" Roger stared at him. "*Twelve?*"

"Yes, Your Highness," Jin admitted. Twelve was the lowest Imperial Security rating possible for a field agent of the IBI.

"Agent Jin," Subianto said gently, "how many assignments have you had in the field?"

There was an extended pause, and then Jin swallowed.

"Marduk was my first solo field assignment, Ma'am," he said, gazing at the wall six centimeters above her head.

"Holy Christ," Roger muttered. "In that case, Ms. Subianto, I would say Agent Jin is one hell of a credit to your Academy!"

"And it also explains why I don't recognize your name." Subianto smiled faintly. "On the other hand, I have to agree with the Prince, Agent Jin. You've done well. Very well."

"Thank you, Ma'am," Jin sighed. "You understand . . ."

"I do," Subianto said, smiling openly now. "And, I'm sorry, but you're still officially in the cold until we can figure out some way to bring you in again."

"Oh, I think we can do something about that in about two days," Roger said. "God willing. And if nothing goes drastically wrong."

"Jesus, look at the signature on that van!" the monitor tech said. "Hey, Sergeant Gunnar, look at this!"

"Imperial permit IFF," the supervisor replied.

"I know, but . . . geez, that's some serious firepower."

The supervisor frowned and used her toot to dial the van.

"Vehicle Mike-Lima-Echo-Three-Five-Niner-Six, approaching Imperial City northeast, this is ImpCity PD Perimeter Security," she said. "Request nature of mission and destination."

Trey tapped the van's communicator and smiled at the female officer in the ICPD uniform who appeared in the HUD.

"Hey; thought you'd be calling," he said. "Firecat, LLC, Trey Jacobi. We're doing a demo for the Imperial Festival. Check your records."

The supervisor frowned and looked inward with the expression of someone communing with her toot, then nodded.

"Got it," she said. "You can understand why we were wondering. You're radiating wide enough they're probably picking you up at Moonbase."

"Not a problem." Trey chuckled. "Happens all the time."

"Mind if I come by for the demo?" Gunnar asked.

"Not at all. Monday, 9 A.M., Imperial City Combat Range. They say there's going to be a big crowd, so I'd get there early."

"Can I use your name to get a good seat?"

"Absolutely," Trey replied. "Take care," he added as he cut the connection.

"Be an even better demo tomorrow," Bill said from the passenger's seat. "And not at the range."

"Couldn't exactly invite her to that," Dave replied from the back. "Today, ladies and gentlemen, we're going to demonstrate how to smear a group of heavily armed mobsters and retreat before the police arrive," he added in a fast, high, weird voice. "Failure to properly plan and conduct the operation will result in severe penalties," he added in a deep, somber baritone. "If any of the members of your organization are captured, or killed, the department will disavow all knowledge of your existence. This van will self-destruct in five seconds."

"Could somebody *please* shut him up?" Clovis said from the seat next to Dave. "Before we're one short on the mission?"

"Well!" Dave said in a squeaky, teenaged female voice. "I don't think that's a very nice thing to say! I swear, some of the dates I agree to go on..."

"I'm gonna kill him," Clovis muttered "I swear it. This time, he's gonna bite it."

"B-b-but *Cloooovis*," Dave whined, "I thought you were my *friend*!"

The airvan pulled up in front of a hastily rented warehouse several blocks from the Greenbrier facility, then floated inside as the doors slid open. It eased to a stop in the middle of the empty warehouse, and Roger watched as Catrone's "friends" unloaded.

The driver looked remarkably like Roger had before his bod-mod. Shorter—he was probably 170 centimeters—but with long blond hair that was slightly curly and fell to the middle of his back, and a chiseled, handsome face. He moved with the robotic stride of a well-trained fighter, light on his feet, and had hugely muscled forearms.

"Trey Jacobi," he said, crossing to where Roger waited beside Catrone.

"Trey's a very good general operator," Catrone said, "and a former local magistrate. He's also our defense lawyer, so watch him."

"Who's my newest client?" Trey asked, holding out his hand to Roger.

"This is Mr. Chung," Catrone replied. "He's...a good friend.

A very important person to me. He'd probably handle this on his own, but he has a pressing business engagement tomorrow."

The individual who climbed out of the driver's side rear door was a huge moose of a man, with close-cropped hair. He strode over like a soldier and stopped, coming to parade rest.

"Dave Watson," Catrone said. "He's a reserve officer with the San-Angeles PD."

"Pleased to meet you." Dave stuck out his hand, shook Roger's, and then resumed his position of parade rest, his face stern and sober.

"This is Bill Copectra," Catrone continued, as a short, stocky man came around the front of the van. "He does electronics."

"Hey, Tomcat," Bill said. "You're going to owe us one very goddammed big one for this. If you had a daughter, that would be the down payment."

"I know," Catrone replied, shaking his head.

"I had a hot date for this weekend, too," Bill continued.

"You've always got a date," the last man said. He was a bit taller than Bill, and wider, with oaklike shoulders, short-cut black hair, and a wide, flat face. He walked with a rolling stride which suggested to Roger either a sailor or someone who spent a lot of time on civanback. Make that horseback, this being Old Earth.

"This is Clovis Oyler," Catrone said. "Deputy officer with the Ogala department. Entry."

"That's usually my spot," Roger said, nodding as he shook Oyler's hand. "Charge?"

"Usually a modified bead gun," Oyler replied. "You can't stay on the door with a charge. And there's not many doors that won't go down with a blast from a twelve-millimeter bead."

"With a twelve-millimeter, you're not going to have many shots left," Roger pointed out.

"If you need more then three or four, you're in the wrong room," Oyler answered, as if explaining to a child.

"Tac-teams." Roger looked at Catrone and nodded. "Not combat soldiers. For your general information, Mr. Oyler, I usually do the entry in a tac-suit or powered armor and ride the entry charge through. Sometime we'll see who's faster," he added with a grin.

"Told you there was a difference," Catrone said. "And Clovis' technique does tend to leave more people alive and unmangled on the other side of the door."

He shrugged, then turned back to Copectra.

"Bill, we've got an address. We need a surveillance setup. Dave will emplace—taps and external wire. We need a schematic on the building and a count on the hostiles. Clovis, while Bill and Dave take care of that, you do weapons prep. Trey, you do initial layout."

"What are you going to be doing?" Trey asked with a frown. Catrone normally took layout himself.

"I've got another operation to work on," Catrone replied. "I'll be here for the brief, and on the op."

"What's the other op?" Trey asked. "I'm asking as your counsel, here, you understand."

"One of the kind where, if we need an attorney, he won't do us much good," Roger replied.

"Prince Jackson," General Gianetto said over the secure com link, "we have a problem."

"What?" Adoula responded. "Or, rather, what now?"

"Something's going on in Home Fleet. There've been a lot of rumors about what's happening in the Palace, some of them closer to reality than I like. I think your security isn't the best, Prince Jackson."

"It's as good as it can get," Adoula said. "But rumors aren't a problem."

"They are when the Navy gets this stirred up," Gianetto noted. "But this is more than just rumors. CID picked up a rumor about a mutiny brewing among the Marines. They're planning something—something around the time of the Imperial Festival. And I don't like the codename one bit. It's 'Fatted Calf.'"

Adoula paused and shook his head.

"Something from the Bible?" he asked incredulously. "You want me to worry about a Marine mutiny based on the *Bible*?"

"It's from the parable of the *prodigal son*, Your Highness," Gianetto said angrily. "Prodigal son. You roast the fatted calf when the *prodigal son* returns."

"Roger's dead," Adoula said flatly. "You *arranged* that death, General."

"I know. And if he'd survived, he should have turned up some-where within the first few weeks after his 'accident.' But it looks like *somebody* believes he's alive."

"Prince Roger is *dead*," Adoula repeated. "And even if he weren't, so what? Do you think that that airhead could have staged a counter-coup? That anyone would have *followed* him? For God's sake, Gen-eral, he was *New Madrid's* son! No wonder he was an idiot. What was the phrase you used about one of the officers I suggested? He couldn't have led a platoon of Marines into a brothel."

"The same can't be said for Armand Pahner," Gianetto replied. "And Pahner would fight for the *Empress*, not Roger. Roger would just be the figurehead. And I'm telling you, something is going down. The Associations are stirring, the Marines are contemplat-ing mutiny, and Helmut is moving *somewhere*. We have a serious situation here."

"So what are you doing about it?" Adoula demanded.

"What's the most critical point we have to secure?"

"The Empress," Adoula said. "And myself."

"Okay," Gianetto replied. "I'll beef up security around Imperial City. Where I'll get it from is going to be an interesting question, since we don't have that many ground forces we know are loyal. But I'll figure it out. Beef up security around the Palace, as well. As for you, you need to be *moving* the day of the Festival."

"I'm supposed to be a participant," Adoula said with a frown. "But I'll send my regrets."

"Do that," Gianetto said dryly. "At the last minute, if you want a professional suggestion."

"What about the Marines?" Adoula asked.

"I'll replace Brailowsky," Gianetto said. "And have a little chat with him."

"Okay," Eleanora said, breaking into one of the final planning sessions. "We have a real problem."

"What?" Roger asked.

"Sergeant Major Brailowsky was just arrested, and the Marine web sites are all talking about Fatted Calf. I think Kjerulf was a little free with information."

"Shit." Roger looked at the clock. "Twelve more hours."

"Ask me for anything but time," Catrone replied.

"They're going to sweat him," Marinau said. "He's resistant to interrogation, but you can get anything out of anybody eventually."

"He's going to be in the Moonbase brig," Rosenberg said. "That's lousy with Navy SPs. We can't just spring him quietly."

"Greenberg is still in place," Roger pointed out. "If he knows Kjerulf is on our side, and Brailowsky would have to, since they're talking about 'Fatted Calf,' then we'll lose Kjerulf, as well. And they'll know it's going down sometime around the Festival."

"And Kjerulf knows it has to do with Mardukans," Eleanora said with a wince.

"And there's now a warning order on the IBI datanet," Tebic said, looking up from his station. "A coup attempt planned for around the Imperial Festival."

"They know everything important," Catrone said flatly, shaking his head. "We should abort."

Everyone looked at Roger. That was what Catrone realized later—much later. Even *he* looked at Roger. Who was looking sightlessly at the far wall.

"No," the prince said after a long pause. "Never take council of your fears. They know about Helmut, but that was obvious. They suspect I may be alive, but they don't know about Miranda."

He paused and consulted his toot.

"We move it up," he continued, his voice crisp. "It'll take time for them to do anything. Orders have to be cut, plans have to be made, squadrons moved, questions answered. Temu," he looked at Jin, "you've been managing the parade permits. Can we jump the queue? Get the Parade Marshal to move us forward to first thing in the morning?"

"We can if you're willing to risk slipping a little cash into someone's pocket," Jin said after a moment, "and I think I know which pocket to fill. But there's a chance he might smell a big enough rat to raise the alarm."

"Assess the odds," Roger said, and the extremely junior IBI officer closed his eyes for fifteen seconds of intense thought.

"Maybe one in five he'll smell something, but no more than one in ten that he'll do anything except ask for more cash if he does," he said finally, and Roger frowned. Then the prince shrugged.

"Not good, but under the circumstances, better than waiting for Brailowsky to be sweated," he decided, and turned to the other IBI agents.

"Okay, Fatted Calf is the codeword, apparently. Tebic, can you insert something covertly on the Marine sites—the ones they read?"

"Easy," Tebic said.

"Codeword Fatted Calf. Insert it so it will read out at oh-seven-hundred. That's seven hours from now. That's the kickoff time."

"What about Helmut?" Catrone asked.

"Nothing we can do about that," Roger said. "He was scheduled to turn up at ten, and that's when he'll turn up. I hope."

Catrone nodded at the prince's qualifier. Unfortunately, they still hadn't gotten any confirmation from Helmut that he'd even received Roger's instructions, much less that he'd be able to comply with them.

"We don't know anything for sure about Helmut at this point," Roger continued, "but we do know we *need* Kjerulf. He and Moonbase are right on top of us. If he can't at least confuse things up there long enough for us to take the Palace, we're all dead, anyway. And if we wait for Helmut, we lose Kjerulf."

He shrugged, and Catrone nodded. Not so much in agreement as in acceptance. Roger nodded back, then returned his attention to Tebic.

"On the Moonbase net," he said. "Add: Get Brailowsky."

"Got it."

"You sure about that?" Catrone asked. "Security is going to be monitoring."

"Let them," said the prince who'd fought his way halfway around a planet. "We don't leave our people. Ever."

"We need one more thing," Roger said. It was a clear Saturday in October, the first day of the Imperial Festival. A day when the weather computers knew damned well to make sure the weather in Imperial City was *perfect*. Clear, crisp, and beautiful, the sun just below the horizon in Imperial City. The Day. Roger was staring unseeingly at the schematic of the Palace, fingering the skintight black suit that was worn under armor.

"Yeah, backup," Catrone said, looking at the plan one more time.

It was going to be tight, especially with the Bad Guys expecting it. And they were all tired. They'd intended to get some sleep before the mission kicked off, but what with last-minute details and moving it up . . .

"No, I was talking about Nimashet," Roger said, and swallowed. "They're going to kill her the moment your team hits."

"Not if they think it's the cops," Catrone pointed out. "They're not going to want a dead body on their hands on top of everything else. I'm more worried about Adoula killing your mother, Roger. And you should be, too."

"We can't count on that," Roger said, ignoring the jab. "Remember what Subianto said about Siminov—a polished mad-dog, remember? And as much as you say your team is the best of the best, they're not *my* best. And my best, Mr. Catrone, is pretty damned good. And I do know one person I *can* count on."

"We don't need another complication," Catrone said.

"You'll like this one," Roger said, and grinned ferally.

Pedi Karuse liked to dress up. She especially liked the variety available on Old Earth, and she'd decided on a nice gold-blonde dress that matched the color of her horns. It had been fitted by a very skilled seamstress—she'd had to be to figure out how to design a dress for a pregnant Mardukan that didn't look decidedly odd. Pedi had matched it off with a pair of sandals that clearly revealed the fact that Mardukans had talons instead of nails on their feet. The talons were painted pink, to match the ones on her fingers. Her horns had also been expertly polished only a few hours before, by a very nice Pinopan woman named Mae Su, who normally did manicures. Humans had all sorts of dyes and colors, but she'd stayed with blonde this time. She was considering dying them red, since one of the humans said she was a natural redhead personality, whatever that meant. But for now, she was a blonde.

There was the problem of Mardukan temperature regulation, of course. In general, they had none. Mardukans were defined by Doc Dobrescu, who'd become the preeminent (if more or less unknown) authority on Mardukan physiology, as "damned near as cold-blooded as a toad." Toads, by and large, do not do well on cold mornings in October in Imperial City. Most of the

Mardukans dealt with this by wearing environment suits, but they were so . . . utilitarian.

Pedi dealt with this sartorial dilemma—and the frigid environment—in several ways. First, she'd been studying *din-shon* exercises with Cord since she'd first met him. *Dinshon* was a discipline Cord's people used to control their internal temperature, a form of homeopathic art. Part of it was herbal, but most of it was a mental discipline. It could help in the Mardukan Mountains, where the temperatures often dropped to what humans considered "pleasant" and Mardukans considered "freezing." Given that this particular morning was what *humans* considered "freezing," Mardukans didn't even have a fitting descriptive phrase short of "some sort of icy Hell."

Dinshon exercises could help her manage even this bitter cold, but only for a few minutes. So she'd come up with some additional refinements.

Around her wrists—all four—and ankles, she had tight leather bands, with a matching collar around her neck. The accouterments made her look something like a Krath Servant of the Flame, which wasn't remotely a pleasant association, but the *important* part was that the bands covered heat strips that were hot enough to be on the edge of burning. More strips covered her belly and packed around the developing fetuses on her back.

With those and the *dinshon* exercises, she should be good for a couple of hours. And no icky, unfashionable environment suit.

All in all, she looked to be in the very height of style, if you ignored the slight reflection from the poly-saccharide mucoid coating on her skin, as she stepped daintily out of the airtaxi and pranced up to the front door of the Caepio Neighborhood Association Headquarters.

"My name is Pedi Karuse," she said in her best Imperial, nodding at the two men. One of them was almost as tall as she was. If she'd been wearing heels, she would have towered over even him, but he was big . . . for a human. "I'm here to see Mr. Siminov. I'm aware that he's in."

"The Boss don't talk to any scummy walk-in off the street," the shorter of the two said. "Get lost."

"Tell him I'm an emissary from Mr. Chung," Pedi said, doing her best to smile. It wasn't a natural expression for Mardukans, with their limited facial muscles, and it came out as more of a grimace. "And he'd really like to speak to me. It's important. To him."

The guard spoke into his throat mike and waited, then nodded.

"Somebody's coming," he said. "You wait here."

"Of course," Pedi said, and giggled. "It's not like we're going to wander around back, is it?"

"Not with a scummy," the bigger guard said with a scowl.

"You never know till you try it," Pedi said, and wiggled her hips. It was another nonnatural action, but she'd watched human females enough to get the general idea.

The person who came to the door was wearing a suit. It looked badly tailored, but that was probably the body under it. Pedi had seen pictures of a terrestrial creature called a "gorilla," and this guy looked as if he'd just fallen out of the tree . . . and hit his head on the way down.

"Come on," the gorilla look-alike said, opening the door and stepping aside. "The Boss is just up. He hasn't even had his coffee. He hates to be kept waiting when he hasn't had his coffee."

There was a loud buzz as Pedi stopped into the corridor, and the gorilla scowled ferociously.

"Hold it!" he said, surprise and menace warring in his voice. "You got *weapons.*"

"Well, of course I've got weapons," Pedi said, giggling again as three more men stepped into the corridor. "I'm *dressed*, aren't I?"

"You got to hand them over," the gorilla said with the expression of someone who'd never understood jokes, anyway.

"What?" Pedi asked. "All of them?"

"*All* of 'em," the gorilla growled.

"Well, all right," Pedi sighed. "But the Boss is going to be waiting for some time, then."

She reached through the upper slits on her dress and drew out two swords. They were short for a Mardukan, which made them about as long as a cavalry sabre, and similarly curved. She flipped them and offered the hilts to the gorilla.

When he'd taken those, she started pulling out everything else. Two curved daggers, the size of human short swords. A punch-dagger on the inside of either thigh. Two daggers at the neck, and two more secreted in various spots that required a certain amount of reaching. Last, she handed over four sets of brass knuckles, a cosh, and four rolls of Imperial quarter-credits.

"That's it?" the gorilla asked, his arms full.

"Well . . ." She reached up and under her skirt and withdrew a long punch-stiletto. It was slightly sticky. "*Now* that's it. My father would kill me for handing them over so tamely, too.

"Just set it on the pile," the gorilla said. When she had, he offered the armload to one of the other guards and ran a wand over her, carefully. There were still a couple of things he didn't like. She had another roll of credits, for example, and a nail file. It was about two decimeters long, with a wickedly sharp point.

"I've got to have *something* to do my horns with!" she said, aghast, as he confiscated that.

"Not in here," the gorilla said. "Okay, now you can see the Boss."

"I'd better get it all back," she said to the guard with the armful of ironmongery.

"I'm going to love watching you put it all back," the guard replied cheerfully as he carted it into one of the side rooms and dropped it on a convenient table with a semimusical clang.

"So, what's it like, working for Mr. Siminov?" Pedi asked as they walked to the elevator.

"It's a job," the gorilla said.

"Anyplace in an organization like this for a woman?"

"You know how to use any of that stuff?" the guard asked, punching for the third floor.

"Pretty much," Pedi answered truthfully. "Pretty much. Always learning, you know."

"Then, yeah, I guess so," the gorilla said as the doors closed.

"She's in," Bill said.

"One more body to keep from killing." Clovis shook his head. "I hate distractions."

"'Just follow the yellow brick road!'" Davis said in a munchkin voice. "'Just follow the yellow brick road! Follow the, follow the, follow the, follow the, follow the yellow brick road! Just follow—'"

"I've got live ammo," Clovis said, shifting slightly. "Don't tempt me."

"Can it," Tomcat said, reaching up and lowering the visor on his helmet. "Forty-five seconds."

Honal wiggled to try to get some more space in the seat. He failed, and snarled as he began punching buttons.

"Damned dwarfs," he muttered.

"Say again, Red Six," the communicator said.

"Nothing, Captain," Honal replied.

"Outer doors opening," Rosenberg said. "Move to inner door positions."

"Dwarfs," Honal muttered again, making sure he wasn't broadcasting, and picked up on the antigravity. "A race of dwarfs." But at least they made cool toys to play with, he thought, and pressed the button to transmit.

"Red Six, light," he said, then flipped the lever to lift the landing skids and pulled the stingship out of its bay, turning out to line up with the doors to the warehouse. They were still in the underground facility, but once out of the cover of the bunkers' concealing depth of earth, they were going to light up every beacon in Imperial City.

It was time to *party.*

"Three, four, five," Roger counted as he trotted along the damp passageway. Water rose up to the lip of the catwalk, and the slippery concrete surface was covered with slime.

The passage was an ancient "subway," a means of mass transit that had predated grav-tubes. Imperial City's unending expansion had left it behind long before the Dagger Years, and the Palace—whether by accident or Miranda MacClintock's design—was right over a spot that used to be called "Union Station."

Roger was counting side passages, and stopped at seven.

"Time to get the mission face on," he said, looking at his team of Mardukans and retired Empress' Own. The latter were mostly sounding a bit puffed by the three-kilometer run, but they checked their equipment and armed their bead and plasma cannon with the ease of years of practice.

Roger consulted his toot one last time, then opened what

looked like an ancient fuse box. Inside was a not much more modern keypad. Hoping like hell that the electronics had held up in the damp, he drew a deep breath and punched in a long code.

Metal scraped, and the wall began to move away.

Roger stepped into the darkness, followed by twelve Mardukans in battle armor, a half-dozen former Empress' Own, likewise armored, and one slightly bewildered dog-lizard.

"Your first meeting is in twenty-three minutes, with Mr. Van den Vondel," Adoula's administrative assistant said as the prince entered the limousine. "After that—"

"Cancel it," Adoula said. "Duauf, head for the Richen house."

"Yes, sir," the chauffeur said, lifting the limo off the platform and inserting it deftly into traffic.

"But . . . but, Your Highness," the girl said, flushing. "You have a number of appointments, and the Imperial Festival is—"

"I think we'll watch the parade from home this year," he said, looking out the window. Dawn was just breaking.

The Imperial Festival celebrated the overthrow of the Dagger Lords and the establishment of the Imperial Throne, five hundred and ninety years before. The Dagger Lord forces had been "officially" beaten on October fifth; the removal of minor local adherents, most of whom had been dealt with by dropping rocks on their heads, was ignored. For reasons known to only a few specialized historians, Miranda MacClintock had stomped all over any use of the term "October Revolution." She had, however, initiated the Imperial Festival, and it remained a yearly celebration of the continuation of the MacClintock line and the Empire of Man.

The Festival was having a bit of a problem being festive this year. The crowds for the fireworks the night before had been unruly, and a large group of them had pressed into Imperial Park, calling for the Empress. They'd been dispersed, but the police were less than certain that something else, possibly worse, wouldn't happen today.

The Mardukans unloading from trailers, however, were simply a sight to boggle the eye. The beasts they were leading down the cargo ramps were like something from the Jurassic, and the Mardukans were supposedly—and the saddles and bridles bore it out—planning on riding them. The riders were big guys, even for Mardukans, wearing polished mail, of all things, and steel helmets. The police eyed the swords they wore—cultural artifacts, fully in keeping with the Festival and, what was more, tied in place with cords—and hoped they weren't going to be a problem.

The same went for the infantry types. They bore long pikes and antique chemical rifles over their backs. One of the sergeants from the local police went over and checked to make certain they didn't have any propellants on them. Scanners weren't tuned for old-fashioned black powder, and they looked as if they knew which end the bullet came out. They didn't have any ammunition, but he checked out the rifles anyway, just out of personal interest. They were complicated breechloaders, and one of the Mardukans demonstrated the way his broke open and was loaded. The ease with which he handled the rifle spoke to the cop of long practice, which was troubling, since they were supposedly a group of waiters from a local restaurant.

But when they unloaded the last beast, he nearly called for backup. The thing was the size of an elephant, and *clearly* not happy to be here. It was bellowing and pawing the ground, and the rider on its back seemed to be having very little effect on its behavior. It appeared to be searching for something, and it suddenly rumbled to life, padding with ground-shaking tread over to Officer Jorgensen.

Jorgensen blanched as the thing sniffed at his hair. It could take off his head with one bite from its big beak, but it only sniffed, then burbled unhappily. It spun around, far more lightly than anything that large should move, and bellowed. Loudly. It did *not* sound happy.

Finally, one of the big riders in armor gave it a piece of cloth that looked as if it might have been ripped from a combat suit. The beast sniffed at it, and snuffled on it, then settled down, still looking around, but mollified.

It was a good thing the crowds were still so sparse, Jorgensen thought. Maybe that was why the parade marshal had swapped these guys around to the head of the parade from somewhere near the tail? To get them and their critters through and out before the presence and noise of bigger crowds turned the cranky beasts even crankier?

Nah, it couldn't be anything that reasonable, he thought. Not with all the other crap going on this year.

But at least it was going to be an *interesting* Festival.

"Here he comes," Macek said, glancing up from the panel he'd pulled apart and sliding the multitool back into its holster on his maintenance tech's belt.

Macek and Bebi had both been stationed with the Moonbase Marine contingent in an earlier tour, which was why they'd been picked for this job. They didn't like it, but they were professionals, and they'd followed Roger through too many bloodsoaked battlefields to care about one bought-and-paid-for admiral.

"What about the aide?" Bebi asked.

"Leave her," Macek said, glancing at the attractive brunette lieutenant and pushing down his goggles. "Stunner."

Bebi nodded, withdrew the bead pistol from the opened maintenance panel, and turned. Greenberg had just enough time to identify the weapon in his assassin's hand before the stream of hypervelocity beads turned his head into gory spray. The lieutenant beside him opened her mouth as her admiral's brains and blood were deposited across her in a red-and-gray mist, but Macek raised his stunner before she could do anything more.

"Sorry about that, Ma'am," he said, and fired.

Both men dropped their weapons and put their hands on their heads as Marine guards pounded suddenly down the corridor, bead pistols drawn and very angry looks on their faces.

"Hello," Macek said.

"You mother-fu—!"

"Fatted Calf," Bebi interrupted conversationally, lowering his hands. "Mean anything to you?"

"Inner doors opening," Rosenberg said. "Initiate."

The Shadow Wolves swept forward, bursting from their hiding place in the very heart of Imperial City. As soon as he'd cleared the inner doors and had full communications capability, Honal keyed the circuit for all squadrons.

"Arise *civan* brothers!" he cried. "Fell deeds await! Now for wrath, now for ruin, and a red dawn!"

Roger had taught him that. He didn't know where the prince had picked it up—probably some ancient human history—but it was a great line, and deserved to be repeated.

"Oh, shit," Phelps said.

"What now?" Gunnar inquired with a yawn.

"Multiple signatures!" Phelps snapped. "Military grade. Three loca—four . . . *five* locations, two in the Western Ranges! Three of them are *inside* the city!"

"*What?*" Gunnar jerked upright in her station chair, keying up a repeater on her console. "Oh, my God! Not again."

"Where in the hell did they *come* from?" Phelps demanded.

"No idea," Gunnar replied. "But five gets you ten where they're *headed*." She started tapping in a set of commands, only to stop as her connection light blinked out. A fraction of an instant later, there was a rumble from the bulding's subbasement.

"Primary communications link down," Corporal Ludjevit said tersely. "Secondary down, too. Sergeant, we're cut off."

"Find out why!" Gunnar said. "Shit, can't we communicate at *all?*"

"Only if you want to use a phone," Ludjevit told her.

"Then use the fucking *phone!*"

"Luddite."

"Say what you will about all these human devices," Krindi Fain observed, blowing out the match, "there's a certain thrill to gunpowder."

The main communications node for the Imperial City Police Department had just encountered two kilos of the aforementioned gunpowder. The gunpowder had won.

"Humans taught us that, too," Erkum said, scratching at the base of one horn. "Right?"

"Oh, *be* a spoilsport," Krindi replied. "Time to get out of here."

"Right this way," Tebic said. "Getting in was easy." It had been, thanks to IBI-provided clearance for the "technicians." "Getting out, we have to take the sewers."

Imperial City was the best defended spot in the galaxy. Everyone knew that. What most were unaware of, however, was that it was defended primarily against *space* attack. Defensive emplacements ringed the city, and some were located in its very heart, for that matter. But they were designed to engage incoming hostile weapons at near orbital levels.

There were far fewer defenses near the ground.

The stingships used that chink in the capital's armor for all it was worth. Aircars had been grounded automatically, as soon as the city police network went down. That meant the traffic which would normally have been in their way was parked on the ground, drivers cursing at systems that simply wouldn't work. That didn't mean the air was free, just less cluttered by *moving* crap.

Honal banked the stingship around one of the city's innumerable skyscrapers and triggered a smart round. The round went upwards, then back, and impacted on Prince Jackson's office as Honal dove under a grav-tube and made another bank down 47th Street.

A police car at the intersection of 47th and Troelsen Avenue sent a stream of beads his way, but they bounced off the stingship's ChromSten armor like raindrops. Honal didn't even respond. The police, whether they knew it or not, were effectively neutrals in this battle, and he saved his ammo for more important things.

Such as the defensive emplacements at the edge of Imperial Park.

His sensors peaked as one of those emplacements locked onto him, and he triggered two HARM missiles at the radar. They screamed off the Shadow Wolf's wing racks, and he banked again—hard—to put another skyscraper between him and the defenses. The HARM missiles flew straight and true, riding the radar emissions into the defensive missile pods, and rolling fireballs blew the pods into scrap.

But one of the pods had already fired, and an anti-air missile locked onto his stingship and made the turn down 41st Street, howling after him.

A threat warning blazed in Honal's head-up display as the

pursuing missile's homing systems went active. He glanced at the HUD's icons, then dropped the ship down to barely a hundred meters and kicked his afterburners to full thrust. The Shadow Wolf's turbines screamed as the stingship went hurtling down the broad avenue at the heart of the capital city of the Empire of Man, but the missile was lighter, faster, and much more modern. It closed quickly, arrowing in for the kill, and Honal waited carefully. He needed it close behind him, close enough that it couldn't—

He hauled up, riding his afterburners through a climbing loop on a pillar of thunder. His stingship's belly almost scraped the side of yet another skyscraper, and the semismart missile followed its target. It cut the corner to destroy the stingship, slicing across the chord of the Shadow Wolf's flight path . . . and vanished in a sudden blossom of flame as it ran straight into the grav-tube Honal had looped inside of.

"Yes!" Honal rolled the ship and headed for Montorsi Avenue and the next target on his list. "I am Honal C'Thon Radas, Heir to the Barony of—!"

"Red Six," Rosenberg said dryly over the com. "You've got another seeker on your tail. Might want to pay a little attention to that."

"Captain Wallenstein," the duty communications tech said in the clipped, calm voice of professional training. "We're receiving reports of a military-grade attack on Imperial City. IBI communications and Imperial City Police are down. The Defense Headquarters is in communication with us, and the defenses around the Palace are reporting attack by stingships."

"Contact Carrier Squadron Fourteen," Gustav Wallenstein said, turning to look at his repeater display as the same information began to come up there. "Have them—"

"Belay that order," a crisp voice said.

Wallenstein's head snapped around, and his face twisted with fury as Captain Kjerulf stepped into the Moonbase Operations Room.

"What?" Wallenstein demanded, coming to his feet. "*What* did you just say?!"

"I said to belay that order," Kjerulf repeated. "Nobody's moving anywhere."

"*Minotaur, Gloria, Lancelot,* and *Holbein* are moving," a sensor tech said, as if to contradict the chief of staff. "Course projections indicate they're moving to interdict the planetary orbitals."

"Fine," Kjerulf replied, never taking his eyes from Wallenstein. "What's happening on Old Earth is no concern of ours."

"The hell it's not!" Wallenstein shouted, and looked at the guards. "Captain Kjerulf is under arrest!"

"By whose orders?" Kjerulf inquired coolly. "I've got you by date of rank."

"By Admiral Greenberg's orders," Wallenstein sneered. "We've had our eye on you, Kjerulf. Sergeant, I *order* you to arrest this traitor!"

"Why does treason never prosper?" Kjerulf asked lightly, as the Marine guard remained at her post. "Because if it prospers, none dare call it treason. Well, Wallenstein, you've prospered for the last few months, but not today. Sergeant?"

"Sir?"

"Fatted Calf."

"Yes, Sir." The Marine drew her sidearm. "Captain Wallenstein, you are under arrest for treason against the Empire. Anything you say, etc. Let's save the rest until we have you in a nice interrogation cell, shall we?"

"Captain," the com tech said as a slumping Wallenstein was led out of the room, "there's a call on his secure line from Prince Jackson. He's asking for Admiral Greenberg."

"Is he?" Kjerulf smiled thinly. "That particular call might be a little difficult to put through, Chief. I suppose *I'd* better take it, instead."

He seated himself in the chair Wallenstein had vacated and keyed the communication circuit with a tap.

"And good morning to you, Prince Jackson," he said cheerfully as the prince's scowling face appeared on his com display. "What can I do for the Imperial Navy Minister this fine morning?"

"Can the crap, Kjerulf," Adoula snarled. The data hack in the display's lower corner indicated that it was coming from an aircar. "Get me Greenberg. And have Carrier Squadron Fourteen moved in close to Old Earth. Prince Roger's back, and he's trying another coup. The Empress' Own needs Navy support."

"Sorry, Prince Jackson," Kjerulf said. "I'm afraid that, as a civilian member of the government, you're not in my chain of command. And Admiral Greenberg is unavailable at the moment."

"Why is he unavailable?" Adoula demanded, suddenly wary.

"I think he just got a fatal dose of bead-poisoning," Kjerulf said calmly. "And before you trot out General Gianetto—who, unlike you Mr. Navy Minister, is theoretically in my direct line of command—you can feel free to tell him that he's up for the next dose."

"I'll have your head for this, Kjerulf!"

"You're going to find that hard going," Kjerulf told him. "And if we lose, you're gonna have to wait in line. Have a nice day, Your Highness."

He hit the key and cut Adoula off.

"Right, listen up, troops," he said, turning his command chair to face the Ops Room staff and tipping it back. "Does anyone really believe that the first coup was Prince Roger?" He looked around at the assembled expressions, and nodded. "Good. Because the fact is that Adoula led the coup, and he's been keeping the Empress hostage ever since, right?"

"Yes, Sir," one of the techs—a master chief with over twenty years worth of hash marks on his cuff—said. "I'm glad somebody's finally willing to say it out loud."

"Well, you can all make your decision right now," Kjerulf said. "Until very recently, Adoula thought Roger was dead. He's not. He's back, and he's got blood in his eye. Forget everything you've seen on the news programs about the Well-Dressed Prince. Bottom line, he's a MacClintock—and a *true* MacClintock, what's more. The Marines are with us. The captains of the *Gloria, Minotaur, Lancelot,* and *Holbein* are with us, and Admiral Helmut is on the way. He's probably going to be a day late and a credit short, because we had to start the ball early. Anyone who is *not* willing to stand his post—and that's probably going to mean missiles on our heads—head for Luna City, pronto. Anyone willing to stay is more than welcome."

He looked around, one eyebrow raised.

"I'm staying," the com tech said, turning back to her board. "Better to die like a spacer than work for that bastard Adoula."

"Amen," another of the petty officers said.

"Very well," Kjerulf said as the rest of them nodded and muttered their assent. "Send a message to all Fleet Marine contingents. The codeword is: Fatted Calf."

"I love Imperial Festival," Siminov said as Despreaux's float chair was wheeled into the room by the gorilla. "Bookies are busy, whores are busy, and drug sales are up fifteen percent."

Despreaux glowered at him over her gag, then turned to look at Pedi.

"So, as you see, Ms. Karuse," Siminov continued, "Ms. Stewart is unharmed."

"Well, Mr. Chung sent me over to negotiate," Pedi said, grimacing again in an attempt to smile and rubbing her horns suggestively with her fingertips. "You see, he just doesn't *have* a million credits sitting around at the moment. He's willing to offer a hundred thousand immediately, as what he calls the 'vig,' and pay the rest in a few days, if all goes well. In two weeks, at the outside."

"Well, I'm sorry you've come all this way for nothing," Siminov said. "The deal is nonnegotiable. Especially since my emissary went missing," he added harshly. "Perhaps *you* should go missing, Ms. Karuse," he suggested. "That would only— What was that?"

A distant explosion rattled the building, and Siminov and his gorilla looked at one another with perplexed expressions.

"Damn," Pedi said mildly, glancing at her watch. "Already?"

The gang lord and his bodyguards were still trying to figure out what they'd just heard when she slapped Despreaux's chair, throwing it across the room, and dropped forward. All four of her hands hit the floor in front of her feet, and she kicked back with both legs.

Gorilla and his brother went flying back against the wall. They slammed into it—hard—and Pedi pushed off with her lower hands and flipped backwards. She flew through the air, landing in front of the two guards even as they began to reach into their jackets for their bead pistols. Her upper elbows slammed back to connect with their faces, and her lower hands reached down and back. Her more powerful false-hands gripped tight, picked them up by their thighs, and threw them off their feet. They landed on the backs of their skulls with bone-jarring force.

She somersaulted forward, thanking the gods of the Fire Mountains for a high ceiling, and flipped across the desk. All four hands balanced her on its surface as her feet smashed into Siminov, sending him backward to slam against the wall before he could raise the bead pistol he'd pulled from a drawer. He hit with stunning force, and the pistol went flying into a corner of the office.

Pedi somersaulted again, backwards this time, and ended up back between the guards. She grabbed gorilla's hair, tilted his head back so that his throat was extended and unguarded, and flipped the back of her horns across it with a head twist. The sharpened recurve opened it in a fountain of blood, faster than a knife, and she tossed the bleeding body aside and kicked the other guard on to his stomach. She stamped down with one foot to break his neck, then calmly reached over and locked the door.

"Roger thought you might underestimate a woman," she said gently as she strolled back across the room.

Siminov stared at her, stunned by his abrupt encounter with his office wall and even more by the totally unanticipated carnage about him. He was still staring when she picked him up with one lower hand and threw him across the room. He made the violent acquaintance of yet another wall and oozed down it to the floor in a heap, moaning and clutching an arm which had acquired a sudden unnatural bend just below the elbow.

"He especially thought you might underestimate a pregnant one, even if she was a Mardukan," Pedi went on genially. "And, I'll admit, if you were dealing with one of those beaten-down Krath wusses, you might have been having a different conversation."

She picked Despreaux up, heavy float chair and all, and used the sharpened side of her horns to cut the tape holding the human woman to the chair.

"But you're not dealing with one of them," she continued, walking over to where Siminov was trying to get to his feet. His eyes widened at the sight of the bloodsoaked Mardukan looming over him. "I am Pedi Dorson Acos Lefan Karuse, Daughter of the King of the Mudh Hemh Vale, called the Light of the Vales," she ended softly, leaning down so that her face was barely two centimeters from his, "and *that*, my friend, is a *civan* of a different color, indeed."

✧   ✧   ✧

"You seem like a nice guy," Rastar said, lifting the inquisitive sergeant by his body armor in one true-hand as the earbud hidden under his cavalry helmet carried him Honal's message. He flipped his right false-hand in a gesture of apology and ripped the bead pistol off the cop's belt with his free true-hand. "I'm very sorry to do this."

He turned with the sergeant in front of him and pointed the pistol at the other police in the squad which had been watching the Mardukans.

"Please don't," he continued in excellent Imperial as hands jerked reflexively towards holsters. "I'm really quite good with one of these. Just toss them on the ground."

"Like hell," Peterson's second in command said, his hand on his pistol.

"Always the hard way," Rastar sighed, and squeezed his trigger. The bead blew the holstered weapon right out from under the corporal's hand, and the cop bellowed in shock—not unmingled with terror—and jerked his ferociously stinging fingers up to cradle them against his breastplate.

"No!" Rastar snapped as two of the other cops started to draw their own weapons. "He's not injured. But you have a very small area at the top of your armor where you're vulnerable. I can kill every one of you before you draw. Trust me on this."

"And you won't get a chance to, anyway," one of the Diasprans said, lowering a razor-sharp pike until it rested on one of the cop's shoulders. The small group of police looked around . . . into a solid wall of pikes.

Two more Diasprans stepped forward and began collecting weapons. They tossed them to Rastar, who caught the flying pistols neatly as the Diasprans secured the police.

"How many guns do you *need*?" Peterson demanded.

"I generally use four," Rastar said, "but larger caliber. They're on their way." He mounted his *civan* and looked at the Palace, a kilometer away. "This isn't going to be pretty, though."

"Two-gun mojo can't hit the broadside of a barn," one of the cops said angrily.

"Two-gun mojo?" Rastar asked, turning the *civan*.

"Firing two guns at once, you idiot," the sergeant said. "I cannot *believe* this is happening!"

"*Two* guns?"

Rastar turned to look at the police aircar, and his hands flashed. Four expropriated bead pistols materialized in his grip as if by magic and he emptied all four magazines. It sounded as if he were firing on full automatic, but when he was done, there were four holes, none of them much larger than a single bead, punched neatly through the aircar's side panel.

"Two guns are for humans," he said mockingly as he reloaded from one of the officers' expropriated ammunition pouches. Then he turned towards the Palace and drew his sword as the first explosion detonated in the background.

"Charge!"

Jakrit Kiymet keyed her communicator as an explosion rumbled in the distance.

"Gate Three," she said, frowning at the line of trucks setting up for the Festival.

"Military shuttles and stingships detected in Imperial City air space," the command post said tautly. "Be ready for an attack."

"Oh, great," she muttered, looking around. She'd been pulled from guarding Adoula Industries warehouses and made a member of the Empress' Own. That was usually a job for Marines, but she'd known better than to ask questions when she was told to "volunteer." Still, it didn't take a Marine to know that defending the Palace from stingships in her current position—standing in front of the gate, armed with a bead rifle—was going to be rather difficult.

"What am *I* supposed to do about stingships?" she demanded in biting tones.

"You can anticipate a ground assault, as well," the sergeant in the distant, and heavily fortified, command post said sarcastically. "The Palace stingship squadron is powering up, and the response team is getting into armor. All you have to do is stand your post until relieved."

"Great," she repeated, and looked over at Diem Merrill. "Stand our post until relieved."

"Isn't that what we do anyway?" the other guard replied with a chuckle. Then he stopped chuckling and stared. "What the . . . ?"

A line of riders mounted on—dinosaurs?—was thundering

across the open ground of the Park. They appeared to be waving swords, and they were followed by a line of infantry with the biggest spears either of the guards had ever seen. And . . .

"What in the hell *is* that thing?" Kiymet shouted.

"I don't know," Merrill replied. "But I think you ought to tell them to go active!"

"Command Post, this is Gate Three!"

"And . . . time."

Bill swung the airvan out of traffic and dropped it like a hawk at the back door of the "neighborhood association."

Dave had opened the side door as they dropped, and Trey put two beads into each of the guards as Clovis rolled out of the vehicle under his line of fire. The entry specialist hit the ground before the airvan was all the way down, and crossed the alley at a run. He put the muzzle of his short, heavy-caliber bead gun against the lock of the door and squeezed the trigger. Metal cladding shrieked and sprayed splinters in a fan pattern as the twelve-millimeter bead punched effortlessly through it. One bead for the deadbolt, one for the handle, and then Dave kicked the door open as he hurtled past Clovis and charged through it.

Three guards spilled out of the room just inside the entryway. Their response time was excellent, but not excellent enough, and Clovis dropped to one knee, taking down all three of them as Dave went past.

"Corridor one, clear," he said.

Roger keyed the last of a long series of boxes and lifted the plasma cannon. He and his team were ninety seconds behind schedule.

"Show time," he muttered as the door slid backwards, and then up.

The power-armored guard outside the Palace command post door whirled in astonishment as the solid wall of the deeply buried corridor abruptly gaped wide. His reflexes, however, were excellent, and he was already lifting his own heavy bead gun when Roger fired. The plasma blast took off the guard's legs and sent him flipping through the air, and Roger's second shot took out the other guard while the first was still in midair.

That left the CP door itself. The portal was heavily armored with ChromSten, but Roger had dealt with that sort of problem before. He keyed the plasma gun to bypass the safety protocols and pointed it at the door, sending out a continuous blast of plasma. The abuse risked overheating the firing chamber and blowing the gun, and probably its user, to hell. It also made the weapon useless for further firing, even if it survived. But this time, the gun held up, and the compressed metal door ended up with a body-sized hole through its center, while the corridor looked like a rainy day on the Amazon—or a normal Mardukan afternoon—as the Palace sprinkler system came to life.

Roger dropped the now useless cannon and let Kaaper take the entry while he followed at the four position. It felt odd to follow someone else in, but Catrone had been right. Roger was the only person they literally could not afford to lose if some idiot decided to play hero. But there were no lunatics inside the command post. None of them were armored, and although they had bead pistols, they knew better than to try them against armor.

"Round 'em up," Roger said, and strode over to the command chair.

"Out," he said over his armor's external speakers.

"Like hell," the mercenary in the chair said.

Roger raised a bead pistol, then shrugged inside his armor.

"I'd really like to kill you," he said, "but it's unnecessary."

He reached out and picked the post commander up by his tunic. The burly mercenary might as well have been weightless, as far as Roger's armor's "muscles" were concerned, and the prince tossed him across the room contemptuously. The erstwhile commander slammed into the bunker's armored wall with a chopped-off scream, then slithered bonelessly down it. Roger didn't even glance at him. He was too busy punching a code on the command chair's console.

"Identification: MacClintock, Roger," he said. "Assuming control."

"Voiceprint does not match authorized ID," the computer responded. "MacClintock, Roger, listed as missing, presumed dead. All codes for MacClintock, Roger, deactivated. Authorization: MacClintock, Alexandra, Empress."

"Okay, you stupid piece of electronics," Roger snarled.

"Identification: MacClintock, Miranda, override Alpha-One-Four-Niner-Beta-Uniform-Three-Seven-Uniform-Zulu-Five-Six-Papa-Mike-One-Seven-Victor-Delta-Five. Our sword is yours."

There was a long—all of three or four seconds—pause. Then—

"Override confirmed," the computer chimed.

"Deactivate all automated defenses," Roger said. "Lock out all overrides to my voice. Temporary identity: MacClintock, Roger . . . Heir Primus."

The automatic bead guns on the Palace walls opened up. They took down the dozen *civan* immediately behind Rastar in a single burst and traversed for a second.

Then they stopped.

"Thank you, My Prince," Rastar said under his breath. "Thank you for giving my people their lives, twice over."

Civan ran with long, loping strides, heads down and flipping tails balancing them behind. Rastar lay forward over his own beast's neck, all alone now and far out in front of the others. Only Patty had managed to keep pace with him, and the bead guns which had cut down his troopers had wounded her, as well. The big *flar-ta* was more enraged than hurt, however, and Rastar heard her thunderous bellows overtaking him from behind. He drew all four bead guns as they neared the gate, but the two guards at the gate, after a single burst of fire aimed at nothing in particular, turned around and hit the gate controls. The portal opened, and they darted through it.

The gate had opened just far enough to admit them, and it began closing immediately. Couldn't have that.

"*Eson!*" Rastar bellowed to the mahout on Patty's back.

Patty had had a very bad month.

First, the only rider with whom she'd ever had a decent sense of rapport had disappeared, replaced by someone who acted the same way, but just didn't *smell* right. Then she'd been loaded on ships—horrible things—prodded, led around, carted to different planets, unloaded, loaded again, and generally not treated at all as she'd come to expect. And most of the time the food had been simply *awful.* Worst of all, she hadn't even been able to let her frustration out. She hadn't been permitted to kill anything at all since before even the last breeding season.

Now she saw her chance. She'd been pointed at those little targets, and they were getting away. Yes, she'd been pinpricked, but *flar-ta* were heavily armored on the front, lightly armored on the sides, and rather massive. The bleeding wounds lined across her left shoulder, any one of which would have killed a human, weren't really slowing her down. And as the human guards tried to escape from her wrath, and the idiot on her back prodded at the soft spot on her neck, she sped into the unstoppable killing gallop of the *flar-ta* and lowered her head to ram the gate.

The twin leaves of Gate Three were marble sheathing over a solid core of ChromSten. If they'd been shut and locked, no animal in the galaxy could have budged them. But the integral, massive plasteel bolts had been disengaged to let the fleeing guards pass, and the only thing holding them at the moment was the hydraulic system which normally moved them. Those hydraulics were rather heavy—they had to be, to manage the weight of the ChromSten gate panels—but they weren't nearly heavy enough for what was coming at them.

The impact sound was like a flat, hard explosion. Marble sheathing shattered, one of Patty's horns snapped off . . . and the moving gates flew backward.

The mahout on Patty's back went flying through the air, and Patty herself stopped dead in her tracks. She rocked backward heavily as her rear legs collapsed, then sat there, shaking her head muzzily and giving out a low bellow of distress.

Rastar reached the gate, still far ahead of any of the others, and he reined in his *civan* and leapt from the saddle before it had slid to a stop.

The *flar-ta* had prevented the gates from closing, but her huge bulk had the archway *leading* to the gate half-blocked. There was little room to get past her—barely room for two or three *civan* riders at a time—and even as he watched, the hydraulics recovered and the armored panels started to close again. He darted forward, drew one of his daggers, and slammed it into the narrow crack under the left-hand gate. The panel continued to move for a moment, but then the blade caught. The gate rode up it, grinding forward, scoring a deep gouge into the courtyard's pavement. Then there was a crunching sound, and it stopped moving.

He repeated the maneuver with the right-hand gate, then drew his bead pistols as rounds begin to crack around his head. Humans in combat suits, which could stop rounds from bead pistols, were pouring into the courtyard from the Empress' Own's barracks. Most of them looked pretty confused, but the stalled *flar-ta* and the Mardukan were obvious targets.

More beads whipcracked past him, dozens of them. But if he allowed them to push him back, regain control of the gateway even momentarily, they would be able to unjam the gates and close them after all. In which case, the assault on the North Courtyard would fail . . . and Roger and everyone with him would die.

In the final analysis, human politics meant very little to Rastar. What mattered to him were fealty; his sworn word; the bonds of friendship, loyalty, and love; and his debt to the leader who had saved what remained of his people and destroyed the murderers of his city. And so, as the ever-thickening hail of fire shrieked around his ears and pocked and spalled the Palace's wall's marble cladding, he raised all four pistols and opened fire. He wasted none of his rounds on torso or body shots which would have been defeated by his foes' combat suits. Instead, he searched out the lightly armored spot at the throat, the vulnerable chink, no larger than a human's hand.

The combat-suited mercenaries recruited to replace the slaughtered Empress' Own weren't combat troops, whatever uniform they might wear. They were totally unprepared for anything like *this*, and those in the front ranks looked on in disbelief as bead after bead punched home, ripping through the one spot where their protective suits were too thin to stop pistol fire. *No one* could do what that towering scummy was doing.

Humans went down by twos and threes, but there were scores of them. Even as Rastar began dropping them, their companions poured fire back at him, and the calf of his left leg exploded as a rifle bead smashed it. Another bead found his lower right arm. His mail slowed the hypervelocity projectile, but couldn't possibly stop it, and the arm dropped, useless. Another slammed through his breastplate, low on the left side, and he slumped back against the *flar-ta*, three pistols still firing, still killing. More beads cracked and screamed about him, but he kept firing as his *civan* brothers thundered across the final meters of the Park to reach him. He heard their war cries, the sounds of the trumpets sweeping up behind him, as he had upon so many battlefields before, and another bead smashed his left upper arm.

He had only two pistols now, and they were heavy, so heavy. He could barely hold them up and a strange haze blurred his vision. He knew he was finally missing his targets—something which had never happened before—but there were still beads in his magazines, and he sent them howling towards his foes.

Another bead hit him somewhere in the torso, and another hit his lower left arm, but there were fewer humans now, as well, and his *civan* brothers were here at last. He had held long enough, and the riders of Therdan poured past him, forcing their way through the gate, taking brutal casualties to close with the humans where their swords could come into play. Combat suits might stop high velocity projectiles, but not cold steel in the hands of the Riders of the North, and Prince Jackson's mercenaries staggered back in panicky terror as the towering Mardukans and screaming *civan* rampaged through them and reaped a gory harvest.

And the Diasprans were there as well, climbing over the *flarta*, charging forward with level pikes while others picked up the weapons of fallen human guards. They were there. They were through the gate.

He set down his last pistol, the pistol that had been light as a feather and now was heavy as a mountain, and lay back against the leg of the *flar-ta* which had carried his Prince, his friend, so far, so far.

And there, on an alien plain, in the gateway of the palace he had held for long enough, long enough, did Rastar Komas Ta'Norton, last Prince of fallen Therdan, die.

"What's happening?"

"Looks like a dogfight in Imperial City, Sir," Admiral Prokourov's intelligence officer said. "I don't know who against who, yet. And we've got the communications lag, so—"

A priority message icon flashed on the admiral's communicator console, and Prokourov tapped the accept key.

"Prok," General Lawrence Gianetto said from the screen, five minutes after the message had been transmitted from his office on Old Earth. "Roger's back. He's trying to take the Palace. We've got stingships and powered armor on our backs. Get into orbit and prepare to give fire support to the Empress' Own."

"Right." The admiral nodded unhappily. "I don't suppose I could get that order direct from the Empress, could I?"

Larry Gianetto scowled at the wallpaper in the two quadrants of his com display dedicated to CarRon 14 and CarRon 12. That bastard Kjerulf had locked him out of the Moonbase communications system completely, and the general made a firm resolution to have the system architecture thoroughly overhauled after the current situation had been dealt with. And after he'd personally seen Kjerulf dangling in a wire noose.

At the same time, and even through his fury, he knew it wasn't really the system's fault. His office was in Terran Defense HQ, which was the administrative heart of the Imperial military, but Moonbase was the Sol System's operational headquarters. That was why Greenberg had been on Luna instead of with one of his squadrons; because, in effect, Moonbase was the permanently designated, centrally placed flagship of Home Fleet. Every recon platform, system sensor, and dedicated command loop was routed through Moonbase, which was also the toughest, nastiest fortress ever designed by humans. Getting it back from Kjerulf, even after the attack on the Palace was dealt with, was going to be a gold-plated bitch, unless Gianetto had more loyalists in the garrison than he thought he did.

But for the moment, that meant that in a single blow, Kjerulf had blinded Gianetto's eyes. *He* was getting the take from every sensor scattered around the system; Gianetto and his loyal squadron commanders had only what their own sensors could see. And it also meant Gianetto had to individually contact each squadron commander through alternate channels. Channels which he was not at all certain were going to be proof against Moonbase's eavesdropping, despite their encryption software.

He drummed on his desk nervously. It was going to take five minutes for Prokourov's and Gajelis' acknowledgments of his movement orders to reach him. And the signal-lag to his other squadrons was at least four times that long. He grimaced as he admitted that Greenberg had had a point after all when he'd pointed out that communications delay out to him. He'd brushed it aside at the time—after all, he'd known all about it for his entire professional career, hadn't he? But it turned out that what he'd known intellectually about its implications for naval operations and what he'd really understood weren't necessarily the same thing. He was a Marine. He'd always left the business of coordinating naval movements up to the Navy pukes, just as he'd left it to Greenberg. His own tactical communication loops had always been much shorter, with signal lag measured in no more than several seconds. He hadn't really allowed for order-response cycles this tortoiselike, and he wasn't emotionally suited to sitting here waiting for messages to pass back and forth with such glacial slowness.

He glowered at the other holographic displays floating in his superbly equipped office, and this time his scowl was a snarl. Light-speed transmission rates weren't the only things that could contribute to uncertainty. Finding someone—anyone!—who knew what the hell was going on could do the same thing. And despite all of the sophisticated communications equipment at his disposal, he didn't have a *clue* yet what was happening at the Palace. Except that it was bad.

Very bad.

"Plasma rifles!" Trey snarled, rolling back from the corridor as a blast cooked the far wall. "Nobody said they had *plasma guns!*"

"Plasma in the morning makes me happy!" Dave caroled in a high tenor. "Plasma in my eyyyyes can make me cryyyyyy!"

"Bill?" Catrone said.

"They just started popping up," the technician replied over Catrone's helmet com. "Seven sources. They must have had them shielded in the basement someplace. Three closing. Two in Alpha Quadrant, moving right.

"Then they've got the stairs," Catrone said. They'd made it to the second floor, but now they were getting pinned down and surrounded by heavier firepower.

"I'm down to twenty rounds," Clovis said, thumbing in another magazine. "Starting to see what your friend meant about combat troops. Which is the *only* reason I'm not killing Dave right now!"

"Yeah, we need some serious firepower," Catrone agreed tightly. "But—"

"Tomcat," Bill said. "Stand by. Help's on the way."

"Did *you* know they had plasma guns?" Despreaux asked as she triggered another burst at the left side of the doorway.

"No," Pedi said, aiming carefully at a leg which had exposed itself on the right side of the door. She missed . . . again. "Did you?"

"No," Despreaux said tightly.

"It's not like you could have told us, or anything," Pedi said, deciding to just spray and pray. Most of the rounds hit the wall, which they had discovered was armored plasteel. "So, if you did know, you can admit it. Just to me. Between friends."

"I *didn't*," Despreaux said angrily. "Okay?"

"All right, all right," Pedi said pacifically. "How do you reload one of these things, again?"

"Look, just . . . stay down and let me do the shooting," Despreaux said. "Okay?"

"Okay," Pedi replied with a pout. "I wish I had my swords."

"I wish I had my Roger," Despreaux said unhappily.

"Look, Erkum," Krindi said gently, eyeing the weapon his friend was carrying. "Let me do the shooting, all right? You just watch my back."

He looked up at the towering noncom one last time, while a small, still voice in the back of his brain asked him if this was *really* a good idea. Erkum was the only person, even among the Mardukans, who could have carried one of the light tank cannon the Alphanes had supplied—*and* its power pack—without benefit of powered armor. The sheer intimidation factor of seeing that coming at them should be enough to convince Siminov's goons to be elsewhere. Of course, there *were* possible downsides to the proposition. . . .

"Watch my back," he repeated firmly.

"Okay, Krindi," Erkum said, then kicked in the front door of the Neighborhood Association and stepped through it, tank cannon held mid-shoulder-high and leveled. The sudden intrusion froze the group of guards at the other end of the corridor for a moment as they turned, and their eyes widened in horror as they caught sight of him. Then he pulled the trigger.

The round came nowhere near the humans. Instead, it blew out the corridor's entire left wall, opening up half a dozen rooms on that side, then impacted on a structural girder and exploded in a ball of plasma.

Pol's finger, unfortunately, had clamped down on the trigger, and two more plasma bolts shrieked from his muzzle, blowing out a thirty-meter hole that engulfed the ceiling and most of the *right* wall, as well. The building was instantly aflame, but at least between them, the follow-up bolts had managed to take out most of the guards who'd been his nominal targets.

"Water *damn it*, Erkum!" Krindi dropped to one knee and expertly double-tapped the only human still standing with his bead rifle. "I told you *not* to fire!"

"Sorry," Erkum said. "I'm just getting used to this thing. I'll do better."

"Don't *try!*" Krindi yelled.

"Ooooo! There's one!" Erkum said as a guard skittered to a halt, looking at them through the flames of several eviscerated rooms on the right side of the mangled passageway. The human raised his weapon, thought better of it, and tried to run.

Erkum aimed carefully, and the round—following more or less the damage path to the *left* of their position—went through the room and hit a stove in the kitchen on the back wall, blowing a hole out the back of the building and into the one on the other side of the service alley, which promptly began spouting flames of its own. If the running guard had even noticed the shot, it wasn't evident.

Erkum tried again ... and opened up a new hole in the ceiling. Then his finger hit the firing button to no avail as the cannon's internal protocols locked it down long enough to cool to safe operating levels.

"I'm out of bullets," he said wistfully. "How do you reload this thing?"

"Just ... use it as a club," Krindi said, running to the end of the corridor with Erkum on his heels. Despite this planet's hellish climate, he was pretty sure he wouldn't have needed his environment suit anymore. The building was getting hot as hell.

"What the hell was that?" Clovis shouted.

"I don't know," Trey said, checking right, "but this place is *seriously* on fire!" He fired once, and then again. "Clear."

"I'm melting!" Dave shouted in a cracked falsetto. "I'm melllllt-ing!" he added, taking down two guards who had just rounded a corner at the run.

"Up," Catrone said. "Whatever it was, it's given us an opening. Let's take it."

He tapped Dave on the shoulder and pointed right.

"Daddy, don't touch me there, please?" Dave said in a little kid's voice as he bounded down the corridor and skidded around the corner on his stomach. He cracked out three rounds from the bead gun and then waved.

"Corridor clear," he said in a cold and remote voice.

"Office of the Prime Minister," a harassed woman said, not looking up at the screen. Sounds of other confused conversations came through from behind her, evidence of a crowded communications center without a clue of what was happening.

Eleanora cursed the fact that the only current number she had was the standard public line.

"I need to speak to the Prime Minister," she said pointedly.

"I'm sorry, Ma'am," the receptionist said. "The Prime Minister is a busy man, and we're all just a little preoccupied here. Perhaps you could call back some other time."

She started to reach for the disconnect key, and Eleanora spoke sharply.

"My name is Eleanora O'Casey," she said. "I am chief of staff to Prince Roger Ramius MacClintock. Does that ring any bells?"

The woman looked up at last, her eyes widening, then shrugged.

"Prove it," she said, her voice as sharp as Eleanora's. "We get all sorts of cranks. And I've seen pictures of Ms. O'Casey. They don't look a thing like *you*."

"Are you aware that there's a battle going on in the city?"

"Who isn't?"

"Well, if Prime Minister Yang wants to know what's going on, you'd better put me through to him."

"Damn it," Adoula snarled into the com screen. "*Damn* it! It really is that little bastard Roger, isn't it?"

"It looks that way," Gianetto agreed. "We haven't captured anyone who's actually talked to him, but there's a widespread belief that he's back, and more his mother's son than his father's, if you get my drift. And they may be right. If I didn't know exactly where she's been and what her condition is, I'd say this plan had Alexandra's markings all over it. Especially the assassination of Greenberg. If it hadn't been for that . . ." He shrugged. "The point is, I'd say there's an excellent chance that they're going to at least get control of the Palace. And they've already taken out your office downtown. I'd be surprised if they hadn't made arrangements to deal with your other probable locations."

"Very well," Adoula said. "I understand. You know the plan."

He switched off the communicator and sat for just a moment, looking around his home. It was a pleasant place, and it pained him to think of giving it up forever. But sometimes sacrifices had to be made, and he could always build another house.

He stood up and went to the door, looking through it into the office on the far side.

"Yes, sir?" his administrative assistant said, looking up with obvious relief. "There are a number of messages, some of them pretty urgent, and I think—"

"Yes, I'm sure," Adoula said, frowning thoughtfully. "It's all most disturbing—*most* disturbing. I'm going to step out for a moment, get a breath of fresh air and clear my brain. When I come back, we'll handle those messages."

"Yes, sir," the woman said with an even more relieved smile.

She really was rather attractive, the prince reflected. But attractive administrative assistants were a decicred a dozen.

Adoula walked back to his own office, and out the French doors to the patio. From there it was a short walk through the garden to the back lawn, where a shuttle waited.

"Time for us to go visit the *Hannah*, Duauf," he said, nodding to his chauffeur/pilot as he stepped aboard.

The chauffeur nodded, and Jackson settled back into his

comfortable seat and pressed a button on the armrest. The sizable charge of cataclysmite under his mansion's foundations detonated in a blinding-white fireball that virtually vaporized the building, all of the incriminating records stored on site, and his entire home office and domestic staff.

A tragedy, he thought, but a necessary one. And not just to tie up loose ends.

Admiral Prokourov spent the ten-minute delay while he waited for Gianetto's response to his own reply dictating messages to his squadron to prepare for movement. He also sent one other message of his own to another address while he waited. When the general's reply came, it was more or less what he'd anticipated.

"You've got the frigging order from *me*." Obviously, Gianetto had also been giving orders on another screen while he waited, but he snapped his head back to glare into the monitor and snarled the reply as soon as he heard the admiral. "And if you don't think you can do the job, I'll find someone who *will*! We don't have time to dick around, Prok!"

"Four hours-plus from our current position," Prokourov said with a shrug. "We'll start moving—"

The admiral paused as his shipboard office's hatch opened, and his eyes widened as he saw the bead pistol in the Marine sergeant's hand.

The Marine walked over and glanced at the monitor, then smiled.

"General Gianetto," he said solicitously. "What a pleasant surprise! You may be unhappy to hear this, but Carrier Squadron Twelve isn't going anywhere, you traitorous son of a bitch!"

He keyed the communicator off long before the general even heard the words, much less had a chance to formulate a reply. Then he turned to Prokourov. He opened his mouth, but the admiral gestured at the gun in his hand.

"Thank you, Sergeant," Prokourov said, "but that won't be necessary."

"Oh?" the sergeant said warily, and glanced over his shoulder. There was one other Marine at the hatch, but the rest of the flagship's Marine detachment was spread out attending to other duties, involving things like bridges and engineering spaces.

"Oh," Prokourov replied. "Do you *know* what's going on, Sergeant?"

"No, Sir," the sergeant replied. He started to lower his bead pistol, then paused, eyeing the admiral warily. "All I know is that we were supposed to do everything we could to prevent Home Fleet from moving to the support of the Palace and, especially, of General Gianetto."

"So what's your chain of command?" the intel officer asked with a frown.

"Dunno, Sir. Word is that the Prince's back, and he's taking a crack at getting his mother out. I know he's a shit, but, damn it, Sirs!"

"Yes, Sergeant," Admiral Prokourov said. "Damn it, indeed. Look, put down the pistol. We're on your side." He looked at the intel officer with a raised eyebrow. "Let me rephrase that. *I'm* on your side. Tuzcu?"

"I'd sure as hell like to know that whatever's going on has a *chance*!" The intel officer grimaced. "Certainly before I *commit*, for God's sake!"

"Sir," the sergeant said, lowering his pistol, "the whole Fleet Marine Force is on the Prince's side. Of the Empress', that is. Sergeant Major Brailowsky—"

"So that's why he was arrested," Prokourov said.

"Yes, Sir." The sergeant shrugged and holstered his pistol. "You serious about helping, Sir?" he added, keeping his hand close to the weapon.

"I'll admit I'm not sure *what* I'm helping, Sergeant," the admiral said carefully. "What we have right now is a total cluster fuck, and I would deeply like to get it unclustered. And as it happens, I've already contacted Moonbase to see what *they* have to say."

"I can guess Greenberg's reaction," the Marine growled sourly.

"That's assuming Greenberg is still in command," Prokourov noted. "Which I tend to doubt, since our movement orders came direct from Admiral Gianetto, not the fleet commander. It's possible, I suppose, that Greenberg was simply too busy doing something else to give us a call, but I expect he's suffered a mischief by now. And if he hasn't, you might as well just shoot me with that pistol, because if their planning—whoever 'they' are—is *that* bad . . ."

❖   ❖   ❖

"Incoming call from Admiral Prokourov."

"My screen," Kjerulf said, and looked down as Prokourov appeared on his main com display.

"Connect me to Admiral Greenberg, please," the admiral said. "I need confirmation of instructions from the Navy Minister's office."

"This is Kjerulf," he said, looking at Prokourov's profile. "I'm sorry, Admiral, but Admiral Greenberg is unavailable at this time."

Prokourov had his pickup off, and was speaking to someone off-screen while he waited out the transmission delay. He didn't appear flustered, but, then, he rarely did, and Kjerulf turned off his own pickup as he noted a blip on his repeater.

"Carrier Squadron Fourteen is moving," Sensor Three reported. "Big phase signature. They're headed out-system at one-point-six-four KPS squared."

"Understood," Kjerulf said, and looked back down at Prokourov's profile waiting out the interminable communications lag. He'd expected CarRon 14 to move as quickly as it got the word, but Prokorouv's CarRon 12 had become just as critical as he'd feared, because Greenberg *had* changed the lockout codes on the base's offensive missile launchers.

It was another one of those reasonable little safety precations which was turning around and biting everyone on the ass in the current chaotic situation. Modern missiles had a range at burn-out of well over twelve million kilometers and reached almost ten percent of light-speed, and a few dozen of those fired against Old Earth—whether accidentally or by some lunatic—would pretty much require the human race to find a new place to call home, even without warheads. So it only made sense to ensure that releasing them for use was not a trivial process. Unfortunately, it had allowed Greenberg to make sure no one could fire them against any *other* target—like traitorous ships of the Imperial Navy supporting one Jackson Adoula's usurpation of the Throne—without the command code only he knew. And he was no longer available to provide it.

Fortunately, he hadn't done the same thing to Moonbase's countermissile launchers, so the base could at least still defend itself against bombardment. But it couldn't fire a single shot at anything outside the limited envelope of its energy weapons, which meant the four carriers of Fatted Calf Squadron were on their own. Things were going to be ugly enough against CarRon 14's *six* carriers; if CarRon 12 weighed in with four more of them, it would be bad. If they continued to sit things out, at least it would only be four-against-six, and that was doable ... maybe.

The other squadrons were still too way the hell far out-system to intervene. So far. And they also had longer signal delays. Wu's Squadron Six was all the way out on the other side of the sun, over forty light-minutes from Old Earth orbit. Thirteenth, Eleventh, and Fifteenth were all closer, but round-trip signal time even to them was over forty-three minutes. And, of course, their sensors had the same delay. They couldn't know yet what was happening on the planet, which meant none of them had had to commit yet. But they would. For that matter, they could already be moving, and he wouldn't know it until *his* light-speed sensors reported it.

He closed his eyes, thinking hard for a moment, then opened them again and glanced at his senior com tech.

"We still have contact with the civilian com net planet-side?"

"Yes, Sir."

"Then look up a number in Imperial city. Marduk ... something. House, maybe. Anyway, it's a restaurant. Tell them where you're calling from and ask for anybody who has a *clue* what's going on! Ask for ... ask for Ms. Nejad."

"Aye, aye, Sir," the noncom said in the tone of someone suppressing an urge to giggle hysterically.

"Marduk House," the Mardukan said in very broken Imperial.

"I need to speak to Ms. Nejad," an exasperated Kjerulf said.

"Kjerulf," Prokourov said on the other monitor, responding to Kjerulf's last transmission at last. "I'd sort of like a straight answer on this. Where's Greenberg? And what do you know about the fighting dirt-side?"

"She busy," the Mardukan said. "She no talk."

"Sir," a sensor tech said, "CarRon Twelve's just lit off its phase drive. It's moving in-system at one-six-four gravities."

Kjerulf's jaw clenched. So much for CarRon 12's neutrality. He glared at the Mardukan on his com display.

"Tell her it's Captain Kjerulf," the captain snapped. "She'll talk to me. Tell her!"

"I tell," the Mardukan said. He walked away from the pickup, and Kjerulf wheeled away from his own to the monitor with Prokourov on it.

"Greenberg's *dead*," he barked. He said it more harshly than he'd intended to, but he was a bit stressed. "As for the rest, Admiral, if you want to support Adoula, then you just *bring it on!*"

"Mr. Prime Minister, understand me. Roger is not the boy you knew," Eleanora said firmly, holding onto her temper with both hands. It had taken almost fifteen minutes just to get the pompous, self-serving jackass on the line, and he'd been fending off anything remotely smacking of taking a stand for at least five more minutes. "What's more important, you have to know what's been going on in the Palace."

"Know and suspect are two different things, Ms. O'Casey," Yang replied in his cultured Old Terran accent. "I've met with the Empress several times since the first of Roger's coup attempts—"

"That was *not* Roger," Eleanora said flatly. "I was *with* Roger, and he was on *Marduk*."

"So you say," the Prime Minister said smoothly. "Nonetheless, the evidence—"

"As soon as we take the Palace, all I ask is a team of independent witnesses to her Majesty's condition—"

"Guy named Kjerulf on the other line," one of the Diaspran infantrymen said. They'd moved to an office suite in an old commercial building, well away from the warehouse, which they'd known was going to be blown the moment the stingships lifted. All calls to the warehouse and restaurant were being forwarded, over deceptive links, to the office. "Says he wants to talk to Ms. Nejad. That's you, right?"

"Got it," Eleanora said, holding up her hand. "That's all I'm asking," she continued to the Prime Minister.

"And agreeing to it would be tantamount to supporting you," Yang pointed out. "We'll have to see what we see. I don't care for the Prince, and don't care to have him as my Emperor. And I've seen no data that supports your contention that he was on Marduk."

"Give me a more private contact number, and I'll dump you

the raw file. And the presentation. Furthermore, we had Harvard Mansul from the IAS with us for part of it as independent corroboration, and an IBI agent for a third independent data source. There's plenty of documentation. And you *know* the Empress was being conditioned. You'd met her too many times before to think she was acting normally."

"As I said, Ms. O'Casey, it will be quite impossible for me, as Prime Minister, to . . ."

"Roger, this is Marinau, do you read?"

"Yes," Roger panted as he ran down the corridor. Automated systems had gone to local control, and he triggered a round at a plasma cannon that popped out of the wall. The cannon—and at least six cubic meters of Palace wall—disappeared before it could swivel and target his group. Another curtain of water erupted from overhead and splashed around his team's armored feet as they pounded onward.

"We've got the courtyard, but the shuttles are late," Marinau said over the sound of heavy firing.

"I've got the doors open up there," Roger snarled. "What more do you want?"

He paused and went to a knee, covering, as they reached another intersection and the team went past him. Plasma fire erupted from one of the side corridors, and the Mardukan who'd been crossing it was cut in half.

"Can you detach anyone?" Marinau asked. "We're getting slaughtered up here!"

"No," Roger said, his over-controled voice like ice as he imagined the hell the unarmored Mardukans were facing. He'd fought with them across two continents, bled with them and faced death at their side. But right now, they had their job, and he had his. "Contact Rosenberg. See what the holdup is. Continue the mission. Roger out."

The corridor intersection had been taken, at the cost of another armored Mardukan and one of the Empress' Own. They were down to fifteen bodies, and less than halfway to his mother's quarters.

It was going to be tight.

Catrone held onto the desk as another titanic explosion rocked the building.

"What in the hell *is* that?" he asked as the armored room shuddered and seemed to lean to the right.

"I think I know," Despreaux said tightly. The rescue team had made it to Siminov's office, but they were pinned down again, with guards on both ends of the corridor covering the door.

"Me, too. And I'm going to *kill* Krindi for letting Erkum anywhere *near* a plasma gun," Pedi added, stroking her horns nervously.

"No way out, there, Boss," Clovis said, ducking back as bead rounds caromed off the doorway.

Trey was being tended to behind the desk after taking a bead through the thigh. The nasty hit had pulverized the femoral bone and cut the femoral artery, but Dave had an IV running and a tourniquet in place.

"A tisket, a tasket, a head in a basket," Dave said in a high voice. "No matter how you try, it cannot answer the questions you ask it!"

"Have you got any idea where we are?" Krindi asked over the crackling roar of flames. Fortunately, their environment suits were flame resistant, and they'd lowered their face shields and activated their filters. But the air was getting low on oxygen, and even inside the suits, it was bloody hot.

"Second floor?" Erkum suggested uncertainly. He was training the gun around, delighted to have it operational again as he looked for targets.

"Third floor, third floor," Krindi muttered, looking up. "Oh, hell. Erkum, look, very carefully..."

Catrone grabbed Despreaux as the rocking concussion of an explosion slammed into the room. The entire office seemed to lift and then drop, sliding downward and to the side in an uncontrolled fall as the desk toppled towards the right wall. It crunched to a halt at an angle, listing to the right.

Dave threw himself over Trey, trying to get a finger hold on the carpet.

Pedi rolled onto her stomach, gripped a fold of the deep-pile carpet in her teeth, and flung out all four arms. She managed to snag Catrone with her lower right, Dave and Trey with the upper left, and Clovis, as he slid past, with her upper right.

"Okay," she muttered through tightly clenched teeth. "What do we do now?" The floor her lips were pressed against was getting distinctly warm.

"Slip sliding away," Dave sang in a high tenor, holding onto the unconscious Trey with one arm and gripping the carpet between thumb and forefinger with the other hand. "Slip sliding away, hey!"

"I hate classical music," Clovis said as he drew a knife and very slowly lifted it in Dave's direction, then slapped it into the carpet as a temporary piton. "I really, really do . . ."

Honal banked left, almost clipping a building with his tail, then flipped right and down the next road, then left again, and pulled up sharply, rolling the stingship over on its back. As the Empress' Own stingship rounded the corner, he let it have a burst from his forward plasma guns and rolled back upright.

"Way's clear," he said. "Roll the shuttles!"

"Where's Alpha Six?" Flight Ops asked as Honal flew over the remains of the stingship sticking out of a building. Only the tail was visible, with the markings of a squadron commander.

"Alpha Six won't be joining us," Honal said, pulling up and over the building in salute to a fallen comrade. "Roll the shuttles."

Time to go and join Rastar. He was probably having fun at the gate.

"At least the Navy is still out of it," Ops said. "Rolling shuttles now."

"Citizens of the Empire!"

Prince Jackson Adoula's face appeared on every active info-terminal in Imperial city. He looked grave, concerned, yet grimly determined, and uniformed men and women bustled purposefully about behind him as he sat at a command station. Holo displays in the background showed smoke towering over the unmistakable silhouette of the Palace.

"Citizens of the Empire, it is my grave responsibility to confirm the initial reports already circulating through the datanet. The traitor, Roger MacClintock, has indeed returned to launch yet another attempt to seize the Throne. Not content with the murder of his own brother, sister, and nieces and nephews, he is now attempting to seize the Palace and the person of the Empress herself.

"I urge all citizens not to panic. The valiant soldiers of the Empress' Own are fighting courageously to defend her person. We do not yet know how the traitors managed to initially penetrate Palace security, but I fear we have confirmation that at least some Navy elements have been suborned into supporting this treasonous act of violence.

"All government ministers and all members of Parliament are being dispersed to places of safety. This precaution is necessary because it is evident that this time the traitors are targeting more than simply the Palace. My own offices in the Imperial Tower were destroyed by a precision-guided weapon in the opening moments of the attack, and my home—and my staff, many of whom, as you know, have been with me for years—was totally destroyed within minutes of the start of the attack on the Palace."

A spasm of obvious pain twisted his features for a moment, but he regained his composure after a visible struggle and looked squarely into the pickup.

"I swear to you that this monumental treachery, this act of treason against not only the Empire, not simply the Empress, but against Roger MacClintock's own family, shall not succeed or go unpunished. Again, I urge all loyal citizens to remain calm, to stay tuned to their information channels, and to stand ready to obey the instructions of the military and police authorities."

He stared out of the thousands upon thousands of displays throughout Imperial City, his expression resolute, as the image faded to a standard Navy Department wallpaper.

"Calm down, Kjer," Prokourov said ten minutes after Kjerulf's reply, calmly ignoring the outburst. "I'm *probably* on your side. Taking out Greenberg was a necessity, distasteful as it may have been. But I want to know what *you* know, what you suspect, and what's going on."

"Ms. Nejad, she still busy," the Mardukan said, coming back into the monitor's field of view. "Gonna be staying busy."

"Tell her to get *un*busy!" Kjerulf snapped. "All right, Admiral.

All I really ask is that you keep out of this. My main worry is CarRon Fourteen. We've shut down the Moonbase fighter wing, and it turns out that they're pretty unhappy with Gianetto, anyway. I've got a small squadron of loyal ships holding the orbitals. All I need is for the rest of the squadrons to stay out of it."

He turned off his mike and looked over at Tactical.

"Any more movement?"

"No, Sir," Sensor Five said. "But Communications just intercepted a clear-language transmission from Defense HQ to all the outer-system squadrons. General Gianetto's declared a state of insurrection, informed them that Moonbase is in mutinous hands, and ordered a least-time concentration in Old Earth orbit."

"Crap," Kjerulf muttered, and keyed his mike. "Admiral Prokourov, I take that back. We may need active support—"

"Captain Kjerulf," Eleanora O'Casey said, appearing on his other monitor. "What's happening?"

The door looked like oak. And, in fact, it was—a centimeter slab of polished oak over a ChromSten core. Most bank vaults would have been flimsy by comparison, but it was the last major blast door between them and Roger's mother. And, unfortunately, it was on internal control.

Roger lifted the plasma cannon—his third since the assault began—and aimed at the door.

"My treat, Your Highness," one of the Mardukans said, carefully but inexorably pushing Roger away from the door.

The prince nodded and stepped back, automatically checking to be sure the team was watching in every direction. They were down to ten, including himself. But there should be only two more corridors between them and his mother, and if the information in the command center's computers was correct, there were no automated defenses and no armored guards still in front of them. They were there. If only she was alive.

The Mardukan carefully keyed in the sequence to override the safety protocols, then triggered a stream of plasma from the tank cannon at the door. But that door had been intended to protect the Empress of Man. It was extraordinarily thick, and it resisted the blasts. It bulged inward, but it held stubbornly through seven consecutive shots.

On the eighth shot, the overheated firing chamber detonated.

Roger felt himself lifted up by a giant and slammed through the merely mortal walls of the approach corridor. He came to a halt two rooms away, in one he recognized in confusion as a servant's chambers.

"I don't sleep with the help," he said muzzily, picking himself out of the rumpled tapestries and ancient statuary.

"Your Highness?" someone said.

He tried to put a finger into one of his ears, both of which were ringing badly, but his armor's helmet stopped him. So he shook his head, instead.

"I *don't* sleep with the help," he repeated, and then he realized the room was on fire. The overworked sprinkler system was sending a fresh downpour over him, but plasma flash had a tendency to start *really* hot fires. These continued to blaze away, adding billowing waves of steam to the hellish environment.

"What am I doing here?" he asked, looking around and backing away from the flames. "Why is the room on fire?"

"Your Highness!" the voice said again, then someone took his elbow.

"Dogzard," Roger said suddenly, and darted back into the flames. "*Dogzard!*" He shouted, using his armor's external amplifiers.

The scorched dog-lizard came creeping out from under a mattress, a couple of rooms away, wearing a sheepish expression. She'd been following well behind the group. From her relatively minor damage, she'd probably run and hidden at the explosion.

"How many?" Roger said, shaking his head again and looking at the person who'd called him. It was Master Sergeant Penalosa, Raoux's second in command. "Where's Raoux?"

"Down," Penalosa said. "Hurt bad. We've got five left, Sir."

"Plus me and you?" Roger asked, pulling up a casualty list. "No, *including* me and you," he answered himself.

"Yes, Sir," the master sergeant replied tightly.

"Okay," Roger said, and then swore as a blast of plasma came *out* of the small hole his Mardukan had managed to blow in the door. So much for the CP's information that there were no guards beyond. "What are we on? *Plan Z?*" he said. "No, no, calm, right? Got to be calm."

"Yes, Sir," the sergeant said.

"Plan Z it is, then," Roger said. "Follow me."

"Sir, we just lost the feed from the system recon net," Senior Captain Marjorie Erhardt, CO HMS *Carlyle* said.

"We have, have we?" Admiral Henry Niedermayer frowned thoughtfully and checked the time display. "Any explanation of why, Captain?"

"No, Sir. The feed just went down."

"Um. Obviously something is happening in-system, isn't it?" Niedermayer mused.

"Yes, Sir. And it's not supposed to be," Erhardt agreed grimly.

"No, but it was allowed for," Niedermayer pointed out in return, with maddening imperturbability.

"Should we head in-system, Sir?" Erhardt pressed.

"No, we should not," the admiral said with just a hint of frost. "You know our orders as well as I do, Captain. We have no idea exactly what's going on on Old Earth right this minute, and any precipitous action on our part could simply make things enormously worse. No, we'll stay right here. But go ahead and bring the task group to readiness for movement—*low-powered* movement. Given the timing, we may need to adjust our position slightly, and I want strict emissions control if we do."

Larry Gianetto's face was grim as the icons and sidebars in his displays changed. Whatever his political loyalties, he was a professional Marine officer, one of the best around when it came to his own specialty, and keeping track of the apparently overwhelming information flow was second nature to him.

Which meant he could see exactly how bad things looked.

The attack on the Palace had been only minutes old when he ordered additional Marines into the capital to suppress it. Now, over half an hour later, not a single unit had moved. Not one. Some were simply sitting in place, either refusing to acknowledge movement orders or stalling for time by requesting endless "clarification." But others were stopped where they were because their personnel were too busy shooting at each other to obey. And most worrying of all, even in the units which had tried to obey his orders, the personnel loyal to him seemed to be badly outnumbered.

If the defenders already in the Palace couldn't stop these lunatics, then it was highly unlikely that anyone else on the planet would be willing to help him retake it afterward.

He looked at a side monitor, showing a fresh broadcast from Prince Jackson, and bared his teeth in a cynical, mirthless smile. The viewing public had no way of knowing that the bustling command post behind Adoula did not exist outside one of the most sophisticated VR software packages in existence. By now, Adoula was actually aboard the *Hannah P. McAllister*, an apparently down-at-the-heels tramp freighter in orbit around the planet. His public statements were recorded aboard the ship, beamed down to a secure ground station, plugged into the VR software, and then rebroadcast through the public information channels with real-time images from the Palace inserted. The illusion that Adoula was actually still in the city—or, at least, near at hand—was seamless and perfect.

And if things continued to to go to hell in a handbasket the way they were, it was about time Gianetto started considering implementing his own bug-out strategy.

"Christ, the cavalry at last," Marinau said as the first shuttle landed in the courtyard. He and what was left of his teams and the Mardukans had held the North Courtyard over twice as long as the ops plan had specified. They'd paid cash for it, too. But at least the bogus Empress' Own's armored reaction squad had gone in pursuit of Roger, thank God! And thank God the so-called troops Adoula had found as replacements weren't real combat troops. If they had been, there would have been *no one* left to greet the incoming shuttle.

It came under heavy fire, but from small arms and armor-portable cannon only. The heavy antiair/antispace emplacements had all been knocked out, and the shuttle was giving as good as it got. It laid down a hail of heavy plasma blasts on the positions which had the attackers pinned down, and as big—*huge*—armored Mardukans piled out of the hatches, more fire came from the sky, dropping across the positions of the mercenaries still holding the Palace.

"No," Kuddusi said, raising up to fire a stream of beads at the defensive positions. "The cavalry went in *first*."

"Let's move," Marinau said. "Punch left."

✧   ✧   ✧

"Where are we going?" Penalosa asked as Roger led them down an apparently deserted corridor.

"To here." Roger stopped by an ancient picture of a group of men chasing foxes. He lifted an ornamental candlestick out of a sconce, and a door opened in the wall.

"This is a shortcut to Mother's room," he said.

"Then why in hell didn't we use it *before*?" Penalosa demanded.

"Because," Roger thumbed a sensor ball and tossed it into the passageway, "I'm pretty sure Adoula knows about it."

"Holy . . ." Penalosa muttered, blanching behind her armored visor as the sensor ball's findings were relayed to her HUD. There were more than a dozen defense-points in the short corridor. Even as she watched, one of them destroyed the sensor ball.

"Yep," Roger agreed, "and they're on Adoula's IFF." He keyed his communicator. "Jin, you getting anywhere?"

"Negative, Your Highness," Jin admitted. "I've been trying to crack Adoula's defensive net, but it's heavily encrypted. He's using a two-thousand-bit—"

"You know I don't go for the technical gobbledygook," Roger said. "A simple 'no' would suffice. You see what we see?"

"Yes, Sir," Jin said, looking at the relayed readouts.

"Suggestions?"

"Find another route?"

"There aren't any," Roger muttered, and switched frequencies. "God damn it." He hefted the replacement plasma cannon he'd picked up and tossed it to Penalosa. "If this doesn't work, get to Mother. Somehow," he added, and drew both pistols.

"*No!*" Penalosa dropped the cannon and grabbed vainly for the prince as he leapt into the corridor.

"That's it," Gianetto said. "I won't say it's all over but the shouting, but there are insertion teams deep into the Palace, they've secured an LZ inside the inner parameter, and they're lifting in additional troops. CarRon 14's moving, and so are Prokourov and

La Paz. Unfortunately, I don't have a single goddamned idea what Prokourov is going to do when he gets here, and he's going to get here well before CarRon 13. The ground units here planetside are either refusing to move at all, or else fighting internally about whose orders to take, and the commanders loyal to *us* don't seem to be winning. That means Gajelis is the closest available relief—with the head start he got, he's going to be here about twenty minutes before CarRon 12, even if Prokourov's feeling loyal to us. And it's still going to take Gajelis another three hours-plus to get here. We may still be able to turn this thing around—or at least decapitate the opposition—if we can get control of the orbitals, but in the meantime, we're royally screwed dirtside. It's time to leave, Your Highness."

"I cannot *believe* that little shit could put something like this together!" Adoula snarled.

"It doesn't matter whether it was him, or someone else. Or even whether or not he's really still alive," Gianetto pointed out. "What matters is that the shit has well and truly hit the fan. I'll be issuing the official dispersal order in ten minutes."

"Understood," Adoula replied, and looked at his loyal chauffeur once again. "Duauf, go inform the captain that we'll be leaving shortly."

"At once, Your Highness," the chauffeur murmured, and Adoula nodded. It was so good to have at least *one* competent subordinate, he reflected. Then he pursed his lips in irritation as another thought occurred to him. One more thing to take care of, he thought irritatedly. Loose ends everywhere.

"We're holding the inner perimeter, Your Highness," "Major" Khalid said. "But we've lost the stingship squadron, and they're shuttling in reinforcements. They've got us cut off from the main Palace, and so far, they've thrown back every try to break out we've made. We need support, Sir. Soon."

"It looks bad," Adoula said, his face serious. "But the Navy units I control are on the way. They've got enough firepower to get you out of there. But given how complicated and fluid the situation is, I'm afraid these rebels may get their hands on the Empress and the replicator, and we can't have that. Kill the Empress at once. Dump the replicator."

"Yes, Sir," Khalid said, but he also frowned. "What about us?"

"As soon as the Navy gets there, they'll land shuttles to pull you out," Adoula said. "I can't afford to lose you, Khalid. We've got too much more work to do. Kill the Empress now, then all you have to do is hold out for—" The prince ostentatiously considered his toot. "Hold for another forty minutes," he said. "Can you do that?"

"Yes, Your Highness," the "major" said, squaring his shoulders. "I'm glad you haven't forgotten us."

"Of course not," Adoula said, and cut the circuit. He looked into the dead display for an instant. "Most definitely not," he said softly.

The defensive systems in the secret passage, light and heavy plasma and bead cannon, were momentarily confused. The figure was giving off the IFF of the local defenders, as last updated. In automatic mode, that didn't matter—not here, in *this* corridor. But the intruder had paused outside the systems' area of immediate responsibility, where matters were a little ambiguous. Did its mere presence in the corridor's entrance represent an unauthorized incursion? If not, its IFF meant it was not a legitimate target, but if it *was* an incursion . . .

The systems' computers were still trying to decide when beads started cracking down-range, destroying the first two emplacements. At which point, they made up their collective electronic minds and opened fire.

Roger considered it just another test.

Over the last year the Playboy Prince who'd set out so unwillingly for Leviathan had learned that life put obstacles in one's path, and one either went around them, if possible . . . or *through* them, if necessary. This fell under the category of "necessary," and there weren't enough bodies left to just throw them in and soak up the losses to take out the emplacements. More than that, he'd proven himself to be better at fast, close combat than any of the rest of the team. Ergo, this was one of those times when he *had* to put himself in jeopardy.

He'd killed three of the defensive weapons before they were

all up and tracking on him. He killed a fourth, concentrating on the eight heavy emplacements, before the first stream of beads hit him. They knocked him backward, but couldn't penetrate the ChromSten armor. He got that bead cannon, and then a plasma gun gushed at his feet. He'd seen it tracking, and jumped, getting it while he was in the air. But when he came down, he stumbled, trying to avoid another stream of plasma, and fell to the side. He got the fifth emplacement before the first Raider could make it through the door.

Funny. He'd thought you were supposed to get cold at the time like this. But he was hot. Terribly hot.

"This really sucks," Despreaux said, coughing on smoke.

The wall, floor—whatever—of Siminov's office was too hot to touch now. So they'd climbed onto the edge of the desk, dragging Trey and the semiconscious Siminov with them. Some of the smoke came from the lower edge of the desk, which was beginning to smolder. When that caught fire, as it was bound to eventually, they were all going to be in rather desperate straits.

Despreaux happened to be the one looking at the door when the hand appeared.

It fumbled for a grip, and she raised her pistol before she noticed that the hand was both very large and covered in an environment suit glove.

"Hold fire!" she barked as Krindi chinned himself up over the edge of the door frame.

"So, *there* you are," the Diaspran said, showing his teeth in a Mardukan-style pseudosmile behind his mask. "We've been looking all *over* for you."

"What took you so long?" Pedi asked angrily.

"I figured there was time," Krindi said, dragging himself fully through the doorway. "You were born to hang."

"Roger, just lie still!" Penalosa was saying.

"Hell with that." Roger got to his feet—or tried to. His lower left leg felt strangely numb, but he got got as far as his right knee, then pushed himself upright.

And promptly toppled over sideways again.

"Oh," he said, looking at the left leg which had refused to support him. Not surprisingly, perhaps, since it was pretty much gone just below the knee. "Now, that's a hell of a thing. Good nannies, though. I don't feel a thing."

"Just stay down!" Penalosa said sharply.

"No." Roger got up again, more cautiously. He looked around and picked up a bead cannon from a suit of armor with a large, smoking hole through its breastplate. "Let's go."

"God *damn it*, Your Highness!"

"Just a thing, Master Sergeant," Roger said. "Just a thing. Can I have an arm, though?"

"We've got the corridor suppressed," Penalosa said as the two damaged suits of armor limped slowly and painfully down the narrow passageway.

"I noticed," Roger said, when they came to the end. It was another ChromSten door.

"But there's this," Penalosa said. "And not only are we about out of plasma cannon, but these are awful tight quarters for try-ing your little trick. Not to mention that . . . nobody's too happy about trying it again, anyway."

"Nobody" being Penalosa herself and one of the Mardukans, since the other two suits had bought it destroying the last two installations after Roger had gotten the first six.

"Yes, understandable," Roger said. "But unlike the last door, Master Sergeant, this one is *original* installation." He bared his teeth behind his visor. "Open Sesame," he said.

And the door opened upwards.

"Attention all vessels in planetary orbit! This is Terran Defense HQ! Hostile naval units are approaching Old Earth, ETA approxi-mately eleven-thirty-seven hours Capital Time. All civilian traffic is immediately directed and ordered to clear planetary orbit at once. Repeat, all civilian traffic is immediately directed and ordered to clear planetary orbit at once. Be advised that heavy fire is to be anticipated and that any vessel in a position to pose a threat to Imperial City will be deemed hostile and treated accordingly. Repeat, all civilian traffic is immediately directed and ordered to clear planetary orbit at once, by order of Ter-ran Defense HQ!"

"Well, about damned time," Captain Kjerulf muttered as the grim-faced rear admiral on the display screen spoke. The recorded message began to replay, and he turned back to the thousand and one details demanding his attention with a sense of profound relief. He'd been more than a little concerned about the collateral damage which would almost inevitably occur when a full-scale naval engagement walked across the orbital patterns of the teeming commerce which always surrounded Old Earth. At least he didn't have to worry about *that* anymore.

"And it's about time," Prince Jackson Adoula muttered as *Hannah P. McAllister* made haste to obey the nondiscretionary order. There were, quite literally, hundreds of vessels in Old Earth orbit; now they scattered, like shoals of mackerel before the slashing attack of a pod of porpoises. Adoula's vessel was only one more insignificant blip amid the confusion of that sudden exodus, with absolutely nothing to distinguish her from any of the others.

Aside from the fact—not yet especially evident—that *her* course would eventually carry her to *meet* CarRon 14 well short of the planet.

Getting to Siminov's office door was the biggest trick, since the floor was too hot to cross without third-degree burns. Fortunately, Krindi could walk on it in his environment suit, and he could lower them to Erkum, who was standing in a more or less fire-free spot on the ground floor. The gigantic noncom's height, coupled with the fact that the office had dropped most of the way through the second floor, made it a relatively easy stretch from that point.

Krindi got all of them out and down just before the last supports gave way and the armored room collapsed crashingly into the building's basement.

"God, I'm glad to be out of *there*," Despreaux said. "On the other hand, I really don't want to burn to death, either."

"Not a problem," Krindi said. "Erkum, gimme."

He hefted his towering sidekick's weapon only with extreme difficulty, but this wasn't something to be trusted to Erkum's enthusiastic notions of marksmanship. Despite its weight, he managed to get it pointed at the side of the building which was least enveloped in flames. Then he triggered a single round.

The plasma bolt took out the walls on either side and blew a nine-meter hole in the back wall. It would have set the building behind Siminov's on fire, if that hadn't already been taken care of some time ago.

"Door," Krindi observed as he pulled the power pack out of the plasma gun and tossed the weapon down into the flaming basement. "Now let's get the polluted water out of here."

They scrambled through the plasma-carved passage and into the alleyway between the blazing buildings, then turned and headed for the alley's mouth. Erkum carried Trey and the well-trussed Siminov, and all of them stayed low, trying to avoid flaming debris until they stumbled out into the fresh morning air at last.

And found themselves looking into the gun muzzles of at least a dozen Imperial City Police.

"I don't know who in the hell you people are," the ICPD sergeant in charge of the squad said, covering them from behind his aircar. "And I don't know what in the hell you've been doing," he continued, looking at the team's body armor and the Mardukans in their scorched environment suits, "but you're all under arrest!"

Despreaux started to say something, then stopped and looked up at the armored assault shuttle sliding quietly down the sky. A large crowd had gathered to watch the buildings burn, since the municipal firemen had wisely decided to *let* them burn as long as plasma fire was being thrown around, and the shuttle had to maneuver a bit to find a spot to land. Despreaux saw a very familiar face at the controls as it settled on its countergravity, and Doc Dobrescu tossed her a salute as the shuttle's plasma cannon trained around to cover the police holding them at gunpoint.

The rear hatch opened, and four Mardukans in battle armor unloaded. They took up a combat circle, two of them also sort of pointing their bead and plasma cannon nonchalantly in the general direction of the police.

And then a final figure stepped out of the shuttle. A slight figure, in a blue dress fetchingly topped off by an IBI SWAT jacket.

Buseh Subianto slid easily between the Mardukans and walked over to the ICPD sergeant . . . who was now ostentatiously pointing his own weapon skyward and trying to decide if placing it on the ground would be an even better bet.

"Good job, Sergeant," Subianto said, patting him on the shoulder. "Thank you for your assistance in this little operation. We'll just be picking up our team and going."

"IBI?" the sergeant's question came out more than half-strangled. "*IBI?*" he repeated in a shout, when he'd gotten his breath.

"Yes," Subianto said lightly.

"You could have *told* us!"

"Sergeant, Sergeant, Sergeant . . ." the Deputy Assistant to the Assistant Deputy Director, Counterintelligence Division, of the Imperial Bureau of Investigation said. "You *know* ImpCity data security isn't that good. Don't you?"

"But . . ." The cop turned and looked at the group by the flaming building. "*You burned the building down!* Hell, you set the entire *block* on fire!"

"Mistakes happen." Subianto shrugged.

"*Mistakes?!*" The sergeant threw his hands up. "They were using a *tank* cannon! A *plasma* tank cannon!"

Erkum ostentatiously interlaced his fingers in front of him and began twiddling all four thumbs. He also tried his best to whistle. It was not something Mardukan lips were designed for.

The sergeant looked at the Mardukans and the very old-fashioned combat shuttle.

"What in the hell *is* this?"

"Sergeant," Subianto said politely, "have you ever heard the term 'above your pay grade'?" The sergeant looked ready to implode on the spot, and she patted his shoulder again. "Look," she said soothingly, "I'm from the IBI. I'm here to help you."

Roger limped down the paneled corridor, using the bead cannon as a crutch and followed by Penalosa and the single remaining Mardukan. Dogzard, still in a deep funk, trailed along dead last. From time to time, Roger stopped and either broke down a door or had the Mardukan do it for him.

A guard in a standard combat suit stepped into the corridor and lifted a bead gun, firing a stream of projectiles that bounced screamingly off of Roger's armor.

"Oh, get *real*," the prince snarled, shifting to external speakers as he grabbed the guard by the collar and lifted him off the ground. "Where's my mother?!"

The strangling guard dropped his weapon and kicked futilely at Roger's armor, gurgling and making motions that he didn't know. Roger snarled again, tossed him aside, and limped on down the corridor as fast as he could.

"Split up!" he said. "Find my mother."

"Your Highness!" Penalosa protested. "We can't leave you unpro—"

"*Find her!*"

"Pity to waste you," Khalid said, flipping a knife in his hand as he approached the half-naked Empress on the huge bed. "On the other hand, you don't get many chances at Imperial poontang," he added, unsealing his trousers. "I suppose I might as well take one more. Don't worry—I'll be quick."

"Get it over with," Alexandra said angrily, pulling at the manacle on her left wrist. "But if you kill me, you'll be hounded throughout the galaxy!"

"Not with Prince Jackson protecting me," Khalid laughed.

He stepped forward, but before he reached the bed, the door burst suddenly open and an armored figure, missing part of one leg, leaned in through the broken panel.

"Mother?!" it shouted, and somehow the bead pistol holstered at its side had teleported into its right hand. It was the fastest draw Khalid had ever seen, and the mercenary's belly muscles clenched as the pistol's muzzle aligned squarely on the bridge of his nose. He started to open his mouth, and—

The bead pistol whined an "empty magazine" signal.

"*Son of a BITCH!*" Roger shouted, and threw the empty pistol at the man standing over his lingerie-clad mother with a knife. The other man dodged, and the pistol flew by his head and smashed into the wall as Roger stomped forward as quickly as he could on his improvised crutch.

Khalid made an instant evaluation of the relative value of obeying Adoula or saving his own life. Evaluation completed, he dropped the knife and pulled out a one-shot.

The contact-range anti-armor device was about the size of a large, prespace flashlight and operated on the principle of an ancient "squash head" antitank round. It couldn't penetrate battle armor's ChromSten, so it attacked the less impenetrable plasteel liner which supported the ChromSten matrix by transmitting the shockwave of a contact detonated hundred-gram charge of plasticized cataclysmite *through* the ChromSten to blast a "scab" of the liner right through the body of who ever happened to be wearing the armor. Its user had to come literally within arm's reach of his target, but if he could survive to get that close, the device was perfectly capable of killing someone through any battle armor ever made.

Roger had faced one-shots twice before. One, in the hand of a Krath raider, had badly injured—indeed, almost killed—him, despite armor almost identical to that which he was currently wearing. The second, in the much more skilled hands of a Saint commando, had killed his mentor, his father-in-truth, Armand Pahner. And with one leg, and out of ammunition, there wasn't a damned thing he could do but take the shot and hope like hell he managed to survive again.

Dogzard was still badly depressed, but she was beginning to feel more cheerful. Her God had gone missing, replaced by a stranger, but there was something about the rooms around her now—a smell, an almost psychic sense—which told her that her God might come back. These rooms didn't smell the *same* as her God, but the scents which filled them were elusively similar. There were hints all about her that whispered of her God, and she snuffled at the wood paneling and the furniture as they passed it. She'd never been in this place before, but somehow, incredible as it seemed, she might actually be coming home.

In the meantime, she continued to follow the stranger who said he was God. He hadn't seemed very much like God up until the past little bit. Just recently, however, he'd started acting much more as God had always acted before. The smells of cooking flesh and burning buildings were those she associated with the passage of her God, and she'd stopped and sniffed a couple of corpses along the way. She'd been shouted at, as usual, and she'd obeyed the might-be-God voice, albeit reluctantly. It didn't seem right to let all that perfectly good meat and sweet, sweet blood go to waste, but it was a dog-lizard's life, no question.

Now she was excited. She smelled, not her God, but someone who smelled much the same. Someone who might know her God, and if she was a good dog-lizard, might bring her back to her God.

She pushed up beside the one-legged stranger in the doorway. The smell was coming from the bed in the room beyond. It wasn't her God, but it was close, and the female on the bed smelled of anger, just like her God often did. Yet there was fear, too, and Dogzard knew the fear was directed at the man beside the bed. The man holding a Bad Thing.

Suddenly, Dogzard had more important things to worry about than impostors who claimed they were God.

Roger bounced off the wall as six hundred kilos of raging Dogzard brushed him aside with a blood-chilling snarl and charged into the room. He managed to catch himself without quite falling, and his head whipped around just in time to see the results.

"Holy Allah!" Khalid gasped as a red-and-black *thing* knocked the armored man out of its way and charged. He tried to hit it with the one-shot, but it was too close, moving too fast. His arm swung, stabbing the weapon at the creature's side, but a charging shoulder hit his forearm, sending the weapon flying out of his grasp. And then there was no time, no time at all.

Roger pushed himself off the wall as Dogzard lifted her stained muzzle. Her powerful jaws had literally decapitated the other man, and the dog-lizard gave Roger a half-shamed glance, then grabbed the body and pulled it behind the couch. There was a crunch, and a ripping sound.

Roger limped toward the bed, hobbling on his bead cannon and pulling off his helmet.

"Mother," he said, eyes blurred with tears. "Mother?"

Alexandra stared up at him, and his heart twisted as the combat fugue release him and the Empress' condition truly registered.

His memories of his mother included all too few personal, informal moments. For him, she had always been a distant, almost god-like figure. An authoritarian deity whose approval he hungered for above all things . . . and had known he would never win. Cool, reserved, always immaculate and in command of herself. That was how he remembered his mother.

But this woman was none of those things, and raw, red-fanged fury rose suddenly within him as he took in the scanty lingerie, the chains permanently affixed to her bed, and the bruises—the many, many bruises and welts—her clothing would have hidden . . . if she'd had any clothing on. He remembered what Catrone had said about the day they told him how Adoula had controlled her. Adoula . . . and his father.

He looked into her eyes, and what he saw there shocked him almost more than her physical condition. There was anger in them, fury and defiance. But there was more than that. There was fear. And there was confusion. It was as if her stare was flickering in and out of focus. One breath he saw the furious anger, the sense of who she was and her hatred for the ones who had done this to her. And in the next breath, she was simply . . . gone. Someone else looked out of those same eyes at him. Someone quivering with terror. Someone uncertain of who she was, or why she was there. They wavered back and forth, those two people, and somewhere deep inside, behind the flickering, blurred interface, she *knew*. Knew that she was broken, helpless, reduced from the distant figure, the avatar of strength and authority who had always been the mother he knew now he had helplessly adored even as he tried futilely to somehow win her love in return.

"Oh, Mother," he whispered, his expression as clenched as his heart, and reached the bed towards her. "Oh, Mother."

"W-who are you?" the Empress demanded in a harsh, wavering whisper, and his jaw tightened. Of course. She couldn't possibly recognize him behind the disguising body-mod of Augustus Chung.

"It's me, Mother," he said. "It's Roger."

"Who?" She blinked at him, as if she were fighting to focus on his face, not to find some sort of internal focus in the swirling chaos of her own mind.

"Roger, Mother," he said softly, reaching out to touch her shoulder at last. "I know I look different, but I'm Roger."

"Roger?" She blinked again. For an instant, a fleeting moment, her eyes were clear. But then the focus vanished, replaced by confusion and a sudden, dark whirlwind of fear.

"Roger!" she repeated. "*Roger?!*"

She twisted frantically, fighting her chains with all of their strength.

"No! *No!* Stay away!"

"*Mother!*" Roger flinched back physically from the revulsion and terror in his mother's face.

"I saw you!" she shouted at him. "I *saw* you kill John! And you killed my grandchildren! Butcher! *Murderer!*"

"Mother, it wasn't me!" he protested. "You *know* it wasn't me! I wasn't even *here*, Mother!"

"Yes—yes you were! You look different now, but I saw you then!"

Roger reached out to her again, only to stop, shocked, as she screamed and twisted away from him. Dogzard rose up, looking over the back of the couch, and growled at him.

"Mother," he said to the screaming woman. "Mother! *Please!*"

She didn't even hear him. He could tell that. But then, abruptly, the scream was cut short, and Alexandra froze. Her expression changed abruptly, and she looked at her son, cocked her head, and smiled. It was a terrible smile. A dark-eyed smile which mingled desire, invitation, and stark fear in equal measure.

"Are you here for Lazar? Did he send you?" she asked in a quieter voice, and arched her spine suggestively. "They told me someone would be coming, but I . . . forget the faces sometimes," she continued, dropping her eyes. "But why are you wearing armor? I hope you're not going to be rough. I'll be good, really I will—I promise! Tell Lazar you don't have to be rough, please. *Please!* Really, you *don't*," she continued on a rising note.

Then her eyes came back up, and the screaming began again.

"Penalosa!" Roger yelled, putting the helmet back on as his mother continued to scream and Dogzard rose from her kill menacingly. "*Penalosa!* Damn it! Get somebody else *in* here!"

When the police had secured the scene and the firefighters could get to work—mostly keeping the fire from spreading; Siminov's building and the two on either side of it were already a total loss—Subianto walked over to where Despreaux and Catrone were breathing something purple at the rear of a Fire Department medical vehicle.

"You two need to get moving," she said, bending down and speaking quietly into their ears. "There's a problem at the Palace."

"What do you think he's going to do, Sir?" Commander Talbert asked quietly.

He sat beside Admiral Victor Gajelis on the admiral's flagship, the Imperial Navy carrier HMS *Trujillo*, studying the tactical readouts. Carrier Squadron Fourteen had been under acceleration towards Old Earth for thirty-one minutes at the maximum hundred and sixty-four gravities its carriers could sustain. Their velocity was up to almost five thousand kilometers per second, and they'd traveled almost seven million kilometers, but they still had *eighty-five* million kilometers—and another three hours and thirty-eight minutes—to go. They could have made the entire voyage in less than two hours, but not if they wanted to decelerate into orbit around the planet when they reached it. On a least-time course, they would have gone scorching past the planet at over seventeen thousand kilometers per second, which would have left them in a piss-poor position to do anything about *holding* the planet for their admiral's patron.

At the moment, however, Talbert wasn't much concerned with what his own squadron's units were going to do. His attention was on the information relayed from General Gianetto about Carrier Squadron Twelve.

"What the hell do you *think* he's going to do?" Gajelis grunted. "If he planned on helping us out, there wouldn't have been any reason for him to cut off communications with Gianetto in the first place, now would there?"

"Maybe it was only temporary, Sir," Talbert said diffidently. "You know some of our own units had problems with their Marine detachments, and Prokourov's squadron's personnel weren't anywhere near as handpicked as ours were. If his Marines tried to stop him and it took him a while to regain control..."

"Be nice if that was what happened," Gajelis growled. "But I doubt it did. Even if Prokourov wanted to take back control after he'd lost it, I don't think it mattered. I never did trust him, whatever the Prince thought."

"Do you think he was part of whatever's happening from the beginning, then, Sir?"

"I doubt it," Gajelis said grudgingly. "If he had been, he wouldn't have just sat there for almost twenty minutes. He'd have been moving towards Old Earth as soon as those other four traitors started moving."

He glowered at the frozen secondary tactical plot where the information relayed by Terran Defense HQ's near-space sensors showed the four carriers which had taken up positions around the planet. Those sensors were no longer reporting, thanks to the point defense systems which had systematically eliminated any platforms not hard-linked to Moonbase, but they'd lasted long enough to tell Gajelis exactly who was waiting for him.

Talbert glanced sideways at his boss. The commander didn't much care for the way this entire thing was shaping up. Like Gajelis, he knew who was in command over there, and he wasn't especially happy about it. Nor did he expect to enjoy the orders he anticipated once Carrier Squadron Fourteen managed to secure the planetary orbitals. But he didn't have much choice. He'd sold his soul to Adoula too long ago to entertain second thoughts now.

At least they didn't need the destroyed sensor platforms to keep an eye on Prokourov. Ship-to-ship detection range for carriers under phase drive was almost thirty light-minutes, and Carrier Squadron Twelve was less than ten light-minutes from *Trujillo*. They wouldn't be able to detect any of Prokourov's parasites at this range—maximum detection range against a cruiser was only eight light-minutes—but they could see exactly what Prokourov's carriers were doing.

Still, he'd have felt a lot more confident it he'd been able to tell exactly what was happening in Old Earth orbit. Corvu Atilius was a wily old fox, and Senior Captain Gloria Demesne, Atilius' cruiser commander, was even worse. Six-to-four odds or not, he wasn't looking forward to tangling with them. Especially not if Prokourov was about to bring a fresh carrier squadron in on their asses.

"Admiral," a communications rating said, "we have an incoming message for you on your private channel."

Gajelis looked up, then grunted.

"Earbud only," he said, then sat back and listened stolidly for almost two minutes. Finally, he nodded to the com rating at the end of the message and looked at Talbert.

"Well," he said grimly, "at least we know what we're going to be doing after we get there."

Francesco Prokourov leaned back in his command chair, considering his own tactical plot. The situation was getting... interesting. Not to his particular surprise, the other carriers of his squadron and his parasite skippers were more than willing to follow his orders. A few of them had opted to pretend they were doing so only out of fear of the squadron's Marine detachments, which was a fairly silly (if human) attempt to cover themselves if worse came to worst. But while Prokourov might not be another Helmut, he'd always had a knack for inspiring loyalty—or at least trust—in his subordinates. Now those subordinates were prepared to follow his lead through the chaos looming before them, and he only hoped he was leading them to victory and not pointless destruction.

Either way, though, he was leading them towards their *duty*, and that was just going to have to do.

But he had every intention of combining duty and survival, and unlike Gajelis, he had access to all of Moonbase's tactical information, which gave him a far tighter grasp on the details than Gajelis or the other Adoula loyalists in the system could possibly have. For example, he knew that Gajelis had not yet punched his cruisers (or had not as of ten minutes earlier), which made a fair amount of sense, and that Admiral La Paz's Thirteenth Squadron—or what was left of it after the original Fatted Calf defections—was coming in from astern of him. But La Paz was going to be a nonissue, whatever happened. His lonely pair of carriers wasn't going to make a great deal of difference after Gajelis' six and the combined eight of Fatted Calf and CarRon 12 had chewed each other up. Besides, CarRon 13 was at least six hours behind CarRon 12.

No, the really interesting question was what was going to happen when Gajelis crunched into Fatted Calf Squadron, and at the moment it was fairly obvious that Gajelis—who, despite his first name, was not a particularly imaginative commander—was hewing to a standard tactical approach.

Each of his carriers carried twenty-four sublight parasite cruisers and one hundred and twenty-five fighters, which gave him a total of one hundred and forty-four cruisers and seven hundred and fifty fighters, but the carriers alone represented thirty-eight percent of his ship-to-ship missile launchers, thirty-two percent of his energy weapons, forty percent of his close-in laser point defense clusters, and forty-eight percent of his countermissile launchers. Not only that, but the carriers were immensely more heavily armored, their energy weapons were six times the size of a cruiser's broadside energy mounts, and their shipkiller missiles were bigger, longer-ranged, and equipped with both more destructive warheads and far superior penetration aids and EW. And as one more minor consideration, carriers—whose hulls had two hundred times the volume of any parasite cruiser—had enormously more capable fire control systems and general computer support.

Cruisers, with better than three and a half times the huge carriers' acceleration rate, were the Imperial Navy's chosen offensive platforms. They could get in more quickly, and no ponderous, unwieldy starship had the acceleration to avoid them inside the Tsukayama Limit of a star system. But they were also far more fragile, and their magazine capacities were much lower. And outside the antimissile basket of their carriers, they were far more vulnerable to long-ranged missile kills, even from other cruisers, far less starships. So although Gajelis was essentially a cruiser commander at heart, he was holding his parasites until his carriers could get close enough to support them when they went in against Fatted Calf.

It was exactly what the Book called for, and given what Gajelis knew, it was also a smart, if cautious, move.

Of course, Gajelis didn't know *everything*, now did he?

"Find New Madrid," Roger said coldly.

He was out of his armor, but still wore the skin-tight cat-suit normally worn under it. The combination of the cat-suit's built in tourniquet and his own highly capable nanite pack had sealed the stump of his left leg, suppressed the pain, and pulled his body forcibly out of shock. None of which had done anything at all for the white-hot fury which filled him.

"Find him," he said softly. "Find him *now.*"

He looked around at the human and Mardukan faces gathered about him in the Empress' private audience room. Their owners' smoke- and bloodstained uniforms and gouged and seared battle armor were as out of place against their elegant surroundings as his own smoke- and sweat-stinking cat-suit, but the bizarre contrast didn't interest him at all at the moment. His mind was too full of the woman, three doors down the hall, who screamed whenever she saw a man's face.

"Where's Rastar?" he asked.

"Dead, Your Highness," one of the Vasin said with a salute. "He fell taking the gate."

"Oh, God *damn* it." Roger closed his eyes and felt his jaw muscles ridge at the sudden spasm of pain he hadn't felt when he lost his leg. A spasm he knew was going to be repeated again and again when the casualty totals were finally added up.

"Catrone? Nimashet?" he asked, his voice harsh and flat with a fear he was unprepared to admit even to himself.

"They've got them," a master sergeant from the Empress' Own—the *real* Empress' Own—replied. "They're on their way. So are Ms. O'Casey and Sergeant Major Kosutic."

"Good," Roger said. "Good."

He stood a moment, nostrils flaring, then shook himself and looked back at his companions again.

"Find New Madrid," he repeated in an icy voice. "That slimy bastard will be skulking around somewhere. Look for an over-dressed servant. And tell Kosutic, when she gets here—go to the Empress. My mother's safety is Kosutic's charge for now."

"Yes, Your Highness," the master sergeant said, and began whispering into his communicator.

"You know," Kjerulf commented to the command room in general, "I've decided I'm rather glad Admiral Prokourov is on our side."

"Amen to that, Sir," the senior Tactical rating said fervently, smiling admiringly at his readouts. Prokourov had punched his cruisers—*and* his fighters—twenty minutes after he got his squadron moving. For a cold-start launch with no previous warn-ing, that was very respectable timing, and it spoke well of his people's readiness to accept his orders. Now those cruisers and fighters were boring ahead at four hundred and fifty gravities, better than two and a half times his carriers' acceleration, but barely three-quarters of their own maximum. At that rate, and employing strict emissions control discipline, shipboard detection range against them dropped to barely four light-minutes. But it meant that they would still reach Old Earth orbit in just over two hours, while CarRon 14 was still better than *three* hours out on its current flight profile. They'd get there far in advance of their own carriers, but they would double Fatted Calf's parasite strength, which would more than offset Gajelis' numerical advantage, especially with the Fatted Calf carriers to support them.

Of course, it was extremely probable that Gajelis would still pick them up before they got clear to Old Earth, but nothing he could do could get his *carriers* there any sooner, and knowing Gajelis...

"They've got the Palace," Larry Gianetto said bleakly from Admiral Gajelis' com display. His voice was inaudible to anyone else on *Trujillo*'s flag deck, but it came clearly over the admiral's earbud.

"Yes, Sir," Gajelis said aloud. He was aware of the need to pick his words carefully, lest one of his weaker-kneed subordinates waver in his duty, especially if he had time to stew over it.

"They're still playing it carefully. They haven't claimed or confirmed—or denied—that that little bastard Roger is back, but the rumors are spreading like wildfire, anyway. And they *have* sent out light armored vehicles and assault shuttles to bring in the Prime Minister, the other Cabinet ministers, and the leaders of the major parties in both the Lords and the Commons, as well as at least a dozen major journalists," Gianetto continued. "Once they've had a chance to get the Empress independently examined, we're all screwed. Unless, of course, we make sure that the results of that examination never become known."

"I understand, Sir."

"Be sure you do, Victor." Gianetto's voice was bleaker than ever as he gazed into the pickup of the com unit aboard the inconspicuous vessel carrying him away from the planet. "The only way to keep everything from falling apart is to take out the Palace and all of these bastards from orbit. Which is going to mean taking out an almighty big chunk of Imperial City, as well. It's on record that 'Roger' already blew up Prince Jackson's home and downtown office in an effort to kill him. If the Palace goes, as far as anyone will know once we get done spinning the story, it'll be because our valiant defenders managed to hold him off long enough for the Navy to arrive. At which point he either suicided to avoid capture, or—even better—hit the Palace with a KEW of his own and managed to escape in the confusion. You understand what I'm telling you, Victor? And that it has the Prince's approval?"

"Yes, Sir. I've already heard from Prince Jackson, and he entirely concurs."

Roger had gotten one of the Mardukans to find a broken pike, and he was leaning on that when New Madrid was brought in. Roger had to admit that he truly did look a good bit like his father. They'd never actually met before. Pity that the meeting was going to be so short, he thought coldly.

"Give me a sword," he said to the nearest Vasin as two Diaspran infantrymen threw his father at his feet.

The Earl of New Madrid was trembling, his terrified face streaked with sweat, and he stared mutely up at Roger as the Mardukan handed him the blade. The cavalry sabre would have been a two-handed sword for almost any human, but Roger held it in one hand, rock steady as he slid the tip of the blade under his father's chin.

"I'm curious, *Father*," he said. "I wonder why my mother would *scream* at the sight of me? Why she should *expect* to see men she can't even remember in her bedroom? Why she's covered in bruises and burns? Why she thinks someone who looks just like *me* killed my brother John in front of her? Do you think you might know the answers to those questions, Father?"

"Please, Roger," New Madrid whimpered, shaking uncontrollably. "*Please!* I—I'm your *father!*"

"'Bad seed' they called me," Roger half-whispered. "Behind my back, usually. Often enough to my face. I wondered what could make them *hate* me so? What could make my own *mother* hate me so? Now I know, don't I, *Father*? Well, Father, when a doctor finds a cancer, he cuts it out." Roger dropped the pike and raised the sword overhead in two hands, balancing on his good foot. "And I'm going to *cut you out!*"

"*NO!*" Nimashet Despreaux screamed from the doorway.

"I have the *right!*" Roger spat, not looking at her, trying not to see her, the sword held over his head and catching the light. "*Do you know what he's done?!*"

"Yes, Roger. I do," Despreaux said quietly. She stepped into the room and walked over to stand between Roger and his father. "And I know you. You can't do this. If you push me aside—if you *could* do it—I'll walk. You said it. Carefully, quietly. No muss. No fuss. We try him, and sentence him, and then slip the poison into his arm. But you *will not* cut off his head in a presence room. No one will ever trust you again if you do. *I* won't trust you."

"Nimashet, for the love of *God*," Roger whispered, trembling, his eyes pleading with her. "*Please*, stand aside."

"No," she said, in a voice of soft steel that was as loving as it was inflexible.

"Roger," Eleanora said from the doorway, "the Prime Minister is going to be here in about . . . oh, ninety seconds." She frowned. "I really think it would be better, in both the short and the long run, if you didn't greet him covered in your father's blood."

"Besides," Catrone said, standing beside her in the door, "if anybody gets him, I do. And you told me I couldn't do him."

"I said you couldn't *torture* him," Roger replied, sword still upraised.

"You also said we'd do it by the Book," Catrone said. "Are you going back on your word?"

Silence hovered in the presence room, a silence broken only by the terrified whimpers of the man kneeling at Roger's feet. And then, finally, Roger spoke again.

"No," he said. "No, Tomcat. I'm not."

He lowered the sword, letting it fall to a rest-arms position, and looked at the cavalryman who'd handed it to him

"Vasin?"

"Your Highness?"

"May I keep this?" Roger asked, looking at the sword. "It's a blade from your homeland, a blade you carried beside your dead Prince—beside my *friend*—for more kilometers than any of your people had ever traveled before. I know what that means. But . . . may I keep it?"

The Mardukan waved both true-hands in a graceful gesture of acceptance and permission.

"It was the blade of my fathers," he said, "handed down over many generations. It came to Therdan at the raising of the city's first wall, and it was there when my Prince hewed a road to life for our women and children as the city died behind us. It is old, Your Highness, steeped in the honor of my people. But I think your request would have pleased my Prince, and I would be honored to place it and its lineage in the hand of such a war leader."

"Thank you," Roger said quietly, still gazing at the blade. "I will hang it somewhere where I can see it every day. It will be a reminder that, sometimes, a sword is best not used."

The Prime Minister stepped into the room and paused at the tableau which greeted him. The soldiers, watching a man holding a sword. New Madrid on his knees, sobbing, held in place by two of the Mardukans.

"I am looking for the Prince," the Prime Minister said, looking at the woman who claimed to be Eleanora O'Casey. "For the *supposed* Prince, that is."

Roger's head turned. The movement was eerily reminiscent of a falcon's smoothly abrupt motion, and the modded brown eyes which locked on the Prime Minister were as lethal as any feathered predator's had ever been.

"I am Prince Roger Ramius Sergei Alexander Chiang Mac-Clintock," he said flatly. "And you, I suppose, would be my mother's Prime Minister?"

"Can you positively identify yourself?" the Prime Minister said dismissively, looking at the man in the soiled cat-suit, holding a sword and balancing on one foot like some sort of neobarbarian. It looked like something out of one of those tacky, lowbrow so-called "historical" novels. Or like a comedy routine.

"It's not something a person would lie about," Roger growled. "Not here, not now." He hopped around to face the Prime Minister, managing somehow to keep the sword balanced as he did. "I'm Roger, Heir Primus. Face that fact. Whether my mother recovers from her ordeal or not—the ordeal she went through while you sat on your fat, spotty, safe, no-risk-taking *ass* and did *nothing*—I *will* be Emperor. If not soon, then someday. Is that clear?"

"I suppose," the Prime Minister said tightly, his lips thinning.

"And if I recall my civics lessons," Roger continued, glaring at the older man, "the Prime Minister must command not simply a majority in Parliament, but also the Emperor's acceptance. He serves, does he not, at the Emperor's pleasure?"

"Yes," the Prime Minister said, lip curled ever so slightly. "But the precedent for removal by an Emperor hasn't been part of our constitutional tradition in ov—"

Roger tossed the sword into the air. He caught it by the pommel, and his arm snapped forward. The sword flew from his hand and hissed past the Prime Minister's head, no more than four centimeters from his left ear lobe, and slammed into the presence chamber's wall like a hammer. It stood there, vibrating, and the Prime Minister's jaw dropped as Roger glared at him.

"I don't much *care* about precedent," Roger told him, "*and I'm not very pleased with you!*"

"God *damn* it!" Victor Gajelis snarled under his breath as the new icons appeared suddenly in his plot. He knew exactly what they were, not that the knowledge made him feel any better about it.

"CIC confirms, Sir," Commander Talbert told him. "That looks like every single one of CarRon 12's cruisers. Prokourov must've punched them twenty-five minutes ago, because they're already up to almost eleven thousand KPS."

Gajelis' mouth tightened as he considered the tactical situation. Frankly, in his considered opinion, it sucked.

By sending his cruisers in at reduced acceleration, Prokourov had managed to get their velocity up to almost two thousand kilometers per second more than CarRon 14's. They were still seven million kilometers—almost eight—further from Old Earth orbit, but their greater velocity meant they would actually arrive well before Carrier Squadron Fourteen. Of course, they were *only* cruisers, but there were ninety-six of them.

No fancy cruiser tricks were going to get Prokourov's *carriers* to the planet before Gajelis' own carriers, not with CarRon 14's twenty-minute head start. But CarRon 12's missiles would have the range to cover anything in orbit around the planet for over an hour before they actually reached the planet's orbital shell. Accuracy wouldn't be very good at such extended ranges, but to carry out his own mission orders, Gajelis had to get within no more than three or four hundred thousand kilometers of the planet. He couldn't guarantee the accuracy Gianetto and Adoula had specified from any greater range, even assuming that he could get missiles through the defensive fire of the ships already in planetary orbit. Besides, it was going to be difficult to make it look as if *Prince Roger's* adherents had done the deed if Moonbase had detailed sensor readings showing shipkillers from CarRon 14 hitting atmosphere. No, he had to get close enough to do it with KEW, and that meant advancing into Prokourov's carriers' missile envelope.

Unless . . .

He thought furiously. Almost two hours had passed since the attack on the Palace began. His communications sections were monitoring the confused babble of news reports and speculation boiling through the planetary datanet, and it was obvious that opinion was hardening behind the belief that it was, indeed, Prince Roger. At the moment, however, most of the commentary seemed to incline towards the belief that it was simply a case of the nefarious Traitor Prince returning for a second attempt. The notion that it was an attempt to rescue the Empress was still being greeted with skepticism, but that was going to change as soon as the first independent report of the Empress' condition got out. That was going to take time, but there was no way to know how much of it.

"Punch the cruisers," he said flatly. "Maximum acceleration."

Talbert glanced at him, then passed along the order.

"What about the fighters, Sir?" he asked after a moment.

"Send them in, too," Gajelis said. "Configure them for CSP to cover the cruisers."

"Yes, Sir."

Gajelis didn't miss the brief hesitation before the commander's acknowledgment, but he ignored it. He didn't like committing his cruisers this early, but his own ships and Prokourov's carriers were still eight light-minutes apart, which meant it would take eight minutes for Prokourov to learn that Cruiser Flotilla One-Forty had launched. Eight minutes in which Gajelis' cruisers would be free to accelerate at their maximum velocity. Even assuming Prokourov went to maximum acceleration on his own cruisers the instant they detected CruFlot 140—which he undoubtedly would—Gajelis' cruisers would have built enough acceleration, coupled with the distance CarRon 14 had traveled before launching them, to arrive four minutes before CruFlot 120. And CarRon 14 would be twenty minutes closer to the planet when that happened.

Gajelis' cruisers would be outside the effective range of his carriers' antimissile defenses, but they would be *inside* the basket for his carriers' shipkillers. The same thing would be true for Prokourov's carriers, but Prokourov's targeting solutions would be nowhere near as good. It wasn't an ideal solution, by any means, but, then, there *wasn't* an ideal solution to this particular tactical problem. And if he could get his own cruisers into energy range of the four so-called "Fatted Calf Squadron" carriers covering the planet, he could hammer them, especially with his own *six* carriers' attack missiles piling in on top of the cruisers' fire.

He was going to lose most of his own cruisers in the process, of course, especially with Prokourov's cruisers coming in on them so rapidly. He had no doubt that that was what had prompted Talbert's hesitation. But it was also what cruisers were for. He didn't like it, but he'd come up through cruisers himself. He'd understood how the process worked then, and so would his cruiser skippers now.

Who also all knew they were dead men if Adoula went down.

"They've punched their cruisers," Kjerulf said from the com display.

"Yeah, we sort of noticed," Captain Atilius responded dryly. If the older officer had shown any hesitation about committing himself in the first place, there was no sign of it now. He was like an old warhorse, Kjerulf thought, faintly amused even now, despite all that was happening. Corvu Atilius probably should have made admiral decades ago, but he'd always been too tactical-minded, too focused on maneuvers and tactical doctrine to play the political game properly. "Roughhewn" was a term which had been used to describe his personality entirely too often over the course of his career, but he was definitely the right man in the right place as Fatted Calf Squadron's senior officer. He actually seemed to be looking *forward* to what was coming.

"I always knew Gajelis had shit for brains," Atilius continued. He shook his head. "He's going to get reamed."

"Maybe," Chantal Soheile said from her quadrant of the conferenced display. "But so are we. And it's not like he's got a lot of alternatives." She shook her head in turn. "He's got the edge in carriers and missile power. Basically, the only real option he's got is to pile in on top of us and tried to bulldoze us out of the way before Prokourov can get here."

"Sure," Atilius agreed. "But I guarantee you he'll be sending in his fighters configured for combat space patrol. It's the way his head works. He just doesn't see them as shipkillers—not the way he does cruisers. Besides," he bared his teeth, "his guys are going to have to deal with *Gloria*, aren't they?"

"CruFlot 140's punched, Sir," a sensor technician reported. "Max accel."

"Have they, indeed?" Senior Captain Benjamin Weintraub, CO, Cruiser Flotilla One-Twenty, replied. His ships were eighteen light-seconds ahead of their carriers, and he saw no reason to waste an additional half-minute waiting for Admiral Prokourov's instructions. "Take us to maximum acceleration," he said.

Captain Senior-Grade Gloria Demesne, CO HMS *Bellingham*, narrowed her hazel eyes and considered the tactical plot as she leaned back in her command chair and sipped her coffee. It was hot, strong and black, with just a pinch of salt. Black gang coffee, just the way she liked it. Which couldn't be said for the tactical situation.

CruFlot 150—well, actually, it was component parts of four separate squadrons, but CruRon 153 was the senior squadron, Gloria was 153's CO, "CruFlot Fatted Calf" sounded pretty fucking stupid, and they by-God had to call it *something*—faced half again its own numbers. Not good. Not good at all, but what the hell? At least help was on its way, and if they couldn't take a joke, they shouldn't have joined.

Imperial cruisers carried powerful beam weapons, but for the opening phase of any battle, they relied on the contents of their missile magazines, filled with hypervelocity, fission-fusion contact and standoff X-ray missiles. They fought in data-linked networks, in which each ship was capable of local or external control of the engagement "basket." But for all their speed and firepower, their ChromSten armor was lighter than most military starships boasted and they lacked the multiply redundant systems tunnel drive ships could carry. The far larger FTL vessels were much more sluggish in maneuver, but they were undeniably powerful units, especially in defense. Although cruisers' acceleration meant they could chase the big bruisers down, doing so was always a risky proposition. And, despite the percentage of their internal volume given over to missile stowage, cruisers had much less magazine space than their larger motherships. Nor could they match a carrier's missile defenses, and that might be important. Because Carrier Squadron Fourteen was in the process of making a critical mistake.

Whether through simple stupidity—she'd never had thought much of Admiral Gajelis' brains—or because they were in a hurry, the hundred and forty-four ships of Cruiser Flotilla 140 were charging straight on in at 6.2 KPS^2.

Obviously, Gajelis wanted to get them into range for precision KEW strikes on the Palace, which meant brushing the four Fatted Calf carriers—and their cruisers—out of his way. But his more sluggish carriers were dropping further and further behind the speeding cruisers—they'd been almost eight and a half million kilometers behind when the cruisers made turnover. By the time CruFlot 140 entered effective missile range of Old Earth orbit, they'd be over *twenty-seven* and a half million kilometers back.

Of course, missile engagement envelopes were flexible. Both cruiser-sized and capital ship shipkillers could pull three thousand gravities of acceleration. The difference was that capital missiles, fired from the launchers which only ships the size of carriers mounted, could pull that acceleration for fifteen minutes, whereas cruiser missiles were good for only ten. That gave the larger missiles an effective range from rest of over twelve million kilometers before burnout, whereas a cruiser missile had an effective range before burnout of around 2,700,000 kilometers. Platform speeds at launch radically affected those ranges, however, and so did the fact that missile drives could be switched off and then on again, allowing lengthy ballistic "coasting" flight profiles to provide what were for all intents and purposes unlimited range . . . against nonevading targets. Against targets which could evade, and which also mounted the most sophisticated electronic warfare systems available, *effective* ranges were far shorter. Then there was little matter of active antimissile defenses.

Except that in this particular case, countermissiles from Gajelis' *carriers* weren't going to be a factor. CarRon 14's longer-ranged capital missiles could reach past its cruisers to range on Desmesne's ships and the Fatted Calf carriers, but their *counter*missiles would be unable to intercept the fire directed at their cruisers. That meant CruFlot 140 was more vulnerable than CruFlot 150, which was stuck in relatively tight to its own carriers, since a carrier mounted twenty-seven times the countermissile tubes a cruiser did. Gajelis' carriers and cruisers between them mounted roughly fifty-six hundred shipkiller tubes to Fatted Calf's combined thirty-seven hundred, but Fatted Calf had the cover of almost nine thousand *counter*missile tubes to CruFlot 140's seven thousand. And, even more importantly, no cruiser could match the targeting capability and fire control sophistication of an all-up carrier, which meant Fatted Calf's countermissile fire was going to be far more effective on a bird-for-bird basis. Not to mention the fact that each carrier mounted almost thirty-five hundred close-in laser point defense clusters, none of which would be available to CruFlot 140.

Gajelis had obviously decided to expend his cruisers in an effort to inflict crippling damage on Fatted Calf before his carriers came into range of Demesne's cruisers. He could "stack" shipkillers from his carriers to some extent by launching them in fairly tight waves, with preprogrammed ballistic segments of staggered lengths so that they arrived in CruFlot 140's control basket as a single salvo. It was going to be ugly if—*when*—he did, but the capital missiles would be significantly less accurate staging through the fire control of mere cruisers. And if something nasty happened to be happening to his advanced fire control platforms, it would throw a sizable spanner into the works.

It wasn't as if he had an enormous number of options, she reflected. For that matter, Fatted Calf didn't have a huge number of options, either. But a lot depended on the way the two sides chose to *exercise* their options.

The details. It was always in the details.

"Emergence . . . now," Astrogation said.

"It will take some time for us to get hard word on what's going on in the system," Admiral Helmut said, glancing over at Julian. They were in the Fleet CIC, watching the tactical plots and wondering if the trick was going to work.

"Sir, no response to standard tactical interrogation, of the outer shell platforms," the senior Tactical Officer reported after several minutes. "We're getting what appears to be a priority lockout."

"Directed specifically against us?" Helmut asked sharply.

"I can't say for certain, Sir," the Taco replied.

"In that case, contact Moonbase directly. Tell them who we are, and ask them to turn the lights back on for us."

"Sir," Marciel Poertena's executive officer said just a bit nervously, "far be it from me to second-guess the Admiral, but do you really think he knows what he's doing here?"

"Don't be pocking silly," Poertena said. "Of course he does. I t'ink."

He looked at his display. HMS *Capodista* would never, in the wildest drug dream, be considered a *war*ship. She was a freighter. A bulk cargo carrier. The only thing remotely military about her was her propulsion, since she had to be able to keep up with the fleet elements she'd been designed to serve. Which, unfortunately, meant that her tunnel and phase drive plants were both powerful enough for the Dark Lord of the Sixth's current brainstorm.

At the moment, she, *Ozaki*, and *Adebayo* were squawking the transponders of HMS *Trenchant*, *Kershaw*, and *Hrolf Kraki*, otherwise known as Carrier Squadron Sixty-Three. Nor were they the only service ships which had somehow inexplicably acquired the transponder codes of their betters.

"Of course he does," Captain Poertena muttered again, touching the crucifix under his uniform tunic.

✧　　✧　　✧

"What the hell is that?!" Admiral Ernesto La Paz demanded as a fresh rash of icons appeared in his tactical display. It was basically a rhetorical question, since there was only one thing it really could be.

"Major tunnel drive footprint astern of us!" Tactical called out at almost the same instant. "Eighteen point sources, right on the Tsukayama Limit."

"Eighteen." La Paz and his chief of staff looked at each other.

"It's got to be Helmut," the chief of staff said.

"And isn't that just peachy," La Paz snarled. He glowered at the display for several more seconds, then turned his head.

"Communications, dump a continuous tactical stream to all other squadrons."

"Aye, aye, Sir."

"Maneuvering, come twenty degrees to starboard, same plane. Astrogation, start calculating your first transit to Point Able."

"Sir," the Tactical Officer announced suddenly, "we have two phase drive signatures directly in front of us, range approximately four-point-five light-minutes. BattleComp reads their IFF as *Courageous* and *Damocles*. They're accelerating towards the inner system at one-point-six-four KPS squared. Current velocity, one-three-point-three thousand KPS."

"Ah, yes," Helmut murmured. "That would be our friend Ernesto. But only two ships? And already up to over thirteen thousand?"

He tapped his right thumb and forefinger together in front of him, whistling softly. Then he smiled thinly at Julian.

"It would appear that the party started without us, Sergeant Julian. How irritating."

"*Courageous* and *Damocles* are changing course, Sir," the Taco said. "They're coming to starboard."

"Of course they are," Helmut snorted. "La Paz isn't about to fight at one-to-nine odds! And he knows damned well we can't catch them if he just keeps running. No doubt he'd like us to try to do just that, though."

He glanced at Julian again and snorted at the Marine's obviously confused expression.

"I keep forgetting you don't know your ass from your elbow

where naval maneuvers are concerned, Sergeant," he said dryly. "At least a part of what's happening is obvious enough. The attack on the Palace must have kicked off at least six hours ahead of schedule, because *we* arrived within one minute of our projected schedule, despite our little side excursion, and to have reached that velocity, CarRon 13 must have been underway for a bit over two and a half hours. And since it would have taken over twenty minutes for movement orders from Old Earth to reach La Paz, that gives us a pretty tight lock on when the balloon must have gone up. And we, unfortunately, are still nine-point-eight hours away from Old Earth. So it would appear that the plan to divert Adoula's squadrons away from the planet *before* the attack isn't really likely to work."

Julian's face tightened, but the admiral shook his head.

"Doesn't mean he's failed, Sergeant," he said, with a gentleness he seldom showed. "In fact, all the evidence suggests the attack on the Palace itself probably succeeded."

"*What* evidence?" Julian demanded.

"The fact that the system reconnaissance platforms have been locked out, that La Paz was obviously headed in-system just as fast as he could go, and that his carrier squadron is down to only two ships," Helmut said.

"The recon lockout had to have come from Moonbase—that's the only communications node with the reach to shut down the entire system. And if Adoula were in control of the situation, he certainly wouldn't be ordering his own units locked out of the system reconnaissance platforms. So the lockout order almost certainly came from someone supporting Prince Roger ... which means *his* partisans have control of Moonbase.

"The fact that La Paz was headed in-system suggests the same thing—Adoula and Gianetto are calling in their loyalists, and they wouldn't be doing that unless they needed the firepower because of the situation on the Old Earth.

"And the fact that La Paz is down to only two ships—that half his squadron is someplace else—suggests that someone has been doing a little creative force structure reshuffling. My money for the reshuffler is on Kjerulf. Which would also make sense of Moonbase's defection from the Adoula camp."

"Sir," the Taco put in, "we're also picking up additional phase drive signatures. Looks like four carriers coming in from out-system—we're too far out for IFF—about half a light-minute out from Old Earth, decelerating towards orbit. We've got six more signatures coming out from the inner-system, decelerating towards the same destination."

"Gajelis and . . . Prokourov," Helmut said thoughtfully. He glanced at Julian again. "The six coming out from sunward have to be Gajelis and CarRon 14. I'm guessing the other four are CarRon 12, which *probably* means Prokourov's decided to back your Prince. I can't think of any reason even Gianetto would think he needed ten carriers and over two hundred cruisers to deal with an attack on the Palace. Mind you, I could be wrong. He always did believe in bigger hammers."

"Incoming. Many vampires incoming!" Tactical announced.

Gloria Demesne only nodded to herself. It had been obvious what was coming for the last thirty minutes. CruFlot 140 was still over fifteen minutes out, just entering its own missile range of Fatted Calf, but Gajelis' carriers had started launching over a half-hour before. Now their big, nasty missiles were stacking up in CruFlot 140's control basket, and the cruisers themselves had just gone to maximum rate fire. No wonder even the computers were having trouble trying to tally up the total.

She understood exactly what Gajelis was thinking. This was a bid to overwhelm Fatted Calf with firepower while his own carriers were safely out of harm's way. Fatted Calf's carriers had the range to engage CarRon 14, but the chances of a hit at this range, especially without cruisers of their own out there to provide final course corrections were . . . poor, to say the least. And even any of their birds which might have scored hits would still have to get through CarRon 14's missile defenses. The term "snowball in hell" came forcibly to mind when she considered that scenario. So at the moment, he was free to concentrate *his* fire on the targets of his choice from a position of relative immunity.

For as long as his own cruisers lasted, anyway.

It might just work, but it might not, too, especially given the range at which his cruisers had opened fire. Their missiles would be coming in at high terminal velocities, but crowding the very limits of their designed fire control and with a ten-second signal lag in fire control telemetry, which gave away accuracy. The Imperial Navy's electronic warfare capabilities were good, even against people who had exactly the same equipment. It took the computational capabilities of a major platform to distinguish between real and false targets reliably. The sensors and AI loaded into shipkiller missiles were highly capable, but not as capable as those of the cruiser or carrier which had launched them, so firing at such extreme range meant Gajelis was accepting poorer terminal guidance due to the delay in telemetry corrections.

The sheer size of the salvos he was throwing was also going to have an effect. It wasn't going to catastrophically overwhelm the fire control capability of his cruisers, but it was going to overload it, which meant the computers would have less time to spend coaxing each missile into the best attack solution. If she knew Gajelis, he was going to concentrate a lot of that fire—especially the heavier missiles from his carriers—on Fatted Calf's carriers, instead of hammering the lighter cruisers. There were arguments in favor of either tactic, but Fatted Calf had no intention of wasting *any* of its birds on carriers. Not at this range. Demesne intended to kill cruisers, ruthlessly crushing the smaller, weaker platforms while they were out of their carriers' cover, and Captain Atilius, Fatted Calf's acting CO, just happened to be *Minotaur*'s skipper. Which meant the rest of the squadron's carriers, as well as its cruisers, were conforming to Desmesne's tactical direction.

Which was also why none of Fatted Calf's units had fired a single shot yet. At this range, it would take almost five minutes for CruFlot 140's missiles to reach Fatted Calf, and at their maximum rate fire the cruisers would shoot themselves dry in about fifteen minutes. They'd put a lot of missiles into space over those twenty minutes, but she had a lot of point defense to deal with them. If she waited to fire until the distance to Gajelis' cruisers fell to decisive range, *Bellingham* and her consorts would be able to control *their* missiles all the way in, which meant they'd be at least twenty-five percent more effective. Of course, they'd have to survive Gajelis' fire before they launched, but every silver lining had its cloud.

"Open fire, Captain?" Ensign Scargall asked. The young officer's taut voice was higher pitched than usual and her face was pale as she looked at her readouts, and Gloria didn't blame her a bit.

There were already well over forty-five thousand missiles on the way, and *still* none of Fatted Calf's ships had opened fire.

"No, Ensign," Gloria said in a husky voice. She punched in a command, and the bridge was filled with a throbbing beat as she pulled out a pseudo-nic stick. She brushed a lock of red hair out of her eyes and puffed on the stick, lighting it.

"Hold your fire," she said. "Let them come. Come to me, my love," she whispered. "*Fifteen thousand tears I've cried . . .*" She'd had a hell of a singing voice, once. Before the pseudo-nic smoke had killed it. But every silver lining had its cloud. "*Screaming deceiving and bleeding for you . . .*"

"They're fighting dumb, Admiral," Commander Talbert said.

"Not much else they can do," Gajelis shrugged. "They have to come to meet us to keep us away from the planet. In fact, the only thing that surprises me is that they haven't cut the cruisers loose to intercept our cruisers even further out."

"They have to be worried about keeping us as far out as possible, Sir," Talbert said, "but they've had over three hours to get their forces deployed. They ought to be further out than this by now. And where are their fighters?"

"They probably didn't know exactly when this was coming," Gajelis said, and grimaced. "That's the problem with coups, Commander—it's harder than hell to make sure everyone's ready to kick off at the right moment. They're probably having to make this up as they go along, and they know we're just the first squadron they're going to have on their backs. So they're playing it as cautious as they can, but they still can't afford to wait us out and let us get into kinetic range of Imperial City. As for the fighters, they're obviously holding them aboard the carriers. Given the force imbalance, they'll want to send them in with maximum Leviathan loads. In a minute or two, they'll punch them to come in across the cruisers, from either system north or south."

"Atilius is tricky," Talbert pointed out. "And Demesne is worse. This isn't their style, Sir."

"There's no *style* to a battle like this, Commander," the admiral said, frowning. "You just throw fire until one side retires or is *gone*. We've got more firepower; we'll win."

"Yes, Sir," Talbert said, trying to project a little enthusiasm.

It was hard. Especially knowing that Prokourov's cruisers were going to be close enough to start "adjusting" the force imbalance in about another ten minutes. "I suppose there is a certain quality to quantity."

"Fatted Calf Squadron has just flushed its fighters," Tactical said.

"See?" the admiral said. "Flip a coin whether they go in over the cruisers, or under."

"Here they come!"

Not exactly a professional announcement, there, Demesne thought. But under the circumstances, a pardonable slip.

The volume of space to sunward of Old Earth was a hurricane of raging destruction. Countermissiles, roaring out at thirty-five hundred gravities, charged headlong to meet a solid wall of incoming shipkillers. Proximity warheads began to erupt, flashing like prespace flash guns at some championship sporting event. Stroboscopic bubbles of nuclear fury boiled like brimstone flaring through the chinks in the front gate of Hell. The interceptions began over a million kilometers out, ripping huge holes in the comber of shipkillers racing towards Fatted Calf, but the vortex of destruction thundered unstoppably onward. Eighty-four *thousand* missiles had been fired at only one hundred targets, and nothing in the universe could have stopped them all.

Point defense laser clusters opened fire as the range fell to seventy thousand kilometers, and the fury of destruction redoubled. CruFlot 140's missiles were coming in at twenty-seven thousand kilometers per second, which gave the lasers less than three seconds to engage, but at least tracking had had plenty of time to set up the firing solutions. Demesne's cruisers' point defense was lethally effective, and the four carriers' fire was even more deadly.

Laser heads began to detonate. Against ChromSten-armored ships, even those as light as cruisers, even the most powerful bomb-pumped laser had a standoff range of less than ten thousand kilometers; against a carrier, maximum effect of standoff range was barely half that. Cruisers began to take hits, belching atmosphere and debris, but Demesne and Atilius had been right. Over seventy percent of the incoming missiles were targeted on the carriers, a hundred thousand kilometers *behind* the cruisers.

CruFlot 150 turned, keeping its better broadside sensors positioned to engage the missiles which had already run past it, even as its ships took their own hammering. And they *did* take a hammering. Thirty percent of eighty-four thousand was "only" two hundred and sixty missiles per cruiser, and even with poor firing solutions and the carriers' support—what they could spare from their own self-defense—an awful lot of them got through.

Lieutenant Alfy Washington lay back in his seat, looking up at the stars through his glassteel canopy, his arms crossed. Fighters, and especially fighters on minimum power, had *very* little signature. Spotting them at more than a light-second or so required visual tracking, and space fighters were a light-absorbing matte black for a reason. But they were very, very fast. At an acceleration rate of eight KPS², they could pile on velocity in a hurry, and even their phase drive signatures were hard to notice at interplanetary distances.

He checked his toot and nodded silently at the data that was being fed to his division over the hair-fine whisker laser.

"Christ, Gajelis is dumb as a rock," he muttered, lying back again and closing his eyes. "And I'm glad as hell I'm not in cruisers."

HMS *Bellingham* rocked as another blast of coherent radiation slammed into her armored flank.

"Tubes Ten and Fourteen off-line," Tactical said tightly. "Heavy jamming from the enemy squadron, but we've still got control of the missiles."

For all their toughness, cruisers were nowhere near so heavily armored as carriers. Even a capital ship graser—or the forward-bearing spinal mount weapon of a cruiser like *Bellingham*—couldn't hope to penetrate a capital ship's armor at any range beyond forty thousand kilometers. Missile hatches and weapons bays were more vulnerable, since they necessarily represented openings in the ship's armored skin, but even they were heavily cofferdammed with ChromSten bulkheads to contain damage. For all practical purposes, an energy-armored combat had to get to within eighty thousand kilometers if it hoped to inflict damage, and to half of that if it wanted decisive results. Missiles had to get even closer, but, then again, missiles didn't care whether or not they survived the experience.

Cruisers, unfortunately, were a bit easier to kill, and *Bellingham* bucked again as yet more enemy fire smashed into her.

"Heavy damage, port forward!" Damage Control snapped. "Hull breach, Frames Thirty-Seven to Forty-six. Magazine Three open to space."

"That's okay. We got the birds out first," Demesne said, rubbing the arms of her station chair. Her tubes were flushed, and all she was doing now was surviving long enough to counter the Adoula squadron's ECM through the birds' guidance links. "Just let them stay dumb a *little* longer...."

"Here comes anoth—" Tactical said, and then *Bellingham* heaved like a storm-sick windjammer.

The combat information center flexed and buckled, groaning as some furious giant twisted it between his hands, and Demesne felt her station chair rip loose from its mounts as the lights went out. The next thing she knew, she was on her side, still strapped to the chair, and one of her arms felt ... pretty bad.

"Damage Control?" she croaked as she hit the quick release with her good hand. That was when she noticed the compartment was also in microgravity.

"XO?"

Nobody else in CIC seemed to be moving. Ensign Scargall was still in her station chair, sitting upright, but she ended just above the waist. What was left of her was held in place by a lap belt. The others looked to have been done by blast and debris. What a damn shame.

"Bit of a scar, there, Ensign," Demesne said. She was more than a little woozy herself, and she caught herself giggling in reaction.

"Captain?" her first officer replied in a startled voice. "I thought you were gone, Ma'am!"

"Bad pennies, XO. Bad pennies," she said. "How bad is it?"

"Heavy damage to Fusion Three and Five. CIC took a hit—I guess that's pretty obvious. Alternate CIC is up and functioning. Damage teams are on the way to your location."

"We're still fighting?" she asked, grasping a piece of scrap metal which had once been a million-credit weapons control station. Oh, well. There were others. Hopefully.

"Still in the game," the XO said. "Local gravity disruptions."

"Right." Demesne pushed herself across the shattered compartment to the armored hatch. It was warped, and the readouts on the access panel were dead. She considered the problem for a moment, then pulled herself along the bulkhead to the large hole in the armor which had been supposed to protect CIC. She'd just about reached the ragged-edged hole when there was a flutter, and she got her feet under her just as gravity came back on. It was about half power, but better than floating.

She considered the breached bulkhead with a frown. The hole, while undeniably large, wasn't exactly what anyone might call neat. The passageway outside CIC had been pretty thoroughly chewed up, and there was a gap—over a meter wide—in the deck. That didn't seem all that far, but this particular gap lit up the darkened passageway like an old-fashioned light bulb with the cheery red of near molten metal. Besides, she was in no shape to jump any gaps under the best of conditions, and the jagged, knifelike projections fanging the bulkhead hole scarcely qualified as "the best" of anything. She didn't like to think about what they'd do to her unarmored shipsuit if she tried to get up a run to vault across the gap and didn't hit the hole dead center. She couldn't afford any nasty little punctures, anymore than she could afford to come up short on that handy-dandy frying pan. The compartment's atmosphere had been evacuated—not surprisingly, since she could see stars through the meter-and-a-half hole in the passageway's deckhead if she leaned over and looked up. The frigging hole had been punched halfway through *her* ship! And it wasn't the only one, she suspected. That would have made her cranky, if she'd been the type.

But this wasn't the time to be thinking about that. The problem at hand was how to get out of CIC and to the alternate bridge. And, okay, admit it—she wasn't tracking really well. Probably the pain from the broken arm. Or maybe being thrown across the compartment.

She was still considering her condition—and the condition of her ship, which was just as bad or worse—when an armored Marine suddenly poked his head around the edge of the hole from the other side.

"Holy crap!" the Marine said on the local circuit. "Captain Demesne? You're *alive?*"

"Am I standing here?" she snapped in a gravel voice. "Is this a red suit? Does anybody *else* get a Santa suit?"

"No, Ma'am," the Marine said. "I mean, yes, Ma'am. I mean—"

"Oh, quit stuttering and lie down," Demesne said, pointing to the glowing edges of the gap.

"Ma'am?" the Marine said, clearly confused.

"Lie down across the gap," Demesne said, slowly and carefully, as it speaking to a child.

"Yes, Ma'am," the Marine said. He set down his plasma cannon and lay down across the gap obediently.

Captain Demesne considered him for a moment, then crawled carefully across his armored back, slithering out of CIC and towards her duty.

Commander Bogdan jinked her fighter to the side as a missile from one of the cruisers to planetary north flashed towards her squadron. But the cruisers weren't putting up their regular fight after the hammering they'd taken from CruFlot 140's fire.

That was good, but her business wasn't with Fatted Calf's cruisers. Her job was to intercept the Fatted Calf fighters before they got close enough to launch their Leviathan anti-ship missiles.

Fleet fighters were basically the smallest hull which could be wrapped around a Protessa-Sheehan phased gravity drive and the Frederickson-Hsu countergravity field which damped the man-killing effects of the phase drive. The size of the Navy's current Eagle III fighter also happened to be the largest volume which could be enclosed in a field capable of a full eight hundred gravities of acceleration.

All of that propulsion hardware, coupled with life support requirements, the necessary flight computers and other electronics, and a light forward-firing laser armament, left exactly zero internal volume, and the Eagle III was capable of only extremely limited atmospheric maneuvers. The phase drive would not function in atmosphere, and although the counter-grav could provide lift (after a fashion) it wasn't really configured for that, either. Nor did the fighter's emergency reaction thrusters begin to provide the brute power of something like an assault shuttle. Then again, the reaction drive assault shuttles had the internal volume for a *lot* of payload, whereas the volume requirements of the fighter's drive systems meant that all of its payload had to be carried externally.

Depending on the exact external ordnance loads selected, an Eagle III could carry up to five of the big, smart Leviathans. They were shorter-legged than ship-to-ship weapons. At 4,200 gravities, they accelerated forty percent faster than shipboard antiship missiles, but they had a maximum powered endurance of only three minutes. And, unlike ship-launched shipkillers, their stripped-down size left them with a drive which could not be turned on and off at will. Which meant they had a powered envelope from rest of approximately 667,000 kilometers and a terminal velocity from rest of 7,560 KPS. They were also much smaller targets...with *very* capable ECM and penaids. In short, they might be short-ranged and less flexible, but they were bastards to stop with point defense, so keeping them away from the carriers was a prime mission. And this time, everything was going right.

The fighters from the Fatted Calf units were slashing in at high acceleration, intent on closing the range to CruFlot 140 before launching, but Bogdan's fighters were armed specifically for an antifighter engagement, unburdened by the bulky shipillers. They could have carried up to fourteen Astaroth antifighter/antiship-killer missiles in place of those five Leviathans. Or, as in Bogdan's fighters' case, eight Astaroths and two Foxhawk decoy missiles. That would give them a decisive advantage in the furball, and they'd punched with perfect timing to intercept the mission. The Fatted Calf fighters had another fourteen thousand kilometers to go before they could launch on the cruisers. And by then, Bogdan's squadron would be all over them, like a tiger on...a fatted calf.

"Coming up on initial launch," Bogdan said, prepping her Astaroths.

"Commander," Peyravi in Division 4 said suddenly. "Commander! Visual ID! *Those aren't fighters!*"

Bogdan blanched and set her visual systems to auto-track, trying to spot the targets. Finally, as something occluded a star, she got a hard lock, and swore.

"Son of a *bitch*." She switched to Fleet frequency. "Son of a bitch, son of a bitch, son of a—Mickey, Mickey, Mickey!" she shouted, calling for a priority override to the carrier squadron's

CIC. "These are Foxhawk-Two *drones*! Repeat, they're Foxhawk-Deuces!"

"Blacksheep, Blacksheep," Washington's com said suddenly.

The Adoula fighter squadrons would have gotten close enough for a visual on the Foxhawks by now. The ship-launched version of the standard fighter decoys was big and powerful, but not big enough to fool sensors forever, and that meant it was time to go. Washington adjusted his chair to a better combat configuration and started bringing his systems online.

"Yes, Sir," he said, deepening his voice. "Three bags full . . ."

Admiral Gajelis had just heard the "Mickey" call when the lieutenant commander at Tactical nodded.

"Eagle fighters lighting off," she said. "They must've been blacked down. North polar three-one-five. Closing at four-three-seven-five! Range, two-five-three-two-five-zero!"

"Leviathan guidance systems coming on-line!" a sensor tech said. "Raid count is two hundred . . . five hundred . . . *fifteen* hundred bogeys! Vampire! Vampire, vampire—we have missile separation! Seven-five thousand—I say again, seven-five-zero-zero vampires inbound! Impact in six seconds!"

Commander Talbert's belly muscles locked solid. *Fifteen hundred fighters?* That was impossible! Unless—

"Punch all defense missiles, maximum launch!" Gajelis snapped. "And get the fighters back here!"

"Like there's time," Commander Talbert muttered as he passed on the orders.

Gloria Demesne charged into her alternate bridge just as the fighter ambush sprang. It wasn't just Fatted Calf's fighters. Prokourov had sent his own fighters ahead under maximum acceleration even before he got his cruisers into space. And Kjerulf's Moonbase fighters had reported for duty over an hour ago. There'd been plenty of time to get the speedy little parasites into position and shut down their emissions. Now they poured their heavy loads of Leviathans into the unsuspecting carriers from what amounted to knife-range.

Normally, fighter missiles had very little chance of significantly injuring a massively armored carrier. But, then again, normally the carrier's commander wasn't stupid enough to let fifteen hundred fighters get within twenty-five thousand kilometers of them with a closing velocity of over four thousand kilometers per second.

"Oh, no," Captain Demesne said softly. "You're not going *anywhere.*"

The Fatted Calf fighters, their racks flushed and empty, had gone to max deceleration on a heading back to their carriers leaving the field to the opposing cruisers. CruFlot 140, however, was badly out of position ... and hopelessly screwed.

Both cruiser forces had taken heavy losses—Demesne had lost fifty-seven of her ninety-six ships—but CruFlot 140 had lost eighty-eight. They were down to fifty-six to her thirty-nine, they'd exhausted their own shipkillers, and even if their carriers had been in range to cover them with countermissiles, they were too busy fighting for their own lives against the fighter ambush to worry about their parasites. Which meant that the cruisers' only real option was to bore on in for the kill on CruFlot 150's remaining cruisers, hoping to reach beam range, where their numerical advantage could still make itself felt. Unfortunately for them, Demesne's readouts indicated that all of them were gushing air. Worse, from their perspective, they were well inside the missile envelope of the Fatted Calf carriers.

Those carriers hadn't gotten off unscathed in the missile holocaust. Captain Julius Fenrec's *Gloria* was out of it. She'd been shot to pieces—not such a good omen for certain cruiser skippers, perhaps; Demesne's mouth twisted wryly at the thought—and her surviving personnel were evacuating as rapidly as possible. It was an even bet whether or not they'd all get off before her runaway Fusion Twelve's containment failed. But the other three carriers of the improvised squadron were still in action, and unlike *Gloria,* their damage was essentially superficial. They'd lost very few of their missile launchers, and while their fighters hammered Gajelis' carriers, they were free to engage the surviving enemy cruisers undistracted by anything else. And that, Gloria Demesne thought, would be all they wrote.

Of course, in the meantime, there were all those missiles the fighters had sent scorching into CarRon 14's teeth. Which ought to begin arriving ... right ... about ...

"Detonations on the carriers," the assistant tactical officer said. "Multiple detonations! Holy shit, *Melshikov* is just *gone!*"

"Admiral," Lieutenant Commander Clinton, at Tactical Two said, coughing on the smoke eddying about the compartment. CIC hadn't lost environment, and she still had her helmet latched back. "*Melshikov* is gone, and *Porter* reports critical damage. Everybody else is still intact ... more or less."

Victor Gajelis ground his teeth together in fury. Fighters. Who would have believed *fighters* could inflict that much damage?

He glared at *Trujillo*'s damage control schematic. The fighter strike had concentrated heavily on *Melshikov* and *Porter*, and for all intents and purposes, destroyed both of them. *Porter* was still technically intact, but she'd lost two-thirds of her combat capability, her phase drive was badly damaged, and her tunnel drive had been completely disabled. She could neither survive in combat nor avoid it, and if he didn't order her abandoned, he might as well shoot her entire crew himself.

"It looks like *Gloria* is abandoning," Clinton added, and the admiral nodded in acknowledgment. At least they'd gotten one of the bastards in return, but that didn't magically erase his own losses or mean his other four carriers had escaped unscathed. *Trujillo* was probably the least damaged of the lot, and she'd been hammered hard. She'd lost a quarter of her missile launchers, almost as many of her grasers, and a third of her point defense clusters, and she was still an hour and a half short of Old Earth.

"Sir," Commander Talbert said quietly, "look at Tactical Three."

Gajelis' eyes flicked sideways, and his jaw clenched even tighter as the last of his parasite cruisers was blown apart.

"Three of Fatted Calf's carriers are still intact, Sir," Talbert pointed out in that same, quiet voice. "Prokourov's cruisers will be in planetary orbit in another four minutes—with full magazines—and his carriers will be here in less than two hours."

Gajelis grunted in irate acknowledgment. A little voice deep inside told him it was time to give it up, but he could still do it. Yes, his ships were damaged, but *Gloria* was gone completely now—the explosion had been bright enough to be picked out clearly at twenty six million kilometers—and the three carriers still guarding the planetary orbitals were as badly damaged as his *four* surviving carriers. And the Fatted Calf cruisers had been effectively gutted, while their fighters were dodging around for their lives with his own in pursuit. He'd have to deal with Prokourov's cruisers, as well as Atilius' carriers, but it would still have been little worse than an even fight, if not for Prokourov's carriers. Still, if he went back to maximum acceleration, just blew past Old Earth and took out the Palace in passing . . .

"We have system recon platform access, Admiral," Tactical called out.

"Incoming encrypted message from Moonbase," Communications chimed in.

"Admiral," Tactical went on, without a break, "system platforms report heavy phase drive emissions closing on Old Earth," Tactical called out. "Lots of electronics, Sir. Electronics are encrypted, and we're having a hard time sorting it out. Looks like three squadrons. We're getting IFF off of them. One of them is CarRon 14, but the other two are squawking 'Fatted Calf One' and 'Fatted Calf Two.'"

"'Fatted Calf?'" Julian repeated with a puzzled frown.

"It's t'e pocking Bible," Poertena said excitedly. "You roast t'e pocking patted calp when t'e prodigal son returns."

"Indeed," Helmut agreed with a smile. "Sergeant Julian, you really need to brush up on your general reading." He studied the icons on his repeater plot. "Three ships in one squadron, noted only as Fatted Calf. And all of Twelfth Squadron, which is broadcasting as Fatted Calf Two."

"Intel update complete," Tactical said.

"Admiral La Paz reports a tunnel drive footprint, Sir. A bunch of them. It looks like another fleet." Silence hovered for a handful of seconds, and then Lieutenant Commander Clinton cleared her throat. "Confirmed, Sir. Admiral La Paz's count puts it at eighteen ships."

Gajelis looked at his own display as the central computers updated it, then shook his head.

"It's not going to be one of Prince Jackson's forces," he muttered. "Not that big and coming in from there."

"Helmut," Commander Talbert said.

"Helmut," Gajelis agreed bitterly. "Dark Lord of the Sixth. *Damn* that traitorous bastard!"

Commander Talbert wisely avoided pointing out that "traitorous" was, perhaps, a double-edged concept at this particular moment.

"We'll have to withdraw," the admiral continued.

"Withdraw to *where*?" Talbert demanded, unable to keep his anger totally out of his voice.

"Arrangements have been made," Gajelis said flatly. "Signal the squadron to break off and head for the TD limit. Flight Plan Leonidas. I need to make a call."

"So much for time," Helmut sighed, and punched a command into his repeater. A much larger hologram came up, covered with icons which were so much gibberish to Julian. "Ah, there's what we're after!" the admiral said, reaching into the hologram and "tapping" a finger through some of the symbols. The hologram's scale was so small that they scarcely seemed to be moving at all, but the vector codes beside them said otherwise.

"What is it?" Julian asked.

"Fourteenth Squadron," Helmut replied. "Well . . ."

He frowned and brought up a sidebar list and studied it briefly.

"It *was* Fourteenth Squadron," he continued. "Now, it's Fourteenth missing two carriers. Took a bit of a beating, apparently, but still the ones we want."

"Why them?" Julian asked.

"People, Sergeant. People," Helmut sighed. "It's not the ships, it's the minds within them. Fourteenth is Adoula's most loyal squadron. Where *else* would the Prince run to? The one squadron that would beat feet the instant my fleet turned up and Adoula got on board, which is why I had Admiral Niedermayer come in where he did."

"Is it going to work?"

"Well, we'll just have to see, won't we?" Helmut shrugged. "The bad guys aren't precisely where they should be—thanks to the fact that your Prince had to start early. Remind me to discuss the importance of maintaining operational schedules with him." The admiral bared his teeth in a tight smile. "As it is, we'll just have to wait and see. It'll be some time, either way." He banished the plotting hologram and brought up a 3-D chessboard, instead. "Do you play, Sergeant?"

"I wish I could have welcomed you aboard under better circumstances, Your Highness," Victor Gajelis said in a harsh, grating voice as Prince Jackson was shown into his day cabin. The admiral bent his head in a bow, and Adoula forced himself not to swear at him. It had become painfully obvious that Gajelis was not the best flag officer in the Imperial Navy. Unfortunately, all of the ones better than him seemed to be working for the other side, which meant the prince was just going to have to make do.

"You had no way of knowing Prokourov was going to turn traitor," he said as Gajelis straightened. "Neither did General Gianetto and I. And I still don't see how they coordinated this closely with Helmut. I know you could still have turned it around, if it hadn't been for *his* arrival, Victor."

"Thank you, Your Highness," Gajelis said. "My people gave as good as they got. But with Prokourov going over to the other side and bringing Helmut's numbers up even more—"

"Not just Prokourov, I'm afraid," Adoula said more heavily. "Admiral Wu turned *her* coat, too. She didn't have it all her own way. Captain Ramsey refused to obey the orders to go over to the other side, but all three of her other carriers supported her. *Hippogriff* is gone, but Ramsey hammered *Chimera* and *Halkett* pretty severely before she went. But that leaves only Eleventh, Thirteenth, and Fifteenth to support you—thirteen carriers for us, against twenty-six for them, counting the Home Fleet defections. No, Admiral, you were right to break off when you did. Time to get out with what we can and reassemble for a counterattack. General Gianetto and I have already transmitted the order to our other squadrons. Admiral Mahmut will rendezvous with you on your way to the Tsukayama Limit. Admiral La Paz and Admiral Brettle will proceed independently to the rendezvous."

✧　　✧　　✧

"CarRon 14's changed course, Sir," Tactical said twenty-seven minutes later. "It's broken off."

"Has it?" Helmut replied without looking up from the chessboard as he considered Julian's last move. He moved one of his own rooks in response, then glanced at the Tactical officer. "He's headed for system north, yes?"

"Yes, Sir." The Taco seemed completely unsurprised by Helmut's apparent clairvoyance.

"Good." The admiral looked back at the chessboard. "Your move, I believe, Sergeant?"

"How did you know, Sir?" Julian asked quietly. Helmut glanced up at him, one eyebrow quirked, and Julian gestured at the tactical officer. "How did you know he'd go north?"

"Gajelis is from Auroria Province on Old Earth," Helmut replied. "He's a swimmer. What does a swimmer do when he's been down too long?"

"He goes for the surface," Julian said.

"And that's what he's doing—trying to break for the surface." Helmut nodded at the tactical display. "When he breaks vertically for the TD sphere, four times out of five he has his ships go up." He shrugged. "Never forget, Sergeant. Predictability is one of the few truly unforgivable tactical sins. As Admiral Niedermayer will demonstrate in about eight hours."

"Excuse me, Admiral, but we have a problem," a tight-faced Commander Talbert said as he entered the briefing room where Adoula and Gajelis had been conferring electronically with Admiral Minerou Mahmut. The three carriers of Mahmut's CarRon 15 had rendezvoused with CarRon 14 less than ten minutes earlier. Now both squadrons were proceeding in company for the Tsukayama Limit, less than four light-minutes ahead of them.

"What sort of problem?" Gajelis demanded testily. On their current flight profile, they were less than twenty-five minutes from the limit.

"Seven phase drive signatures just lit off ahead of us, Sir," Talbert said flatly. "Range two-point-five light-minutes."

"Damn it!" Adoula snarled. "Who?"

"Unknown at this time, Sir," Talbert said. "They're not squawking IFF, but phase signature strengths indicate that they're carriers."

"Seven," Gajelis said anxiously. "And fresh, presumably." He looked at the prince and grimaced. "We're . . . not in good shape."

"Avoid them!" Adoula said. "Just get to the nearest TD point and *jump*."

"It's not that easy, Your Highness," Talbert said with a sigh. "We can jump out from anywhere on the TD sphere, but they're sitting almost bang center of where we were *going* to jump, and they were obviously prepositioned. They just fired up their drives—the best em-con in the galaxy couldn't have hidden carrier phase drives from us at this range if they'd been on-line. It's like they read our minds, or something."

"*Helmut*," Gajelis snarled. "The son of a bitch must've dropped them at least four or five light-days out, outside our sensor shell. Then he sent them in sublight on a profile that brought them in under such low power the perimeter platforms never saw them coming! But how in hell did he know *where* to deploy them, damn it?!"

"I don't know, Sir," Talbert said. "But however he did it, they're inside any vector change we can manage. We've got velocity directly *towards* their position—forty-six thousand KPS of it. We can jink round a little bit, try to feint them off, but we're already nine million kilometers inside their missile range. The geometry gives even their *cruisers* over thirty million kilometers' range against our closing velocity, and we're only forty-five million out. By now they've already launched cruisers—probably their fighters, too—and they're only holding their missile fire till they can generate better firing solutions and get their cruiser missiles into range. And at our velocity, we're going to end up in *energy* range of them in another sixteen minutes."

"Launch decoy drones," Gajelis said. "Launch fighters for cover, and launch the cruisers, those that are spaceworthy. You, too, Minerou," he added to the admiral on his com display.

"Agreed," Mahmut said. "On my way to CIC. I'll check back in when I get there."

The display blanked, and Gajelis looked back up at Talbert.

"Go," he said sharply. "I'll join you in CIC in a minute."

"Yes, Sir." Talbert nodded and left quickly.

"You're going to fight?" Adoula asked incredulously.

"We'll *have* to," Gajelis replied. "You heard Talbert, Your Highness. We'll have to engage them."

"No, as a matter of fact, you *won't*," the Prince replied. "Have the rest of your forces engage, but getting me to Kellerman is the priority. This ship will avoid action and get out of the system. Have the others cover you."

"That's a bit—" Gajelis began angrily.

"Those are your *orders*, Admiral," Adoula replied. "Follow them!"

"This is going to be interesting," Admiral Niedermayer remarked. "Observe *Trujillo*," he continued. "Breaking off as predicted."

"Sometimes the Admiral scares me, Sir," Senior Captain Erhardt replied. "How did he know Gajelis was going to head *here*?"

"Magic, Marge. Magic," Niedermayer told the commander of his flagship. "Unfortunately, it would appear he was also correct about Adoula."

Niedermayer's flagship had been tapped back into the system recon net ever since Captain Kjerulf had reconfigured his lockout to allow Sixth Fleet access. He'd used that advantage to adjust his ships' position slightly, but it really hadn't been necessary. As Erhardt's last remark indicated, Admiral Helmut had called Adoula's and Gajelis' response almost perfectly. Only the timing had changed . . . and Helmut had gotten them here early enough for the timing not to be a problem.

"I can't believe the rest of them are just going to come right on in to *cover* him." Erhardt shook her head, staring at the plot where six of the seven enemy carriers had altered heading to accelerate directly towards them even as the seventh accelerated directly *away* from them. "The bastard is running out on them, and they're still going to fight for him?"

"Jackson Adoula is a physical coward, Marge," Niedermayer said. "Oh, I'm sure he's found some other way to justify it, even to himself. After all, he's the 'indispensable man,' isn't he? Without his stronghold in the Sagittarius Sector, it'd all the over but the shouting once the Prince retakes the Palace. So, much as I may despise him, there really is a certain logic in getting him away."

"Logic, Sir?!" Erhardt looked at him in something very like disbelief, and it was his turn to shake his head.

Marjorie Erhardt was very good at her job. She was also fairly young for her rank, and she had a falcon's fierce directness, coupled with an even fiercer loyalty to the Empress and the Empire. All of that made her an extremely dangerous weapon, but it also gave her a certain degree of tunnel vision. Henry Niedermayer remembered another young, fiery captain who'd suffered from the same sort of narrowness of focus. Then-Vice Admiral Angus Helmut had taken that young captain in hand and expanded his perspective without ever compromising his integrity, which left Niedermayer with an obligation to repay the debt by doing the same thing for Erhardt. And he still had a few minutes to do it in.

"The fact that they're fighting for a bad cause doesn't make them cowards, Marge," he said, just a trifle coldly. She looked at him, and he grimaced.

"One of the worst things any military commander can do is to allow contempt for his adversaries to lead him into underestimating them or their determination," he told her. "And Adoula didn't seduce them all by dangling money in front of them. At least some of them signed on because they agreed with him that the Empire was in trouble and didn't understand what the Empress was doing about it.

"And however they got into his camp in the first place, they all recognize the stakes they agreed to play for. They're guilty of High Treason, Marge. The penalty for that is death. They may realize perfectly well that their so-called 'leader' is about to bug out on them, but that doesn't change their options. And even without *Trujillo* they've got only one less carrier than we do. You think they are just going to surrender and face the firing squads when at least some of them may be able to fight their way past us?"

"Put that way, no, Sir," Erhardt replied after a moment. "But they're *not* going to get past us, are they?"

"No, Captain Erhardt, they're not," Niedermayer agreed. "And it's time to show them why they're not."

"Holy Mary, Mother of God," Admiral Minerou Mahmut breathed as his tactical plot abruptly updated. The icons of the seven carriers waiting for him were suddenly joined by an incredible rash of smaller crimson icons.

"Bogeys," his flagship's Tactical Officer announced in the flat, hard voice of a professional rigidly suppressing panic through training and raw discipline. "Multiple cruiser-range phase drive signatures. BattleComp makes it three hundred-plus." More light codes blinked to sudden baleful life. "Update! Fighter-range phase drive detection. Minimum seven-fifty."

Mahmut swallowed hard. Helmut. That incredible bastard couldn't have more than a single cruiser flotilla with the force which would be settling into Old Earth orbit within the next twenty-five minutes. He'd dropped the others—*all* the others—off with the carrier squadrons he'd detached for his damned ambush!

Even now, with the proof staring him in the face, Mahmut could scarcely believe that even *Helmut* would try something that insane. If it hadn't worked out—if he'd been forced into combat against a concentrated Home Fleet—the absence of his cruiser strength, especially with the carrier squadrons diverted as well, would have been decisive.

Which didn't change the fact that Mahmut's six carriers, seventy-two cruisers, and five hundred remaining fighters were about to get brutally hammered.

He spared a moment to glance at the secondary plot where *Trujillo* was still generating delta V at her maximum acceleration. The distance between her and the rest of the formation was up to almost a million kilometers, and to get at her, Helmut's ships would have to get through Mahmut's. A part of the admiral was tempted to order his ships to stand down, to surrender them and let the Sixth Fleet task group have clean shots at *Trujillo*. But if he'd been in command on the other side, he wouldn't have been accepting any surrenders under the circumstances. His own small task group's crossing velocity was so great that it would have been impossible for anyone from the other side to match vectors and put boarding parties onto his ships before they crossed the Tsukayama Limit and disappeared into tunnel-space.

Besides, some of them might actually make it.

Commander Roger "Cobalt" McBain was a contented man. To his way of thinking, he was at the pinnacle of his career. CAG of a Navy fighter group was all he'd ever wanted to be.

Technically, his actual position was that of "Commander 643rd

Fighter Group," the hundred and twenty-five fighters assigned to HMS *Centaur*. CAG was an older term, which had stood for the title of "Commander Attack Group" until three or four Navy reorganizations ago. There were those who claimed that the acronym's actual origin was to be found in the title of "Commander *Air* Group," which went clear back to the days when ships had battled on oceans, and the fighters had been air-intake jet-powered machines. McBain wasn't sure about that—his interest in ancient history was strictly minimal—but he didn't really care. Over the years, the position had had many names, but none of them had stuck in the tradition-minded Navy the way "CAG" had. If one fighter pilot said to another, "Oh, he's the CAG," whether the ships were old jets or stingships or space fighters, everyone knew what he meant.

From his present position, he might well be promoted to command of an entire carrier squadron's fighter wing, which would be nice—in its way—but far more of an administrative post. He'd get much less cockpit time as a wing CAG, although it would look good on his resume. From there, he might claw his way into command of a carrier, or squadron, or even a fleet. But from his point of view, and right now it was damned panoramic, CAG was as good as a job got. A part of him wished he was with the rest of the squadron's fighter wing, preparing to jump Adoula's main body. But most of him was perfectly content to be exactly where he was.

And it was interesting to watch Admiral Niedermayer at his work. Obviously, the Old Man had learned a lot from Admiral Helmut . . . although McBain had never realized before that clairvoyance could be taught. But it must be possible. If it wasn't, how could Niedermayer have predicted where HMS *Trujillo* would be accurately enough to deploy the 643rd ten full hours *before* Gajelis and Adoula ever arrived?

"Start warming up the plasma conduits," Mahmut said. "Any cruisers that make it through are to be recovered by any available carrier."

"Yes, Sir," his flag captain acknowledged crisply, even though both of them knew how unlikely any of their units were to survive the next few minutes.

✧   ✧   ✧

"Open fire," Admiral Niedermayer said, almost conversationally, and the next best thing to eleven thousand missile launchers spat fire. Four hundred fighters armed with antifighter missiles salvoed their ordnance at Mahmut's fighters, and another three hundred and fifty sent over seventeen hundred Leviathans at his cruisers. None of the ship-launched missiles bothered with the sublight parasites, however. Ultimately, the cruisers and fighters had no escape if the tunnel drive ships were crippled or destroyed, and Niedermayer's fire control concentrated on the carriers with merciless professionalism. He'd waited until the range was down to just over ten million kilometers. At that range, and at their current closing velocity, that gave him just under four minutes to engage with missiles before they entered energy range. In that four minutes, each of his cruisers fired a hundred and fifty missiles, and each of his carriers fired over four thousand. The next best thing to eighty thousand missiles slammed into the defenses protecting Minerou Mahmut's carriers.

At such short range, countermissiles were far less effective than usual. They simply didn't have the tracking time as the offensive fire slashed across their engagement envelope, and they stopped perhaps thirty percent of the incoming birds. Point defense clusters fired desperately, and there were thousands of them. But they, too, were fatally short of engagement time. They stopped another forty percent... which meant that "only" twenty-four thousand got through.

Maximum effective standoff range for even a capital shipkiller laser head against a starship was little more than seven thousand kilometers. At that range, however, they could blast through even ChromSten armor, and they did. Carriers were tough, the toughest mobile structures ever designed and built by human beings, but there were limits in all things. Armor yielded only stubbornly, even under that incredible pounding, but it *did* yield. Atmosphere streamed from ruptured compartments. Weapon mounts were blotted away. Power runs arced and exploded as energy blew back through them. Their own fire ripped back at their enemies, but Niedermayer's sheer wealth of point defense blunted the far lighter salvoes Mahmut's outnumbered ships could throw, and his carriers' armor shook off the relative handful of hits which got through to it.

By the time CarRon 15 and what was left of CarRon 14 reached energy range, three of its seven carriers and forty-one of its seventy-two cruisers had been destroyed outright.

By the time the traitorous carrier squadrons crossed the track of Niedermayer's task force, exactly eleven badly damaged cruisers and one totally crippled carrier survived.

"Admiral," Lieutenant Commander Clinton said with a gulp. "We just got swept by lidar! Point source, Delta quadrant four-one-five."

"What does *that* mean?" Adoula demanded sharply. He was sitting in a hastily rigged command chair next to the admiral's.

"It means someone's out there," Gajelis snapped. He'd left his handful of cruisers and fighters behind to assist Mahmut. His flagship was going to be fighting whoever it was with only onboard weapons.

"Captain Devarnachan is sweeping," Tactical said. "Emissions! Raid designated Sierra Five. One hundred twenty-five fighters, closing from Delta Four-One-Five."

"Damn Helmut!" Gajelis snarled. "*Damn him!*"

"Leviathans! Six hundred twenty-five vampires!"

"Three minutes to Tsukayama Limit," Astrogation announced tautly.

"They'll only get one shot," Gajelis said, breathing hard. "Hang on, Your Highness . . ."

"Damn and blast," McBain snarled as the distinctive signature of a TD drive formed. At such short range and with such short flight times, *Trujillo's* countermissiles had been effectively useless, and over fifty of the Leviathans had managed to get through the carrier's desperately firing point defense lasers. They'd ripped hell out of her, and he'd hoped that would be enough to cripple her, but carriers were pretty damned tough.

"We got a piece of her, Cobalt," his XO replied. "A big one. And Admiral Niedermayer kicked hell out of the rest of them. Doesn't look like any of *them* got away."

"I know, Allison," McBain said angrily, though his anger certainly wasn't directed at *her*. "But a piece wasn't enough." He sighed, then shook himself. "Oh, well, we did our best. And you're right, we did get a piece of her. Let's turn 'em around and head back to the barn. Beer's on me."

"Damn straight it is!" Commander Stanley agreed with a laugh. Then, as their fighters swept around through a graceful turn and began decelerating back towards their carriers, her tone turned more thoughtful. "Wonder how things went at the Palace?"

"Your Highness, your mother's been through . . . a terrible ordeal," the psychiatrist said. He was a specialist in pharmacological damage. "Normally, we'd stabilize her with targeted medications. But given the . . . vile concoctions they used on her, not to mention the damage to her implant—"

"Which is very severe," the implant specialist interrupted. "It's shutting down and resetting itself frequently, almost randomly, because of general system failures. And it's dumping data at random, as well. It has to be hell inside her head, Your Highness."

"And nothing can be done about it?" Roger asked.

"These damned paranoid ones you people have, they're designed to be unremovable, Your Highness," the specialist said, with a shrug which expressed his helpless frustration. "I know why, but seeing what happens when something like this goes wrong—"

"It didn't '*go wrong*,'" Roger said flatly. "It was made to fail. And when I get my hands on the people who did that, I intend to . . . discuss it with them in some detail. But for right now, answer my question. Is there anything at all we can do to get this . . . this *thing* out of my mother's head?"

"No," the specialist said heavily. "The only thing we could do would be to attempt surgical removal, Your Highness, and I'd give her a less than even chance of surviving the procedure. Which doesn't even consider the probability of additional, serious neurological damage."

"And the implant, of course, responds to brain action, Your Highness," the psychiatrist noted. "And since the brain action is highly confused at the moment—"

"Doc?" Roger said impatiently, looking at Dobrescu.

"Roger, I don't even have a degree," Dobrescu protested. "I'm a *shuttle pilot*."

"Doc, damn it, do not give me that old song and dance," Roger snapped.

"All right." Dobrescu threw his hands into the air almost angrily. "You want my interpretation of what they're telling you? She's totally pocked in the head, all right? Wackers. Maybe the big brains—the people who *do* have the degrees—can do something for her eventually. But right now, she's in one minute, out the next. I don't even know when you can see her, Roger. She's still asking for New Madrid, whether she's . . . in or out. In reality, or out in la-la land. When she's in, she wants his head. She knows she's the Empress, she knows she's in bad shape, she knows who did it to her, and she wants him dead. I've tried to point out that you're back, but she's still mixing it up with New Madrid. With all the drugs and physical duress, on top of the way they butchered her toot, they've got her half convinced even when she's got some contact with reality that you *were* in on the plot. And when she's in la-la land . . ."

"I was there to see enough of that." Roger's face tightened, and he looked at Catrone. "Tomcat?"

"Christ, Your Highness," Catrone said. "Don't put this on me!"

"That was the deal," Roger told him. "As you asked me, not so long ago, are you going back on your word?"

Catrone stared at him for several seconds, then shrugged.

"When she's in, she's *in*," he said. "All the way in. She's still got a few problems," he conceded, raising a hand at Dobrescu, "but she knows she's Empress. And *she's* not willing to step aside." He looked at Roger, his face hard. "I'm sorry, Roger. It's not because I don't trust you, but she's my *Empress*. I'm not going against her, not when she still knows who she is. Not when it's too early to know whether or not she can get better."

"Very well," Roger said, his voice cold. "But if she's in charge, she needs to get back into the saddle. Things are in very bad shape, and we need her up," he continued, looking at the doctors. "There are people she *has* to meet."

"That would be . . . unwise," the psychiatrist said. "The strain could—"

"Either she can take it, or she can't," Roger said flatly. "Ask *her*. I'm out of this decision loop, starting right now."

"Like hell," Catrone said angrily. "Are you going to go off into one of your Roger sulks? You can't just throw the weight of the entire Empire onto her shoulders, damn it! She's *sick*. She just needs some *recovery* time, goddamn it!"

"Tomcat, I can't just make the galaxy *stop* while she gets better!" Roger snapped. "Okay. This was *your* decision—that was the deal. And for all I know, you've made exactly the right one. But if she's Empress, she has got to *be* Empress, and that means *she* needs to determine what *I* do."

"But—"

"No '*buts*,' damn it! You know as well as I do how unsettled the situation is right now. Sure, we've got Helmut in orbit, and Prokourov and Kjerulf supporting us, but you've seen the coverage, just like me. Some of the newsies are doing their best to be dispassionate and impartial, but only a handful, and the *rest* of the rumors—"

He broke off with a frustrated snarl, then shook himself.

"Adoula did a damned good job of painting *me* as the one behind the first coup for public opinion," he said flatly. "Hell, you heard Doc—they've got *her* half-convinced! It's going to take time for everybody—*anybody*—to begin to understand what really happened. I know that. And I also know that's actually a pocking good argument in favor of Mother remaining in charge. If *she's* on the Throne, then obviously I'm not trying to take it away from her, right? So I *agree* with you about that, damn it! And I don't care if she makes me her one hundred percent alternate, which as Heir Primus *should* be my job right now, or just hands me the shit details to reduce her load while *she* tries to do the job. Hell, I don't care if she tells me to get off-planet and go back to Marduk! But for me to work for her, to help her, I have to at least be able to *talk* to her, Sergeant Major. And right now, I can't even do *that!*"

"Okay, okay!" Catrone held up his hands, as if he were physically fending Roger off. "Point taken, Your Highness—*point!*" He paused and drew a deep breath. "I'll see about a meeting. Not in private—that would probably be bad. A group meeting. You're right, there *are* people she has to see. The new Navy Minister. The Prime Minister. Helmut. I'll set up a meeting—an *easy* one," he added, looking at the doctors.

"A short meeting with people she knows," the psychiatrist said.

"That may help her stabilize. It's an environment she understands. But *short*. Nonstressful."

"Agreed," Roger said curtly.

"And you'll be in it," Catrone said.

"I can't wait."

"Your clothes survived," Despreaux said from the bed.

"Sixty *million* credits worth of damage." Roger sighed, tossing his cane onto the foot of the bed and flopping down next to her. They'd gotten their old bodies back. Sort of. Despreaux had opted for...a bit of upper body enhancement, and she'd kept the hair. She'd decided that she liked being blonde, even if it didn't set off Roger's coloring as well as her earlier dark brown had.

Roger, on the other hand, was back to plain old Roger. Well, plain old Roger just starting to regenerate the calf of his leg. Two meters, long blond hair, green eyes. Deep frown...

"Sixty million," he repeated. "And that's just to the *Palace*."

"And then there's the rumor that there are dozens of secret ways in." Despreaux shuddered. "We need to get those blocked—and make damned sure everyone *knows* they're blocked."

"Working on it." Roger sighed again. "And we need a new Empress' Own. Replacement equipment. Work on the damage we did to the com facilities...Christ."

"If it were an easy job, it wouldn't take us," Despreaux told him with a crooked smile.

"And we need something else." Roger's tone was serious enough that her half-smile faded.

"What?"

"An heir," he said quietly.

The replicator had been found, turned over, the fetus poured out onto the floor and crushed. Roger had felt strange looking down at the pathetic, ruined body of the brother he would never know. They'd found the culprit among the surviving mercenaries—the DNA on his trousers had been a dead giveaway—and he was awaiting trial for regicide.

"Whooo," Despreaux said, letting out her breath. "That's a big thing to spring on a poor old farm girl! I'd hoped to have kids someday, your kids as a matter of fact, but..."

"Seriously," he said, sitting up on the bed. "We need an heir of the body, out of the replicator, viable to take the Throne. Hell, we need duplicates. Things are bad right now. I hope like hell that—"

"I understand," Despreaux said, reaching up to touch his cheek. "I'll stop in at the clinic tomorrow. I'm sure they'll take me in without an appointment."

"You know," Roger said, sliding down to hold her in his arms, "there's another way to get things started . . ."

"God, I thought once I got you in bed, it would be *easy*." She hit him with a pillow. "Little did I realize what a crazed sex maniac hid under that just plain *crazed* exterior!"

"I've got *years* of catching up," Roger replied, laughing. "And there's no time like the present."

"Sergeant Major Catrone," Alexandra VII sighed as Tomcat entered the sitting room.

She wore a high-necked gown, and her hair was simply but exquisitely styled. She looked every centimeter the Empress, but there were still shadowy bruises around her wrists. They had almost—*almost*—vanished, and he knew the medics had almost completely healed the . . . other marks on her body, as well. But they were still there, and something stirred and bared its fangs deep at the heart of him as she touched a control to raise the back of her float chair into a sitting position, and held out a hand.

"I'm so glad to see you," she said.

"All you need to do is call, Your Majesty." Catrone dropped to one knee instead of taking the proffered hand. "I am, and always have been, your servant."

"Oh, get up, Tomcat." Alexandra laughed, and laughed harder at his expression. "What? You thought I didn't know your nickname?" She grinned. "You were a bachelor for many years when you served me; I learned *all* about your nickname." She held out her hand again, fiercely. "Take my hand, Tomcat."

"Majesty," he said, and took it, dropping back to one knee again beside her chair and holding it.

"I haven't been . . . well enough to tell you," Alexandra said, staring at him, "what a *relief* it was to see your face. My one true paladin, there by my side once again. It was like a light in the darkness—and it was such an *awful* darkness," she ended angrily.

"Majesty," Catrone said, embarrassed. "I'm sorry it took us so long. We wanted—we *all* wanted—to move sooner, but until Roger—"

"Roger!" the Empress shouted, snatching back her hand and crossing her arms. "Everyone wants to talk about *Roger*! The prodigal son returned—ha! *Fatted calf!* I'd like to roast *him!*"

"Majesty, control yourself," Catrone said, gently but firmly. "Whatever you knew, or thought you knew, about Roger, you must take him as he is now. Fatted Calf would have been impossible without him. Not just because of the hidden protocols in his mind, either. Because of his leadership, his vision, his determination. His planning. He handled a dozen different actions as if they were one. Perfect combat gestalt, the best I've ever seen. And all he thought of was *you*, Your Majesty, from the first moment I told him what they were *doing* to you. His anger . . ."

The sergeant major shook his head.

"Only one thing kept him from killing New Madrid out of hand. I truly believe only one thing *could* have kept him from doing it, and it wasn't the Empire, Your Majesty. It was his fiancée. He loves you, Your Majesty. He loves his mother. He isn't his father's son; he's yours."

Alexandra looked at him for a moment, then looked away and shrugged, the movement angry, frustrated, possibly even a bit uncertain.

"I hear you, Tomcat. Maybe you really believe that. Maybe it's even true. But when I see him, I see his father's face. Why, of all my children, did *he* have to be the only one to survive?"

"Luck," Catrone said with a shrug of his own. "Excellent bodyguards. And perhaps most of all the fact that, I'm sorry, he's one of the hardest, coldest bastards House MacClintock has ever coughed up."

"Certainly a bastard," Alexandra agreed astringently. "But how I *wish* John were still alive! I knew I could trust him. Trust his good judgment, trust his reasoning."

"With all due respect, Your Majesty," Catrone said with a swallow, "John was a good man. A smart one, and as honest as he could be, working in this snake pit. A . . . decent fighter, and someone I would have been proud to serve one day as Emperor. But . . . Adoula got away. He's calling in all the fleets he controls, and proclaiming that *we're* the ones using drugs and torture to control you now that we've gotten you into *our* hands. We're in the midst of a civil war, and if there's one MacClintock, besides you, who I'd trust at the helm in a civil war, it's Roger. More than John. More even then Alex."

"So you say," Alexandra replied. "But I don't—"

"—why, Sergeant Major Catrone! What a pleasant surprise!" she said delightedly, her face blossoming into a huge smile. "Have you come for a visit?"

"Yes, Your Majesty," Catrone said evenly, his face wooden.

"Well, I hope you've had a good conversation with my friend, the Earl of New Madrid," Alexandra continued. "He's returned to my side at last, my one true love. So surprising that he's such a good man, with a son who's so evil. But, tell me, how are your horses? You raise horses now, don't you?"

"They're well, Your Majesty," he said, standing with a wince. His knees weren't what they used to be.

"I'm afraid I have a meeting in a few minutes with Our loyal servant, Prince Jackson," the Empress said, waving him to a chair. "But I certainly have time to speak to my most favored former retainer. So, tell me—"

"How is she?" Eleanora said, taking Catrone's arm to halt him briefly before they entered the room.

"Tracking," Catrone replied. "Fine at the moment."

"Let's hope this goes well," Eleanora sighed. "Please God it goes well."

"For your side or for her?" Catrone asked bitterly.

"We're on the *same* side, Sergeant Major!" Eleanora snapped. "Remember that."

"I know. I try, but—" Catrone shrugged, pain darkening his eyes. "But sometimes it's hard."

"You love her," Eleanora said gently. "Too much, I think."

"That I do," Catrone whispered. His face clenched for a moment, and then he shook himself. "Where's the Prince?" he asked in a determinedly lighter tone.

"Late," Eleanora said, her lips pursed in irritation.

They entered the conference room and took their seats. Their late entry did not pass unremarked, and they drew a stern look from the Empress at the head of the long, polished table. The room was lined with windows, looking out over one of the south gardens, and bright sunlight filled it with a warm glow. The Prime Minister had one end of the conference table and the Empress had the other. The new Navy Minister was also present; as was Admiral Helmut, who was temporarily holding down the position of CNO; the Finance Minister; Julian, who was still in some undefined billet; and Despreaux, who was in another. And, of course, there was one empty chair.

"And where is Roger?" Alexandra asked coldly.

The door opened, and Roger limped in. He wore a custom-tailored suit of bright yellow, a forest-green ascot, and a straw hat. The regeneration of his leg was still in its very early stages, and he leaned on a color-coordinated cane as he bowed.

"Sorry I'm late," he said, tugging on a leash. "Dogzard insisted on a walk, so I took her to visit Patty. And she didn't want to come back again . . . naturally. Come *on*, you stupid beast," he continued as he practically dragged the creature into the room. She hissed at most of the people sitting around the table, then saw the Empress and produced a happy little whine of pleasure.

Eleanora was watching Alexandra's face and sighed mentally as she saw the quick flicker of the Empress' eyes. In some ways, Eleanora wished Roger had retained his Augustus Chung body-mod. That had been impossible, of course, if only because of the public-relations considerations. But every time the Empress saw him, it was as if she had to remind herself physically that he was not his father even before she could deal with the ambiguity of her feelings where *he* was concerned.

"Sorry," Roger repeated as he finally managed to wrestle Dogzard across to the chair set aside for him. "Just because I let her eat one person . . . Sit," he commanded. "Sit! Quit looking at the Prime Minister that way, it's not respectful. Sit. Lie down. Good Dogzard."

The prince settled into his own chair, hung his cane over its back, looked around the table, and set his hat in front of him.

"Where were we?"

"I *think* we were about to discuss Navy repairs and consolidations," Alexandra said, raising one eyebrow. "Now that you're here..."

The meeting had been going on for an hour, which was longer than Catrone had feared, and far shorter than he'd hoped.

"Between making sure the Saints don't snap up systems and holding back Adoula, there just aren't enough ships to go around," Andrew Shue, Baron Talesian and the new Navy Minister, said, and threw up his hands.

"Then we make faces," Roger said, leaning sideways to pet Dogzard. "We bluff. We only have to keep them off our backs for... what? Eighteen months? Long enough for the shipyards to start pushing out the new carriers."

"Which will be *ruinously* expensive," Jasper O'Higgins, the Finance Minister said.

"We're at war," Roger replied coldly. "War is waste. Most of those expensive ships of yours are going to be scrap floating among the stars in two years, anyway. Mr. O'Higgins. The point is to have them, and then to use them as judiciously as humanly possible. But we have to have them, first, and to do that, we have to keep our enemies off our backs long enough for them to be built."

"They'll be used judiciously," Helmut said. "I know Gajelis. He's a bigger-hammer commander. 'Quantity has a quality of its own.' I'd be surprised if we couldn't give him at least two-to-one in damage levels. Admittedly, even those numbers are terrible enough. A lot of our boys and girls are going to die. But..."

The diminutive admiral shrugged, and the Empress grimaced.

"And Adoula has shipyards of his own," she said angrily. "I wish I could strangle my father for letting any of them get built outside the central worlds, especially in Adoula's backyard!"

"We could always... send an emissary to Adoula," the Prime Minister suggested, only to pause as Dogzard's hiss cut him off.

"Down!" Roger said to the dog-lizard, then looked at Yang. "Methinks my pet dislikes your suggestion, Mr. Prime Minister. And so do I."

"You yourself just pointed out that we have to buy time, Your Highness," the Prime Minister said coldly. "Negotiations—even, or especially, negotiations we don't intend to go anywhere—might be one way to buy that time. And if it should turn out that there actually was some sort of feasible arrangement, a *modus vivendi*, why—"

"Now I *know* I don't like it," Roger said, his voice several degrees colder than the Prime Minister's.

"Nor do I," Alexandra said. Her voice was less chill than her son's, but undeniably frosty. "Adoula is in a state of rebellion. If he succeeds in breaking off permanently—or even merely seems to have temporarily succeeded—others *will* try to do the same. Before long, the Empire will end up as a scattered group of feuding worlds, and all *we* may hold will be a few systems. And the expense at that point will be enormous. No, Roger has a point," she conceded, looking at him balefully nonetheless. "We can make faces. Bluff. But we will *not* take any step which even suggests we might ever treat with Adoula as if he were a legitimate head of state. Instead, we'll send—"

"—and I'm very much looking forward to the Imperial Festival, my love."

Her voice changed abruptly, crisp decisiveness melting into cloying sweetness, and she gazed at Roger with soulful eyes.

"As am I," Roger said. *His* expression had frozen into an iron mask as the Empress' had changed to one of adoration. "It is about that time, isn't it?"

"Oh, yes, my dear," the Empress crooned. "What will you be wearing? I want to make sure we're simply the *loveliest* couple—"

"I'm not sure, yet," Roger interrupted calmly, gently. "But I think, Alexandra, that this meeting's gone on long enough, don't you?" He waved to one of the guards by the door. "Let me call your ladies in waiting. That way you can make yourself fresh and beautiful again," he added, glancing sideways at Catrone, who gave a brief nod of approval.

When the docile Empress had been led from the room, Roger stood and swept the people still seated around the conference table with eyes of emerald ice.

"Not a word," he said. "Not one pocking damned *word*. Meeting *adjourned*."

✧   ✧   ✧

"Well?" Roger said, looking up from yet another of the endless reports floating in the holographic display above his desk. Decisions *had* to be made, and by default, he was making them, despite the fact that his mother had yet to define precisely what authority, if any, was his. Nobody was raising the issue, however.

Not more than once.

"It's a bad one," Catrone said.

His face was drawn, his eyes worried, as he sat down in one of the office's float chairs at Roger's wave.

"Really bad," he continued. "She's . . . changing. She's not asking for Adoula as much, not since we got the worst of the drugs scrubbed out of her system and told her he's gone off to his sector for a while. She still asking for New Madrid, but . . ." Catrone swallowed, and his face worked. "But not as often."

"What's wrong?" Roger asked.

"Christ, Your Highness," Catrone said in an anguished voice, dropping his face into his hands. "Now she's coming on to *me*! That *bastard*. That *stinking* bastard!"

"Pock!" Roger leaned back and grabbed his ponytail.

He stared at the older man for several seconds, then inhaled deeply.

"Tomcat, I know how hard this is for you. But you *have* to stay with her. You have to stay with us!"

"I will," Catrone said. He raised his head, tears running down his face. "If I leave, who *knows* what she'll latch onto? But, God! Roger, it's *hard*!"

"Be her paladin, Tomcat," Roger said then, his face set. "If needs be, damn it, be *more* than her paladin."

"Roger!"

"You just said it yourself. If you're not there for her, someone else will be. Someone who's not as good a man as you are. Someone I can't trust like you. Someone *she* can't trust like you. You're on this post until relieved, Sergeant Major. Is that understood? And you'll do whatever it takes to stand your post, Marine. Clear?"

"Clear," Catrone grated. "Order received and understood, and I will comply. You bastard."

"That I am." Roger grinned tightly. "Literally and figuratively. The last bastard standing. The flag of the *Basik's* Own wears a bar sinister proudly. We carried it across two continents, and to Old Earth, and into this very damned Palace, and we did *anything necessary* to complete the mission. Welcome to the Regiment. Now you know what it means to be one of us."

"And I think we should inform Mistress Tompkins that I'll need a new dress, don't you?" Alexandra said softly.

"Yes, Your Majesty," Lady Russell agreed.

They sat in a gazebo, watching cold rain fall beyond the force screen. Lady Russell was expertly sewing a tapestry, while the Empress mangled a needlepoint of a puppy in a basket.

"I'll never know how you do that so well," the Empress said, smiling politely.

"Years of practice, Your Majesty," Lady Russell replied.

"I'll have many years to practice—

"—two carrier squadrons to the Marduk System," Alexandra said, her face hard. "Given what Roger's said about—"

She stopped, and looked around, frowning.

"Where am I?" she asked in a voice which was suddenly cold and dead.

"The gazebo, Your Majesty," Lady Russell said softly, and looked at her half-fearfully. "Are you well?"

"I was in the conference room," Alexandra said tightly. "I was in a *meeting*! It was *sunny*! Where's the *meeting*? Where are the *people*? Why is it *raining*?"

"That—" Lady Russell swallowed. "Your Majesty, that was two days ago."

"Oh, my God," Alexandra whispered, and looked at the material in her lap. "What *is* this?"

"Needlepoint?" Lady Russell asked, reaching unobtrusively for her communicator.

"It's bloody awful, is what it is!" Alexandra spun the hoop across the gazebo. "Get me Sergeant Major Catrone!"

"Sit, Sergeant Major," Alexandra said, and pointed to the seat Lady Russell had vacated.

"Your Majesty," Tomcat said.

At Roger's order, Catrone had once more donned the blue and red of the Empress' Own, at his old rank of sergeant major. He wore dress uniform, and the golden aiguillette hanging from his shoulder indicated Gold Battalion, the personal command—and bodyguard—of the reigning monarch. Empress Alexandra VII, in this case.

"What happened in the meeting, Sergeant Major?" Alexandra rubbed her face furiously. "I was *in* the meeting, and then I was here, in the gazebo. What happened to me? Who's *doing* this to me?"

"First of all," Catrone said carefully, "no one is doing anything to you, Your Majesty. It's already been done."

She stopped rubbing and sat still, her hands still over her eyes, and he continued.

"Your Majesty, you have two mental states, as we've tried to explain to you before." He waved a hand at her. "This state. Alexandra the Seventh, Empress of the Empire of Man. Fully functional. As good a sovereign as I've ever served. Twice the sovereign her father ever was."

"Thank you for the soft soap, Tomcat," Alexandra said mockingly, eyes still covered. "And my other . . . state?"

"The other," he said even more carefully, then paused. "Well, Your Majesty, in the other you're . . . pliable. You still occasionally ask for your 'good friend,' the Earl of New Madrid, and refer to Prince Jackson as 'Our loyal Prince Jackson.'"

"Oh, God," she said.

"Do you really want it all?" Catrone asked. "Face facts, Your Majesty. You're still in a pretty delicate condition."

"I want it all." She sighed, lowering her hands at last. Then her face firmed, and she met his eye levelly. "All. What happened?"

"In your other state—"

"What do you call that?" she interrupted. "If you call . . . this one Alexandra. *Do* you call it Alexandra, Tomcat?"

"Yes, Your Majesty," he said firmly. "This is the Empress Alexandra. The woman I gave my service to long ago."

"And the other?"

"Well," Catrone winced. "We just call it la-la-land. The doctors have a long technical name—"

"I can imagine," she said dryly. "Do I know I'm Empress?"

"Yes, Your Majesty." Catrone's swallowed. "But, frankly, we just ignore anything you tell us to do. You generally don't give any orders, though."

He paused.

"What *do* I do?" she asked.

"Whatever you're told," Catrone said, his face hard. "About the only positive contribution you make is to ask when your very special friend will be back. And if he's not around, you hit on me, Your Majesty."

"Oh, Christ, Thomas." Her face went blank, and tears formed in her eyes. "Oh, Christ. I'm so sorry!"

"I'm not." Catrone shrugged. "I'm not happy that this has happened to you, Your Majesty, but I'm glad it's me. I've never seen you do it to any other male . . ." He paused again, then shrugged. "Except Roger."

"*What?!*"

"You think he's New Madrid," Catrone said. "You said *all.*"

"And I meant it," Alexandra ground out. She inhaled deeply, nostrils flaring, and leaned back in her chair. "You said I was out for two days?"

"Yes, Your Majesty. We just left you with your ladies. You were . . . monitored by the guards to make sure none of them started giving suggestions."

"Good," Alexandra said firmly. Then she softened, and looked at him oddly. "Thomas?"

"Yes, Your Majesty?"

Her voice was much softer, and he watched her expression carefully, wondering if she'd wandered off again.

"I'm me," she said, and astonished him with a grin. "I could see the question in your eyes. But I have a very serious question of my own, one I'd like an honest answer to. What did my son tell *you* to do? About my come-ons?"

Catrone's hands worked on the arms of his chair, and he stared out at the rain for several long moments. Then he looked back at her and raised his eyes to meet her gray ones.

"He ordered me to do whatever was necessary to keep you from finding some other . . . gentleman companion," he said bluntly. "The doctors all agreed that any such . . . gentleman companion could tell you to give any order he thought up when you're in your la-la state."

"My God, he *is* a bastard, isn't he?" There was actually a bubble of delight in Alexandra's voice, and she shook her head and rubbed the bridge of her nose. "I'm having a hard time framing this next question, Thomas. Did he do that . . . ?"

"He did it for the good of the Empire," Catrone said, his tone as blunt as before. "And he did it knowing the trial I'd face. He told me my term of service is now until one of us dies."

"And you accepted that order?" Alexandra asked calmly.

"I've always served you, Your Majesty," Catrone said, looking suddenly very old and tired. "I always will. But, yes. When Roger gave that order, I obeyed it as if it had come from the mouth of my Emperor."

"Good," she said. "Good. If he can command that loyalty, that service from you—from my strength and my paladin—then, yes, perhaps I have misjudged him."

She paused, and her lips worked, trying not to smile.

"Thomas . . . ?"

"No," he said.

"You don't know what I was going to ask," she pointed out.

"Yes, I do," he said. "And the answer is: No. We never have."

"Tempted?" she asked.

He looked up, his eyes hot, almost angry, and half-glared at her. One cheek muscle twitched, and Alexandra smiled warmly.

"I'll take that as a yes," she said, leaning back in her chair, and cradled her chin in one hand, index finger tapping at her cheek. "You've remarried, haven't you, Tomcat?"

"Yes," Tomcat replied warily.

"Pity."

"What's this about, Catrone?" Roger demanded as he strode down the corridor. "Damn it, I'm up to my eyeballs in work. We're *all* up to our eyeballs in work."

"She's tracking right now," Catrone replied. "She has something she wants to say, and when she calls, you go."

"I'm just getting used to being treated like an adult," Roger snapped. "I'm not happy about being treated like a child again."

"You're not," Eleanora said as she joined them from a cross-corridor. Despreaux was with her, trotting to keep up with the shorter woman, and having a hell of a time doing so in court shoes.

"No, you're not," Roger's fiancée echoed, hopping on one foot and falling behind as she finally gave up and ripped the shoes off. "You're being treated like her Heir. She has something important to say."

The shoes came off, and she carried them in one hand by their straps as she hurried to catch back up.

"It's not just you, Roger," Eleanora said, nodding at Despreaux in thanks. "All of your Companions, your staff, Catrone, the Prime Minister, the full Cabinet, and the leaders of the major parties in both Lords and Commons."

"And in the throne room," Roger growled. "It's a pocking barn! Why the throne room?"

"I don't know," Julian said as he joined them, "but she called for the Imperial Regalia."

Krindi Fain, Honal, and Doc Dobrescu followed in Julian's wake, and Roger glanced at all four of them sourly.

"You guys, too?" he asked as they reached the doors of the throne room.

"Us, too," Julian agreed. "But the Prime Minister and a few of the others have already been in there for over half an hour."

"Crap," Roger said. "Tomcat, you're sure she's not in la-la-land?" he asked, holding up his hand to stop the footman who'd been about to open the door.

"Hasn't been for a day and a half," Catrone replied. "I don't think it's going to stick, but . . ."

"But we'd better get whatever this is over with while it does, right?" Roger said, lowering his hand and nodding at the flunky.

"Right," Catrone agreed as the throne room door swung open.

The throne room of the Empire of Man was a must-see on any tour of the Palace. It was a hundred meters long, and it had escaped the fighting almost completely unscathed. The soaring ceiling, with its magnificent fresco depicting the rise of Man and of the Empire, was intact, suspended sixty meters in the air by flying buttresses that seemed far too thin to support the weight. But they were ChromSten, representing the power and glory that had supported that rise.

More murals covered the walls, inlaid in precious gems. Spaceflight. Medicine. Chemistry. Trade. The arts. All that it meant to be "Man" was represented upon those walls, evoked by the finest artists humanity had produced. There was nothing abstract, nothing surreal—just the simple depiction of the works which made Man what he was.

The floor was a solid sheet of polished glassteel, clear as distilled water, impervious to wear, unblemished and unmarred by the thousands upon thousands of feet which had crossed it in the half-millennium and more of the Empire's existence. It was two centimeters thick, that glistening floor, protecting the stone beneath. Strange, patchwork-looking stone. The stones composing that patchwork had been removed, carefully, one by one, from all of the great works of Terra. In each case, the stone which was removed had been replaced with one which matched it perfectly, and each of those irregular, varicolored stones—each tile in the throne room's true floor—was labeled and identified. The Parthenon. The Colosseum. The Forbidden City. Machu Piccu. Temples and theaters and cathedrals. Stones from the pyramids of Cheops and of the Mayans. Stones from the Inca, and from the great works of Africa. Stones from the walls where aboriginal peoples had worshiped their ancestors. Stones from the Great Wall, carrying with them, perhaps, the tortured souls of the millions who had died to build it. Thousands of stones, all of them bringing the souls who had worshiped at them and built them alive in this one place, the center of it all.

The Throne of Man itself was placed upon a dais formed by the ChromSten-armored hatch cover from a missile tube. That hatch cover came from *Freedom's Fury*, the renamed cruiser from whose command deck Miranda I, the first Empress of Man, had led the battle to throw the Dagger Lords off Old Earth and reestablish functioning and growing civilization in the galaxy. Fourteen steps led up to the throne, each of precious metals or gems. But the sere, scarred ChromSten of the ship outshone them all.

The Throne itself was even simpler, only an old, battered, antique command chair from the same ship. Over the years, it had been necessary to rebuild it more than once. But each master craftsman chosen for the task had taken meticulous care to reproduce exactly the same scarring, the same scorching, as the one Miranda the First, Miranda the Great, had sat upon through those awful battles. And it did have those scars, those burns. Right

down to the clumsily carved initials, "AS," which had been cut
into the side of the chair even before Miranda MacClintock and
her followers cut their way to the flight deck of what had been
a Dagger Lord ship to turn it against its erstwhile owners.

Alexandra VII, the seventeenth MacClintock in direct succession
from Miranda I to sit upon that chair, sat upon it now. Roger
saw her in the distance as they entered the room—a regal, distant figure, much like the mother he remembered of old. The
Imperial Crown glittered upon her head, and she wore a long
train of purple-trimmed, snow-white ice-tiger fur, and held the
Scepter in one gloved hand. There were others present, dozens of
them, although they seemed lost and lonely in the throne room's
vastness, and Roger slowed his pace.

He walked forward, and his staff spread out to either side.
Despreaux walked at his right, holding her hated shoes in her
hand and fidgeting with them. Then came Julian, tugging on the
civilian suit he was just learning to wear. And Honal, wearing the
combat suit of a stingship pilot.

Eleanora O'Casey walked to his left, calm and dignified, more
accustomed to this room than even Roger. Then Doc Dobrescu,
uncomfortable in formal clothes. Krindi Fain, still in his leather
harness and kilt. And directly behind him was D'nal Cord—slave,
mentor, bodyguard, friend—and Pedi Karuse.

Thomas Catrone walked behind the two Mardukans, but Roger
sensed still others behind him. D'estres and Gronningen. Dokkum, Pentzikis and Bosum. Captain Krasnitsky, of the *DeGlopper*, who'd blown up his own ship to take the second cruiser
with him. Ima Hooker, and even Ensign Guha, *DeGlopper's*
unwitting toombie saboteur. Kane and Sawato. Rastar, waving
a sword as his *civan* cat-walked to the side. The list went on
and on, but most especially, he felt a friendly, fatherly hand on
his shoulder. The sensation was so strong he actually looked
to the side, and for a moment, with something other than his
eyes, he saw Armand Pahner's face, calm and sober, ready to
face any challenge for his Prince and his Empire. And beside
Pahner, Kostas Matsugae stood looking on, wondering whether
Roger was well-dressed enough for a formal audience, and tut-
tutting over Despreaux's shoes.

He reached the first balk line, where a subject stopped and

knelt to the Empress, and kept walking, pressed by an urgency in his mind, pushed forward by his ghosts. He passed the second line, and the third. The fourth. Until he reached the fifth and last, where his staff spread out on either hand behind him. And then, at last, he dropped to both knees and bowed his head.

"Your Majesty," he said. "You summoned; I am come."

Alexandra looked down at the top of his bowed head, then looked at the companions who had followed him into her presence. She paused in her perusal at sight of Despreaux's shoes and smiled, faintly, as if in complete understanding. Then she nodded.

"We are Alexandra Harriet Katryn Griselda Tian MacClintock, eighth Empress of Man, eighteenth of Our House to hold the Crown. We have at times, lately, been unwell. Our judgment has been severely affected. But in this place, at this time We are who We are. At any time, this may change, but at this moment We are in Our right mind, as so attested by attending physicians and as proven in conversation with Our Prime Minister and other ministers, here gathered."

She paused, and looked around the throne room—not simply at Roger and his companions, but at all the others assembled there and nodded slightly.

"There have been eighteen Emperors and Empresses, stretching back to Miranda the First. Some of us have died in battle, as have our sons and daughters." She paused sadly as she remembered her own children and grandchildren. "Some of us have died young, some old. Some of us have died in our beds—"

"And some in other beds," Julian muttered under his breath.

"—and some in accidents. But *all* of us have died, metaphorically, right here," she said, thumping her left hand on the armrest of the ancient command chair. "No MacClintock Emperor or Empress has ever abdicated." She paused, her jaw flexing angrily, and looked again at Roger's bowed head.

"Until now."

She yanked the heavy train out of her attendants' hands and stood, wrapping it around her left arm until she had some capability of independent movement. Then she walked down the fourteen steps to the glassteel floor.

"Roger," she snapped, "get your butt over here."

Roger looked up, his face hard, and one muscle twitched in

his cheek. But he stood at her command and walked to the base of the stairs.

"A coronation would take weeks to arrange," Alexandra said, looking him in the eye, her face as hard as his. "And we don't have the time, do we?"

"No," Roger said coldly. He'd wanted to have a conversation with his mother when he returned. This wasn't it.

"Fine," Alexandra said. "In that case, we'll skip the ceremony. Hold out your right hand."

Roger did, still looking her in the eye, and she slapped the Scepter into his hand, hard.

"Scepter," she spat. "Symbol of the Armed Forces of the Empire, of which you are now Commander-in-Chief. Originally a simple device for crushing the skulls of your enemies. Use it wisely. Never crush too many skulls; by the same token, never crush too few."

She struggled out of the heavy ice-tiger fur train and walked around to throw it over his shoulders. She was tall, for a woman, but she still had to rise on the balls of her feet to get it into place. Then she stepped back around in front of him and fastened it at his throat.

"Big heavy damned cloak," she snapped. "I can't remember what it's a symbol of, but it's going to be a pain in your imperial ass."

Last, she removed the Crown and rammed it onto his head, hard. It had been sized to her head for the day of her own coronation, and it was far too small for Roger. It perched on top of his head like an over-small hat.

"Crown," she said bitterly. "Originally a symbol of the helmets kings wore in battle so the enemy knew who to shoot. Pretty much the same purpose today."

She stepped back and nodded.

"Congratulations. You're now the Emperor. With all the authority and horrible responsibility that entails."

Roger's eyes stayed locked on hers, hard, angry. So much lay between them, so much pain, so much distrust. And now the steamroller of history, the responsibility which had claimed eighteen generations of their family, perched on *his* head, lay draped about *his* shoulders, weighted *his* right hand. Unwanted, feared, and yet his—the responsibility he could not renounce, to which he had given so many of his dead, and to which he must sacrifice not simply his own life, but Nimashet Despreaux's and their children's, as well.

"Thank you, Mother," he said coldly.

"Wear them in good health," Alexandra said harshly.

She stood, meeting his gaze, and then, slowly—so slowly—her face crumpled. Her lips trembled, and suddenly she threw herself into his arms and wrapped her own about him.

"Oh, God, my son, my only son," she sobbed into his chest. "*Please* wear them in better health than I!"

Roger looked at the useless club in his hand and tossed it, overhand, to Honal, who fielded it as if it were radioactive. Then he sat down on the steps of the Throne of Man, wrapped his arms around his mother and held her in his lap, with infinite tenderness, as she sobbed out her grief and loss—the loss of her reign, of her children, of her mind—on her only child's shoulder.

FIC SF WEB
Weber, David,
We few /
33910009151318   new
$26.00   01/11/05

DATE			